In Agony Until the End of the World

In Agony Until the End of the World

A Novel of the American Civil War

DANIEL B. HINSHAW

RESOURCE *Publications* · Eugene, Oregon

Resource Publications
An Imprint of Wipf and Stock Publishers
199 W. 8th Ave., Suite 3
Eugene, OR 97401

www.wipfandstock.com

PAPERBACK ISBN: 978-1-7252-7417-4
HARDCOVER ISBN: 978-1-7252-7418-1
EBOOK ISBN: 978-1-7252-7419-8

12/01/25

The cover art: *Absolution Under Fire* by Paul Henry Wood, 1891, is reproduced
with the permission of the Raclin Murphy Museum of Art, University of Notre
Dame.

Beginning with innovations introduced during the American Civil War, the triage and care of seriously ill and wounded combatants has steadily improved, mitigating the loss of life. Yet the deeper aspects of suffering experienced by those *who shall have borne the battle* continue to leave their mark on the lives of military veterans. Over the course of our professional lives as physicians, my wife and I have had the profound privilege to offer our combined skills in surgery, psychiatry, and palliative medicine to help alleviate the physical, psychological, social, and spiritual suffering of US military veterans of the major conflicts of the twentieth and early twenty-first centuries. It is to their memory and to the memory of their predecessors who answered the call of duty, honor, and country that this book is dedicated.

"If slavery be the destined sword in the hand of the destroying angel which is to sever the ties of this Union, the same sword will cut in sunder the bonds of slavery itself. As 'calamitous' as a civil war would be, so glorious would be its final issue, that, as God shall judge me, I dare not say that it is not to be desired."

FROM THE DIARY OF JOHN QUINCY ADAMS, 1820

"This war has been permitted by the Almighty to come upon us as a judgment and the North must suffer as well as the South, for we are partners in the national sin. I believe that this war will not end until the great sin of slavery is removed from our land."

LEVI COFFIN, QUAKER ABOLITIONIST

"In times like the present, men should utter nothing for which they would not willingly be responsible through time and in eternity."

ABRAHAM LINCOLN, 1862

CONTENTS

PREFACE

Nearly two decades before Southern secession was precipitated by Abraham Lincoln's election in 1860, a theological crisis laid the *religious* foundation for the Civil War. Major Protestant denominations, including Baptists, Methodists, and Presbyterians, split into northern and southern branches over the biblical justification for slavery—*religious* secession preceded *political* secession. The historian Mark Noll has ironically observed that the "Book that made the nation was destroying the nation; the nation that had taken to the Book was rescued not by the Book but by the force of arms."[1] It would be very difficult to fully understand the conflict, and what motivated the combatants who fought and died between 1861 and 1865, without an appreciation of the role of religious faith. In comparison with contemporary American culture, mid-nineteenth-century America was overwhelmingly religious, with a very strong evangelical Protestant flavor.[2]

Suffering has always been a defining aspect of human life and death. For Americans, the epitome of our collective suffering as a nation remains the Civil War, in which predominantly devout, religious people prayed to the same God for victory as they proceeded to slaughter each other in massive numbers. Yet, for every soldier killed on the battlefield, two would die from disease, at a time when the nature of infection and the principles of antisepsis were just beginning to be appreciated.

In its many facets, suffering has always been a challenge for the medical profession, especially when the profession has sometimes been too preoccupied with fixing broken bodies to recognize broken souls. Whereas modern medicine has so much more to offer for the mending of broken bodies than our professional predecessors during the Civil

1. Noll, *Civil War as a Theological Crisis*, 8.
2. Noll, *Civil War as a Theological Crisis*, 12.

War, we still struggle as they did to address the deeper psychological, social, and spiritual wounds of our suffering patients. In *This Republic of Suffering: Death and the American Civil War*,[3] the historian Drew Gilpin Faust has shifted our gaze from military tactics and the clever (and not-so-clever) strategies of generals to the universal experience that defined the Civil War for all who were touched by it—death and its inseparable companion, suffering.

As a surgeon and palliative care physician, the author has offered a story here about the encounter with suffering and death in the Civil War seen primarily through the eyes of the medical profession, the charitable organizations, and the non-combatant volunteers who ministered with the limited tools available to relieve the massive suffering of the combatants and refugees. While several of the characters are fictional, many of the individuals highlighted in the novel were real persons whose remarkable stories may be unfamiliar to readers of more traditional accounts about the Civil War.

While this novel does stand alone, a prior novel, *Neither Bond nor Free*, gives an account of several fictional characters' lives in the Antebellum period prior to their appearance in this story. Recognizing the distressing nature of the "N-word," the author has employed its use only when essential for the integrity of the narrative, with *n____r* being substituted on the printed page. Extensive chapter notes are available at the back of the book for readers who would like to know more about some of the topics and historical individuals presented in individual chapters.

---

3. Faust, *This Republic of Suffering*.

ACKNOWLEDGMENTS

WHILE MUCH OF THE research for historical fiction is amenable to solitary searches among primary and secondary sources online, the most pleasant and gratifying aspects of the effort have been those which require direct human interactions as well as travel. One of our great national treasures is the National Park Service (NPS). I want to express my gratitude to the many kind staff and docents at the following NPS Civil War battlefields: the two-site Shiloh National Military Park and Corinth Contraband Camp, TN & MS; Antietam National Battlefield, MD; Gettysburg National Military Park, PA; Fredericksburg & Spotsylvania National Military Park, VA; Wilderness Battlefield, VA; Cold Harbor and Richmond National Battlefield Parks, VA; and Petersburg National Battlefield, VA. In addition to the NPS, other independent museums have been great resources during the writing process, including Fort Pillow State Historic Park, TN; Seminary Ridge Museum, Gettysburg, PA; the American Civil War Museum, Richmond, VA; and especially the National Museum of Civil War Medicine (NMCWM), Frederick, MD. That so many museums dedicated to preserving our collective memory of this national cataclysm exist and are thriving represents a powerful testimony to the enduring interest and respect for this shared moment of suffering in our nation's history. A special thanks goes to the Reverend James Mathiesen and his wife in Danville, VA. My wife and I very much enjoyed their hospitality and Rev. Mathiesen's account of Danville history during a visit to learn more about the philanthropic work of Rev. George Dame, the rector of the Episcopal church in Danville during the Civil War.

I would like to express my deep gratitude to the following individuals for their careful review of the manuscript and insightful comments:

Mark Noll, Professor Emeritus of the History of American Christianity at the University of Notre Dame. Professor Noll's careful and thoughtful review of the nineteenth-century religious currents that have been depicted in the story was invaluable, as I strove to locate the spiritual/religious worldview of my characters solidly within the mid-nineteenth century. As a result of his extremely helpful feedback, debates during the Civil War regarding the scriptural justification for chattel slavery and the intellectual milieu underlying the beginnings of the modern eugenics movement are placed in their historical context.

Dr. Greg Hinshaw, presiding clerk of the Indiana Yearly Meeting of the Society of Friends, offered invaluable observations regarding the appropriate nineteenth-century terminology used by Quakers in describing their faith and doctrine. I am especially grateful to him for alerting me to the travail of Southern Quakers, who suffered greatly for their *Testimony Against War* at the hands of the Confederate government.

Michael Knierim, PhD Candidate in Classical Studies, University of Illinois at Champaign/Urbana. I am indebted to Mr. Knierim for his careful reading of the manuscript and his expert assistance as a translator for those passages containing Latin.

Michael Kehoe, Marketing Sales Director (Retired), University Press of Kansas, Lawrence, KS. I am thankful for Mr. Kehoe's careful reading and feedback regarding the manuscript. His encouragement and sage advice have now helped guide to completion this second volume in a planned trilogy.

Terry Reimer, NMCWM Director of Research. Ms. Reimer's love of Civil War medical history is infectious. I cannot begin to express my deep appreciation for the great expertise, patience, and attention to detail Ms. Reimer has consistently shown in response to my many questions as this project has evolved. Her thorough review of the manuscript and helpful suggestions have added greatly to the authenticity of the text. Needless to say, any residual historical errors are solely the author's responsibility.

Finally, I am deeply grateful to my wife, Jane, whose continuing encouragement and excellent editorial skills helped bring this story to fruition.

PART ONE

"When ocean-clouds over inland hills
Sweep storming in late autumn brown,
And horror the sodden valley fills,
And the spire falls crashing in the town,
I muse upon my country's ills—
The tempest bursting from the waste of Time
On the world's fairest hope linked with man's foulest crime . . ."

HERMAN MELVILLE, FROM *BATTLE PIECES*, 1866

CHAPTER ONE

"All I can say this was a Battle . . ."

GEN. WILLIAM TECUMSEH SHERMAN
IN A LETTER TO HIS WIFE, APRIL 11, 1862

HEAVEN COULD BUT WEEP to see her children slaughter one another; so, the rain fell. Mingling with and diluting the pervasive blood, small rivulets merged into larger channels in a persistent effort to wash away the crimson stain of strife. The steady drumbeat of water pelting the earth was interrupted by the periodic explosions of shells that temporarily drowned out the groans, oaths, and cries for mercy, or for mothers too far away to hear. A more individual tattoo beat within the breast of many dying there that, in ever-more-rapid cadence, far exceeded the staccato drumming of the rain upon the earth. Like the wild ecstatic dance of a dervish, it proceeded faster and faster—and then silence; but only for a moment, as others picked up the refrain, for Death was not satisfied.

Offering an antiphonal response to the outside cacophony, another *choir* in a nearby house joined in, mingling the screams of the wounded, shouts of surgeons barking orders, and singing of saws, followed by the regular thudding of amputated limbs upon a wooden floor. A rain-soaked figure quietly entered the house in search of respite from the deluge and chaotic sounds outside, only to encounter the products of an earlier chaos at close quarters. Finding no peace, General Ulysses S. Grant stumbled back out into the wet and darkness, finding refuge under the spreading arms of an oak tree, where a fitful sleep overtook him late that night of April 6, 1862.

A war altogether different from that strategized by generals and fought by armies was being waged in that small field hospital. With the

3

limited knowledge and weapons available, the warriors engaged in this conflict had the temerity to fight not against a human foe but against that ultimate enemy, Death. Theirs was the paradoxical necessity to frequently commit violence to reverse the effects of violence. For those seriously wounded by the implements of war and *fortunate* enough to survive, they would discover that their battle had only just begun. The foes with which they must now contend were putrefaction, gangrene, and in some cases, medical incompetence.

Adding to that night's woes, a young medical officer found himself caught up in a conflict not of his choosing with the senior surgeon of his regiment, whose ignorance of medicine and paucity of surgical skills had become patently manifest to his younger subordinate. As Dr. Isaac Burgess, assistant surgeon, assisted Dr. Davis P. Hill, surgeon of the 36th Indiana Volunteer Infantry on that fateful night, a recurring thought haunted him. Dr. Hill seemed to fully subscribe to the axiom of the great medieval French surgeon Henri de Mondeville that a surgeon must be prepared to "cut like an executioner," while failing to remember the same surgeon's insistence on the gentle handling of wounded tissues.

"You and your damn notions, Burgess; it's perfectly obvious that this leg should be amputated immediately."

"Sir, how have you come to that conclusion? Our preliminary examination has demonstrated no fracture. If we can control the bleeding, it should be possible to identify and ligate the offending artery and potentially save this soldier's leg."

"Goddam Quaker, are you questioning my judgment?" Dr. Hill glowered at his younger associate. Turning toward the head of the operating table, which consisted of some flat boards laid in parallel fashion over the tops of two barrels, he asked an assistant surgeon from the 6th Ohio Infantry who was helping them, "So, Dr. Bedell, what do you think of this hare-brained scheme of my Quaker associate? When time is of the essence, why should we be engaged in such tomfoolery?"

"Dr. Hill, before I administered chloroform to this soldier, he begged me to save his leg. I told him we would do all that we could to save it. Why not let Dr. Burgess do what he proposes? After all, not to be impertinent—how much experience do most physicians entering military service have in determining when and how amputations should be performed?"

"What insolence! Are you questioning my abilities, Dr. Bedell?"

"No sir, just your experience in addressing these kinds of injuries. I believe this is the 36th Indiana's first taste of combat, is it not? Don't worry. I suspect there will be plenty of other opportunities to perform amputations tonight. Dr. Burgess's plan for preserving this soldier's leg seems quite reasonable to me."

"Are you now conspiring with this damn abolitionist against me, sir? You both should remember that I am the senior medical officer here, and I will not tolerate insubordination!" With a mixture of indignation and relief, Dr. Hill threw down the filthy, blood-stained rag with which he had been wiping his face, and reaching for a flask hidden within his coat pocket, stalked off. As he left, he sent one parting verbal salvo over his shoulder: "Have it your way, you damn rascals. But if it don't go well, don't expect any support from me!"

After Dr. Hill's unceremonious departure, Isaac gave his colleague Israel Bedell a quick glance tinged with gratitude. Nodding to a private who was restraining the unconscious but lightly anesthetized, restless patient to renew his efforts, Isaac said, "Dr. Bedell, after I reposition the tourniquet, let's see what might be done for this soldier, short of an amputation." With his colleague's assistance, Isaac Burgess was able to tie off both ends of the severed artery, debride, and dress the wound.

"Dr. Burgess, that was a fine bit of operating."

"Thank you, Dr. Bedell, but it was truly a joint effort."

"Please call me by my given name, Israel. We should be on thoroughly intimate terms after what we just accomplished. You seem to have more experience treating these kinds of injuries than most of our surgeons when they first encounter combat."

"Thank you, Israel. Also, please call me Isaac. My medical school thesis was on amputations, a product of direct experience with several patients requiring amputations under my mentor Dr. Moses Gunn at the University of Michigan. I just hope that putrefaction and gangrene don't set in."

"Well, his foot is still warm, but it'll require close observation over the next several days. Right now, Isaac, it appears our expertise is needed for others," Israel said as the door opened and orderlies brought two more very wet, wounded soldiers into the makeshift hospital.

"How is it out on the battlefield?" Isaac inquired. "Have you been able to get to the wounded with all the shelling from our gunboats?"

"Between the shelling and the rain, it's one hell of a muddy, blood-soaked mess, sir. A lot of the men have given up tryin' to retrieve the wounded, it's jes' too dangerous. We picked up these fellers during a lull in the shelling." Peering down with the light of a lantern for a closer look at the men he had helped rescue, he exclaimed, "Why, they're both secesh! Tom, we risked our necks for a couple of traitorous Rebs!" Waving his hand in disgust, the orderly turned aside, spat on the floor, and said, "Tom, let's go get some rest so we can kill some Rebs tomorrah, to make up for the ones we saved tonight." Feeling impelled to speak, Isaac said, "Thank you for bringing these wounded men to us. Now that they are our prisoners, it is our duty to care for them."

"Beggin' yer pardon sir, but ye shoulda seen these devils this morning when they came outta nowhere, screaming like banshees from hell itself! They warn't so peaceable then as they are now. Tom and me, we were jes' settin' down for a nice breakfast, and these uninvited guests came to join us. You cain't imagine how fast we had to skedaddle. Why, we had to leave all that nice bacon behind on the double-quick, knowin' that these traitors would be enjoyin' it. We spent the rest of the day trying to keep these Southern boys from driving us into the Tennessee River." At this point, his silent partner spoke up and declared, "I'm mighty thankful fer Genrul Sherman; he held us together and saved us from bein' wiped out by the damn Rebs!"

As the volume of wounded increased, of necessity, the two assistant surgeons worked independently at separate operating tables, drafting additional private soldiers to assist them with anesthesia, lighting, and wound exposure. Amputations of shattered arms and legs being their most common operation, a crude medical counterpoint developed in which a rhythm of "chloroform!," "restrain!," followed shortly by the percussive thud of another discarded limb, was quickly harmonized with a very similar rhythm at the next table. Sustaining the counterpoint was the added refrain: "More wounded!" An occasional note of dissonance would interrupt the macabre contrapuntal harmony when their senior colleague, the ill-tempered Dr. Hill, would briefly appear, flit about the room, offering unsolicited advice that became gradually more incoherent with the passage of time. Harmony would then be restored as he departed to take frequent breaks for cigars and additional swigs from his flask of whiskey.

Just before three o'clock in the morning, as the young surgeons were completing their last operations of the night, Isaac's commanding officer, Colonel Grose, entered the hospital in the company of the medical director of the 4th Division, Dr. Bernard Irwin. Colonel Grose cringed as he surveyed the cramped interior of the operating room, which had acquired an admixture of noisome odors from old blood, sweating bodies, emesis, and other human evacuations. "I wonder where our illustrious surgeon Dr. Hill is; probably drunk somewhere," he muttered half under his breath. Hearing the colonel's comment, Israel exchanged a meaningful glance with Isaac, who tried to avoid responding with a smirk.

Inspired by the horrific environment that confronted them, Dr. Irwin observed with growing intensity, "Colonel, I wish we had better accommodations to offer our wounded soldiers. I am afraid that the rigors of transport upriver to general hospitals in the North will be too much to bear for many of our wounded, and they may needlessly die after otherwise successful operations. There is no need to expose our brave soldiers to the harsh elements and crowding on deck of our naval vessels when with proper preparation, we should be able to provide the care they need in immediate proximity to the battlefield. Pending the outcome of today's battle, I intend to establish a proper field hospital here at Pittsburg Landing for the 4th division of the Army of the Ohio, with clean water, adequate sanitation, and housing for the wounded."

As Isaac stretched out his six-foot frame on the last bit of unclaimed floor beside his colleague's already-recumbent form, he tried to relax, but sleep evaded him. This was his first real taste of battle since the 36th Indiana Volunteer Infantry had been mustered into service on September 16, 1861. Other than a brief skirmish in early February, his medical duties had been primarily consumed, up to this point, in taking care of many young men with communicable illnesses, especially measles, easily acquired and spread by the crowding in the military camps.

A pleasant breakfast had been interrupted by the distant sounds of cannon and musketry coming to their camp at Savannah, about eight miles from Pittsburg Landing. But for some inexplicable reason they only received the order to march toward the battle about 1 p.m. on that fateful Sunday in early April 1862. Isaac recalled the unnerving experience of encountering large numbers of soldiers in blue seeking shelter from the battle, skulking at the base of the two-hundred-foot height above the landing. After being ferried across the Tennessee River, his regiment had not expected to encounter several thousand soldiers, who, with faces contorted by terror, were loudly pronouncing their impending doom if they proceeded further in the direction of the enemy. Their division commander, General William "Bull" Nelson, had ordered the skulkers to stand aside so that *soldiers* could make their way up the hill. Isaac remembered his own struggle to suppress the contagion of fear that rose to greet and envelop him as he heard their shouts: "You'll see."

"You will come back or be killed."

"It's murder."

Isaac was amazed by how rapidly the fear had dissipated as the regiment, responding to encouraging words from Lieutenant Colonel Carey and Colonel Grose, quickened its pace toward the summit and the sounds of battle. Despite acrid smoke obscuring the scene before him, he found his place, with his assigned stretcher-bearers behind the advancing lines of soldiers. Late that Sunday afternoon, the 36th Indiana was given the singular honor of being the only unit of the Army of the Ohio to participate in the first day's combat. Only later had he learned the details of their assignment—to help break a final desperate Rebel attempt to drive the Union forces into the Tennessee River. Before they were fully in line of battle, Isaac's attention was diverted from the shouts of the company commanders to commands of a higher order—the cries of suffering humanity.

About one hundred yards to the left and ahead of Isaac, the flight of a cannonball caused a momentary break in the line of advancing soldiers, who quickly closed ranks. This was followed by screams of pain coming from the same direction. As Isaac and his attendants began to run toward the screams, to his horror, another cannonball swept past to his right, causing several officers to dive for cover but not soon enough to prevent the decapitation of one mounted officer, an aide to General Grant. Although simultaneously drawn in opposite directions, the cold logic of battlefield medicine—first those who might live, then the dying and dead—helped him resume course in the direction of the screams.

The intensity of the injured soldier's screams had diminished dramatically by the time Isaac arrived at his side and were largely replaced by a soft moaning. The young surgeon worked quickly, using tourniquets to control further bleeding from both legs, which the cannonball had almost completely severed below the knee. A very large pool of blood had already formed in the short time it took for Isaac to reach the wounded soldier. With the tourniquets in place and the bleeding temporarily controlled, Isaac directed the stretcher-bearers to quickly carry the wounded soldier to the rear. Not fully realizing the extent or severity of his injuries, the wounded man, in a moment of lucidity, stared directly into Isaac's eyes and whispered, "How serious is it, Doc?" Isaac winced as he remembered that being distracted by the sight of another wounded man fifty yards ahead, he had responded, "You must make your peace with God, soldier." *If only I had offered some additional words of encouragement*, he thought as he lay there, sleep still evading him.

He recalled how as the regiment ascended a rise, the Rebels came into view. As if on cue, both sides started to fire their muskets at each other. In his inexperience, he had moved closer to the main advance than he should have as a medical officer. As a result, he heard for the first time the strange and eerie whiz of musket balls around him, as well as the sickening thud when they contacted human flesh. Reflexively, he had raised his arm and ducked his head to face the storm of the Rebels' firing line. When a company commander concerned for his safety ordered him to the rear, he was embarrassed but grateful. The imperative to move quickly from one wounded soldier to the next had been so all-consuming that only later from a safe distance was he able to fully appreciate the terrors of the battlefield.

As he reflected on the evening's activities in the makeshift hospital, he grimaced as he thought of his ongoing conflict with Dr. Hill. He could not help but see from early in their professional association that his superior officer was grossly incompetent. But as a well-connected War Democrat who offered crucial support to the Republican governor's efforts to form a Union party, he had managed to acquire an early commission at the rank of full surgeon without undergoing the usual formal testing required in the Army. From the beginning, Isaac had been frustrated by Dr. Hill's tacit expectation that his junior medical officer should accept sole responsibility for any deficiencies in the medical care of the regiment regardless of their actual source, while also meekly enduring the abuse that Dr. Hill directed his way. A wry smile came to his lips as he recalled the beginning of his troubles with Dr. Hill, in which he had inadvertently reverted to the plain speech of the Society of Friends when the surgeon was present, saying "thee" instead of "you" during a conversation with his fellow medical officer. "Ah, so you *are* one of those damn Quaker abolitionists who started this war!" Dr. Hill had exclaimed, as he recognized in Isaac the very embodiment of all that was wrong with the Republic. "If you wretched abolitionists had only obeyed the laws of the land, we might still enjoy a peaceful union with our Southern brethren, and they would not have been driven to commit the treason of secession."

Isaac learned from a later conversation with Colonel Grose that Dr. Hill, although a resident of Indiana, was the sole heir of his aunt's

Kentucky plantation, which included many slaves. Colonel Grose, who was a keen observer of those under his authority, recognized the conflict between his two medical officers and sympathized greatly with Isaac but also felt constrained by the powerful relationship that existed between Governor Morton of Indiana and Dr. Hill. As Isaac finally began to drift toward the realm of dreams and nightmares, he felt deep gratitude for his colleague of the evening, Dr. Bedell.

CHAPTER TWO

"I have read a fiery gospel writ in burnished rows of steel . . ."
JULIA WARD HOWE, FEBRUARY 1862

"ISAAC, DR. BURGESS, WAKE up! Alas, our brief nap is over." For a short moment between sleep and wakefulness, Isaac was completely disoriented; but the overwhelming smells of blood and sweat, the sight of severed limbs on the floor in the corner of the room, and the sound of moans from wounded soldiers in the next room quickly brought him back to reality. Rubbing his eyes, he recognized his colleague of the prior night's work, Israel Bedell, who flashed a grin at him and added, "I s'pose my rude interruption of your sleep must've spoiled a lovely dream of some fair maiden. Oh, but are young Quaker men allowed to dream about fair maidens?" Blushing, Isaac protested, "Young Quaker men are subject to all the same temptations as others."

"I figured as much. By the way, why does your colleague, Dr. Hill seem to hate you so?"

"He blames abolitionists, including Quakers like me, for driving the Southern states to secede. He claims to fight for the restoration of the old Union as it was prior to secession."

"And you, Dr. Burgess, are you one of those *damned abolitionists*?" Israel intoned in a sonorous voice as he pulled on his boots but then burst out laughing. Isaac, his face again reddening, but not from embarrassment, responded stiffly, "Dr. Bedell, I am not sure I understand the humor you find in the question. I am, indeed, an abolitionist. Ultimately, this war is about slavery. Dr. Hill is angry because he knows it to be so, and his personal interests are threatened. The Union cannot and will not be restored in its old form with this evil at its core."

"Isaac, please do not take offense. I couldn't help but find some humor in the nasty conflict between you and Dr. Hill. I think his unpleasantness towards you stems not so much from political or even moral convictions but jealousy. He knows you're a competent physician, while it is quite evident that he is a fraud. It must be quite a trial to work under such a tyrant."

"Israel, thank you for explaining yourself. I apologize for speaking with such feeling. May I ask why you are serving as a medical officer?"

"Isaac, I can only admire your commitment as a Quaker pacifist to take up the uniform of the United States Army. To be quite honest, my primary reasons for serving as a medical officer are not nearly so noble. To be sure, I would like to see this treasonous Rebellion crushed, and I would not object at all to the end of the degrading institution of slavery. But if you ask me to give you my most honest reason for serving, I must confess that the possibility of improving my medical skills, while helping some poor suffering bastards, are sufficient reasons for me."

Their conversation was cut short as an orderly from Colonel Grose poked his head in the door and, speaking directly to Isaac, said, "Colonel Grose sends his compliments and requests that you be ready to move forward with the regiment in ten minutes. Please alert Dr. Hill." Turning to Dr. Bedell and offering a hearty handshake, Isaac said, "Thank you, Israel, for your forthright answer to my question. I hope and pray that we will be able to continue our conversation this evening." Grinning, Israel replied, "I can't think of anyone else with whom I would rather be sawing off limbs. Good luck Sawbones!"

After adjusting the green sash worn as an indication of his status as a medical officer and splashing some water on his face, Isaac went in search of Dr. Hill. The tall, thin surgeon, when not disheveled from lack of sleep or from the cumulative filth of marching, the battlefield, and operating, was notable for having fine, even facial features, piercing blue eyes, and a full head of dark brown hair that was complemented by an equally full beard of the same hue. In short, under circumstances of greater order and cleanliness, Isaac Burgess was handsome. Having just achieved his twenty-fourth birthday, he had grown the beard during his final year of medical school, three years earlier, to help create the impression of greater age and maturity. After the previous day's horrors, his features had absorbed a distinct imprint of the pain and suffering he had witnessed, removing the last vestiges of youth from his expression, making the beard superfluous.

"Dr. Hill, please wake up, sir! We have our orders from Colonel Grose. Our regiment will be moving forward to engage the enemy in ten minutes. As happened yesterday, I am prepared to go with the troops and assess the wounded on the battlefield. Sir?" Isaac looked down more closely at the still recumbent form of Dr. Hill, whose flushed face showed no signs of wakefulness but emitted a nauseating odor of alcohol mixed with stale tobacco as he continued to snore loudly in response to Isaac's efforts to awaken him. Motioning to a private who had been detailed to the makeshift hospital, Isaac said, "Dr. Hill will need your help to awaken. Bring some black coffee and a basin of water for him to wash his face, and stay with him until he is fully awake." He then wrote a short note for the snoring surgeon, which explained their orders and his plan of action, while telling the private to make sure it was read by Dr. Hill. After Isaac collected his field pack of medical supplies, he reported in the gray, pre-dawn light to Colonel Grose. After exchanging salutes, the colonel asked him, "Is Dr. Hill ready for duty?"

"He is *getting* ready, sir."

"He is probably still sleeping off all the alcohol he consumed last night," the colonel retorted with disgust. He quickly added, "Dr. Burgess, you are not required to confirm my suspicions, since there is nothing that either of us can do about it."

"Sir, I have taken additional precautions in the event of Dr. Hill's *indisposition* and have spoken to the surgeon of the 6th Ohio and his assistant surgeon, whom you met last evening. They are both willing to provide support in the care of our regiment's casualties, as needed."

"Thank you for your foresight, Dr. Burgess. Please join the other officers in my tent as I review the plan of battle."

Turning to his fellow officers and pointing to a map in the light of a lamp hanging in his tent, Colonel Grose said, "Allow me to quickly review our orders, coming from Colonel Ammen, brigade commander. Gentlemen, as you know, we are the extreme left of the Union line. The plan is for a general advance across our entire front to drive the Rebel forces from yesterday's battlefield. Although we have the advantage of superior numbers, we should assume that the Rebels, who yesterday were so close to a complete victory, will not give ground readily. Indeed, I fully expect that they will attempt to turn our left flank. Once I give the signal to advance, it will be important to deploy skirmishers not only in our front but also on our left, remaining ever-vigilant for a Rebel flank attack."

As quietly as possible, the regiment formed in line of battle as the gray of the eastern sky began to lighten. At 5:30 a.m. they began their advance across the battlefield of the preceding day. As Isaac now followed some yards behind the soldiers at the rear of the regiment, he could hear muffled exclamations of surprise, followed by swearing from some as they moved forward cautiously in the dim light of dawn. Perplexed by their reactions, Isaac quickly learned the reason for their exclamations as he nearly stepped on the recumbent form of a dead soldier. He would have to pick his way carefully through a carpet of corpses lying silent and stiff before him and his comrades, stark reminders of the nature of the current day's business.

As he stepped cautiously among the dead, reflecting on the previous night's useless shelling of the battlefield, he was struck by the needless waste of human life. *Some of these men might still live and breathe, but for the thoughtlessness of our commanders! If only we could have sent more details out to look for the wounded last night, instead of filling the last moments of many a soldier with the terrifying sounds and violence of shells bursting around them.*

His musings were interrupted by a slight noise that he heard off to his right. At first, he dismissed it as the rustling sound created by the living brushing up against the dead, since so many advancing soldiers could not help but contact the myriad numbers of corpses strewn randomly on the battlefield. After moving in the direction of the sound, he again heard the same rustling sound, but louder now and coming from an area where the regiment had already passed. In the dim light, he moved methodically from one recumbent form to another, searching for signs of life but only encountering cold, silent flesh. His searching acquired a frantic quality as the rustling sound persisted, grew more distinct, and was now accompanied by a low guttural sound. *Someone must still be alive nearby and struggling to breathe!* he thought anxiously. As he drew closer, he realized that the rustling and guttural sounds had somehow divided and were emanating from not only his right but also behind and in front of him. With a growing sense of horror accompanied by waves of nausea, the revolting revelation came all at once. These were not the sounds of the wounded struggling for life but the satisfied snorting and rooting of wild pigs feasting on the dead. Isaac had no choice but to reluctantly beat a hasty retreat in the direction of his regiment before he attracted the attention of the porcine horde. As he hurried to catch up with his comrades, he could not avoid pondering the fate of this day's combatants. He shuddered to think of the wild pigs who weren't concerned about states' rights or human freedom. *Surely, they would be quite happy regardless of the outcome of the fighting. They are not prejudiced—Confederate or Union flesh—it is all the same to them.*

After advancing for about a half-mile, the regiment encountered the Confederate forces near the road to Corinth, Mississippi. As Colonel Grose had warned, there were several attempts that morning to turn the Union left, which he countered effectively by sending additional skirmishers. By late morning, Isaac saw that the rest of the regiment, in conjunction with the 24th Ohio and 15th Illinois, were moving forward to assault the enemy near a broken-down fence. He directed his stretcher-bearers to set up an aid station about four hundred yards in the rear of the fence, since most of the casualties were coming from this direction. Isaac's attention then became absorbed with the steady flow of wounded men arriving for evaluation. A well-defined pattern developed as the stretcher-bearers would arrive carrying freshly wounded soldiers. He would first determine the gravity of the injury from its location, extent of the damage, and the apparent condition of the wounded soldier. He had instructed his assistants to make it their priority to quickly bring soldiers with gunshot wounds in the arms or legs for urgent assessment, since there was a reasonable chance of survival if treatment could be instituted quickly. For soldiers presenting with deep wounds to the chest or abdomen, which were likely to have a mortal outcome, his primary goal was to relieve their pain as quickly as possible, sending a silent prayer for their survival (or at least a peaceful death) heavenward, as he directed their transfer to the rear.

The pace of his work would at times be disturbed when a wounded soldier would present himself without the help of the stretcher-bearers. Isaac was initially tempted to assume that if a soldier could present under his own strength without assistance, he must not be seriously injured. He was quickly disabused of this notion when a young soldier, who could not be more than sixteen or seventeen years of age, walked up to the aid station and politely said, "Excuse me, sir. I think my left arm's been injured. Could you please take a look at it?" Looking up after having just placed powdered morphine in the leg wound of another soldier to provide some pain relief, Isaac was startled by the strangely incongruous sight of a quiet youth standing patiently before him with a tattered, blood-soaked left shirt sleeve bereft of the forearm and hand, which had so recently occupied it. Isaac shouted to one of the stretcher-bearers,

"Quick, bring me a tourniquet!" Turning his full attention to his young patient, he directed the wounded soldier to sit down on a nearby tree stump. Giving Isaac a plaintive look, the wounded boy asked, "Doctor, is there anything you can do to fix my arm? I'm left-handed, and I owe my mother a letter. I was hoping to write her about the battle tonight." As he secured the tourniquet on the boy's upper arm, Isaac said, "I'll help you write your mother."

Later, around one o'clock in the afternoon, Isaac's attention was suddenly wrenched away from his duties by a thunderous shout that rolled back over him from the point of conflict. Looking up, he witnessed the Union line, comprised of his regiment in combination with elements of the 24th Ohio and 15th Illinois, surge forward like a giant ocean wave crashing on to rocks. But these *rocks* gave way as the human wave in blue continued its inexorable forward movement. In a matter of minutes, the Confederate line began to dissolve and then reform as a rapid southward retreat of the Rebel forces along the road to Corinth, Mississippi.

"Dr. Burgess, our boys have routed the Rebs! Come an' see, how they've skedaddled," one of Isaac's assistants shouted exultantly. Motioning for the stretcher-bearer to come closer, Isaac responded, "Start searching the battlefield for survivors."

As he carefully picked his way through the debris of battle, Isaac encountered a jumble of abandoned weapons, disembodied limbs and other body parts, the corpses of men and horses, and the occasional recumbent human form still claiming active citizenship in the land of the living. He and his stretcher-bearers were met by dazed confederates being herded at bayonet point to the rear by soldiers from their regiment. With increasing proximity to the scene of the fighting, there was a noticeable decline in the proportion of wounded and dead wearing Union blue as the number of those dressed in gray and butternut increased. Isaac's attention was drawn away by excited voices emanating from a group of Confederate prisoners about fifty yards ahead. The captured soldiers seemed to be resisting the orders of their captors to proceed to the rear.

"Hey, you Secesh, stand up and get away from that body!"

Several Confederate soldiers who were crouching over a body on the ground appeared to ignore the order given by a Union sergeant. It was only after he repeated the order, accompanied by some choice language, that they reluctantly stood up and warily eyed him and the other Union soldiers with him.

"Sergeant, what seems to be the problem here?" Isaac asked with growing interest. Turning around, the sergeant recognized Isaac's green sash and with evident relief in his voice, said, "Doc, there is a Rebel captain here—not sure if he's dead or alive." Observing how assiduously the Confederate prisoners crowded around their stricken officer, Isaac said, "Please, allow me to examine your captain."

The tight ring of Rebel prisoners slowly opened, allowing Isaac to approach and kneel at the side of the Confederate captain. Isaac's quick inspection revealed a wound at the base of the neck on the right side.

"Is he dead, Doc?" one of the Confederate soldiers asked diffidently. By way of response, the wounded Confederate officer moaned but did not speak when Isaac, with the help of one of the Rebel prisoners, gently rotated him to examine his back. Looking up at the Confederate prisoners still hovering around their wounded officer, Isaac found the stolid expressions on their faces rather disconcerting.

"Ah, there is no exit wound," Isaac noted out loud. Addressing the Confederate prisoners, he asked, "Were there other wounded soldiers near your captain?"

"Why do you ask, suh?"

"Because the blood soaking the ground around him is not his. He has been bleeding but it is all internal—inside his body."

"Yes. To get at 'im, we had to move a couple fellers who got shot up pretty bad," one of the Rebel prisoners answered, pointing to some mangled corpses lying nearby. And then for a brief instant lowering the mask of impassivity, he gave Isaac an anxious look and added, "D'ya think he'll live, Doc?"

"Gunshot wounds to the neck are very serious. I fear he has lost considerable blood; indeed, he may still be bleeding. If the bleeding stops soon, he may survive, although putrefaction and inflammation may set in. Also, it is unclear whether nerves in this region or his spine itself may be injured, which could be disastrous." Seeing the puzzled expressions on the faces of the prisoners, he added, "I apologize for all the medical detail. Your captain's condition is very serious. But we'll do everything possible to help him survive." Isaac's attempt to reassure the captive Rebel soldiers of his good intentions on behalf of their wounded captain was met only with silence, their faces retaining a persistent inscrutability.

"What's your captain's name?"

"Captain Fitzhugh Wormeley of the 24th Tennessee."

"Sergeant, my stretcher-bearers are preoccupied assisting other wounded on the field. Could you detail two men to help carry Captain Wormeley back to our hospital tent?" Isaac requested. "Yes, sir. Harry and Joe, you heard the doctor. Git a stretcher and carry the prisoner back to camp." After the Rebel prisoners had been marched off under guard, the sergeant turned to Isaac and said, "Doc, there's sumthin mighty peculiar 'bout them Rebel soldiers and their captain." Equally puzzled, Isaac could only offer the sergeant a quick nod of agreement as he rushed off in search of other wounded.

"Dr. Hill, why did you elect to *not* explore this young soldier's arm?" Isaac asked with growing exasperation. "We don't know the condition of what remains after the traumatic amputation."

"Oh Burgess, you amaze me! Last night you were anxious to avoid amputation, and now you are advocating aggressive measures, when it is clearly obvious that the wound is not bleeding—indeed, the shell already performed the amputation. What more is there for us to do? I say, we should not meddle with it," was Dr. Hill's supercilious response.

"It is precisely because his wound is *not* bleeding that I am concerned. I worry that putrefaction will likely develop if non-vital tissue remains in the wound. Also, without securing the severed blood vessels, how can we be certain they won't bleed later?" Isaac retorted with mounting anger. Arbitrary decisions being the bulwark of incompetence, the senior surgeon, summoning a full measure of officiousness, pronounced his verdict: "Burgess, I won't tolerate any more impertinent questions. There will be no operating on this soldier's wound until such time as I decide." Increasingly aware of his junior medical officer's clinical and operative skills, Davis P. Hill was more than happy to take credit for Isaac Burgess's successful outcomes while at the same time realizing the threat posed by a subordinate who was *too successful*. He mused, *How better to address this administrative problem than by being decisive? Yes, I am quite satisfied. As for the patient, the poor bastard is probably doomed anyway. The important issue at hand is to periodically remind this damn Quaker of the chain of command!*

Isaac sat down on a stool beside the young soldier's cot and buried his face in his hands. Would the miracle of surviving a traumatic battlefield amputation slip away because of his superior officer's arrogant incompetence and neglect? When he had briefly examined the wound on the battlefield, he could clearly see ragged edges that had been soiled by dirt carried by the explosive shell fragment that caused the injury. *Surely, even Dr. Hill could at least understand the importance of cleaning the wound,* he thought with smoldering anger. His angry musings were interrupted by a weak voice coming from the cot. When he separated his hands, Isaac saw to his surprise that the subject of all his concern was awake and was attempting to capture his attention.

"Doctor, were you able to help me?"

"What's your name, soldier?"

"Amos, sir."

"Amos, do you remember anything, since I saw you on the battlefield?"

"When they brought me here, another doctor took a quick look at me and said that I wasn't going to have an operation, that the shell already did the operating. Will you still help me write a letter to my mother?"

"Of course, I will." Before addressing Amos' question, Isaac bit his lip, swallowed hard, and looked away to the furthest corner of the tent in which his young patient was housed while searching for comforting yet honest words. The best that he could summon tumbled hastily out of his mouth.

"Amos, do you know what happened to your left hand and forearm on the battlefield today?"

After a very long pause that was punctuated by a stifled sob, Amos replied, in a voice cracking with emotion, "Are they . . . gone? Is that why it feels numb and I can't grasp anything?" Isaac leaned forward, grasping Amos's remaining hand, and said, "I am so sorry, Amos. Are you afraid to look?" The dread in the wounded soldier's eyes, combined with a solitary tear that flowed slowly down his right cheek, answered Isaac's question.

"The other doctor who saw you has decided against an operation at present," Isaac stated as calmly as possible while attempting to suppress his emotions. "How would an operation make any difference, if the shell already did the operating?" Amos asked with some confusion.

"Sometimes, more tissue may need to be removed to allow healing to occur safely."

"Would there be anything left?"

"Hopefully, the rest of you would survive to recover from this terrible wound. We must watch you closely during the next several days. It is still possible that you will need an operation. Amos, how old are you?"

"Seventeen, sir."

Isaac gazed upon the stricken youth, his anger with his senior medical officer temporarily dissolved in the face of the human tragedy before him. *How many more mothers' sons, hovering between life and death, will I encounter before it's all over? Oh, the letter I'll ultimately have to write his mother!* Then, speaking softly and deliberately, he asked, "Amos, what shall we write to your mother, tonight?"

CHAPTER THREE

"Go down, Moses,
Way down in Egypt's land;
Tell old Pharaoh
To let My people go!"

Slave Spiritual

"Ain't you heard dem explosions an' de earth a shakin' so? Why, Missus Penny, dey's de angels announcin' dat de Year o' Jubilee has come! De Good Lawd is settin' us free. From now on, I'm gonna raise mah hammer only to strike de anvil of freedom! Jes' like Moses down in Egypt-land, I say, 'Let mah people go!'"

"But Moses, it was always our intention to give you your freedom, but at the right time, once you have been *fully* prepared for it."

Dere's nuttin' you can do about it, one way or t'other. *It ain't fo' us to decide.* When de good Lawd's spoken, who kin argue wit' Him?" The blacksmith and locally renowned slave preacher of the Magnolias plantation, while being respectful to his young mistress, remained adamant in his apocalyptic pronouncement. Dazed and feeling a deepening sadness tainted by a sense of betrayal, Penelope Wormeley could only watch helplessly as the charismatic slave, Moses, organized and led the exodus of almost every slave on the plantation toward the Union lines only a few miles away.

"Auntie Betsy, I just don't understand how Moses could act as he has," Penelope said disconsolately as she slowly ran her fingers through her three-year-old son's blond hair. Pausing a moment from feeding eighteen-month-old Emily to mop her brow and adjust her head scarf, the old slave cook gave her mistress a look containing equal portions of surprise, pity, and disgust. "Missus Penny, forgive mah impertinence, but did you eber consider dat yo' slave property might have ideas of dere own about freedom?"

"But that's just it. Many times, especially during our Sunday schools together, I have explained to them my great desire to give them their freedom, *once they are prepared to receive it.*"

"Mebbe, dey jes' got tired of waiting fo' de time when *you'd* decide dey's ready to *receive* freedom and realized dat dey's ready to *take* it."

"Haven't we been kind masters? Don't they know how much we love and care about them? Without the food, shelter, and guidance we provide, how can they possibly survive?"

"Missus Penny, dere ain't a slave dat's bin here at de Magnolias dat ain't thankful fo' yo' many kindnesses to dem. But, for a taste of real freedom, dey's ready to take those risks. Cain't you unnerstan dat we git tired of hearing yo' promises of freedom, an' yet we ain't any closer to it?"

"So, Betsy, you don't believe I have been sincere in the promises I have made?"

"Oh no, Missus Penny, we believe *you believe* yo'self wif all yo' heart when you say sech things! But, since Massa Wormeley come, at de rate he sell so many of us down South, dere won't be many left to enjoy de freedom *you believe* you want to gib us!" Upon hearing this painfully accurate indictment of her husband's behavior, the color rose in Penelope's cheeks, and she blurted out, "Well Betsy, why didn't you leave with Moses and the others then?"

"I's jes' a fool, I guess. If'n I leave you now, what will become of you and yo' chillun, Missus Penny?"

"Do you mean to say that you are staying with the children and me because you pity us?"

"Dat jes' about sums it up." Before Penelope could respond to the unsolicited pity of her cook, a knock at the kitchen door interrupted the exchange between the two women. Turning toward the open door, Penelope was startled but also pleasantly surprised to see Moses standing there. With an air of triumph, she turned back to her cook and said, "You see Betsy, they have already returned after being gone for only a day! Moses realized very quickly how foolish it would be to *take* his freedom when not fully ready for it!"

"I's sorry to disappoint you Missus Penny, but I didn't come back to be yo' slave agin. I come to tell you dat Massa Wormeley bin wounded in de fight and is poorly. De Yankees have him in dere hospital. I can take you to 'im, if'n you like."

Seeking a brief respite, an exhausted Isaac Burgess stepped outside of the hospital ward, occupying a large tent, where for nearly twenty-four hours he had been attending to many wounded soldiers from both armies. A break in the clouds that late Tuesday afternoon revealed a brilliant sunset whose evolution from bright orange to a darker, more somber purple absorbed his attention. He was startled out of his reverie by the voice of an orderly: "Doc, there is a secesh woman here who wants to see her wounded husband."

"What's her husband's name?"

"Captain Fitzhugh Wormeley of the 24th Tennessee, sir."

A very pale, anxious, but unexpectedly familiar face greeted Isaac when he approached Penelope Wormeley. Quickly looking up at him, she begged, "Doctor, please take me to my husband. He is Captain Wormeley of the 24th Tennessee Infantry."

"Please come this way, Mrs. Wormeley. Your husband is unconscious, but perhaps he will respond to your voice."

As Penelope Wormeley began to keep solitary vigil at her husband's bedside, a host of memories flooded Isaac's consciousness. This young Southern matron was the same Penelope Endicott he had met ten years before during a visit to the South with his Uncle Levi Coffin. Although he immediately recognized her, the recognition was not mutual on her part. After first speaking to him with no response and then resignedly sitting quietly at her husband's side for several minutes, she turned to Isaac, who lingered nearby. "Doctor, what are your expectations for my husband?"

"Mrs. Wormeley, I am quite concerned about the type of injury he has sustained. The bullet entered at the base of the neck, just above the collar bone on the right side here," pointing to the location on himself, "and there is no exit wound. He has likely lost a considerable amount of blood, which may account for his unconscious state. Since his pulse is quite rapid, I fear the onset of inflammation and putrefaction, which in turn could lead to further bleeding. One encouraging sign is the apparent lack of injury to his lung."

"What more can be done for him, Doctor?"

"When he awakens, we may need to give him some stimulants to treat the shock. In the meantime, we will care for his wound while closely observing his overall condition for any changes. I'm afraid that any attempt to operate directly on the wound might be very dangerous at this time. Good nursing care and prayers are what he needs most right now."

"Thank you, Doctor. With so many wounded soldiers of your own to care for . . . ?" Interrupting her before she could finish asking her question, Isaac stated emphatically, "Mrs. Wormeley, your husband is no longer an enemy combatant. He is my patient and is under my protection, and in such condition, he will receive the same care as any of the other wounded soldiers here, regardless of their loyalties. Furthermore, he is in no condition to be moved at present. His transport would pose a grave additional danger to his life."

Wiping her tears away with her handkerchief, Penelope looked up at the Union surgeon standing near her and, for the first time during their encounter, met and held his gaze, looking intently at him. Taking this as a sign of recognition, Isaac asked her, "Is it possible, Mrs. Wormeley, that we know each other? Is your Christian name Penelope, and are you not an Endicott of the Magnolias plantation, which is near this place?" For a moment in her astonishment, forgetting her husband's desperate plight and the flight of her slaves, she gasped and closely scrutinized the surgeon in his Federal uniform, who held her husband's fate in his hands. Recovering her composure, she replied, "It seems you have carried out your plan to become a physician and now are a surgeon in the Yankee Army. To meet Isaac Burgess again here and under these circumstances, how extraordinary!"

CHAPTER FOUR

"The fate of our cause rests on us here . . . I will hope for the best, knowing that if I am killed that I die fighting for My Country and my rights . . . "

CAPT. GEORGE W. DAWSON, 1ST MISSOURI INFANTRY,
C.S.A. IN A LETTER TO HIS WIFE, APRIL 26, 1862

THE FIRST RAYS OF sunlight caught Dr. Bernard Irwin smiling as he surveyed the orderly rows of tents which formed the nucleus of his growing division field hospital. With possession of the battlefield, he and his colleagues had worked assiduously the past thirty-six hours, operating on the wounded and reclaiming tents, along with other materiel from the old Union camp, once again in Federal hands. As he lifted his cup of coffee, he couldn't help but smile again, toasting their successful efforts with the anticipation of much more yet to be accomplished. The site was well situated, having a stream with potable water nearby and in its center an abandoned farmhouse, which now served as his headquarters. Over a thousand wounded soldiers were already receiving care in the field hospital, and he estimated that he could eventually accommodate twice that number. The wounded would benefit from clean water and good nursing care while avoiding the trauma and uncertainty of evacuation and transport by steamboat to northern cities. His most pressing challenge had been to identify competent surgeons he could trust with the major operations. His pleasant thoughts were interrupted by the familiar voice of one of those competent surgeons, Dr. Isaac Burgess.

"Dr. Irwin, Dr. Bedell and I have finished operating. Do you have any other tasks we should address before we make our rounds?"

"Dr. Burgess, please pardon my plain speech, but you look like hell! First, go get some sleep." Isaac smiled wearily upon hearing his superior officer's plain speech, realizing how little it had in common with the plain speech of his fellow Quakers. Saluting Dr. Irwin, he had to admit the truth of his assessment. *I must, indeed, look a sight,* he thought.

Awakened several hours later by an orderly, he could vividly recall in minute detail the whole panoply of sights, sounds, even smells which had engulfed him during the past few days, and yet he could not shake off a sense of persistent disorientation. Sitting up and daring to examine his reflection in a mirror on the small side table in his tent, he was met by a face that justified Dr. Irwin's blunt assessment earlier that morning. *Who is this pathetic specimen of humanity? It's not just my appearance that has changed. That's a matter to be easily addressed with soap, water, and a comb. No, what deeper transformation has been wrought by my immersion in so much suffering and death? Am I the same Isaac Burgess I was just a few days ago?* He repeated his silent question to the mirror. *Who is this pathetic specimen of humanity?* After attending to his personal toilette with some care, he began his "morning" rounds in the early afternoon.

"Amos, how are you feeling today?"

"It is very strange, Doctor. My left hand feels hot, and at times there are sharp pains in the fingers. But when I look for it and it's not there, I can't understand how I can be feeling such things! Am I losing my mind?"

"No, Amos, you are not mad. The remnants of the nerves that once served your hand and forearm are present in your upper arm and can still transmit sensations to your brain as if your hand and fingers were still intact. With these new symptoms, I think it prudent to change your dressing and examine your wound now." Turning to the hospital steward who was attending a patient nearby, Isaac gave orders to bring clean water, lint dressings, and chloroform for the dressing change, as well as some laudanum for the pain which would follow the procedure. Distressed by the appearance of Amos's wound, Isaac went in search of his senior medical officer, still hoping that he could convince him of the urgent necessity to formally explore the wound.

Casting a glance back at his junior medical officer, Dr. Davis P. Hill scowled at Isaac. "Burgess, I had a winning hand. What kind of mischief are you now up to that should require leaving a very pleasant card game?"

"Sir, I am very concerned about this soldier's wound. Please, let us examine it together," Isaac whispered to his senior colleague, trying to avoid further distressing Amos. Ignoring the anxious look on their patient's face, Dr. Hill loudly exclaimed, "Didn't I tell you to leave this soldier's wound alone?"

"But Dr. Hill, is it not standard practice to daily assess our patients' condition and to examine and dress their wounds? If you would care to examine it, you can see that erysipelas is developing in the stump. In addition to the color change, please note the presence of marked edema, another sign of the incipient inflammation. Unfortunately, a novel pain has made its appearance that may well be related to the changes progressing in the wound. I strongly urge you to surgically explore this wound as soon as possible."

"Burgess, here are your orders regarding this patient. You may continue to daily dress his wound and treat his pain, but you will *not* bother me again with any of your ridiculous pleas to explore his wound." Turning around, Dr. Hill hoped he might still catch the remainder of the card game but not before Isaac had grasped his arm and hissed in his ear, "Dr. Hill, I must follow your orders; but I do so *under protest*. Without prompt exploration of his wound, debridement of the devitalized tissues, and securing of the severed vascular structures, this young soldier will lose his only chance of survival."

"Why, you arrogant puppy! Let go of me, wretch! Don't think that I won't keep a record of your insolence and insubordination. I could have you court-martialed for your behavior."

"Dr. Hill, if you feel that my behavior warrants such action on your part, I welcome the opportunity to defend my professional record while serving in this regiment."

As Isaac relaxed his grip on Davis Hill's sleeve, the senior surgeon quickly moved away from his subordinate while uttering his favorite epithet for Isaac—"Damn Quaker!"—under his breath. After his anger dissipated, Isaac reflected to himself, *Dr. Hill, you will never attempt to court-martial your junior officer for two reasons: you would be exposed for the fraud and quack you are, and you would be hard-pressed to find another to do your work, as well as suffer your abuse, if I were gone. But, for my own sanity, I must seek a transfer to another regiment!*

More diarrhea, Isaac sighed, as he looked up to see yet another soldier approaching during sick call, grimacing and grasping his abdomen. *What is it the boys are calling it down here? Oh yes, the 'Tennessee Quickstep.' Thank God for the opium poppy*, he thought as he handed out the medication to slow the rapid flux and relieve the cramps of a private who had successfully dodged a rendezvous with death on the two preceding days but who could not escape this more mundane threat. As sick call was ending, his ennui was suddenly relieved when one of the orderlies came up and reported, "Doctor Burgess, you requested to be notified of any change in the condition of the wounded Confederate captain. He is awake and in some pain, sir. His wife is asking for you to come and evaluate him."

As Isaac approached Captain Wormeley's bed, he was met by Penelope, who had been at her husband's bedside mopping his brow with a moist cloth. "Isaac . . . Dr. Burgess, he has awakened but seems very confused and agitated," she stated anxiously. "At first, he seemed to recognize me. He grasped my hand tightly and kissed it. When I tried to extricate my hand because the pressure of his grip was becoming painful, he said, 'Mammy Katie, don't leave me. I'm afraid.' What does it all mean; is he dying?"

"Who is Mammy Katie?"

"She was his Negro nurse during his infancy and childhood. He has always spoken of her with great fondness. She died before we were married."

Captain Wormeley interrupted their conversation by trying to climb out of bed. Only with considerable difficulty were Isaac and a hospital attendant able to restrain the delirious captain. He began to insistently call for 'Mammy Katie,' and only quieted somewhat when Penelope allowed him to grasp her hand again, tightly squeezing it until she winced in pain. Isaac called to another attendant to bring laudanum, which he was only able to persuade the delirious captain to swallow after much coaxing by 'Mammy Katie.' As its analgesic and sedating properties slowly took effect, the suffering captain gradually relaxed his grip on his wife's hand and lapsed into a fitful sleep.

While Isaac continued to cautiously restrain the delirious captain, he felt the intensity of the young Southern matron's gaze as she assessed the changes time had wrought in the appearance of her *Friend* from the North. Once his patient showed no more signs of agitation, Isaac gave her his full attention. Before he could speak, Penelope observed, "You're taller than I remember . . . and that full beard. Your eyes finally gave you away—the gentle Quaker boy! Whatever induced you to take up the uniform of a soldier, a Yankee invader at that? Surely, your uncle Levi Coffin must not approve. Am I mistaken about the commitment of the Society of Friends to their Testimony Against War?"

"Mrs. Wormeley, with the perspicacity I remember so well, you have discerned the painful paradox of my life. Indeed, my uncle is quite disappointed in me, as are also my parents. To enter military service, even as a noncombatant medical officer, is abhorrent to many in my parent's generation, among the Society of Friends, and has been a source of considerable controversy among my peers. Even my status in the Society may be in question," Isaac replied with sadness.

"So, putting on the Federal uniform has disrupted those relationships most dear to you. I see you have even abandoned the plain speech of *thy* Quaker brethren—doubtless another casualty of Yankee tyranny!" Penelope added with heightened sarcasm. "Why? What possible good can be achieved? How can you in good conscience be part of an army of conquest? Do you really want to be part of this army of hungry locusts that has come to destroy everything in its path?" Consciously pausing to allow some of the tension to dissipate, Isaac responded slowly, "Perhaps I can be of some small assistance to your husband and you, despite my compromised status as a member of the Society of Friends." Reddening, Penelope quickly protested, "Forgive me; of course, I am grateful for the medical care you are providing my husband." Wishing to shift the focus of their conversation elsewhere, Isaac asked, "Mrs. Wormeley . . . ?"

"Please call me by my Christian name, Penelope."

"Penelope, I remember that when we first became acquainted ten years ago, your fondest desire was to free your slaves at the Magnolias plantation after you had completed preparing them for emancipation. It was a blessed goal. Were you successful in your efforts?" When Isaac's question was met by silence, he looked inquiringly at Penelope, only to be startled by the expression on her face. An equal admixture of anger and embarrassment tinged with despair seemed to suffuse her features, rendering her temporarily speechless.

Penelope, who was usually not at a loss for words, gave a halting reply. "I . . . I don't quite know how to answer your question. My vision for their future has never wavered, and yet . . ." But, warming to her subject, she proceeded with growing vehemence to deflect Isaac's question as a torrent of words tumbled out of her mouth. "This vile Yankee plague has descended upon us and destroyed everything in its path! My husband may die defending his state, our overseer abandoned the Magnolias so as not to 'miss the fun of killing Yankees,' and my dear parents are gone, both having died during a yellow fever outbreak while visiting New Orleans nearly five years ago. Surely you remember the eloquent slave preacher, Moses our blacksmith. Upon hearing the sounds of battle at Pittsburg Landing, he announced to everyone on the plantation that the *Year of Jubilee* has come. As a result, he has led nearly all our able-bodied servants away to the Federal lines. It's quite likely, I may soon be a widow with two small children and one house servant remaining, Betsey our cook, who says she will stay for the moment because she pities me!"

Struck by the gale force wind of the distraught Southern matron's emotional tirade, Isaac could only respond with a look of complete bewilderment as he struggled to form a compassionate reply. "Penelope, I am so sorry to hear of your parents' deaths and of all your suffering." Cautiously, he added, "Do you think it might just be possible that Moses was exercising a prophetic gift in his pronouncement regarding the *Year of Jubilee*? The timing and circumstances may not have been of your choosing, and yet the emancipation of your slaves has come, suddenly and swiftly. Is this not in some sense a fulfillment of your heartfelt desire for them?"

Still flushed, Penelope quickly responded, "It has always been *my* responsibility, indeed *my* right, to emancipate them at the opportune moment of *my* choosing. They will not survive without *my* guidance and protection." Startled by her vehemence, but not silenced, Isaac responded with some irony, "It seems that Moses and your other slaves have ideas of their own about the *opportune* moment for their liberation. Ten years have passed since you expressed your noble goals for your slaves' future emancipation. Were you able to free *any* of your slaves during that period? Has your husband been supportive of your vision?" Stung by this reminder that the fate of *her* slaves was no longer hers alone to determine but also subject to her husband's whims, Penelope angrily responded, "It has always been the sacred right of the Southern States to order and administer their institutions in their own way!"

With the finality of Penelope's invocation of Southern Rights came a pause in their conversation, during which Isaac could only reflect with utter amazement on the profound changes that ten years of polemics and sectional discord had wrought in the idealistic friend he had known. *Oh, Penelope! What has become of your compassion for your slaves? I wonder how many of them have been sold by your husband. This plague of locusts— the Yankee Army, which you understandably detest—is an instrument of liberation. It will accomplish, albeit imperfectly and with great suffering, what you and other well-meaning Southern slaveowners seem only capable of contemplating over a lifetime of hesitation and equivocation. Moses is right. The Year of Jubilee has come accompanied by all the horrors of a civil war.* Speaking softly and with deliberation, Isaac responded by saying, "I only hope that you can eventually see the hand of Providence in all of this."

"I wonder if you will still be so sanguine about the *Year of Jubilee*, when you see the immense suffering and loss of life among the 'liberated' slaves as they are caught up in the conflict," was Penelope's bitter retort. Avoiding further eye contact with Isaac, Penelope suddenly rose and left her unconscious husband and his Yankee physician. Involuntarily, Isaac's gaze and thoughts followed the diminishing and diminished vision of Southern femininity as she receded quickly down the rows of cots flanking her on either side, apparently insensible to the suffering humanity they contained. *Is this the same person whose grace and charm swept all before her as she navigated the crowded dining room on the steamboat where we first met?* he asked himself in perplexity. *Is this really the same woman who as a young maiden taught her slaves the psalms and gently nursed and comforted the dying among them?*

As soon as she was out of sight, Isaac reflected further upon the young Southern matron's words. *How closely her prediction of imminent suffering among the liberated slaves mirrors the concerns which Uncle Levi has so often expressed about rupturing the relationship between master and slave through force rather than through moral suasion*, he marveled. *'The inevitable resentments of the aggrieved former master would create unbearable hardships for the emancipated slave.'* Regretting the unanticipated direction their encounter had taken, Isaac sadly recognized the wide gulf now separating him from his Southern friend. Resuming his rounds, he was unable to escape from a deepening gloom which insisted on joining him as he moved among his patients.

"Amos, wake up! Dr. Burgess is here to see you." But the wounded youth, who was sweating profusely, did not awaken in response to the verbal prompting of his soldier nurse. "How long has he been in this state?" Isaac asked, as he realized that four days had passed since Amos received his wound.

"Sir, he has been unconscious for the past hour and during the prior two hours, he gradually became quite confused—seemed to think he was home—calling repeatedly for his mother."

"His pulse is quite rapid. I am afraid putrefaction has developed in his wound," Isaac responded after a quick assessment. "Ah, what is this? His dressing, which we changed only a few hours ago, is now soaked through with a rust-colored liquid. His blood clots have begun to liquify, and I can only guess what else may have transpired in this neglected wound!" Turning to his assistant, Isaac said in a voice tinged with bitter irony, "We have been authorized to *only* change the dressing. Since it is soaking wet, we can at least replace it with a clean one." As gently as possible, Isaac, with the help of his assistant, removed the soiled dressing from the stump of what remained of Amos's left arm. "Not only has the blood clot liquified, but the underlying soft tissues are no longer recognizable!" Isaac exclaimed, just in time to become the target of a massive hemorrhage that erupted from blood vessels, which had retracted within the necrotic liquifying tissues at the elbow. "Quick now, apply a tourniquet here above the stump!" Isaac shouted to his assistant as he attempted to apply direct pressure to the stump and quell the bleeding.

Surveying the situation after achieving temporary control over the bleeding, Isaac shook his head. "In addition to the putrefaction in his wound, he has now lost a significant amount of blood. It is only a matter of time. Private, I'll stay with him. Thank you for your assistance. Go get some rest."

As he kept vigil that evening at Amos's bedside, a jumble of bitter thoughts pressed in on him. *Here I am sitting beside a young soldier condemned to an early grave, who might have otherwise lived, except for the arrogance and incompetence of Dr. Davis P. Hill.* As he brooded over this and fully indulged other dark thoughts directed at his senior officer, a disturbing series of questions gradually forced their way into Isaac's consciousness, demanding his consideration. *Could poor Amos be a casualty of my conflict with Dr. Hill? How much has arrogance justified as competence on my part contributed to the demise of this seventeen-year-old boy? Could I have been more diplomatic? No matter how I would like to place the responsibility for Amos's imminent death squarely on Dr. Hill's shoulders, this is a tragedy to which I have made my own contribution. Could another surgeon have persuaded him to act in the best interests of this suffering youth?* These and similar questions began to torture Isaac as he struggled to solve an insoluble problem.

A rustling of bed sheets interrupted Isaac's morbid musing. Looking up at Amos's face, he was compelled by the intensity of his patient's gaze to turn and look toward a point on the ceiling of the tent where the delirious soldier's attention was singularly focused. Oblivious to Isaac's presence, the young veteran of Shiloh tried to raise himself up in bed while not shifting his gaze from the ceiling of the tent. Before Isaac could attempt to calm him and restrain his movements, Amos addressed the unseen person whose presence he felt so intensely and said, "I'm coming, Mother!" Dropping back onto the cot, he lapsed into unconsciousness. Fifteen minutes later, he was gone.

"Dear Mrs. ____, it is with deep regret that I write to inform you of the death of your son, Amos. He died a hero's death, from complications of a wound received on the battlefield. He was a devoted son, being ever solicitous of your welfare while under my care. Indeed, his last words in this world were, 'I am coming, Mother . . .'" Isaac paused in his writing and thought, *"I better not mention that her son's heroism was rewarded with medical incompetence."*

Interrupting Isaac's rounds the next day, one of the hospital attendants approached him. "Dr. Burgess, please come take a look at this."

"What is it, Tom?"

"The Rebel officer, who's still quite confused, was thrashing around this morning, sir. When Elias and I wrestled him back to bed, I noticed a red area of skin at the back of his neck, opposite his wound. Over the past several hours the redness has become more pronounced. He also continues to be quite feverish, with a rapid pulse." Pleased with the attentiveness to detail exhibited by the soldier-nurse, Isaac replied, "Let's go examine him."

"Tom, this is an important development. There is fluctuance underlying the erythematous, reddened area of skin. Putrefaction in the wound appears to be *necessitating* or pointing toward the surface. We may be able to help this man by opening this area surgically. Along with the chloroform and knife, bring some lint dressings and clean water to rinse the wound." Incising the fluctuant area of skin at the back of Captain Wormeley's neck, Isaac was gratified to see an initial rush of pus mixed with partially liquified blood clot drain from the wound. Upon gentle irrigation of the wound, he was startled by the appearance of a round musket ball which he retrieved. Tom, who was assisting Isaac, asked, "Dr. Burgess, what's that doing in his wound? All our troops have rifled muskets. I thought he was one of *our* casualties. It ought to have been a Minié ball, not a round musket ball."

"Tom, it seems that our *Southern* officer was wounded by *Southern* arms. This raises some questions in my mind about the Rebel soldiers who hovered around their wounded captain when we first picked him up on the battlefield. Despite their reticence to speak, my impression at the time was that they were deeply concerned for his welfare. Now, I wonder about the nature of that concern . . ."

CHAPTER FIVE

"I would rather live in Siberia, worse still, in Sahara,
than live in a country surrendered to Yankees."
Mary Chesnut, Southern Diarist, April 15, 1862

Awakened the next day by intense pain radiating down his right arm, Fitzhugh Wormeley was surprised to see his wife sitting at his bedside. "Penny, what are you doing here? Where am I?" he asked, gasping between questions in his distress.

"Oh Fitz, you know me!" Penelope exclaimed with relief. "You've been delirious until now. After you were wounded, you became a prisoner of the Yankees. The Confederate Army has retreated toward Corinth. This large tent is part of what the Yankees call a 'field hospital' that they have assembled on the battlefield."

"Oh Penny, my right arm is on fire! It's paralyzed! I can't move it at all!" Penelope's cries for help attracted the attention of Captain Wormeley's hospital attendant who, in turn, went in search of his physician. Isaac, who had been attending to another patient in an adjacent tent (ward) of the field hospital, came as quickly as possible to assess the situation.

"Captain, this should help ease your pain," Isaac announced as he gave his Confederate patient more laudanum. "Please try to move the fingers in your right hand. Try to make a fist. Are you able to flex and extend your arm at the elbow, like this?" Isaac demonstrated the desired maneuvers.

"I can't do anything with my hand or arm! It's useless dead weight!"

"No," Isaac shook his head. Witnessing meaningful, albeit slight, voluntary movement in some of the tested muscles, he expressed modest optimism. "Certainly, the current condition of your right hand and

34

arm must be discouraging, Captain. However, although you cannot yet perceive it, I assure you there is some function present, and where there is function there might be further improvement in time," Isaac explained.

"But the pain, Doctor, what about the terrible fire in my arm? Will it ever go away?" Captain Wormeley asked with increasing anxiety.

Trying to reassure the Rebel captain as best he could without producing false hopes, Isaac said, "Your pain will be treated with tincture of opium or laudanum for as long as you require it. Both the loss of muscle function and the intense pain are from injury to the nerves at the base of your neck. As with the potential for significant return of muscle function, I *hope* that you will also see a gradual diminution of the pain as you heal. The peculiar burning quality of the pain is consistent with injury to the nerves. What remains unknown at present is the full nature of the injury. If it is primarily due to pressure from the blood that has accumulated in the wound, your prognosis should be better than if the injury was due to a combination of direct trauma to the nerves from the musket ball and the pressure exerted by the blood."

Not satisfied with Isaac's long-winded explanation, the injured captain asked, "How long will it take to recover? I depend upon my right arm."

"It is very difficult to predict, but recovery will likely be slow—months, possibly years. Indeed, you may become dependent on opium for relief of chronic pain as well," Isaac said, clarifying his previous statement with this blunt assessment.

"Are you declaring me a cripple, sir? After being paroled and exchanged I must return to the fight for Southern independence!" Fitzhugh Wormeley exclaimed with as much fervor as he could summon while attempting to sit up before flopping back on his hospital cot, totally exhausted.

Isaac slowly replied, "A better description of your current condition is 'disabled.' Your long-term prognosis is unknown at this time, although I am suggesting that there may be real hope of some recovery in the future. If you were serving in the Union Army, I would have to declare you as *unfit for duty* for the foreseeable future. I am sorry, but I expect the medical officers in your own army would make the same determination."

"Oh, my dear husband, condemned to such terrible suffering by the Yankees!" Penelope exclaimed. "A true Southern hero, you have not hesitated to offer your health and future happiness on the altar of our country's honor. As for the Yankee invaders, they have no honor!" Offering no response, Isaac turned to his assistant, Tom, and quietly instructed him regarding additional interventions to enhance the Southern captain's comfort and left the aggrieved pair to reflect on their altered fortunes.

The soldier-nurse, Tom, who had assisted Isaac in retrieving the musket ball from Captain Wormeley's neck, was silently fuming as he brought a cool compress to place on the wounded captain's forehead. Directing a fleeting look of disgust toward his patient's wife, he muttered, half under his breath, "Pride goeth before destruction, and a haughty spirit before a fall."

"What is this—a Yankee soldier scolding me with Holy Scripture? Such impertinence! How dare you question my motivations or cast aspersions on Southern honor!" His Yankee *impertinence* finally getting the better of him, the hospital attendant decided to explore the nature of Southern honor. "Mrs. Wormeley, may I direct your attention to this lead ball, which I assisted the kind Dr. Burgess in retrieving from your husband's neck?" he asked in a firm but polite manner. Still annoyed with the *rude* soldier-nurse, but her native curiosity piqued, Penelope replied, "How can examination of the lead ball that nearly killed my brave husband justify your unfeeling, rude speech? I should insist that another nurse be assigned to my husband."

Unable to repress a smirk, Tom replied, "Whether you request another attendant to care for your wounded husband is of no concern to me; however, *the truth is*. I must insist that you examine the musket ball and comment on its character. Please, tell me what you see, Mrs. Wormeley."

"I see a perfectly round lead ball," Penelope answered, momentarily forgetting her offended dignity. Tom then produced a Minié ball for her examination and again asked her to describe it.

"This second object lacks the perfect roundness of the first. It has a pronounced conical shape. What is the purpose of this exercise?" Penelope's irritation was now mixed with genuine interest.

"Ma'am, the second object you just examined is the standard projectile fired from the rifled muskets issued to the Federal soldiers that were facing your husband's regiment in the recent battle. It is known affectionately as the Minié ball, after its French inventor. The lead ball retrieved from your husband's wound was not fired from a Federal musket."

"What are you implying by all this obfuscation? Surely, it is perfectly obvious that my husband was wounded by the enemy, fulfilling his duty as an officer and a gentleman." Penelope blustered as she attempted a return to the apparent safety of wounded Southern honor. Turning to her husband, who had maintained silence throughout her exchange with his nurse, Penelope demanded, "Fitz, refute this soldier's insolence. Why, he's implying that you were wounded by your own men—an utterly ridiculous thought!" To Penelope's growing dismay, rather than offering a quick rebuttal to his nurse's assertions, the wounded captain's only response was to turn his face to the wall and remain silent.

"Ma'am, we may indeed be a plague of Yankee locusts invading your country, but you may be surprised to discover that even locusts have a sense of honor. For this reason, I felt compelled to reveal the truth, no matter how painful, regarding your husband's wound. Only he and the Rebel soldiers under his command can give a full accounting of what happened. I suspect you will never gain a true understanding, for the simple reason that your Southern notion of honor is so closely tied to pride. Furthermore, while I readily confess to not sparing your sensibilities, Dr. Burgess, in his compassion—even for traitors—had no intention of bringing you grief by revealing the nature and source of your husband's wound."

Penelope, whose flushed face had gradually acquired a distinct pallor during her exchange with the hospital attendant, interjected, "Did Dr. Burgess order you to keep this information from me?"

"No, ma'am, he did not give a direct order but said, almost more to himself than to me, 'The knowledge of this captain's being wounded by his own men can only cause suffering. Without knowing more of the circumstances involved, it might be better for us to keep this information to ourselves.' He clearly was thinking to minimize your suffering, ma'am. But I must confess, when you started ranting about Yankees having no honor, you got my dander up. Now, you may well be right in saying that most of us Yanks are without honor, I certainly won't make any claim to it. But when you cast your aspersions so wide as to include Dr. Burgess . . . well, I just had to respond."

"Mrs. Wormeley . . . Penelope, I am sorry that you learned about the nature of your husband's wound the way you did," Isaac said upon encountering the wounded captain's wife later that day outside the field hospital.

"Were you really trying to spare my feelings by keeping the information about Fitz's wound from me?"

"Yes, I suppose that was a major factor in my reticence to speak to you about it. All that we knew, and still know, from the evidence at hand is that Captain Wormeley was shot by one of his own men. Until he shares more information about the incident, that is *all* we know. It is an unfortunate fact that during the chaos of battle, soldiers may become the inadvertent, accidental targets of fire from their own side. Without additional evidence, it seemed inappropriate to speculate further as to the actual circumstances underlying his injury. Considering your strong emotional response to his injury, it also did not seem like an opportune time for further discussion," Isaac added gently.

"After rashly expressing my contempt for all of you, I am deeply chastened by your careful choice of words now," Penelope said with regret. "Of course, I should expect nothing less from my old Quaker friend. But have you shared with me everything you know about the circumstances of his wounding?" Seeing hesitation on Isaac's part, Penelope pressed her point. "Please tell me everything you know about it. Don't concern yourself anymore with sparing my feelings."

"I can only tell you what I observed on the battlefield at the time of his capture and the impressions arising from that initial encounter. It must be emphasized that my impressions are just that, only impressions. Truly, it is not my desire to cause you further distress." The intense and expectant expression on Penelope's face overcame Isaac's residual hesitation. He went on to describe the clot of Rebel soldiers that surrounded the wounded captain, their initial resistance to leaving his side when ordered to do so, and how Isaac was mystified by what appeared to be such great solicitude for their captain's welfare, albeit marked by their disconcerting reticence to speak. "Penelope, it was extremely difficult to exchange meaningful information with the soldiers. They remained almost entirely silent to a man, except for one soldier who, after some hesitation, asked if the captain would survive. Needless to say, the discovery of the Rebel musket ball in his wound forced me to reconsider even the minute peculiarities of that initial encounter and place them in an entirely different light."

"Were there many Confederate soldiers present?" Penelope asked with growing apprehension. "Hmm . . . there were at least eight," Isaac said after some consideration. "I remember having some anxiety at the time that they actually outnumbered their four captors by two-to-one."

"Were any of the Confederate soldiers who were with my husband wounded?"

"A couple of them appeared to have minor superficial wounds. All of them were walking without difficulty."

"Do you think any of them would still be here at the field hospital?"

"I seriously doubt it. If you wish, I can ask the sergeant who escorted them from the battlefield about their status." His curiosity aroused, Isaac couldn't help asking, "Do you have reasons to be concerned?"

The veil of patriotic Southern defiance began to lift, revealing a deep sadness, even melancholy, in Penelope's expression. Dismayed by the sudden transformation in his friend, Isaac said, "Please, you should sit and rest. Perhaps we should speak more of these issues at another time."

"Thank you, Isaac. I will sit, but if your time allows, I owe you the truth. Tom, the soldier who is serving as nurse for my husband, is a remarkable individual. Please do not chastise him for revealing your discovery to Fitz and me. If one is to retain any sanity in this world gone mad, pretense must eventually succumb to facts. I still hope that *Southern honor* is more than mere pretense, but he was right to challenge me. *Pride does go before destruction* . . . Where should I begin? Perhaps, Isaac, you have been perplexed and disappointed by the Penelope of your renewed acquaintance, wondering where and when the younger idealistic Penelope you met ten years ago was lost. When you began to ask about my cherished project of slave education and gradual emancipation, I was stung by your questions and reacted in a mean-spirited manner, hiding my embarrassed resentment under the cloak of *Southern rights*. For in truth, my efforts at educating my servants for freedom came entirely to naught. By teaching them to hope as Christians, I only added to their misery, when later, after marriage, my husband began to break up families, selling them to pay off a large debt from his family's heavily mortgaged plantation. Where was the liberation to captives promised in the Scriptures? Naively, just like my notions about slave education, I thought *my* Fitz could be educated about the fundamental humanity and dignity of our servants. Rather, it was I who was quickly educated about the iron control he intended to exert over *all his property*, inherited and acquired through his marriage to the Endicott heiress.

"You may have wondered why our lively correspondence ended abruptly back in '56, when I stopped responding to your letters. Oh, how I later regretted that action, for I missed our friendship. You challenged me to consider perspectives so foreign to my experience here in Tennessee, which I desperately needed and even craved, but also increasingly resented."

"But, what of your abolitionist aunt and uncle in Cincinnati, did you not continue your relationship with them?" Isaac interjected. Penelope paused long enough for Isaac to see a tear form at the corner of her eye and slowly begin its journey down her cheek. Giving Isaac a piercing look, she replied in a voice straining with emotion, "Being daily immersed in our section's increasingly strident attitudes, I became convinced that like my Quaker friend, Isaac Burgess, my aunt and uncle had adopted views that represented a dangerous threat to our Southern way of life. Thus, it seemed my only recourse was to cut off all such relationships. Seeing that my mother was becoming more obdurate in her support of our section and its institutions, my father became increasingly reticent to challenge the prevailing assumptions, privately or in public, which at the time I misunderstood as lending his tacit support. Alas, when I lost my dear parents during the outbreak of yellow fever, I was counseled by my remaining Southern relatives to quickly marry, ideally allying one great Southern fortune to another. Fitzhugh Wormeley was a devoted suitor, in whom I convinced myself I saw a kindred spirit. We would unite our fortunes and thereby expand the opportunity for true philanthropy by preparing the servants of not one but *two* great plantations for freedom.

"Isaac, was it not Socrates who offered the sage advice to *know thyself*? I was not only in desperate need of self-knowledge, but neither did I know the man I was about to marry. The idealized man I had created in my imagination was gradually displaced by the real man, with his many good qualities that were unfortunately compounded with many bad. Almost two years before the war broke out, he had settled all the financial debt, making both plantations highly profitable, but at what a cost in human suffering! A third to half of the Magnolia's servants had been sold, many with little regard to preserving family relationships. Ironically, as profits soared, Fitz purchased many new slaves, expanding and replacing the depleted workforce on both plantations but not restoring the human relationships lost forever through the earlier sales.

"If my memory serves me correctly, when we first met, during your travels with your uncle Levi Coffin in southwestern Tennessee and northern Mississippi, you were in search of free-labor cotton and other produce grown without slave labor. Fitzhugh took increasing exception to the free-labor farmers in our district. Indeed, he made it his mission to either buy many of them out or destroy their profitability in the local markets. A favorite saying of his before the war was, 'The genius of the

Southern economy lies in the perfect wedding of capital and labor." In other words, the slaves performing the labor are also the capital supporting the labor. By this time, my entreaties to honor a different vision were met with a puzzled, indulgent incredulity and then finally ignored. As the *fire-eaters* pressed successfully for secession following the election of Lincoln, I finally suppressed that younger Penelope in my efforts to support my section as a loyal patriot, comforting and deluding myself with the pleasant fantasy, *we'll beat the Yankees, establish our liberty, and eventually free our servants at the opportune time on our own terms.*

"As you may have begun to surmise from my question about the Confederate soldiers surrounding my wounded husband, I am afraid that my husband has made a number of enemies in the community through his aggressive business dealings. It is quite possible that some of those poor individuals he had driven from small farms near our plantation may have joined the same regiment in which he has served as a captain.

"Oh, what revelations may come through a small round lead ball! So, Isaac Burgess, my Quaker friend, you are not the only person compromised by this terrible conflict. The personal compromise you have made in bending the Quaker Testimony Against War to the breaking point must be a great source of pain for you. However, you bend it toward a higher good in your commitment to ending slavery. But, what of someone like me? You have just heard the confession of a repentant slaveowner, who truly abhors the very institution—the great *sin*— responsible for this civil war. And yet, if I were to publicly repent of this great evil, I would, in effect, be *declaring war* on my family, my homeland, and my ancestors who inherited this terrible system. Ultimately, I would become a person without family or country, an island of utter desolation and misery in the universe."

Isaac marveled at the surprising about-face of the young Southern matron as she briefly bared her soul to him. He was dumbfounded both by the brutal honesty of her confession and by the tremendous suffering that could only result from accommodating two diametrically opposed lives in the same person—the public persona of the unquestioning Southern patriot and an inner life haunted by a dark unspeakable reality. *What can I say that will help alleviate her pain?* he asked himself. *What a terrible burden it is to live with such profound contradictions, not only in oneself but in one's family, community, and entire civilization!* After the poignant revelation ended, Isaac cautiously attempted a response. "Perhaps, Penelope, there may be more subtle yet effective ways to repent for the sin of slavery that may also be less fraught with conflict." Penelope eyed her Quaker friend with bemused suspicion. "Dr. Isaac Burgess, are you about to propose a solution to my dilemma which is informed by the Quaker Testimony Against War?" she asked with a slight smile.

Relieved to see his friend finally smile, Isaac nodded and said, "The repentance I am proposing would transform you into a *new* kind of Southerner, one freed of the prejudices born of slaveholding. In an earlier conversation, you prophesied great suffering for the Negroes liberated by the violence of the conflict. My uncle once made the same observation, emphasizing how rupturing the relationship between master and slave by force could produce smoldering resentment on the part of the former slaveholders that would persist for generations. As the nature of your relationship to Moses and your other servants is radically transformed by the war, your basic love and concern for them need not change. Indeed, might it not acquire a newfound purity, untainted by any self-interest? Opportunities may even come in which you can still assist them in their new status, no longer as your slave property but as refugees seeking the freedom and full dignity of human beings created in the image of God."

Penelope smiled wanly at Isaac as she slowly and doubtfully shook her head. "Oh, Isaac Burgess, in your passion to save my *tainted* Southern soul, you remind me how much I truly miss the debates that formed much of our former correspondence. I daresay you now know much more of the discord hidden within many a Southern heart that must accommodate the tortured rationalizations so fundamental to sustaining an evil system upon which our whole civilization depends. It is difficult for me to see how I may be able to help my former servants in their struggle when I may be close to becoming a refugee myself, but I promise you this much, Dr. Isaac Burgess: I will remain deeply interested in their welfare. If some opportunity to be of real assistance does come, I pray God will open the way for me. However, I must also be realistic. I may be the last person to whom they would apply for assistance in their new status." *Definitely not the last person*, Isaac thought, as he remembered Penelope's husband.

CHAPTER SIX

"You will say, Christ saith this and the Apostles say this, but what canst thou say? Art thou a child of Light and hast thou walked in the Light, and what thou speakest, is it inwardly from God?"

<small>GEORGE FOX, A FOUNDER OF THE
RELIGIOUS SOCIETY OF FRIENDS, 1652</small>

Adrian, Michigan
June 14, 1862

Dear Isaac,

It was with great relief that I received thy long letter of May 31—we are so hungry for any news from thee here. Even the few lines thou sent immediately after the terrible battle at Pittsburg Landing were a tremendous balm to the intense anxiety for thy safety, which we all felt in hearing of that cataclysmic struggle—so much destruction and suffering! Oh, where will it all lead, when will it end?

Thy repeated protestations that thou dost not share the same level of danger that the soldiers in combat experience hardly gives reassurance. It is very difficult to imagine that bullets discriminate between combatants and noncombatants. Please, dear brother, forgive a devoted sister's scolding. I should be rejoicing, and indeed, I am very thankful that the secessionists abandoned Corinth to the Federal Army without a major battle. I can only hope that this portends a quick end to the bloodshed.

When thou related thy frustrations with thy senior medical officer, I sensed a novel bitterness in thy words, which I fear may be poisoning thy heart. Oh, Isaac, is it not possible that thou art saving and comforting many of our suffering countrymen who otherwise might fare much worse, if thou were not serving in that regiment? Even though thou art suffering unjustly from his constant barrage of insults, by acting wherever possible as a shield between thy nemesis and those in need of competent and compassionate medical care, art thou not following in our Lord's footsteps? I know this cannot possibly answer thy horror at the needless death of thy young patient whose arm was amputated by the cannonball. Thou gave this as one of the more extreme examples of the senior medical officer's despotism. I shudder to think of the other instances of his gross neglect and incompetence which thou hast not mentioned. Ultimately, what can I say in response to thy frustration at the injustice to thee, and more importantly, the frightful care in which thou must participate against thy will and better judgment? Rather than succumbing to the noxious effects of growing anger and cynicism that seem to be nurtured by every encounter with thy senior colleague, perhaps thou art wise to seek transfer to another regiment. My prayer is that the *Inner Light* of Christ will illumine thy path and give thee patience as thou seek to discern His will. I fear that the 36th Indiana Volunteer Infantry may not be the only regiment in the Union Army which harbors despotic and incompetent medical officers. If thy wish for transfer to another regiment is fulfilled, my hope will be that thou will enjoy not only more collegial professional relationships but an environment in which thou will be nourished in spirit, even amid this terrible conflict. Notwithstanding the many frustrations and difficulties which thou hast endured during thy service with this regiment, does not thy placement in the 36th Indiana seem providential, at least in some respects?

How extraordinary to meet Miss Endicott, I should say Mrs. Wormeley, again and under such circumstances! The combination of her husband's wounding, with his resultant disability and the departure of almost all the slaves from the Magnolias plantation to become contrabands, must have overwhelmed her. Reading thy description of her despair has reminded me that I must retain some compassion, even for slaveowners in their distress, while at the same time rejoicing for their slaves who have escaped bondage. I share thy concern that the large number of contrabands coming into the Union lines every day poses an ever-increasing challenge for the army to provide adequate food, shelter, and protection. Certainly, their care will be viewed as an unwelcome burden by many military officers and soldiers who came to fight a war, not to care for liberated slaves. Oh, how my heart aches for them. I am more firmly resolved than ever to come South with Mrs. Haviland and help address their needs, hopefully as a teacher, but ultimately in whatever capacity is required, as soon as it is safely feasible.

Louisa and Sam hope to join me on some of these expeditions, although I fear for their safety as free Negroes. For if any of the refugee camps we are visiting are overrun by Rebel cavalry they might be harmed or enslaved. In any event, dear brother, I promise to seek out Penelope Wormeley and her family. From what she told thee in your last meeting, she plans to stay with an uncle who lives close by Corinth. If the authorities intend to establish a contraband camp at Corinth, perhaps this will create the opportunity for me to finally meet thy old Southern friend. If it is God's will, I may be able to engage her in the blessed work of educating and caring for the contrabands. She might be able to see her original vision come to fruition, albeit through very different means.

With the challenges of delivering mail to armies in the field, I am not sure thou hast heard from Sam yet. After many frustrations, bureaucratic delays, and despite the steadfast support and encouragement of his mentor, Mr. John Mercer Langston, Sam was *refused* admission to the Ohio Bar! Both Sam and Mr. Langston were flabbergasted, since Sam's formal education and training exceed that of most individuals seeking admission to the Ohio Bar. In retrospect, after further informal discussions with other sympathetic legal colleagues, his mentor, Mr. Langston, was told that his own admission to the Ohio Bar was made possible because he was "nearly white." Apparently, factors such as competence and mastery of a profession have little bearing on one's opportunities if one has a dark skin, even in the *enlightened* state of Ohio. The gross injustice of it was a bitter blow to our dear friend. For the present, he continues to serve as Mr. Langston's assistant in his law practice but remains deeply frustrated by his inability to personally advocate for the rights of Negroes to full citizenship or to directly strike a blow against the slave power. He chafes at not being able to serve in the army but somehow retains the hope of eventually securing a commission as an officer. With the prejudice against Negroes among those still governing the legal profession, even in the state of Ohio, I despair of Sam's dreams being fulfilled any time soon. However, Mr. Langston has reassured him that the opportunity for Negroes to serve in the US Army will come in due time. He is convinced that the government will realize soon enough that the contrabands will be able to do more than build fortifications and drive wagons.

Louisa and I are still quite busy teaching refugees at the Raisin Institute with Mrs. Haviland. Uncle Levi has indicated that he intends to soon visit the different contraband camps to personally ascertain the needs of the refugees, so it is possible that I may travel with him. If, as you predict, a contraband camp is established at Corinth, it will be high on my list of destinations to visit. It would be such a blessing to see thee, if thy transfer has not yet occurred. Please write as soon as thou can. Thy safety is constantly a subject of our prayers.

Thy affectionate sister,

Rebecca

Isaac Burgess looked up from reading his sister's letter. He had already received the bad news directly from his best friend Sam Johnson. Unlike his mentor, John Mercer Langston, a mulatto of mixed-race parentage who at times may have passed for being white, his friend Sam was quite dark—there was no denying his African ancestry. While Oberlin College had welcomed black students like Samuel and Louisa Johnson in the years prior to the War, its commitment to the equality of Negroes had been an unusual exception to the prevailing hostility in the North toward free Negroes and those refugees from the South seeking freedom from slavery. From reading Northern newspapers, Isaac was struck by the wide array of attitudes expressed toward the free Negro in the North and more recently directed at the *contrabands* by editors: occasionally compassionate, often indifferent, and not infrequently hostile. Hostility in the North was often centered in the fear that the contrabands would be unleashed by the Lincoln Administration upon Northern cities and, as low-wage labor, would destroy the livelihoods of white workers in the factories. The commonly held belief that Negroes were representatives of an inferior race, which was a foundational principle of the South's "peculiar institution," was largely unquestioned in the North. *How can someone like Sam or Louisa ever advance in a society with such deep-seated prejudices?* Isaac reflected disconsolately. *Perhaps a violent and bloody civil war is the only means by which such a revolution in attitudes can occur. But what does this say about our civilization? Will a black man only be recognized in his full humanity by being as violent and destructive as his white counterpart? And yet, so many of the Negro editors like Frederick Douglass advocate for the arming of black men as soldiers to prove their inherent manhood. What has become of the Testimony Against War which I still hold dear as a Quaker? Hardly a day passes that I am not immersed to greater depths in the violence of which man is capable! Federal gains during the winter and spring are being rapidly eroded by the actions of the Confederate forces in recent weeks, especially through the audacity of Jackson and Lee in Virginia. Perhaps Uncle Levi was right; I should never have put on the uniform of the United States Army. And yet, how can I stand aloof from all the suffering? Who am I to judge Sam in his desire to bear arms on behalf of his brothers and sisters in chains? No, I must accept the painful fact that I am caught up in a maelstrom from which there is no escape, and I must do the best I can.* Isaac's flirtation with despair was interrupted by the voice of a soldier at the entrance to his tent. "Sir, the mail has just arrived, and it appears there are orders for you."

With growing excitement mixed with apprehension, Isaac quickly perused the contents of his orders. *You are directed to report for duty as soon as practicable to the 88th New York Infantry Regiment of the Second Brigade of the First Division of the Second Corps of the Army of the Potomac. . . . You will retain the rank of Assistant Surgeon, US Volunteers.* A wry smile came to Isaac's lips as he digested the full import of his orders. *I am now ordered to join what may be one of the most aggressive, dare I say bloodthirsty, units in the whole Union Army—the Irish Brigade—and Catholics in the bargain! I now move deeper into the maelstrom, but at least I will finally be free of Dr. Hill.*

As Isaac reflected on the implications of his orders, he resolved to send a letter thanking Dr. Moses Gunn for his assistance in the transfer. Just as his sister Rebecca had warned him, so also his old mentor had cautioned Isaac about the possibility of obtaining a position even worse than his current assignment in the 36th Indiana volunteers. Isaac remembered how in one letter, Dr. Gunn had insisted that glory was not to be found in the grim work of a military surgeon. *"I have heard some complain that surgeons are never alluded to after a battle. No, why should they be? Poor, benighted souls; did anyone dream for a moment that a surgeon's field had aught of glory about it? No, the glory consists of carnage and death. The more bloody the battle, the greater the glory. A surgeon may labor harder, must labor longer, may exhibit a higher grade of skill, may exercise the best feelings of our poor human nature, may bind up many a heart as well as limb, but who so poor as to do him honor? There is no glory for our profession. We may brave the pestilence when all others flee; we may remain firm at our posts when death is more imminent than it ever was on the battlefield; but who sings our praise? Does the world know whom the physicians were who fell at Norfolk, when yellow fever depopulated that* town? Does it know who rushed in to fill their places? And of those who survived, can it designate one? Did they survive to receive fame? Yet those men were braver than the bravest military leader, for theirs was bravery unsupported by excitement or by the hope of fame. No, there are none so poor as to do us reverence. And, thank God, there are few of us so unsophisticated as to expect it."

As Isaac remembered his mentor's words, he realized that transfer to the Irish Brigade might be the perfect antidote to any temptation for him to seek personal recognition as a military surgeon. *The glorious deeds of the brave soldiers of the Irish Brigade during the recent Peninsula Campaign in Virginia, and those yet to be heralded by an eager press, will spare the rest of us any notice,* he thought. *It will only remain for us to do our best to mend the heroes' broken bodies, quietly comfort them in their suffering, and thereby find blessed anonymity.*

McMinnville, Tennessee
August 18, 1862

Dear Rebecca,

Thank thee for thy letter dated the 14th of June. The mail finally caught up with me in Middle Tennessee. I write in haste, since I have just received orders for my transfer. But first I will briefly explain why it has been so difficult to exchange mail in a timely fashion. Our regiment, with others, has spent considerable time and energy chasing the Confederate cavalry commander Nathan Bedford Forrest all over this region, only to be humiliated on more than one occasion by his clever tactics and deceptions. Thou may find the following revelation as surprising as I did. After hearing more of his history, I realized that Forrest is the very same individual who invited Uncle Levi and me to attend the medical lecture at the Memphis Medical College ten years ago. Apparently, he became one of the wealthiest men in Memphis through his buying and selling of human beings. I guess his initial scruples about separating families were overcome. At the beginning of the war, he outfitted a cavalry regiment at his own expense and rose rapidly from private to general. Here is but one example of Forrest, the extraordinary cavalry commander. Responsible for protecting the Rebel retreat in the aftermath of Shiloh, he distinguished himself by a daring, almost suicidal cavalry charge against the pursuing Federal forces. He got out ahead of his own troopers and was surrounded by angry Federal soldiers, one of whom shot him point-blank in the hip, raising him in the saddle. Notwithstanding his serious injury, he exercised such presence of mind as to grab one of the frightened soldiers in blue and lifted him up behind his saddle as a shield, thereby securing his retreat to his own troops. Such is the reckless daring of this very dangerous Confederate officer. Suffice it to say, his reputation grows daily as he occupies the energies of increasing numbers of Federal soldiers in his pursuit.

In his most recent letter, Sam hinted that there may be other ways, apart from serving as a lawyer, in which he can support the struggle for Negro freedom and equality. He expressed a desire to visit me at whichever regiment I am assigned in the Army of the Potomac, when and if the transfer occurs. I am not sure what schemes he has in mind, but I fear that they will likely involve significant risk.

Anyway, my important news to share is that my orders for transfer to the Army of the Potomac have arrived . . . I don't know what to expect, but I suspect I will be the first Quaker doctor my Irish patients will have ever encountered. I will send a brief note to Sam informing him of my new regiment. Although at present the brigade is near the capital, I suspect with General Lee on the offensive, my new regiment will soon be on the move.

Ever thy affectionate brother,

Isaac

P.S. Through orderlies coming from the military headquarters in Corinth, I have heard that tremendous plans are being laid to establish a secure contraband camp there. I hope that thou will be able to see it in the coming months.

CHAPTER SEVEN

*"In my regiment, as private soldiers, there were seven first-class
lawyers! Last, but not least, the surgeons of this brigade were among
the first in the army—Dr. Reynolds had no superior."*

FR. WILLIAM CORBY, CHAPLAIN 88TH
NY VOLUNTEER INFANTRY REGIMENT

A DEEP GLOOM HAD settled over the Army of the Potomac, which even
the cheerful warmth of a September sun could not dispel, as the troops
reluctantly left the safety of the capital in pursuit of Lee's invading
Army of Northern Virginia. Not even having their beloved "Little Mac,"
General George B. McClellan, back in full command could provide a
sufficient antidote to the despondency of the combined force, made up
of dispirited units fresh from the disaster of Second Bull Run and exhausted veterans of the failed Peninsula Campaign. And yet the morale
of armies is not merely subject to the personalities of charismatic leaders. More than anything, the spirit of the Army of the Potomac reflected
the collective responses of each soldier, not only to human charisma
but to less exalted—though more powerful—elements within their environment. For the Army's mood underwent a rapid, almost miraculous
transformation within a few days of stepping out on the roads of Western Maryland. The warmth of a *pro-union* Maryland sun was reflected
in the faces of the citizenry, who came out in large numbers to greet
their soldiers in blue. They were no longer despised enemies in Rebel
territory; here, they were welcomed home as defenders and protectors!
It was as a witness and participant in this remarkable metamorphosis
that Dr. Isaac Burgess eventually caught up with the 88th New York Volunteer Infantry on their way to Frederick, Maryland.

Marked by alternating bouts of sleep and wakefulness, Isaac Burgess's journey by rail had offered a much-needed opportunity for rest and reflection. For an Indiana boy whose furthest eastward travel up to this point had been Cleveland, Ohio, Isaac eagerly absorbed the changing landscape from the window of his railway carriage. An intangible quality, subtle, and yet distinctive from his Midwestern experience, became apparent to him as he passed through the many small towns, villages, and farms on his eastern journey to the Federal capital. He puzzled over how to define this quality which so specifically marked his perceptions of the East. He could not help but smile when he finally identified its defining character. *Why, there's a solidity, a sense of permanence about these communities,* he realized. *They have acquired the dignity of age—a notion entirely amusing, I suppose, to a visitor from Europe, with its millennia of history, but for a Westerner like me, whose very existence is infused with the haste of the new, they are indeed old. Yes. Three or more generations of one family occupying the same land constitutes a venerable antiquity here in our young Republic,* he thought. *And yet, will it survive civil war?*

Arriving in the capital, Isaac's warm impressions of rural Eastern America and its *ancient* durability had been quickly displaced. Passing through the outer ring of fortresses surrounding Washington, the fact that the nation was tearing itself apart in a civil war came crashing back into his consciousness. The abrupt transition from charming small-town America, seemingly untouched by the vicissitudes of war, to a capital very nearly under siege was so jarring that he could not help but blurt out, "Am I still in the same country?" Another passenger sitting nearby looked up from reading his newspaper, and seeing Isaac's uniform, commented drily, "This must be your first time in Washington. The capital's been like this for more than a year, at least since the disaster of First Bull Run. And now, a year later, we've had an even worse catastrophe on the same battlefield, compounded by the Rebel invasion! Mark my words," the anonymous prophet of doom added, "the slave power will triumph soon through the competence of generals like Lee and Jackson. Our poor benighted Republic and with it, the light of liberty, will be extinguished from the face of the earth!"

As if the profound dejection which his neighbor on the train had so generously poured into his soul were not enough, Isaac's brief tour of the nation's capital after leaving the train only added to his own gathering melancholy. Searching in the city for his regiment, he felt increasingly smothered by the spirit of despair which seemed to permeate the atmosphere. Learning that the Irish Brigade was already in motion, but hoping to quickly catch up and report for duty, he left the capital on horseback, joining the masses of Federal troops clogging the roads of Western Maryland. Mingling physically with the very scenes of Eastern rural life which had so recently charmed him from his railway carriage served as a tonic, his mood gradually lifting the further from Washington he rode. But more than anything, he was struck by how he and the other soldiers were so susceptible to the kind words and simple generosity of strangers. It seemed a sort of contagion was spreading among the troops, one not wrought by dark and miasmic agencies but rather an epidemic of cheerfulness. How else could young soldiers, so long afflicted by home-sickness, respond to the hugs and kisses of pretty girls bringing home-made treats for "*our* boys in blue"? In his amazement at the rapidity of the transformation, Isaac realized that no matter how much mental effort might be expended, human moods were simply not subject to the dictates of reason. In his musings, as he rode along, he had to acknowledge the obvious, *Human reason cannot compete with the smile of a pretty girl! Indeed, and how contagious is the joy spreading from that smile!* When Isaac heard a young private exclaim, "We're back in God's country!" he found himself in full agreement. *Exchanging the role of invader for that of defender is a most welcome change*, he thought.

Late the next day, arriving in Frederick as the sun was setting, Isaac was finally able to report to Dr. Francis Reynolds, the senior surgeon of the 88th New York Volunteer Infantry. Looking up from the desk at which he was writing a report, the middle-aged Dr. Reynolds surveyed the young Midwestern physician dispassionately. "Well lad, it seems you have been rather keen to transfer to the Army of the Potomac. I must say, you've picked a rather interesting time to make the transition," he added with a tinge of irony. "I am not particularly interested in your reasons for seeking a transfer; however I couldn't help but note that among your letters of reference there was no letter from the senior surgeon of your regiment, Dr. Hill. Notwithstanding that omission, you were highly recommended by your academic mentor and former partner in medical practice, Dr. Moses Gunn. I had the pleasure of Dr. Gunn's professional acquaintance during the recent Peninsular Campaign—a truly remarkable surgeon and gentleman—his endorsement of your qualities as a physician and surgeon is something I am certain he would not give lightly. You may be unaware that Colonel Grose, your regimental and later brigade commander, wrote his own unsolicited letter on your behalf. He perceives your departure as a great loss, emphasizing your competence not only as an operating surgeon but as a physician well-liked and trusted by the officers and men under his command." Pausing, Dr. Reynolds then gave Isaac a piercing look, which evolved into a broad smile. "Did you ever expect that you would end up in an all-Irish Catholic regiment? The good Dr. Gunn also happened to mention in his correspondence that although you're a Quaker, you didn't hesitate to collaborate closely with the Catholic Sisters of Mercy in their charitable labors for the sick and suffering during your time working with him in Detroit. He even went on to suggest from his perspective 'as a High Church Episcopalian' that you might benefit greatly from a closer acquaintance with the Roman Church." Relishing the look of astonishment in Isaac's eyes, Dr. Reynolds laughed heartily and said, "You must be just a wee bit surprised by how much we already know about you," as he rose from the desk to shake Isaac's hand.

"Dr. Reynolds, I . . . don't quite know how to respond to your kind and surprising words," Isaac replied, still nonplussed. "You seem to know much more about me than I you." With a twinkle in his eye, Dr. Reynolds responded, "That's as it should be, my young colleague. We are very glad to have another competent surgeon join the brigade. As for your being a Protestant, we'll forgive you that failing *because* of your Quaker affiliation. When the English were doing their best to starve my fellow countrymen during the great potato famine, your brothers and sisters in the Society of Friends were the only members of that blighted race to offer the poor Irish succor in their distress, for which you will always be remembered in our prayers."

Checking his pocket watch and changing the subject abruptly, the Irish surgeon said, "Dr. Burgess . . . may I call you Isaac? We had better go organize our medical supplies and kits. There are several staff you should also meet, including my brother Laurence, the senior surgeon of our brigade, and I would like for you to become acquainted with the facilities at our disposal here in Frederick. We may need them very soon. Just before you arrived, I was notified that our brigade is to depart early tomorrow toward South Mountain in pursuit of the enemy."

CHAPTER EIGHT

"The days after the battle are a thousand times worse than the day of the battle—and the physical pain is not the greatest pain suffered. How awful it is . . . The dead appear sickening but they suffer no pain. But the poor wounded mutilated soldiers that yet have life and sensation make a most horrid picture. I pray God may stop such infernal work—though perhaps he has sent it upon us for our sins. Great indeed must have been our sins if such is our punishment."

Dr. William Child, Surgeon,
5th New Hampshire Volunteers, September 22, 1862

Dampness reigned, permeating everything. Seeping through the interstices of his uniform, its clammy touch first tickled and then cajoled until fitful sleep finally abandoned Isaac Burgess early on the morning of September 17, 1862. As he rose and stretched his sodden frame, he noticed that there were many others around him for whom a restful repose had not come that night. He shuddered to think that many of his insomniac comrades would find rest soon enough, an uninterrupted tranquility, secure in its permanence. In the profound darkness of the nocturnal drizzle, he could merely sense the presence of the two behemoths resting warily opposite each other, separated only by a small creek bearing the name of Antietam. Because of their proximity to the enemy, the commanders on the Union right had decided against fires, for which the sleepless soldiers compensated by meditatively chewing the grounds of the coffee they would have preferred to drink while awaiting the dawn.

Much of what had happened in the past several days remained a jumble in Isaac's mind. As they had marched toward South Mountain,

54

rumors had passed through the ranks of some extremely valuable information that General McClellan had providentially obtained about the disposition of Lee's army. Hopes ran high that Lee and his Rebel Army might be trapped and even destroyed. By the time Isaac and the other medical officers had reached South Mountain, it was quite evident that there had been ferocious fighting, the Confederate forces yielding ground slowly in their desperate effort to give Lee time to concentrate and thereby protect his scattered army. The Union victory at South Mountain seemed to put the final touches on the transformation in mood of the Army of the Potomac from crushing despair to an almost manic exuberance in their anticipation of victory. The Irish Brigade had been given the honor to take the lead in the pursuit of the fleeing Rebels as they concentrated their forces at the town of Sharpsburg on the Potomac side of Antietam Creek.

The elation flowing through the Army of the Potomac in its pursuit of the Rebel Army was for Isaac evanescent, giving way to sober reflection in the predawn darkness. *Have I been just as intoxicated by the shouts of victory and the sight of fleeing Rebel soldiers as the others?* he asked himself. *Has the restoration of morale in this army been transmuted from patriotic high spirits into the bloodlust of a large predatory beast hungry for slaughter?* he wondered with a growing sense of foreboding. Among the many horrific sights from the fighting at South Mountain, one especially haunted him. Traveling in the wake of the destruction, Isaac had been surprised to find an intact human being, a young Rebel soldier, resting by the roadside propped up against a tree. Inexplicably, there he was quietly reading a book in his lap when everything around him was in tatters—body parts strewn about with blood-staining rocks, bushes, and mother earth. Drawn to the strange vision in all its incongruity, Isaac had dismounted to get a closer look. To his dismay, he discovered that sightless eyes were still directed to a passage marked by the young corpse's bloodied finger—*Blessed are the peacemakers. . . .*

With growing anxiety, he thought, *I must compose myself, or I will be of little assistance to those who will shortly be clinging to life. What did that great early Friend, Isaac Penington, my namesake, always emphasize?* 'Come out of the knowledge and comprehension *about* things, into the *feeling life*; and let that be thy knowledge and wisdom . . . and that will lead thee . . . without reasoning, consulting, or disputing.' *I cannot reason my way through all this madness, but perhaps the compassionate Spirit within will guide me. Oh Lord, help me to transcend knowledge and wisdom and enter that 'feeling life' for the sake of my suffering patients*, he silently prayed.

Isaac's inner counsels were rudely interrupted as the beasts awakened in the mist. At 6 a.m., the sudden flash and thunder of an artillery duel, coupled with the rising sound of musketry off to the right, heralded the beginning of the slaughter he had been dreading. Hooker's Union Army I Corps attacked the left flank of Lee's army with a furious intensity, which was reciprocated by Stonewall Jackson's veterans. Not knowing the details of McClellan's plan of attack, Isaac and his fellow regimental officers were merely informed that Sumner's II Corps, including the Irish Brigade, would soon be engaged in support of the action initiated by the I Corps in conjunction with General Mansfield's XII Corps. As time passed, the definition of *soon* acquired an increasingly elastic character, becoming a source of growing tension among the soldiers as they waited their turn to enter the slaughter pen. When the II Corps was called into action after 9 a.m., General Sumner impetuously lead Reynolds's division into battle before his two other divisions had even crossed the Antietam, hoping to rapidly exploit a perceived weakness on the Confederate left near the small, white-washed church of a German pacifist sect, the Dunkards. A sudden, unanticipated attack by Rebel reinforcements on his left collapsed Sumner's flank before he could reach the little white church. The two remaining divisions of Sumner's II Corps, of which the Irish Brigade was a part, were then directed southward toward a sunken farm road, which—having been deeply rutted by many years of use—formed an excellent defensive position. Here, portions of two Confederate divisions were effectively hidden, defending Lee's center.

Seeing that the brigade was finally going into action, Dr. Reynolds, with Isaac riding beside him, selected a large straw stack near the barn of a farm in the rear of the brigade and said, "Here, we'll set up a temporary field hospital. The straw will provide something clean and comfortable for the wounded lads to lay on as well as serve another purpose for us. It will absorb much blood today." Appreciating the stack's height, Isaac noted, "Hopefully, it will also provide shade for at least some of the wounded. I am afraid that the day will be quite warm now that the clouds and mist have dissipated." As the medical officers began to organize the makeshift hospital, at about 10:30 the order came from General Meagher, the brigade commander, for the soldiers to move forward at the double-quick. Startled by the unexpected sight of a military chaplain galloping past them *toward* the sound of battle, Isaac couldn't help but stare after him. Dr. Reynolds paused from setting up an operating table, smiled, and said, "There goes Fr. Corby, the chaplain of our regiment; he'll likely be asking the boys to make an Act of Contrition, so that he can give them absolution before they face death." Perceiving the confusion manifested in the face of his Quaker colleague, he added, "Ah, now that is the very best medicine! We bind their wounds, but he tends their souls." Isaac could only respond, "Before this moment, I've never seen a military chaplain ride into battle. In my experience, they spend their time offering words of comfort to the sick and wounded in the rear or encourage the soldiers between battles with prayer meetings and Sunday sermons." It was now Dr. Reynolds's face that wore a confused expression. "But who will shepherd their poor suffering souls to the other side at the moment of death, if not a priest? Oh . . . yes, now I see. Forgive my ignorance. For Protestants, I guess the sacraments are not so tangible. If you could be there with the good chaplain right now, you would witness an extraordinary thing. Upon the face of every one of our Irish boys, even if only for the briefest moment following receipt of the priest's absolution for their sins, you would see a look of joy and peace. It is this peace that translates into an unwavering bravery in the face of death."

Quickly, the straw stack became a silent witness to the flood of wounded Irish soldiers rolling back from the Sunken Road, which would this day earn its new epithet, *Bloody Lane*. The 63rd NY Volunteers were the first elements of the Irish Brigade to encounter at close range the concentrated firepower of the Confederate soldiers who, rising suddenly, as if in ambush, collapsed their left flank. As senior regimental officers fell, their more junior colleagues, for as long as they were standing, assumed command, laboring intensively to restore order out of the chaos. Along with the continual ebb and flow of the assaults directed at the Sunken Road, the numbers of wounded, dying, and dead soldiers on the field steadily increased. The unique tactics favored by General Meagher, buck and ball administered through smoothbore muskets at close quarters and followed up with the bayonet, gave ample expression to Irish bravery, while also assuring Irish destruction in large numbers. By this time in the conflict, their Southern adversaries, well-armed with Enfield-rifled muskets, were able to pour a highly accurate, deadly fire into their ranks well before the Irish smoothbores could be effective.

In his efforts to supervise the stretcher-bearers, Isaac left the relative safety of the field hospital, moving closer to the combat zone. Instinctively, as he had done at Shiloh, he raised his arm to shield his face and head from the storm of far-from-spent Minié balls whizzing around him. Smoke moving over the battlefield created a surreal mix in which the blood and gore of men and horses would drift in and out of view, and where the dead and dying were intermingled, with the wounded hobbling to the rear. Accompanying the gruesome vision was a cacophonous mix of exploding shells, the crack of musketry, and the forlorn whinnies and cries of pain from horses and men in their agony.

Disoriented within this rapidly evolving hellscape, Isaac was astonished to recognize, far ahead of his stretcher-bearers and close to the firing line, the figure of Fr. Corby bent over a wounded soldier. Apparently absorbed completely in his pastoral task, the chaplain seemed oblivious to the dangers around him, moving quickly from one soldier in extremis to the next. *How can he be so calm and fearless amid the whizzing bullets and exploding shells?* Isaac wondered as he hugged the earth after a nearby explosion sent him ducking for cover. Gesturing to his stretcher-bearers to return toward the rear with their wounded, Isaac threw one last glance back in the direction of the Catholic chaplain, who—seemingly unperturbed—continued his pastoral rounds in hell.

Heat and glare from an unrelenting midday sun pitilessly dispelled any remaining shadows that had been cast by the straw stack, making the thirst of wounded soldiers and sweating surgeons more acute. Looking up from operating to wipe his brow, Dr. Reynolds sighed and then shouted over the din to Isaac, who was operating nearby, "This heat is quite insufferable. How are you faring, my young Quaker colleague?"

"A bit of cold water would be a luxury right now, although our patients need it the most," Isaac replied. And then he quickly added, with a wry grin, "An old mentor of mine, Dr. Way, would always say that inadequate light is the bane of surgeons. Wouldn't you agree, Dr. Reynolds, that notwithstanding our other frustrations, we are indeed blessed with excellent illumination?" Breaking out into hearty laughter, the profusely sweating Irish surgeon gave Isaac an approving look and said, "Why, for shame, Dr. Reynolds! Here ye be complaining about heat and thirst, while your colleague has been able to summon forth a praiseworthy gratitude for better lighting!" Acknowledging Dr. Reynolds's response with a quick smile, Isaac surveyed the surrounding chaos that had acquired the dignity of 'field hospital.' *In circumstances such as these, one must search diligently for some ray of hope, no matter how trivial,* he thought.

As Bloody Lane was cleared of its defenders, the focus of the action shifted to the Union left, where forces under General Ambrose Burnside's command had been struggling to cross a well-defended bridge over Antietam Creek in their efforts to collapse the right flank of Lee's army. With the relative lull in fighting at the center, Isaac's duties acquired a rhythm in which he supervised the recovery and triage of the Irish wounded from the field, alternating with progressively more time given to operating on those individuals who might benefit from surgical intervention. In brief moments of reflection while wiping his sweating brow, he was grateful to be so fully preoccupied with the work at hand. *Better not to think on it, better to become a medical machine—assess the wounded, dress their wounds, operate where possible, and stay busy; first and foremost I must remain busy—this must be my refuge!* he mused in his attempt to confine himself to being a small cog in that vast machine of war, the Army of the Potomac. And so, Isaac and his colleagues operated into the night, their ministrations continuing through the early morning hours, the better illumination of the day now replaced by lantern light.

As the grey light in the East was being transmuted to the orange red of dawn, the two behemoths, so imposing on the previous dawn but now thoroughly bloodied and exhausted, faced each other warily. Isaac, who had taken a break from operating, sipped hot coffee at the front door of the Roulette farmhouse, which had been appropriated as a Union hospital. After nightfall, the Irish Brigade's surgeons had finally moved their operating indoors from the farm's straw stack. Surveying the scene around him, Isaac realized that there was hardly a patch of ground surrounding the farmhouse and its outbuildings which was not occupied by the wounded. Fully absorbed in the macabre lullaby, composed of the soft moaning intermingled with louder groans and cries of pain coming from the recumbent forms in the yard, he was startled when a lieutenant approached and addressed him, "Sir, I have orders to begin transporting those wounded who are sufficiently stable via ambulance to the hospitals in Frederick." Responding to the look of incredulity on Isaac's face, the lieutenant added, "I realize this must be surprising to you. But, as the officer in command of our brigade's ambulances, I want to assure you that I, along with all the other ambulance officers, received these orders directly from the Medical Director of the Army of the Potomac, Dr. Letterman, himself. If you have any questions, you can take them up with Dr. Letterman over at the Pry Farm." Recovering from his initial surprise, Isaac replied, "Lieutenant, your orders are indeed most welcome. I apologize for my evident incomprehension when you announced your orders. Having wallowed in chaos for the past twenty-four hours, I was not prepared for the possibility that order might be restored." Grinning, the lieutenant responded, "Dr. Letterman, God bless him, means to do just that!" Recovering a modicum of hope, Isaac exclaimed, "Well let's not disappoint him! I'll start making a list of candidates for you immediately."

Being new to the Army of the Potomac, Isaac had not been fully apprised of the changes wrought in medical services by Dr. Jonathan Letterman with the blessing of the Surgeon General, Dr. William Hammond. While Isaac determined potential candidates for transport, Dr. Reynolds, who was working with him, described the reforms introduced by Dr. Letterman, including his advocacy for healthier diets to combat scurvy among the troops but especially his insistence on creation of an ambulance corps under medical control. With the horrific outcome of the previous day's combat, Dr. Letterman now had the opportunity to demonstrate the benefit of timely transport of the wounded to local hospitals for definitive longer-term care.

The etiquette of armies has its own peculiar logic; being the prerogative of generals, it is beyond the ken of the mere mortals in the ranks. In the dance of death, both the killing and the burial of the killed, it is ultimately the generals who define the choreography. After bidding adieu to the first wave of ambulances, Isaac waited with growing impatience for a truce allowing both armies to bury their dead and rescue any among the wounded on the battlefield who still lived. *The longer the generals obsess over their rights, the fewer wounded remaining on the field that will have any chance of survival,* he silently fumed. He had been given the responsibility to oversee the burial details as well as finish the search for wounded survivors of the prior day's fighting in and around the sunken farm road. Though he had been encouraged to rest while awaiting the truce, he could not sleep. His mind, so tightly wound by the intense excitement and stress, could not yield to the realm of dreams and nightmares, not when the living nightmare around him was still so vivid. While sleep evaded him, he upbraided himself for being unable to draw on his inner spiritual resources during the battle, ultimately depending on the distraction of continuous activity to cope with the horrors around him. *Am I afraid to truly embrace the "feeling life" that Isaac Penington extolled so powerfully?* he asked himself. As his thoughts wandered over the scenes of fighting from the previous day, the image of the Catholic chaplain rose before him. *This Papist has more courage in his little finger than I will ever possess in my whole being! How ironic! Without hesitation and at great danger to himself, he ministers to the wounded and dying on the battlefield. His is the "feeling life" par excellence, and yet he probably has never heard of Isaac Penington!* Isaac thought, surprised by his growing admiration for the priest and disgusted with his own weakness.

An eerie silence reigned over the battlefield, where only twenty-four hours earlier, a deafening roar had dominated. Beginning to emanate from the decomposing flesh of horses and men, a sickening, pungent odor embraced Isaac's nostrils. Carrying flags of truce, the search parties under the assistant surgeon's command fanned out as they approached the scene of the Irish Brigade's *Calvary* on the fringes of Bloody Lane. Warily, they eyed clusters of soldiers clad in grey and butternut who were on a similar mission: to *seek the living among the dead*, which had assumed an increasingly futile character for both parties in that place of human butchery. Sadly, as he rapidly assessed the condition of those wounded who were still alive, he realized that almost without exception, their tenuous connection to life was slipping away. He urged his stretcher-bearers to carry them as expeditiously as possible back to the Roulette farm. "When you get there, first call for Fr. Corby. They need his ministrations more than anything the medical profession can offer at this point."

Upon reaching Bloody Lane, Isaac gasped as he viewed its entire length. *There is no part of the road that is not covered with the dead*, he concluded after searching the length again. *What had been a nearly impregnable defensive position, when finally flanked by our troops, became a death trap*, he reflected silently. *Such bravery, and all for a cause unworthy of such valor and sacrifice! How is it possible that such slaughter can happen? To what end? These dead Rebels prayed to the same God, who instructed them and us to "love one another as I have loved you." Has the God who is Love abandoned us to the consummation of our mutual hatred?*

Near where a bend in the sunken road gradually changed its direction toward the Roulette farm in the distance, a group of soldiers in blue, ostensibly under Isaac's command, had apparently forgotten their orders and were stripping a Rebel corpse, looking for souvenirs. Struggling with limbs stiffened by rigor mortis, the soldiers alternated curses with laughter as they made slow progress in their efforts to remove from his dead body what remained of a Rebel officer's dignity: his uniform, sword, revolver, and other personal effects. Horrified, Isaac shouted at them. With growing exasperation, he thought, *how quickly someone who was not so long ago a living, breathing child of God becomes an object to be plundered!*

Repetition of his shouted commands to stop seemed to fall on deaf ears. By the time he reached the scene of the looting, the group of soldiers had dispersed with their trophies. Catching up to one of the soldiers, Isaac attempted to remonstrate with him, but the private would have none of it. "Look over yonder, sir. The Rebs are doing the same to our corpses. These 'ere dead ones were trying their best to kill us yesterday." Pointing proudly to the officer's sword that was now in his possession, he added, "Spoils o' war it is, plain and simple. If'n I'd bin there lyin' stiff on the ground, don't doubt fer a moment that our *friends* in grey would have stripped me clean of anythin' useful or interestin' to them."

It was true. The Union dead were also being picked over by Rebel soldiers; a major difference in their plundering seemed to be a particular interest in acquiring Federal shoes, since shoes of any kind were a luxury for many of the private soldiers of the South. Isaac could only gasp in the full realization that whatever rules might apply in polite society, they were no longer relevant on the battlefield. And then another thought came to him, which made him pause and gasp anew. *As a medical student, I distanced myself from the grisly business of acquiring the anatomic specimens so necessary to our medical education. Plundering the dead for knowledge! I always justified not asking how the bodies were acquired because of the good coming from the knowledge gained. How can I begrudge these poor soldiers their trophies? The monstrosities of which human beings are capable—not only capable of perpetrating but also piously justifying with perfectly sound reasoning!* Between plundering the dead and fraternizing with their mortal enemies of the preceding day, it was challenging for Isaac to focus his restive command on preparing the trenches for the burial of the Union dead as well as the torching of the equine corpses.

Later, he was relieved to finally be back at the Roulette farm, where after a nap, he began to make the rounds of his patients. Coming to an unfortunate soldier who had sustained a gunshot wound to the forehead, exposing the underlying brain, he was joined by the omnipresent chaplain, Fr. Corby. "Dr. Burgess . . . have I addressed you correctly?" he asked with a smile as he offered his hand to Isaac. "Yes, Chaplain Corby, I am Dr. Isaac Burgess. Please call me Isaac," the Quaker physician replied with a smile. Being a good Protestant, he was unable to address the Catholic priest as "Father," choosing instead to use the title "Chaplain," which was not lost on Fr. Corby, who responded with a slight smile to the young Protestant's scruples regarding form of address. Looking at the poor soldier with the head wound, he asked Isaac if there had been any change in the soldier's condition. "Unfortunately, he remains unresponsive to verbal and other stimuli and has not spoken," Isaac explained. "It is disconcerting to look into his eyes and wonder, if he is conscious, what he may be thinking," Isaac added. "Yes, I find that very challenging indeed," was Fr. Corby's response. "By God's mercy, I am certain that he is still susceptible to communication through prayer, so I come by as often as I can to pray with him." Isaac nodded and said, "Thank you, Chaplain Corby, for your extraordinary ministry to all our wounded soldiers. Your bravery under fire in attending to the wounded on the battlefield puts me to shame." To Isaac's great surprise, Fr. Corby demurred, "I'm as much afraid as the next man. Yesterday, as soon as our men began to fall, I dismounted and began to hear their confessions on the spot. It was then I felt the danger even more than when dashing into battle. Every instant bullets whizzed past my head, any one of which, if it had struck me, would have been sufficient to leave me dead on the spot. All I could do was to move from one poor suffering and dying soldier to the next, offering the sacraments of the church almost mechanically in my fear, I'm ashamed to say. Though, with the bullets flying and shells bursting, it was hardly a time for pious reflection or flights of inspiration. No, God is merciful to us terrified mortals. He makes up the difference in the pitiful offerings we give him."

CHAPTER NINE

"Man must be free; if not through the law, then above the law."
MOTTO OF THE *ANGLO-AFRICAN* WEEKLY NEWSPAPER, 1859–65

"In giving freedom to the slave, we assure freedom to the free—honorable alike in what we give, and what we preserve. We shall nobly save, or meanly lose, the last best, hope of earth."
ABRAHAM LINCOLN, DECEMBER 1862

IN THE DAYS FOLLOWING the battle, Frederick underwent a dramatic metamorphosis; indeed, every small town and village in the vicinity of Sharpsburg was affected, becoming components of a vast hospital spreading across Western Maryland. Confederate and Union wounded were distributed widely among churches, large public buildings, farms, and private homes, many of which had been selected as potential hospitals before the battle by the foresight of Dr. Jonathan Letterman. As the remaining wounded soldiers of the Irish Brigade were transferred via ambulance to more permanent accommodations, Isaac and his colleagues bade farewell to their temporary field hospital on the grounds of the Roulette farm. Dr. Reynolds and he were assigned to US General Hospital No. 1 on the outskirts of Frederick, where they continued to care for many of their wounded as well as others, including wounded Rebel soldiers. Two L-shaped stone buildings dating back to the Revolutionary War had been constructed by Hessian prisoners of war. They formed the nucleus of what would evolve quickly into the largest medical facility in the area, with multiple wards constructed on a former parade ground adding to its already extensive size.

A tall, well-dressed young man was hardly noticed amid all the noise and confusion as he confidently approached the desk of the hospital steward at the entrance to US General Hospital No. 1 in the late morning of Monday the 29th of September, 1862. Without looking up, the harried administrator perfunctorily said, "State your business."

"I am here to see Dr. Isaac Burgess, Assistant Surgeon in the 88th New York Volunteer Infantry."

"Do you have an appointment? All our surgeons are quite busy with clinical duties," the steward replied officiously as he continued to write in his ledger.

"No, I do not have a formal appointment. However, I am quite certain that Dr. Burgess will want to see his best friend, Sam Johnson. Here is my business card."

Briefly, interrupting his writing, the steward picked up the business card and read: *Samuel Johnson, A.B., Newspaper Correspondent*. Finally, looking up from his desk to assess the owner of the business card, he exclaimed in a mixture of dismay and disgust, "What is this? Best friend of the good doctor, indeed! Why, you're nothing but an uppity *n____r* putting on airs! Leave the premises immediately, or I'll have the guards throw you out!" Before Samuel Johnson could properly protest, the steward had motioned to two guards, who—with evident pleasure—grabbed him by the arms and, "escorting" him out into the street, gave him a parting shove and kick in the seat of his pants, laughing loudly. One of the hospital guards declared to his comrade, "This is what comes of Lincoln's proclamation. The *n____rs* begin to think they're our equals!" and he then spat to punctuate his disgust at such a thought.

Later, in the early evening, having finished his rounds, Isaac met with the hospital steward to review any outstanding issues from the day before retiring. With considerable efficiency, the steward, Thomas Simpson, identified several impending shortages of medications, including morphine and chloroform. After assuring Isaac that he had already placed urgent orders for the medications and was hopeful of their replenishment by noon the next day, Isaac asked him if there was anything else he wished to report. Pausing to think for a moment, the weary steward laughed and said, "Dr. Burgess, you wouldn't believe the impertinence of some of the Negroes after the President's Proclamation last week. There was a tall, dark-skinned fellow—well-dressed, I might add—who came in here requesting to see you. He claimed to be your best friend. Of course, I had the guards throw him out. Here . . . he left a business card for you."

When Isaac saw the card, he groaned. "Tom, he spoke the truth! He is my best friend, or at least I hope he still is after this incident." Nonplussed by this unexpected turn of events, the hospital steward, who made it his personal goal to avoid any conflicts with his superiors, replied obsequiously, "Sir, I am truly sorry if I have caused you any distress. Seeing him as I did during a very busy day, I suppose I may have made some hasty assumptions about what his real business might be." Then, giving Isaac a sideways glance verging on a smirk, he added, "So, it is true that *he* is your best friend?"

"Yes, from my earliest memories he has always been my best friend. We grew up on adjacent farms in Indiana and later were educated together at Oberlin College in Ohio. That "A.B." on his business card is the very same Bachelor of Arts degree that I also received in the graduating class of 1858. After I matriculated at the medical school of the University of Michigan, he went on to read the law under John Mercer Langston, an attorney in Ohio. Tom, only this morning you mentioned how difficult it has been to recruit more civilians to serve as nurses for the wounded. As part of the Bachelor of Arts curriculum at Oberlin, Samuel Johnson received training in the essential elements of human anatomy and physiology. He is just the kind of person we need. Indeed, if I recall, you were also complaining this morning about the overwhelming nature of your administrative duties as hospital steward. Sam has the practical knowledge and organizational skills that could significantly lessen your burden."

Well, wonders never cease, Tom thought with amazement. *What a fool I am. Of course, a Quaker doctor, likely an abolitionist, might just be the only white man to claim a n____r for his best friend!* Assuming a chastened tone of voice, Tom replied, "Dr. Burgess, I am certain we'll be able to find some duties suitable for your friend's many talents. Please forgive my judgment made in haste." *But I'll be damned, if I give any real responsibility to a n____r,* Tom added silently to himself.

"If I am able to find him and convince him to return and offer his services here, an apology from you might go a long way toward rectifying the situation," Isaac suggested. Tom's response was a stiff nod and inarticulate grunt. *He's a fine doctor, but he asks too much of me,* Tom thought bristling at the notion of formally apologizing to a Negro.

Isaac could not shake the gloom from his thoughts. *Even a competent, and for the most part compassionate, hospital steward thinks nothing of treating Negroes without respect for their humanity. How will this
terrible prejudice against the colored race ever be overcome?* Of necessity,
Isaac's thoughts returned to the practical problem at hand: *How am I to
find Sam? Where would he find lodgings in a Southern town . . . ? Why of
course, he would seek the help of the local Negro church community!* came
the answer after he pondered various possibilities.

Wasting no more time, Isaac promptly walked over to the hospital's
kitchen and the adjacent scullery. Both kitchen and scullery were staffed
primarily with Negro women, which gave Isaac hope that he might learn
from them the locations of the churches in Frederick where Negroes attended. Approaching several black women washing the massive amounts
of dirty laundry generated at the hospital, he made his inquiry. After
several of the women looked up and directed taciturn faces toward Isaac,
an older woman cautiously asked, "Why does you wanna know Massa?"

"I am trying to find a dear friend of mine who may have sought
lodging through one of the Negro churches."

"What kinda friend might dat be, Massa? De church ober on East
Third Street has services only fo' de black folk on Sundays." Finally, realizing the confusion he had caused among the black washerwomen, Isaac
apologized and clarified himself. "I am sorry to confuse you ladies. My
friend is a young black man, tall and likely well-dressed, who may have
come to the church yesterday for worship services and to find a place to
stay here in Frederick. His name is Samuel Johnson, and he is educated
as a lawyer." Seeing the puzzled expressions on their faces, Isaac added,
"Samuel and I grew up as neighbors in Indiana and attended college together in Ohio." This further explanation didn't ameliorate the confusion,
although two of the younger women became animated, and one could
be heard saying to the other, "Why dat's de hansom fella who come to de
church yestiday!" Hearing them, Isaac became hopeful and asked, "Do
you know where the 'handsome fellow' is lodging?" "He likely stayin'
with Deacon Jones 'bout two blocks beyon' de church on East Third
Street," came the reply from one of the younger women.

As Isaac hurried along East Third Street, he was struck by the appearance of the African Methodist Episcopal church, a sturdy two-story
edifice constructed of brick. Venturing two more blocks as instructed,
he began to encounter increasing numbers of Negroes. Frederick's Negro population included some enslaved tradesmen rented out by their

masters and others who were free persons of color. Approaching a middle-aged black woman who had three children in tow, Isaac asked, "Ma'am, do you know where Deacon Jones of the African Methodist Episcopal Church resides?" Pausing to fully appreciate the sight of a *polite* Federal soldier in his blue uniform, she smiled and replied, "I like de color of yo' uniform, suh. Now, you sojer boys are finally gettin' down to the business of freein' mah people." Isaac couldn't help but smile broadly and respond, "That's why I wear this uniform." Remembering Isaac's question, she added, "Oh, you were askin' for Deacon Jones. I'll take you directly to 'im. He happens to be mah husband. If'n you'd be so kind as to knock some sense into his head, I'd be much obliged. He's a thinkin' dat he shud join up when dey start recruitin' Negro sojers, but he forgets dat he has a wife and three chillun."

"I'll do my best, ma'am, to persuade him to stay home." Considering the odd circumstances of their meeting, the deacon's wife, with a mixture of curiosity, and a hint of suspicion, asked, "Why are ye lookin' fo' mah Amos? He ain't in some kinda trouble, is he?" "Oh, ma'am, please accept my apologies. I should have explained my purpose at the beginning of our conversation," Isaac replied. "No. He's not in any trouble at all. I'm looking for a very dear friend of mine, a Negro by the name of Samuel Johnson, who might have approached your husband at the church seeking help to find lodging here in Frederick. Perhaps, if you have met, he mentioned my name, Isaac Burgess."

Growing quite animated, the deacon's wife exclaimed, "Imagine dat! Here I bin talkin' to de bes' friend of de man stayin' wif us, and a white sojer in blue at dat! I jes' come fum de market, where I was buyin' some meat an' vegetables fo' de meal tonight. You mus' join us fo' supper." Arriving at the door to her home, she directed her attention to an open window on the second floor above the door and shouted, "Amos Jones, come open de door. It's Martha. We got ourselves another gues' fo' supper tonight." When Isaac began to protest that he did not want to impose, Martha with a dismissive wave of her hand, said, "It ain't ebry day dat I kin entertain white and black men who are best friends! Now you jes' shush yo'self and come in an' meet yo' ol' friend." But as sound travels fast, the door suddenly burst open, and Sam Johnson was clasping Isaac Burgess in a powerful bear hug before Deacon Jones could even reach the door. Oblivious to the consternation on the faces of Martha, her children, and other colored passersby, the two friends exchanged the greetings of best friends who hadn't seen each other for more than a year. "Dr. Isaac

Burgess, why you are a poor, starved specimen of humanity, if I say so!"
exclaimed Sam in mock horror. "Hasn't Uncle Sam been feeding you
rascals?" Then quickly changing the subject from Isaac's weight loss during federal service, Sam assumed a censorious air, and declaimed, "Dr.
Burgess, you really must do something about the manners and decorum
displayed by your colleagues at US General Hospital No. 1! Having been
the recipient of their less than cordial welcome earlier today, I could
suggest some improvements in their general demeanor," Sam solemnly
pronounced and then broke into hearty laughter, much to Isaac's relief.

"Oh Sam, how glad I am to see you! It has been far too long for old
friends to be separated. I am so ashamed of the treatment you received
at the hospital. Unfortunately, prejudice against Negroes is not limited
to those wearing the uniform of the Confederacy," Isaac said by way of
apology. Surprising Isaac with another laugh, Sam replied, "Men in uniform represent only one segment of the larger community of prejudice
that thrives amid the white populace. I just came here from New York
City, that bastion of culture and civilization. Let me assure you, my dear
friend, that the *hospitality* shown me in that great metropolis by white civilians has fully matched any of the *pleasantries* your military colleagues
have offered to me here in a slave state." Not knowing how to respond,
Isaac could only shake his head in regret.

"Enough about our white 'friends' in the generic sense; I want to
shift my attention to this *particular white Friend* standing in front of me,"
Sam said with a smile as he clapped Isaac on the shoulder. "Isaac, I daresay we have a lot to discuss, even some rays of light and hope that appear
to be breaking through the clouds threatening our nation. But let's not
keep these good people any longer outside their home," he said, motioning for Isaac to enter the deacon's house.

Later during supper, Sam addressed their hosts: "Didn't I tell you
that my best friend would find me?" "You sho' did, Mista Johnson. But
you didn't menshun anyting 'bout 'im bein' a white man," Deacon Jones
replied with awe. "How'd he know where to look fo' you?" Sam grinned
and said, "This is no ordinary white man that you see before you. For
most white people in the North, we *free* Negroes might as well be invisible, the exception being when we're perceived to be *in the way*. However,
for this white man, there are no *invisible* people. In fact, he sees human
beings created in the image of God where other members of his race see
only chattel to be bought and sold, or among the more charitable, an
inferior race possibly deserving of some compassion but certainly not

of citizenship in this grand republic. Being the close friend of our race and serving as a conductor on the Underground Railroad, he's made a thorough study of our ways. Knowing that I am a Christian who ought to be more steadfastly seeking the *Kingdom*, he has reasoned rightly that upon entering Frederick town, I should make my way first to a local Negro church where those of similar complexion find spiritual sustenance. Is my surmise about your methods of detection correct, Isaac?" It was Isaac's turn to laugh as he replied, "To the letter."

"Reading a week ago of President Lincoln's preliminary Emancipation Proclamation to take effect January 1, 1863, in response to the victory at Antietam, was wonderful news," Sam enthused as the two friends began to share their experiences of the preceding year. "At one point, many of us had despaired regarding the president's leadership. Would he finally elevate this conflict from a war to restore a union tainted by slavery to the moral crusade that has been foreordained by Providence?"

Isaac shook his head and responded, "Oh, but the tremendous cost at which emancipation will be purchased! Sam, it is impossible to convey to you the truly horrible nature of the slaughter I witnessed at Antietam and Shiloh. The suffering and loss of life only grows worse as the war progresses. The vicinity of the battlefield was transformed not only into a vast hospital but also a charnel house of unprecedented size. Before I was transferred to the hospital here in Frederick, it was impossible to escape the omnipresent stench from rotting flesh, both human and equine; myriad numbers of horses dutifully carried their human owners into the slaughter. How ironic that two small houses of worship were located at the heart of the fighting in the two major battles I have witnessed thus far: Shiloh, a Methodist meeting house in the Battle at Pittsburg Landing and the small white chapel of a pacifist sect, the Dunkards, at Antietam."

"Isaac, it is so terrible and yet so glorious," Sam exclaimed. "Did not that former slave and great abolitionist orator, Frederick Douglass, once say, *'If there is no struggle, there is no progress'*? Can't you see that those two chapels, and the very different creeds they represent, are at the very heart of this great conflict? It seems very fitting indeed that they should be placed at the center of the battlefields. Was it not, after all, the Southern Protestant churches that seceded from their Northern brethren twenty years ago, long before the Southern states formally departed? From newspaper accounts, I remember reading that Shiloh Meeting House was directly affected by that earlier separation, becoming Southern Methodist. At the other extreme lies the poor little pacifist community of German Dunkards, hardly enthusiastic advocates of states' rights and slavery!"

"You never cease to amaze me, Sam," Isaac responded with wonder. "You have always had the great gift to see profound symbolism emerging from the most doubtful of circumstances. Where my vision has been constrained by cries of pain and the other inexpressible horrors of war, you undoubtedly would find hope, perhaps even a sense of triumph."

Uncertain whether there was a tinge of sarcasm in Isaac's words, Sam replied, "*If there is no struggle . . .* I guess, my friend, that you perceive in me a naïve optimism, unjustified by your actual experience of war, and perhaps that is a fair criticism of my enthusiasm. But certainly, you can appreciate the fact that President Lincoln would not have moved forward with his preliminary Emancipation Proclamation without the Federal victory at Antietam. Notwithstanding the horrific slaughter, a great good may yet come from it. Is this not the first fruits of all the many years of labor on the part of abolitionists? For those of us of African ancestry, the Proclamation has cleared a path for us to participate directly in the struggle as soldiers in Federal uniform, setting the ultimate seal upon our citizenship. If we shed our blood for the preservation of the Union and the destruction of the Southern slave power, how can the full rights of citizens ever be denied us?" At this point, the deacon who had been listening to the conversation with growing interest blurted out, "Nearly half mah life, I bin a slave. Thanks be to the Good Lawd that because ob mah trade as a carpenter, I could save and buy mah freedom an' dat ob Martha befo' we married, so's our chillun could be born free!" And then, with tears streaming down his face, he added, "Dis yere Proclamation of Mista Lincoln come directly fum de Lawd—de President only put it on de paper. Jes' like de good Lawd Hisself lay down His life for all us po' sufferin' sinners, if'n I kin offer mahself so that there be no mo' slavery, I wud do it wif joy in mah heart!"

Isaac, with emotion, tried to answer the impassioned statements of his friend and the deacon. "Gentlemen, how can I respond to such heartfelt eloquence? Indeed, '*God moves in a mysterious way, His wonders to perform . . . .*' Please forgive my despairing assessment of the war. Perhaps I have been too close to its most horrific aspects and thereby blind to the hand of Providence at work, even in the cruelest acts of which human beings are capable." Looking directly at Martha, Isaac then added, "Deacon Jones, I have deep admiration for your willingness to sacrifice yourself upon the altar of freedom for your people. However, I believe there are many ways to support the war effort that you could pursue without putting your family at risk of losing a loving husband, father, and breadwinner. You also have your ministry as a deacon at the African Methodist Episcopal Church to consider. I believe that there are some wounded soldiers being cared for at your church. Since we are in desperate need of caring, competent nurses here in Frederick, you could then offer a ministry of incalculable value by addressing both the physical and spiritual needs of many wounded soldiers without resorting to the violence of war yourself." Turning toward Sam, he added, "I hope to convince Sam to do the same." Looking around the table, he noticed a look of gratitude suffusing Martha's face, while the two men who had listened respectfully to Isaac's concerns both shook their heads almost in unison.

Sam was the first to respond. "Isaac, it had been my intention to serve in the capacity you describe, as well as possibly in other ways, until such time as enlistment in the military is open to Negroes. Ironically, it seems from my experience earlier today that gaining access to the wounded may have its own challenges. My dear pacifist Quaker friend, I think that you still don't fully realize how important military service is to the black man. In some *mysterious*—even Providential—manner, I think it will be the means by which we may finally exorcize the old demons oppressing our souls that have been implanted by generations of enslavement. Even living as free Negroes in the North, that oppression has been perpetuated in more subtle ways by our continued subordination to the dominant race in this country. Only through military service, with all the sacrifices that implies, will we be able to demonstrate our full manhood and provide irrefutable evidence of our equality as members of the human family claiming all the rights of citizenship."

Deeply moved by Sam's impassioned declaration, Deacon Jones placed his right hand on Sam's left forearm and said, "Mista Johnson, you hab de gift. Hab you felt de call fum de Lawd?" Puzzled by the deacon's question, Sam said, "Deacon Jones, I'm not sure of your meaning. Specifically, to what kind of call from the Lord are you referring?" Gazing intently first into Sam's eyes and then into Isaac's, the good deacon shook his head and said, "Ain't it obvious to you—the Lawd's callin' yo' to His ministry! Gawd don't waste sech eloquence on jes' anybody." While Sam's face registered surprise at the deacon's pronouncement, Isaac—grinning—said, "Deacon Jones, you are not the only person to recognize that Samuel Johnson's true vocation is to the ministry. He seems to be the last one to acknowledge the call, though." "Isaac, you do me a disservice,"

Sam protested. "It is true that I have been encouraged by my pastor back home, and by some of my professors at college, to pursue the ministry. Furthermore, after my own fashion, I have felt God's call; I would be a liar if I denied it. But I also have come to understand that my response to that call must first include direct action on my part against the evil in this world. My journey to the Lord's ministry must include suffering, even offering my life, if necessary, on behalf of those for whom I would minister."

"But Sam, is it absolutely necessary to participate directly in the violence of war? Would it not be possible to genuinely suffer on behalf of those for whom you would later minister without being a soldier?" Isaac asked, prodding his friend. "Isn't this the path that our sisters Louisa and Rebecca are taking, as they prepare to teach in the contraband camps?"

Sam smiled and responded, "A wonderful suggestion, my friend. Clearly, our sisters, as the good Lord said, *have chosen the better part, which will not be taken from them.* But Isaac, why didn't you follow your own advice and pursue this more pacific path yourself, instead of causing so much heartache and grief to your parents and uncle, Levi Coffin by volunteering for military service, with its associated risks?" Before Isaac could venture a reply, Sam continued to make his argument. "Earlier I hinted at other routes my service might take before the military avenue opens to me," Sam stated with a cryptic smile. "Isaac, did you look closely at the business card I left with the hospital steward?"

"No, but here it is," and Isaac produced the card that he had hastily pocketed after seeing Sam's name on it. "Ah, Samuel Johnson, A.B., *Newspaper Correspondent*—so Sam, are you working for a newspaper?"

"Newspapers, hopefully. That is why I was visiting New York. The editors of the *Anglo-African*, which is published there, were quite interested in having a Negro correspondent in the field who could give their readers a firsthand account of the action from a Negro perspective. Theirs is the one newspaper that has made a firm commitment to me, although others showed some interest when I visited their offices."

"Sam, this is excellent news. Certainly, you will have an opportunity to utilize your skill as a writer to good effect; although, being close to the action will place you in many dangerous situations."

"Isaac, I only mentioned my journalistic pretensions by way of introducing other, better voices bolstering the argument for Negroes in uniform to fight and suppress this rebellion. I would like to now quote a Negro gentleman, a schoolteacher from Philadelphia, who wrote quite a compelling defense of Negro involvement in the prosecution of this war, which was published in the *Anglo-African*. I believe he strikes at the core of what military service means for all men of color, whether enslaved or nominally free." Pulling a rumpled newspaper from his pocket, Sam read out loud the following: "No nation ever has or ever will be emancipated from slavery . . . but by the sword, wielded too by their own strong arms . . . God will help no one that refuses to help himself . . . If ever-colored men plead for rights or fought for liberty, now of all others is the time. The prejudiced white men North or South never will respect us until they are forced to do it by deeds of our own . . . Without this we will be left a hundred years behind this gigantic age of human progress and development . . . The issue is here; let us prepare to meet it with manly spirit, let us say to the demagogues of the North who would prevent us even now from proving our manhood . . . that we will be armed, we will be schooled in military service . . ."

When Sam finished quoting from the *Anglo-African*, Isaac sighed, and—directing a look of sad resignation toward Martha—said, "You offer powerful, convincing words in support of Negro military service in this conflict, both from what you have quoted but also drawing from your own inner resources, Samuel Johnson. Be it far from me to attempt any refutation of the logic of your argument. After all, here I sit dressed in the very uniform which you desire and are worthier than I to wear. Before you and Deacon Jones put on Union Blue and take up arms in this righteous cause, consider this. While some—like you, Sam—will have no familial commitments, many others of your race who will answer the call to arms will leave wives, children, and other dependent family members to an uncertain fate. Especially, I daresay this will be acutely felt by those refugees from slavery who already are presenting themselves in large numbers to the US Army for protection. Will there be sufficient compassion and competent administration to address the needs of what will likely be enormous numbers of refugees, vulnerable to hunger, exposure, sickness, let alone Rebel military raids, designed to re-enslave them?"

His eyes flashing through the gloom surrounding the dimly lit dining table, Sam—in an impassioned voice—responded, "Sometimes, Isaac, my friend, you can be so annoying when offering reasonable objections!" Turning to Deacon Jones, he added, "Of course, Isaac is correct in foreseeing the many possible, even probable difficulties and dangers attending Negro military service in this terrible war. He gives sound advice to persons like yourself, who have other responsibilities that must be weighed when considering such a decision. As I am essentially free of competing responsibilities, my choice is simple. I would fully respect you if you decide not to enlist when the opportunity presents, for all the reasons Isaac enumerated. But for me, and perhaps for all men of color, we sense on some level that these are apocalyptic times; irresistible forces draw me and others toward the battlefield. Reasonable argument is no longer sufficient to restrain our commitment to action." Deacon Jones, perceiving his wife's increasing agitation, placed his left hand on her right and calmly said, "Mah dear Martha, how I love you and our chillun! Nothin' will change dat, not eben death kin touch de love I hab fo' you. We's gotta do a lot o' prayin' 'bout dis befo' I makes any decision. But I gotta confess dat I agree wif brother Sam here dat dese are apo-ca-lyp-tic times, an' I fear dat mah heart will be torn apart befo' it all is ober." Smiling wanly at his friend, Isaac said, "Sam, I capitulate. The persuasive-ness of your rhetoric has prevailed yet once more. It will be interesting to see what effect your duties as a war correspondent may have upon your enthusiasm. As the defeated party, I would like to take the liberty of changing the subject. Tell me the news concerning your sister Eliza, her husband Tiberius, and your extended Canadian family."

"Oh Isaac you have such a clever way of counterattacking in our de-bates, you rascal!" Sam replied with a grin. "You know full well how Tib is frequently offered to me as an exemplar to emulate by my parents . . ." "And by your sisters, Hattie and Louisa," Isaac interjected triumphantly. "Well, last I heard, Tib . . ." Isaac continued, and then, turning to the Joneses, he apologized—"Tib is Tiberius Johnson's nickname . . ."—and then, resuming his train of thought, "Tib and his half-brother Cicero were still hoping to participate in the development of higher education for Negroes in the United States. Have they acted on this plan?"

"At one point, they had been contemplating a move to Ohio from Canada West to take up teaching responsibilities at Wilberforce Univer-sity, Tib hoping to become a professor of history and Cicero, professor of natural history and mathematics," Sam explained. "But Wilberforce Uni-versity, the only college founded specifically for teaching black students in Ohio, closed earlier this year for financial reasons. It seems that most of its support, ironically, came from Louisiana planters who would send their mulatto sons to the North for an education. The war interrupted that relationship, however. Being themselves the mulatto sons of a Ken-tucky planter, Tib and Cicero felt a special sympathy for the mission of the college. Now they must wait upon events. The elevation of the Negro race through higher education, especially those newly emancipated, re-mains the sole focus of their energies," Sam stated with admiration but added, "I have a different path to follow." Isaac interjected, "What news do you have of their father, Mr. Horton Newby, and Tib's mother, Lid-die?" Sam smiled, and—looking to their hosts—said, "I must apologize for digressing into family business, at least without providing further explanation. It is a rather long and complicated story, but suffice it to say, Mr. Newby, their white father by two different mothers, is a truly re-markable model of reform and repentance who should be emulated by all those who would own other human beings. He freed his slaves, sold his plantation in Kentucky, and has dedicated his remaining years to offering a classical education to refugee children and their interested parents in Buxton, Canada West. The most amazing aspect of his journey has been the reconciliation he has enjoyed with his formerly enslaved children and the final blessing of God on his marriage to Tib's mother, Liddie." Then, anticipating Isaac's next question, he added, "While his sons are seriously contemplating a return to the country of their birth, Horton Newby has solemnly declared that he will only return to the United States at such time that his marriage as a white man to a woman of African ancestry will be fully recognized and legally sanctioned by the laws of the land. On more than one occasion, he has publicly stated his gratitude to the government of Great Britain for its recognition that the love of man and woman can transcend racial origins." Clasping Martha's hand, Deacon Jones marveled at the news from Canada. "Here in Maryland, we don't hear much 'bout de life of Negroes in Canada." Looking directly at his wife, he added, "Martha, dese young men hab shared so many amazin' tings wit' us tonight. Jes' as Doctor Burgess said, quotin' de hymn, de Good Lawd does move in mysterious ways!"

CHAPTER TEN

*"... Men of the North, away with your Balaam-like proclivities,
your trifling with truth and trafficking in principles ... Look upon us
not as outcasts, pariahs, slaves, but as men whom the Almighty has
endowed with the same faculties as yourselves, but in whom your
cruelty has blurred His image and thwarted His intent ..."*

THE *ANGLO-AFRICAN* NEWSPAPER, MAY 11, 1861

MEETING SAM EARLY THE next morning outside the entrance to US General Hospital No. 1, Isaac helped his friend run the gauntlet of guards and the hospital steward. Startled by the reappearance of the black man they had *escorted* off the premises the previous day, now in the company of one of the medical officers and clearly on friendly terms with him, they were further surprised when Isaac made a point of stopping to salute each of them and introduce Sam. "Mr. Johnson has graciously offered to volunteer his services on behalf of our wounded soldiers." Looking up from his desk, Thomas Simpson mumbled a muted apology, citing pressure of time and the challenge of assessing the wide variety of individuals seeking entrance to the hospital. "Oddly enough, my complexion seems to have a negative effect on some persons," Sam responded with irony.

Retreating to Isaac's quarters, the two friends shared an abbreviated breakfast before Isaac took Sam with him on his hospital rounds. "Do you have your free papers with you?" Isaac asked Sam anxiously.

"Yes, they're on my person. But is there any reason to be concerned when the Union Army occupies this region?"

"Sam! Reflect for a moment on the treatment you have received at the hands of Federal soldiers in the last twenty-four hours. Some of these fellows in blue uniforms might be quite happy to kidnap and sell you

77

into slavery. Even if slavery is dying in Western Maryland, it's still fully protected by law here, and we're not that far from Virginia, where the trade in human flesh continues unabated, despite the conflict. Perhaps we should have your papers copied and recorded with the County clerk," Isaac said with continued concern. "Well Isaac, if you really think there is a significant risk, certainly I'll do it," Sam's voice still betraying some incredulity. "Yes, please do it to allay your old friend's anxiety, if nothing else," Isaac implored. "We are on the edge of a universe entirely hostile to the Samuel Johnsons of the world we have known in the West, notwithstanding all the prejudice that still exists in Indiana and Ohio. Speaking of prejudice and gross injustice, Sam, I am so sorry that you were not admitted to the Ohio Bar."

"It came as no shock to me," Sam replied. "Mr. Langston had prepared me well for the anticipated disappointment. After he was admitted to the Ohio Bar, the news came back to him that the judges, in confirming his knowledge and fitness for legal practice, felt justified in their decision because of his light skin." In a voice tinged with undisguised bitterness, Sam added, "When I contemplate the hypocritical pretense of the judges who denied my admission to that same bar, I gain some appreciation for the not-so-amicable greetings I received from the guards and the hospital steward yesterday; at least the latter were authentic in their open hostility. As I told your colleague, Mr. Simpson, it appears that my complexion has a decidedly negative effect on some persons! Mr. Langston, being a grand repository of optimism, is hopeful that many of the old prejudices will drop away as the war progresses. He is insistent that my time will come. I hope he is correct in his analysis of the historical currents that are unfolding."

Noticing that Isaac was checking his pocket watch, Sam abruptly changed the subject. "Before you take me on the grand tour, Isaac, tell me something of your own transformation. In donning the Federal uniform, I see that you have shed the plain speech of the Society of Friends." Isaac smiled sadly at his friend. "It became almost immediately apparent to me that if I were to function at all in an organization with such a rigid hierarchical structure as the US military, I could no longer bear witness to this fundamental aspect of my identity as a member of the Society of Friends. As you know, Sam, the plain speech and plain dress were once radical egalitarian responses inspired by the Gospels to the rigid castes of seventeenth-century England. Today, you have witnessed that as an officer, I *even salute*—the outward transformation from non-conformist

Quaker to compliant soldier is now complete. I have justified this tearing asunder of my identity because a higher demand has been placed upon me—to actively participate in the struggle to achieve freedom for four million enslaved Americans. May God forgive the presumption and arrogance in my choices, which I know have wounded many of those I love."

Grasping Isaac's hand tightly, Sam said with fervor, "My friend, neither of us will pass through these perilous times without being transformed in ways we might never have imagined before the War; I for one honor your sacrifice." Getting up quickly, Isaac replied, "Your presence here at this time is a real tonic for me, Sam. But now, we must begin our rounds."

Over the coming weeks, Sam fully embraced his duties as a nurse, ignoring the many slights, occasionally vociferous protests, and frank hostility of wounded soldiers initially offended by the presence of a black man at their bedside. When a catastrophic hemorrhage was averted by Sam's initiative through his timely placement of a tourniquet, word spread quickly throughout the ward that "this Negro knows what he's about." Even the wounded Rebel soldiers began to soften in their attitudes toward the educated Negro from the North, comparing him to the best traditional healers among the enslaved they had encountered before the War. Indeed, Sam's practical medical knowledge, bolstered by his collegiate studies at Oberlin, set him apart from most of the other civilian volunteer staff at the hospital while at times being nettlesome to the less competent among the formally trained medical staff. Even the hospital steward began to acknowledge Sam's organizational skills, intense work ethic, and intellectual abilities. Isaac was startled late one afternoon, two weeks after Sam's arrival, when Thomas Simpson took him aside and quietly admitted, "Dr. Burgess, the administrative demands placed upon me of late have been extreme. *Uncle Sam* has been pitiless in the vast numbers of forms that he continues to create. Everything, it seems, must be inventoried; your friend, Mr. Johnson, was kind enough to provide invaluable assistance to me yesterday when perceiving my situation. Do you think he would be willing to assume some of these duties on a regular basis in addition to his care of the wounded?" Isaac, smiling at the diffidence exhibited by the hospital steward, replied, "Why don't you ask him directly, Thomas? After all, he is his own man, I cannot speak for him."

In contrast to the growing respect of the enlisted men for Sam and his skills, the officers, however, were not so appreciative of this Negro

presence at their mess, no matter how well educated. After Sam had begun volunteering at the hospital, Isaac had—without a second thought—
invited Sam to come dine with him and the other officers as his civilian
guest. When Sam demurred, expressing concerns about the kind of reception he would likely experience, Isaac insisted. And their reception of
the black scholar, as Sam feared, while not openly hostile, was chilly in
the extreme. Many of the officers, whether medical or not, shared views
regarding the conflict in full sympathy with those of their commanding
general, George McClellan. His goal had always been to put down the
rebellion and restore the Union to its former state, while not interfering
with the South's *Peculiar Institution*. Lincoln's preliminary Emancipation
Proclamation was met with derision and disgust in many quarters within
the Army of the Potomac. Isaac learned of many resignations among officers, who stridently opposed any redefinition of the conflict as a war
of emancipation. He became acutely aware that if his performance as a
medical officer had ever been in question, their chilly welcome of his
black friend would have overflowed into overt hostility directed beyond
Sam toward him, the Quaker doctor whose abolitionism "in their eyes"
was the putative cause of the conflict.

After a successful operation in which Sam, for lack of other qualified medical personnel, assisted Isaac by administering the chloroform
anesthetic, the chilliness toward the Quaker doctor's Negro friend now
transmogrified to a simmering heat which boiled over at the next officer's mess. Before accompanying his friend to the evening meal, Sam
expressed his growing concerns. "I'm afraid that we may have inadvertently crossed the Rubicon with our Irish friends. Did you see the censorious look Dr. Reynolds gave me when he noted my presence in that
operation?" Isaac, who had been distracted by some correspondence,
looked up and replied, "No, Sam, I did not observe your interaction with
Dr. Reynolds. He is one of the kindest, most compassionate physicians
I have encountered so far in my military experience. It is difficult to
imagine that he would harbor ill will toward you or anyone." Smiling
at his friend's naïveté, Sam responded, "Isaac Burgess, is it possible that
you are imputing your own general goodwill to your colleague? All I can
say is that he gave me a look communicating shock and disgust that a
Negro might dare to assist at the operating table. Indeed, the expression
on his face made it clear that taking such liberties would not be tolerated
by any of the other surgeons here."

"Sam, I hope your apprehensions are without foundation or are at least overstated."

"Isaac, I suspect we'll know soon enough. Be prepared for some indigestion coming with our next meal, though."

As Sam surmised, the attack commenced at the officer's mess. The form it took was odd, even circuitous, but as the conversation evolved, it rapidly became clear to both Sam and Isaac that the battle plans had been laid with careful premeditation. To Isaac's surprise and chagrin, his equable friend, Dr. Reynolds, lead the charge. If nothing else, the line of attack was designed with one major aim: to make the Negro understand his place. Of necessity he must observe the proper boundaries that American civilization had long since established regarding those of African ancestry; in short, as a black man, he was not welcome in their company.

Turning toward Sam, Dr. Reynolds fired the initial salvo. "Mr. Johnson, many of us among the officer corps of the Army of the Potomac have followed recent political events with considerable interest—even, dare I say—concern. Perhaps none has been more provocative than the preliminary Emancipation Proclamation coming from Mr. Lincoln last month. I can only imagine that you must have followed these developments with considerable interest, albeit from a different perspective. Ah, but this is tangential to my primary question for you this evening. We have learned from your friend Dr. Burgess of your many scholarly achievements, quite unique and remarkable among members of your race. Considering the recent events to which I have alluded, I think I can speak not only for myself but also my colleagues assembled here that we would be most gratified to hear your opinion, as a Christian scholar, about St. Paul's teaching regarding the proper relationship between slave and master." Having laid down the gauntlet, Dr. Reynolds's face assumed a complacent smile.

Sensing rising anger on his behalf from Isaac's posture, Sam placed his hand on his friend's arm as a silent message to signify: *Isaac, as an advocate, I am fully prepared for this form of combat. Relax. I am not afraid to enter the fray.* Rising to address his adversaries, Sam's expression reflected Dr. Reynolds' smile back on its owner as he said, "Dr. Reynolds, I must thank you for this invitation to speak to you and your colleagues on a subject of great personal interest to me. The association you have made, no matter how tangential as you say, between the president's proclamation and the teaching given to us from the Holy Scriptures on the relation between slaves and masters, is timely indeed. As an American of African ancestry, I am greatly heartened by your evident interest in a topic of universal import to all humanity. Before I respond, may I seek further clarification regarding the nature of your request? Are you interested in my exegesis of the broader Pauline corpus with respect to the subject of relations between masters and slaves or only the traditional passages employed by Southern slaveowners in their efforts to secure the obedience of their enslaved Africans?" The puzzled looks on the face of Dr. Reynolds and the other officers signaled Sam's first small victory. Smiling, he paused while he slowly surveyed his audience. Fr. Corby, who had been making pastoral visits that afternoon in the hospital and having stayed for supper raised his hand slightly. Catching Sam's attention, he answered, "Mr. Johnson, I for one, would be delighted to hear all of your thoughts on this important subject." Sam's smile broadened in gratitude to the chaplain as he continued his speech.

"Perhaps at this point it might be wise to remind ourselves that for every spoken or written word there is a context. Indeed, it may be necessary to consider more than one context, especially regarding much of what is communicated between human beings. For example, let us for a moment reflect upon Paul's Letter to the Ephesians, chapter 6, verses 5 through 9, and his Letter to the Colossians, chapter 3, verses 22 through 24, favorite scriptural passages invoked by slaveowners to justify their role as master over their enslaved Africans. First, it is clear from both examples that slavery was a common condition within the pagan Roman empire. Indeed, I willingly concede that slavery has been a part of the human experience from time immemorial." Sam's discourse was, at this point, interrupted by several voices expressing their approval, "Yes, that's the way it's always been . . . How's he going to extricate his enslaved Southern brethren from that fact!" Pausing to patiently allow the murmuring to subside, Sam continued. "Of course, this first context which I have just acknowledged is that emerging from a culture fostered by a cruel, often inhuman, pagan empire where the value and dignity of a human life was subject to the fate of one's birth or to the vagaries of conquest. And now, after nineteen centuries since the advent of Christ, are we no better? Is our American civilization still in its essence pagan? But I digress. Thanks be to God that this is not the only context in which we must consider the written counsels of the apostle to the gentiles. Paul recognized the practical challenges of bringing the Christian faith to the highly stratified society of the empire, while always keeping in mind the ultimate vision of a unity for all in Christ, in whom *there is neither Jew* nor Greek, there is neither bond nor free . . . as he so beautifully stated in the third chapter of his letter to the Galatians.

"It is of great importance to remember that in his admonition for slaves to obey their masters, the accent is not on the human master *but on Christ*, of whom the earthly master can only be an image, and often a poor one at that. I apologize that I don't know the Catholic translation into English of chapter 6, verses 5 through 9 from Paul's Letter to the Ephesians. Please bear with me as I quote from the Authorized version:

"Servants, be obedient to them that are your masters according to the flesh, with fear and trembling, in singleness of your heart, *as unto Christ*; Not with eyeservice, as menpleasers; but *as the servants of Christ*, doing the will of God from the heart; With good will doing service, *as to the Lord, and not to men*; Knowing that whatsoever good thing any man doeth, the same shall he receive of the Lord, whether he be bond or free. And, *ye masters, do the same things unto them, forbearing threatening: knowing that your Master also is in heaven; neither is there respect of persons with him.*"

"The translators chose to render the Greek word *doulos* as "servant"; but let us be clear—the word means *slave* and would be more accurately translated thus. Note that Paul balanced his admonition to slaves with an equally forceful admonition encouraging masters to moderate their behavior to those subordinated to them, *knowing that your Master also is in heaven; neither is there respect of persons with him.* I won't burden you by quoting the apostle's letter to the Colossians, which essentially repeats the admonition in a similar fashion. So, I would suggest to you that the apostle's counsel was offered to new converts to help them navigate their world as Christians while keeping in mind their respective station in life. It is ridiculous to read it as an endorsement of chattel slavery. Paul's concern in writing his letter was not to overthrow the social order of his time, rather his concern was the revolutionary change being effected in the individual hearts and behavior of Christian converts, which one might reasonably hope would in time have its own transformative effect on the wider culture.

"Let us now return to the apostle's use of this curious Greek word *doulos*. In his letter to the Ephesians, Paul has referred to *your Master . . . in heaven*. Could this imply that *doulos* has a much broader application than merely the context of chattel slavery? Is it not interesting to note that the great apostle confers the title of *doulos Christou—slave of Christ* on himself? Indeed, he applies this title to himself more than once in his epistles, even in his initial greetings in the letters to the Philippians and to Titus. He confers this 'honor' of *slave of Christ* on others as well, including his associates Timothy, Epaphrus, and refers to his friend Tychicus as *syndoulos* or *fellow slave*. Do you begin to see how context is so important?" Angry murmuring erupted among the officers. Finally, Dr. Reynolds turning to Fr. Corby asked, "Father, is there any truth in what this fellow is saying? Did St. Paul actually refer to himself in this way?"

"Yes, Dr. Reynolds, Mr. Johnson is absolutely correct. *Doulos* would more appropriately be translated as *slave* and St. Paul did use the very titles he describes. Furthermore, I am enjoying his presentation very much and I wish that my brother officers would give him a fair hearing. I've rarely heard such a lucid discussion from my own students at Notre Dame. "Please continue with your line of reasoning, Mr. Johnson," Fr. Corby added.

"I fear that my longwinded presentation is exhausting my auditors," was Sam's response to Fr. Corby's invitation to continue. "Therefore, I will limit my further exegesis of *doulos* to only two more examples from the apostle's writings and then with your indulgence, I would like to finish my response to Dr. Reynolds' kind invitation with some short observations about the noble Irish race.

"There was one instance wherein the apostle Paul addressed the issue of slavery directly. His short letter to Philemon is usually *not* a part of the Southern rationale for enslavement of other human beings. As you may remember, a Christian friend of the apostle Paul, Philemon, owned a slave named Onesimus, who ran away from his master and by the Providence of God encountered Paul when the apostle was a prisoner in Rome. Eventually, Onesimus was converted to the Christian faith through Paul's ministry. In his letter, Paul announces the change in Onesimus's condition to his master and then makes some extraordinary assertions. First, Paul beseeches Philemon on behalf of '*my son, Onesimus, whom I have begotten in my bonds.*' But this does not begin to fully describe the bond formed between Paul and this convert slave. Two verses later he goes on to inform Philemon that he is sending the slave Onesimus, who is now Paul's *innermost* self, back to his master. The once *good-for-nothing* slave has now become through his conversion to the Christian faith a dear son to Paul, who, in turn, sends him back to his master no longer as a *doulos*, but as a *hyper doulos* that is *above a slave* as a beloved brother with the clear implication that he ought to be freed. Certainly, the apostle does not order Philemon to manumit Onesimus, but he does tell him that their relationship has been profoundly transformed forever.

"My final observation regarding the apostle's use of the word *doulos* is in the context of his letter to the Philippians, chapter 2, verse 7. This, in my opinion, is the most surprising and profound use of the word, for in Paul's description of the incredible humility of God in becoming a human being through the incarnation, the passage states that Christ emptied Himself, taking the form of a *doulos*, a slave! Yes, some of you may retort that the Bible you read has *servant* in this verse. But the original word is *doulos*, and I submit to you that His humility could be no more compellingly expressed other than by taking the form of a *slave*. Use of *servant* by the translators of this passage has diminished the apostle's revelation regarding the humility of the God who would suffer on behalf of his creatures.

"In closing, I would like to express my admiration for the Irish people. I am fully cognizant that this little exercise you have given me this evening holds another message. I think it can be summarized in language like the following: '*Notwithstanding your intellectual gifts or academic achievements, you remain and will ever remain a member of an inferior race—one by nature unfit to share the company of white persons.*' As a young man at college, I thrilled to read of the valiant struggles extending over centuries of the Irish people to free themselves from the tyranny of the British yoke. I could only feel deep sympathy when I read of the overt prejudice directed at the Irish by their British masters, who in print would declaim frequently on the theme of Irish inferiority, even referring to Irish barbarism.

"Some of you may have seen a small medallion created in the last century by Josiah Wedgwood. On its surface was placed the image of a black slave in chains raising those chained arms in supplication, with the caption 'Am I not a man and a brother?' I look now at your brave faces, reflecting generations of Irish suffering, and ask you, *are we not men and brothers?* There is a charming old Latin aphorism: *corvus oculum corvi non eruit*, meaning 'a crow will not pull out the eye of another crow.' As members of two oppressed races, do we not have more in common than that which separates us? Is the color of my skin so repulsive to you that you cannot warm to the humanity that lies underneath and which nonetheless would honor your noble Irish blood—noble in its suffering? But alas, *homo sum humani a me nihil alienum puto*—'I am a human being, so nothing human is strange to me.'

Preparing to leave, Sam was startled when Fr. Corby rushed up to him, insisting that he stay. Turning to his fellow officers, the chaplain said,

"Since the recent proclamation made by Mr. Lincoln, I have been reflecting on this whole issue of slavery in America. It has been an easy, perhaps even lazy, path for me to follow regarding this army's view of its purpose in this rebellion. Like many of you, I felt the primary, perhaps the only, goal of the Army of the Potomac should be to restore the Union as it was. With Mr. Lincoln's proclamation, my assumptions have been shaken to their core, for I am inclined to see the hand of Providence in momentous events like this, even when I don't understand them. Naturally, as a son of the church, I sought the counsel of my superior, Fr. Sorin, one who is far wiser than I regarding this and many issues. In our correspondence, he alluded to some of the very same observations presented so eloquently by Mr. Johnson. Clearly, the church has had to live within the cultural and legal climate of a given place and time, making accommodations that sometimes were far from the ideal offered us in the gospel of our Lord. First, Fr. Sorin offered me a sweet taste from the Eastern fathers of the church, taken from a commentary on a passage in Ecclesiastes by St. Gregory of Nyssa, that great spiritual father and bishop in the fourth century." Pulling the cherished correspondence out of his pocket, he began to read, "'For what is such a gross example of arrogance . . . as for a human being to think himself the master of his own kind? . . . So, when someone turns the property of God into his own property and arrogates dominion to his own kind, so as to think himself the owner of men and women, what is he doing but overstepping his own nature through pride, regarding himself as something different from his subordinates? . . . You condemn man to slavery, when his nature is free and possesses free will, and you legislate in competition with God, overturning his law for the human species. The one made on the specific terms that he should be the owner of the earth and appointed to government by the Creator—him you bring under the yoke of slavery, as though defying and fighting against the divine decree.'

"In our correspondence, Fr. Sorin also reminded me of the recent encyclical of 1839, in which our Holy Father, Pope Gregory XVI of blessed memory, speaks against slavery in the strongest and most unequivocal terms. If you will please bear with me as I quote the Holy Father: 'We warn and adjure earnestly in the Lord faithful Christians *of every condition* that no one in the future dare to vex anyone, despoil him of his possessions, reduce to servitude, or lend aid and favor to those who give themselves up to these practices, or exercise *that inhuman traffic by which the Blacks, as if they were not men but rather animals,* having been brought into servitude, in no matter what way, are, without any distinction, in contempt of the rights of justice and humanity, bought, sold, and devoted sometimes to the hardest labor.' Of course, I could read you more of the same, but I hope you all understand that what Fr. Sorin has in his wisdom shared with me is fully consonant with what you heard earlier this evening. Turning to Sam, Fr. Corby added, "Thank you, Mr. Johnson, for your erudite answer to Dr. Reynolds's query. I welcome your kind words and well wishes for the suffering Irish race and am honored to be your brother."

CHAPTER ELEVEN

"There is no more consoling sacrament established by our Lord than the Sacrament of Penance—confession. It seems to have, for those who rarely find opportunity to receive it, an infinite charm when unexpectedly brought within their reach."

FR. WILLIAM CORBY, CHAPLAIN, 88TH NY VOLUNTEER INFANTRY

DR. FRANCIS REYNOLDS COULDN'T escape a growing sense of unease. It had been a week since he had been recruited by the other officers 'to put the Negro in his place.' While the objective had been accomplished—the lily-white company at the officer's mess had been restored—he was still dismayed by Fr. Corby's reaction to the event. Not only had the chaplain confirmed the arguments presented by the 'uppity' Negro, even quoting a church father and a recent papal encyclical, but he had made it abundantly clear that he was not afraid to call a black man 'brother.' Furthermore, in defending the 'sanctity' of their dining arrangements, Dr. Reynolds was now acutely aware of a barrier that he had helped erect between himself and his Quaker colleague, which he regretted more with each passing day. For his part, Isaac continued to execute his professional duties with his usual competence, remaining courteous and compassionate to all. Despite their treatment of Samuel Johnson, the Quaker doctor maintained an unperturbed demeanor around his Irish colleagues, only keeping to his room for meals, which he shared with his Negro friend. *If only the Quaker would express anger or resentment at the way his friend has been treated*, he thought. *This quietly going about one's business, as if nothing of import has occurred. Why, it is simply maddening!* During the officer's mess more than a week after the incident, an epiphany came to Dr. Reynolds as he listened to yet another exposition by one of the officers upon the inferiority of the Negro race. *My Quaker colleague has come to realize that we Irish in our pig-headedness aren't worth the breath. After all, we won't even listen to the Holy Father in Rome!*

Looking up from a bedside dressing change the next morning, Dr. Reynolds was transfixed by the penetrating gaze of Fr. Corby as he made his pastoral rounds. "Well Francis, don't you think you might be overdue for a visit to the confessional?" Fr. Corby whispered in the doctor's ear. "It seems to me that you might have a few things troubling your soul." Initially reddening, the Irish doctor's face, which of late had been uncharacteristically gloomy, now brightened, and a broad smile emerged to replace the gloom. He then quietly replied, "Father, it is indeed time I took my medicine. I've been such an ass! Do ye think ye could fit this sinner into your schedule this morning?"

Responding to a knock at the door of his room, Isaac was startled to see Dr. Reynolds standing there with a sheepish look on his face, holding a bottle of wine. "Dr. Burgess . . . Isaac, may I join you and Mr. Johnson?" the Irish doctor asked with uncharacteristic diffidence. Rising from the small table where they had just finished their evening repast, Sam anticipated Isaac's response and said, "Please come in, Dr. Reynolds. You are most welcome. We have been looking forward to your visit."

"Looking forward to my visit . . . ?" Dr. Reynolds' diffident facial expression now collapsed in utter confusion. "Why, of course, how could it be otherwise?" was Sam's confident reply. "Isaac has repeatedly assured me that you are a man of the highest integrity and a doctor with boundless compassion for your fellow man."

"But . . . I have treated you, his best friend, abominably," the Irish doctor protested. "Isaac had every right to call me out for my perfidy, but not a word or even a disapproving look from him! I don't understand it."

"Dr. Reynolds . . . Francis, please don't think that I didn't harbor such impulses," Isaac interjected. "It was only through Sam's restraining influence that I was able to present such a dispassionate response to your behavior and that of the others. The Society of Friends has a tradition of advocating for peace in the world, although, I must confess, in my case I hardly live up to the tradition. And yet, I bear witness that my Baptist friend here is a more faithful advocate for peace than I will ever be. Rather than allowing me to indulge a strong desire to rage at you and the other officers, Sam has calmly reminded me that our earlier training in rhetoric at Oberlin was for the sole purpose of persuasion, *not for condemnation*. I don't mean to embarrass him, but being the excellent lawyer that he is, I should nevertheless like to quote the advice he gave me which quelled my passion. 'As an advocate my task is to present the factual evidence as faithfully and persuasively as I can. *It is the ultimate task of conscience to do the rest.*'"

In the long pause that followed Isaac's interjection, Francis Reynolds caught Sam's gaze and held it. The corners of his mouth forming a faint smile, he finally said, with some trepidation, "Mr. Johnson can you forgive a pigheaded fool of an Irishman?"

"Of course, I can, and I have already forgiven you, Dr. Reynolds," Sam responded with conviction, as he offered a hearty handshake, which was enthusiastically reciprocated. "But, more importantly, have I persuaded you, Dr. Reynolds, that we are *both men and brothers?*"

"Aye, *my brother*, you've persuaded me with a wee bit of help from Fr. Corby and a painful conscience!" And then the Irishman broke into hearty, infectious laughter, in which Sam and Isaac quickly joined. "Indeed, gentlemen, if my conscience were to take bodily form, I'm convinced it would bear a striking resemblance to our good chaplain!"

His initial awkwardness returning, Dr. Reynolds looked down at the bottle of wine in his left hand, drawing the attention of Sam and Isaac to it. "Mr. Johnson . . . may I call you Samuel? I know Isaac is a teetotaler, but I hoped you might join me in a toast to our mutual humanity as a means of reconciliation. This bottle of French wine has accompanied me since I joined the 88th New York Volunteer Infantry regiment. I have saved it for the day when I would be able to celebrate our final victory over the Rebel Army." It was Sam's turn to offer an awkward smile to their encounter. "Dr. Reynolds, this is an extraordinarily kind gesture on your part. It seems premature to celebrate that victory, since an intact Rebel Army still opposes the Army of the Potomac. Shouldn't you continue to preserve it until that glorious day?"

"My conscience, that is Fr. Corby, says otherwise," was the reply, which could not help but be tinged with some regret. Sam gave Dr. Reynolds a puzzled look and said, "I'm not sure I understand, doctor."

"Forgive me . . . I keep forgetting that you Protestants don't know about the Sacraments. Well, ye see . . . there's this little problem of penance. The good father . . . that is Chaplain Corby, when confessing us sinners, he will often assign a penance, hopefully one that will really get to the heart of the matter we've confessed. He has known all about my bottle of wine and its intended use for many months. So, being the wise pastor that he is, after I finished making my confession, he asked me in an ever-so-gentle voice, 'Francis, do you still have that bottle of wine to celebrate the final victory?' Sensing that something was afoot, I cautiously replied, 'Well yes, Father . . . I'm still confident of our final victory over the Rebels.' Now when Fr. Corby pauses during a confession and his voice becomes even softer, ye know the hammer's about to strike! Then he asked me a question. 'Francis, what do you think? Which victory is greater: overcoming a harsh prejudice against another race of men or beating the whole Rebel horde?' 'Well, Father, I suppose ye want me to answer the former rather than the latter,' I replied but quickly added, 'Those Rebs are mighty difficult to beat.' And guess what the good father said: 'All in due time, Francis, the military victory will come, all in due time. But, changing a human heart—now that is a *real* victory, indeed a miracle, worth celebrating!' So, Samuel and Isaac, you see my dilemma. As Fr. Corby has instructed me to do, it is time to offer the penitential libation."

Sam's face was suffused with a mildly amused expression as he responded to Dr. Reynolds' catechizing regarding the sacrament of confession. "May I suggest, Dr. Reynolds, that you yet defer the offering until the final victory over the Rebels. To apprehend the change of heart and tremendous goodwill underlying your willingness to share that bottle of wine with a colored person is sufficient for me. It is as if we have already toasted a newborn friendship transcending our differences. And besides, like my Quaker friend, I also took a temperance pledge as a student at Oberlin, committing myself to receive alcohol only as a stimulant in the case of extreme medical need. Thus, on my honor, that bottle should remain inviolate until the Rebels surrender."

"Oh, now what shall I do?" Dr. Reynolds exclaimed with a genuine mixture of relief and confusion, being torn between joy at the stay of execution regarding his bottle of wine and the anxiety accompanying failure to perform his penance. Thinking quickly, he added, "Is it not true that the word 'temperance' actually signifies *moderation* rather than *abstinence*?"

Sam laughed and replied, "Yes, Dr. Reynolds you are, of course, correct. Isaac and I signed on to the pledge understanding that 'temperance' connoted *abstinence*, with the only exception being for medicinal use. Would not a toast with another, non-spiritous liquid suffice to meet the intent of your penance? Could we not toast each other with coffee?"

"Samuel Johnson, I'll gladly toast you with coffee," Francis Reynolds agreed gratefully. "For my part, I will make sure that Chaplain Corby knows you unhesitatingly offered to share your wine with me," Sam said by way of reassurance. After inadvertently swallowing some coffee grounds during their toast, the Irish doctor screwed up his face and said, "I honor both of you as men of principle. I think this must be the most memorable, as well as least potable, toast I have ever experienced—Perhaps all the better as an act of penance!

"As you might guess, the Irish have greater difficulty with *keeping* than making pledges of abstemiousness. Prior to our entry into combat service, Fr. Dillon, a former chaplain of our Brigade, endeavored mightily to encourage the men of the 63rd New York Volunteer Infantry to take a 'temperance' pledge of the same kind you gentlemen have taken. While most of the regiment, with sincere goodwill, signed on to the pledge, the celebratory activities prior to the brigade's departure from New York proved too strong a temptation for many, leading to misbehavior on the part of intoxicated soldiers and bringing shame on the regiment. Indeed, the 63rd was not allowed to redeem its honor during the Peninsular Campaign." "But they certainly proved their courage and devotion at Antietam!" Isaac interjected. "Aye, they certainly did, through great suffering and loss of life," Dr. Reynolds added.

Reflecting over the bitterness of the coffee with which he had just toasted the Negro race, Francis Reynolds directed a different question at his new friend. "Samuel, I understand from some remarks Isaac made when you first came to join us that in addition to your volunteer work here, you are also serving as a correspondent for a newspaper."

"Yes. Newspaper reporting is my current means of financial support. I am writing for the *Anglo-African*, a newspaper created for an educated, literate Negro readership. As you might imagine, the Negro population of the United States is keenly interested in the progress and ultimate outcome of this war."

"Well, I guess you don't have much to report of an encouraging nature regarding the attitudes of Federal soldiers towards your race," Francis observed sadly. Sam initially hesitated to answer and then—with a faint smile—replied, "I daresay that I'm a bit more optimistic than that. Multiple generations in this country have been nurtured upon the certainty of their superiority to at least one other race of human beings. It is an intoxicating notion, no matter how perverse and false, that many draw comfort from—the 'knowledge' that despite experiencing the worst impoverishment or the most desperate circumstances, a white person can still say, 'At least I'm not one of them.' And yet, I consider myself fortunate indeed to have persuaded at least two leaders in this army to change their minds about the humanity of the Negro race. If the shepherds are won over, surely the sheep will eventually follow. I am fully convinced that once the white man sees what the black man in a blue uniform can do on behalf of freedom and the Union, many more will also be won over. So, Francis, I have sober but cautiously optimistic news for the *Anglo-African* and its readers."

In the weeks that followed, many of Francis Reynolds's colleagues were startled to see him seek out the Negro volunteer's help with bedside wound care and assistance at the operating table. Where before there had been open disdain, a clear respect and even deference began to emerge that did not escape the notice of all the staff. A colleague, bemused by the change in the Irish doctor's behavior, especially noting his growing number of absences from the officer's mess, pressed Francis about the incongruous nature of his actions. The response was quick and direct. "It really is quite simple. As I mentally reviewed Mr. Johnson's eloquent rebuttal to my taunt, all I could perceive was the brilliance of another fellow human being. He is one of only a few among his race who have had the opportunity to pursue a proper education. Can you not see the similarity with our own Irish poor? To what heights might this race of Africans or our own downtrodden Irish brethren scale, if given similar opportunities? Oh, what an arrogant, prejudiced fool I've been! Being of a forgiving disposition, Mr. Johnson and Dr. Burgess have been kind enough to allow me to join them for meals. In the certainty that we shall be called back to our regiment soon, I am anxious to learn as much as I can from this remarkable man."

Francis Reynolds's premonition of imminent change was verified two days later. First, Sam shared the sad news he had just received that his father, Benjamin Johnson, had been declining in health for the past several months. Ben Johnson had insisted on keeping the news from his son, telling Sam's mother that his son's work should not be interrupted on account of his father's *minor* ailment. When Ben's weight and strength continued to decline to the point that he was essentially confined to bed, he finally allowed a letter to be sent summoning Sam home. "Oh, Sam, I am so sorry," Isaac commiserated with his old friend. "I wish that it would be possible for me to go with you and help attend to his medical care."

"You know, Isaac, that Dr. Way will do his best for my father," Sam replied, his eyes glistening. Then, his face brightening, he attempted a smile as he declared, "Isaac, the next time we meet, hopefully I will be wearing the uniform of a Federal officer. After my father regains his health, I will seek a commission as an officer in a Negro infantry regiment. Surely, once the Emancipation Proclamation takes effect on the first of January, the recruitment of Negroes for active military service will begin in earnest."

On the same day in late November that Sam departed for Indiana, Isaac and Francis received orders ending their service at US General Hospital No. 1 in Frederick and directing them to rejoin the Irish Brigade in Virginia. To their surprise, it appeared that the Army of the Potomac's campaigning season might extend into the winter under its new commander, Major General Ambrose Burnside.

CHAPTER TWELVE

"I thought I could almost hear the slow flap of the grim messenger's wings, as one by one he sought and selected his victims for the morning. Sleep, weary one, sleep and rest for tomorrow toil. Oh! Sleep and visit in dreams once more the loved ones nestling at home. They may yet live to dream of you, cold, lifeless and bloody, but this dream soldier is thy last, paint it brightly, dream it well . . ."

CLARA BARTON, DECEMBER 12, 1862

Falmouth, Virginia
December 21, 1862

Dear Rebecca,

By now, I must assume thou hast learned of the disaster that has befallen the Army of the Potomac here at Fredericksburg. Before I give thee my own account, I must apologize for my tardiness in corresponding with thee and the rest of the family. Please share my best wishes and prayers for Ben Johnson's health. Already, it seems an age since I said farewell to Sam late last month as he left Frederick for home to care for his father. Any news thou hast to share regarding the Johnsons in their time of travail would be gratefully received.

On our way to report for duty with the Irish Brigade at Falmouth, Virginia, Dr. Francis Reynolds, the senior surgeon of our regiment, and I stopped briefly in the capital before boarding a transport ship on the first of this month. What for many veterans had become a dull repetitive affair, the voyage down the Potomac River and into the Chesapeake was a source of wonder for me. Sights and sounds of birds in flight, the subtle transition from fresh to salt water gradually detectable for the first time to my sense of olfaction, the vast expanse of shoreline, visible either as virgin forest or prosperous farms, presented such a marked contrast to the reality in which I had been immersed for so long. As my senses became intoxicated by this new harmonious world of beauty, a civil war seemed ludicrous; such conflict among God's creatures in opposition to the very order of nature seemed nothing less than blasphemy. As we approached our destination, the enormous army supply depot at Aquia Creek, the peaceful vision evaporated, and I was quickly returned to the harsh reality of war.

The images confronting us during our fifteen-mile train ride to Falmouth could not have been more different in every respect from those on the Chesapeake. In all directions, we were surrounded by a forlorn landscape, marked by the total desolation that only armies can create. Normally, nature acquires a simple, unadorned beauty with the advent of winter. From our railway carriage we could only see an obscene nakedness in which anything and everything of any conceivable military use had been stripped from the vicinity. Fences had been dismantled and trees cut down to provide wood for fires. Farms and plantations were abandoned; indeed, any signs of animal or human activity were essentially absent. We could only look at each other in dismay after surveying the forbidding world outside our train window. After a few moments, Francis Reynolds smiled at me sardonically and then quoted the poet Dante: "Abandon all hope, ye who enter here." Thus, with a deep sense of foreboding, we left the train at Falmouth.

Initially awed to silence by the sheer immensity of the Army of the Potomac as it spread out along the northern bank of the Rappahannock River, Francis discovered something that made him laugh and say to me, "Well, Isaac, perhaps we shouldn't abandon *all* hope. After all, it appears that our medical director, Dr. Letterman, has been quite busy organizing divisional field hospitals on a grand scale." For upon surveying the army's encampment in greater detail, we were both able to appreciate the presence of row upon row of tent hospital wards which had been well organized to the north of a large imposing mansion, the Lacy House. This mansion, also known as Chatham and dating back to the last century, is well situated on Stafford Heights, above the north bank of the Rappahannock, facing the town of Fredericksburg.

After settling into my quarters, a snug tent equipped with a small makeshift chimney, I took the opportunity to explore our situation before taking up my clinical duties. Standing in the December chill on the second-floor veranda of the Lacy House, I was offered a panoramic view of the historic town of Fredericksburg and the hills beyond, known as Marye's Heights, which were now bristling with Confederate troops and artillery. From what my fellow officers have surmised, General Burnside's original intention had been to surprise the Confederates by moving to the east and, crossing the Rappahannock River, threaten Richmond while offering battle to them on ground of his own choosing. All went according to the general's plans until enormous delays were encountered in delivering the necessary pontoons for the river crossing. Meanwhile, the initiative was lost as General Lee countered the threat by occupying Marye's Heights, leaving not only the rank and file of the Army of the Potomac but also many officers, myself included, wondering what our commanding general would do next. How well I remember overhearing a conversation between our regimental chaplain, William Corby, and one of the brave soldiers of our brigade! The young Irishman, suspecting the worst, said, "Father, they are going to lead us over in front of those guns which we have seen them placing, unhindered, for the past three weeks." The chaplain, a very sensible and good man, replied, "Do not trouble yourself, your generals know better than that." But, dear Rebecca, they apparently did not *know better* for it became evident soon enough that General Burnside's intention was a direct assault on the heavily fortified heights beyond the town.

In the pre-dawn darkness of a foggy and very cold 11th of December, the order to assemble the pontoon bridges spanning the Rappahannock was given. Sadly, those brave men who set to their task quickly became targets for Rebel snipers occupying Fredericksburg. As soon as hammering or other noises of construction could be heard, a fierce fire was directed in that direction. Cries of pain and the rush of feet running back toward the northern shore of the river testified to the effectiveness of the Rebel marksmen. Finally, after the Confederate sniping became intolerable, detachments from the 7th Michigan and 19th and 20th Massachusetts regiments crossed over in some of the same boats intended to form part of the pontoon bridge and assumed the perilous duty of driving the Rebel sharpshooters from the town, ultimately facilitating completion of the bridges. In concert with their efforts, Union artillery began a bombardment of the town, producing momentary bursts of intense light accompanied by loud explosions. The random character and distribution of the bright flashes of light penetrating the deep fog in which the town was shrouded almost acquired a kaleidoscopic quality. But forgive me, dear sister. Reading what I just wrote suggests something of beauty about that destructive act; and yet, it was beautiful as well as terrible!

Dr. Dyer, the divisional surgeon-in-chief at the Lacy House, which was to become a very busy hospital, organized aid stations on the northern side of the Rappahannock as wounded soldiers began to pour back over the newly completed bridges. As the fog lifted, the firing of the Rebel sharpshooters in the town intensified before being silenced by grim house-to-house fighting initiated by the Federal soldiers who had so courageously crossed the river. Here, Rebecca, I must digress to tell thee of an extraordinary woman who was present at the Lacy House.

Perhaps thou hast heard of Clara Barton, a volunteer nurse from Massachusetts? I believe some of the earlier exploits and bravery under fire at Antietam of this middle-aged former schoolteacher have been described in newspaper accounts. In any event, shortly before the battle she arrived from the capital with provisions for "her boys" and showed great energy, as well as fearlessness, throughout the entire battle and its aftermath. On that morning of the 11th, she was standing on the second-floor veranda of the Lacy House attempting to catch a better view of the action across the river, seemingly oblivious to the danger, as Minié balls fired by the Rebels began to hit the mansion around her as well as soldiers in the yard below. Finally, an officer was able, with some difficulty, to persuade her to be escorted to safety. She is well loved and respected by all the soldiers. As the fighting intensified, she would find her way into the thick of it, providing aid and succor even to wounded Rebel soldiers in their suffering—whoever entered her realm of compassion was a subject of her concern. While I was tending the wounded in one of the aid stations that Dr. Dyer had set up near the river, I was startled to see Miss Barton, accompanied by an officer, rushing across the pontoon bridge into the maelstrom. Later, I learned that she had gone to help at an aid station in the burning town. Unfortunately, her chaperone was killed shortly after escorting her to the aid station. That same evening, she was back at the Lacy House ministering to the wounded soldiers who had helped clear the town of Rebel sharpshooters. Such bravery and indefatigable energy—her cheerfulness and calm disposition amid the intense suffering have been quite a tonic to the wounded and their surgeons alike!

Once the town had been cleared of sharpshooters and the pontoon bridges were in place, General Burnside ordered his two grand divisions to cross the Rappahannock. The 2nd (including the Irish Brigade) and 9th Corps crossed upstream into the town while the other grand division crossed further downstream, on to the plains east of the town. Most of this movement occurred on the 12th with little interference from our *hosts* on Marye's Heights. Adding to the already intense anxiety of our soldiers was the macabre and thoroughly disgusting behavior of some professional embalmers, who brazenly approached the men as they crossed the Rappahannock. Considering those brave souls, many of whom were about to meet their Maker, the gross insensitivity of the embalmers' blandishments made my blood boil. One entrepreneur, after handing out his business card, offered his services in case any of them might be making "an early trip home." In such an event, he assured his prospective customers that they would be "nicely boxed up and delivered to loving friends by express, sweet as a nut and in perfect preservation." Needless to say, I could hardly blame our men for the kind of verbal retorts they offered back to their would-be *preservers.*

To the Army's shame, some units (thankfully not our brigade) engaged in a rampage of looting. General Couch, the commander of the 2nd Corps, was mortified by the soldiers' behavior and did his best to put a stop to it. But it was as if Shakespeare's Mark Antony himself were here to "cry 'havoc!' and let slip the dogs of war." Rebecca, I've seen war bring out the best—but often the worst—in men, and this was no exception. Soldiers were smashing family heirlooms and cavorting in ladies' petticoats, presumably under the intoxicating influence of alcohol, although I wonder. The madness of war may be sufficient impetus—youth in the conscious expectation of imminent slaughter and painful death can hardly be expected to exercise rational judgment.

A dense fog enveloped the Army of the Potomac on the morning of the 13th—from the Lacy House we could no longer see the church spires of Fredericksburg, it was so thick. Most of the poor soldiers who had crossed the pontoon bridges on the previous day had been deprived of sleep because the ground had softened and become a wet, muddy mess. To compound their misery, the foggy morning that followed their sleepless night was extremely cold. While finishing a dressing change on the stump of a soldier's limb that I had amputated the prior night, one of our stretcher-bearers came and in great agitation, urged me to come see the "spectacle!"

Indeed, it was a spectacle, for the fog at about ten in the morning on that fateful day had lifted sufficiently to expose rank upon rank of Federal troops lined up with great precision on the plain across from us on the Fredericksburg side of the Rappahannock River. From the distance and perspective gained from the second-floor veranda of the Lacy House, the impression was one of the majesty of soldiers on parade. The sunlight reflected from their gun barrels and bayonets, the regimental flags fluttering in the chilly breeze, for the briefest moment created a scene of enchantment. But, as would soon become painfully apparent, this was no parade ground exercise!

As the regiments of the Irish Brigade and other units of the 2nd Corps were now organizing in Fredericksburg for their planned assaults on Marye's Heights, I was ordered with a team of stretcher-bearers to cross over into the town and form an aid station in anticipation of the casualties that would most certainly come.

Here, Isaac paused in his writing and involuntarily shuddered. *I had better not tell Rebecca about what happened during the bombardment of the troops in the town as they were on their way to form in line of battle at the base of Marye's Heights,* he thought. *But I must give her some sense of the horrors of that day. Well, I won't tell her of the poor Negro woman with her three children who were running towards us on Sophia Street in their desperate effort to escape the bombardment . . . how solid shot from a Rebel battery found its victims, and she and two of her children were no more—only broken fragments of humanity. It was a miracle that at least one survived, wounded but not requiring a major operation.*

Resuming his letter, Isaac continued:

Being famous for his oratorical skills, General Meagher spoke rousing words to each regiment of the Irish Brigade before it departed through the town towards Marye's Heights. Here is a portion of what I heard him say: "In a few moments you will engage the enemy in a most terrible battle, which will probably decide the fate of this glorious, great, and grand country—the home of your adoption . . . you will strike a deadly blow to those wicked traitors who are now but a few hundred yards from you and bring back to this distracted country its former prestige and glory." Always mindful of the power of symbols, and since most of the brigade's tattered green flags had not yet been replaced, the general had each soldier place a sprig of boxwood in their cap to remind them of their Irish heritage. Later, it became a very practical means of identification on the battlefield as well. The 28th Massachusetts Infantry, which only recently had joined the brigade, was the only regiment that day to carry the green banner which so emphatically expressed in Gaelic the Irish soldiers' ancient battle cry; *Faugh a Ballagh*, or *Clear the Way!* By virtue of possessing that important symbol, the new regiment was placed in the middle during the actual assault so that the entire brigade could see and rally to their beloved flag.

As the brigade headed up Sophia Street, fire from Rebel batteries began to take a toll on the men. It seemed as if the ground was continually shaking under us from the relentless bombardment of the town. While we may have initiated the destruction of Fredericksburg, the Rebels managed to complete what we had begun . . .

Isaac again paused in his writing as he recalled, with horror, witnessing and then personally experiencing the concussive force of a shell which, exploding a few yards ahead of him, had dismembered and killed several soldiers, spattering him with their blood. The force of the blast had thrown him against the wall of a house, leaving him stunned for several minutes. He gradually came to himself as he repeatedly heard cries of "Dr. Burgess, are you badly hurt?" from his stretcher-bearers. Looking up, he realized that the Irish Brigade had disappeared around the corner of the next street. "Don't worry about me; you must not lose sight of the brigade," he had told the ambulance team. "I am fine and will follow presently." However, when he had tried to get up, he had felt lightheaded, and—noticing blood dripping from his forehead—against his will, found himself settling back down to a sitting position. As he tried to muster the strength to tentatively rise a second time, he was surprised to see the kind brown eyes of the omnipresent Clara Barton looking down at him. He remembered her saying somewhat reproachfully, "Now doctor, you must not rush yourself. I witnessed what happened, and your left side was slammed against that wall like a battering ram. The wall seems no worse for the encounter, but I'm not so sure about you," she had added with a smile. "You're bleeding from your forehead. Let me help you to the aid station just around the corner so that I can clean the wound and determine its extent." Isaac gratefully remembered her gentle touch as she cleansed his face and forehead with cool water. She had declared, with some relief, "Doctor, most of this blood is not your own, but you do have a nasty abrasion that is oozing a bit on the left side of your forehead, which probably should be bandaged. I suspect that your left side must be one rather large bruise extending from shoulder to ankle. Don't you think one of the other surgeons should examine you in more detail?" she had admonished after bandaging his forehead. But after a quick *thank you*, he had insisted on rejoining his brigade and had limped off down Sophia Street in pursuit, wincing in pain as he went. After taking a few steps, he felt the nurse's hand on his right arm, and she whispered a parting word of caution in his ear: "Doctor, please do be careful. There has already been one mortally wounded physician in this town."

Rubbing his left shoulder, which was still quite sore—Clara Barton's diagnosis of extensive bruising was correct—Isaac thought, *I must not include anything about this in the letter, or Rebecca and the others back home will be overly concerned.* Resuming his writing, he continued:

> We set up an aid station in a small, abandoned house on the outskirts of Fredericksburg near a section called Liberty Town where free blacks lived. Its yard offered a full view of the plain leading up to Marye's Heights and the stone wall at its base, behind which was a sunken road. Oh, the Irish and sunken roads! Did their first encounter at Antietam presage something even worse at Fredericksburg? As we were setting up our aid station, the first assault against the stone wall was quickly broken, and one could see in the distance, many Federal wounded lying on the plain no closer than fifty yards from the stone wall, behind which the Confederate soldiers were directing an unrelenting fire at our troops. The Irish Brigade had been assigned to carry out the second-wave assault directed at the stone wall. Unfortunately, the Federal soldiers had to navigate several obstacles, including a small bridge over a drainage ditch, before they could even form ranks on the plain. To cross the bridge, they could move no more than four abreast. During these maneuvers, the Rebel artillery produced many casualties, which began to flood our aid station. The shelling was so fierce that it made the ground shake even at our aid station.

I won't mention that eventually the explosions were so close and frequent that we were forced to move our aid station back into the town.

> It was an awe-inspiring sight, the Irish Brigade forming ranks on the plain from left to right, the 116th Pennsylvania, 63rd New York, 28th Massachusetts, 88th New York, and 69th New York infantry regiments. They demonstrated such

discipline and grace under the intense artillery barrage of the enemy while the single green flag fluttering in the breeze in front of the 28th Massachusetts rallied them on to their doom! Oh Rebecca, war is more than senseless tragedy—it is a kind of collective madness! Wave after wave of brave soldiers was sent against Marye's Heights, only to be cut down by artillery or the deadly fire coming from the Rebel soldiers protected by the stone wall and sunken road. The closest any Federal soldier got to the wall was fifty yards, and among those who did could be counted many wearing sprigs of boxwood in their caps.

The continuing fire coming from Rebel artillery and the infantry behind the stone wall made it extremely hazardous to collect our wounded. Those soldiers who could attempted to crawl back toward the town, but many were picked off by Rebel sharpshooters when they made any effort to move. One of our stretcher-bearers was gravely wounded as he tried to reach his wounded comrades. It wasn't until nightfall that more soldiers were able to withdraw to the cover of the town. The last image seared into my memory from that terrible day was seeing soldiers' bodies forming a thick carpet of blue across the plain in front of Marye's Heights. Temperatures plunged that night below freezing, and because no truce had been arranged to attend the wounded, we were impotent to relieve the anguish of suffering and dying men. We could only listen with growing despair to their cries of unrelieved pain and thirst. I only learned later that General Burnside had given serious consideration to renewing the attack the next day, thus the neglect of our wounded. How many wounded soldiers, who might otherwise have been saved, froze to death on that hellish night, only God knows!

After collecting as many wounded as we could, our ambulances transported them back through Fredericksburg and over the pontoon bridges to the north side of the Rappahannock under cover of darkness. I spent the rest of that night operating with my senior colleague Dr. Reynolds in the Lacy House.

Isaac paused in his writing and remembered how miserable he had felt by dawn of the next day, Sunday the 14th of December. His colleague, having noticed his limp, and even though Isaac had tried to minimize his injuries, finally insisted on examining him toward morning. "Why, my friend you've got extensive hematomas involving both your left arm and leg and by the look of that discoloration along your lateral chest wall and abdomen, it appears you're one giant bruise!" he observed with concern. Having discovered no evidence of fractures, Dr. Reynolds, nevertheless had insisted that Isaac get some rest, which he did not resist. Resuming his letter, Isaac continued:

> Awakening in the early afternoon on First Day, the 14th, I returned to the Lacy House to assess both the medical and military situation. While occasional shelling from artillery occurred throughout the day, it became clear that no more attempts to take Marye's Heights were planned. As I looked out over the battlefield from the second-floor veranda, there was a striking incongruity in the appearance of the plain beneath Marye's Heights from the vivid image of the prior day. The solid carpet of blue had now become a patchwork quilt, with white blotches interspersed among the blue. The Rebel soldiers had been busy during the night stripping our soldiers of their clothing, leaving them naked to the elements! I could only hope that they had limited their scavenging to the dead.
>
> Another distressing sight awaited me that was much closer in proximity. Almost every inch of space in the Lacy House was occupied with recumbent wounded soldiers, the only exception being made for the operating tables. The poor fellows were terribly uncomfortable, crammed into every nook and cranny. It would take some time for the medical staff to sort out the appropriate disposition for each wounded soldier, but eventually they were placed in the cleaner and less crowded tent wards devised by Dr. Letterman to await eventual transfer to hospitals in the north for those needing additional care and longer periods of recovery.
>
> An extraordinary phenomenon occurred that night. The shimmering colors of the aurora borealis, never before seen so far south, made an appearance. Was it some sort of heavenly sign? I am certain that at least some of the Rebels saw it as God's benediction on their cause, and perhaps a herald of more victories to come. But could the God of peace offer any sort of benediction on such violence born of human folly? For me, this celestial prodigy was indeed a sign—not of heaven's blessing but of divine grief over the mad, destructive impulses of which human beings are capable. I doubt that even such an extraordinary phenomenon can erase the despair written in many a Federal soldier's heart.
>
> Finally, on the 15th, a truce was arranged so that the dead from the "slaughter pen" (our chaplain's apt description of the plain below Marye's Heights) might be buried. Rebecca, the images of military pageantry I described earlier in this letter must now be brought fully into perspective. Examination at close

quarters of the *patchwork quilt* covering the plain below Marye's Heights revealed a scene entirely devoid of glory or pageantry. Forgive me, but I must give thee at least some sense of what will remain seared in my memory until my dying day. Not only were there the naked corpses of Union soldiers—the white blotches of the quilt—now predominating among the few still wearing blue on that field of horror, but innumerable fragments of humanity were scattered there, evincing a forlorn desire of being reunited with their owners. How is one to offer honorable burial under these circumstances? Without the hope of a future resurrection, which seemed so remote in that place of death, how could any mother bereaved by the name *Fredericksburg* retain her sanity?

To be fair to our Southern brethren, I must share with thee a story related to me by one wounded soldier who managed to survive overnight on that hellish plain. He witnessed an exceptional act of compassion, performed not once but repeatedly by one of the Rebel soldiers. Rather than strip the dead and dying Union soldiers of their clothing and other effects that night, one young Confederate climbed over the wall, behind which he had been shooting at our soldiers earlier that day, crossed the chasm of hate, and not without some personal risk, took water to thirsty Union wounded that night. Perhaps his compassionate act is the sign of hope upon which we should all focus our gaze and not on celestial wonders, no matter how spectacular or obscure.

Before closing, I would like to share with thee one more anecdote of the battle. In addition to Miss Barton, I have occasionally met other women at various times who have offered to care for the sick and wounded. Shortly after the battle, Dr. Mary Walker appeared at Lacy House offering her professional services for the care of the wounded. Her dress aroused much curiosity and comment (not entirely positive) by the other medical officers. Not having a formal commission in the US Military, she nonetheless wore a green sash, indicating her status as a surgeon. What was perhaps most peculiar about her apparel was that she wore men's trousers and a modified tunic that extended close to the knee, reminiscent of the Bloomer reform dress. In any event, she cut quite a figure with her quasi-military outfit and quiet confident air. In my encounters with her, she was gentle and competent in the care of wounds. I did not have an opportunity to operate with her, so I cannot speak of her skill in that regard. All in all, she seemed knowledgeable of medicine, compassionate in her care of the wounded, and otherwise a bit eccentric. My colleague, Francis Reynolds, who has largely overcome his prejudice against the Negro through his acquaintance with Sam, looked at her from a distance during our rounds and said to me with a smirk, "I hope, Dr. Burgess, that you're not going to insist that I be cured of my prejudice against women doctors, and especially ones wearing trousers. Having already given up one prejudice this year is quite sufficient for me!"

So, Rebecca, thou canst see that I seek some solace from the nightmare of war in the humor offered by my colleagues. Please extend my most sincere wishes for health and peace to all our loved ones, and that the Emancipation Proclamation on the first of January will bring new hope amid the suffering.

Thy ever-affectionate brother,

Isaac

CHAPTER THIRTEEN

"A good minister met me on the march one day and asked, in all simplicity and earnestness: 'Chaplain, how do you bring your men to Divine service? I see them as I pass your quarters attending by the hundreds, if not thousands . . . I cannot induce my men to attend that way; in fact, very few take any interest in religious services.' 'Why, my dear sir, I do not bring them,' I replied, 'their faith brings them.'"

FR. WILLIAM CORBY, CHAPLAIN, 88TH NY VOLUNTEER INFANTRY

PUSHING ASIDE THE FLAP that served as the *door* to his tent, Isaac gazed in sadness at yet another Virginia sunset. He had just reread—for the fifth time—Sam's letter, in which his friend had recounted the last days of Ben Johnson, whose health had not improved with the advent of his son but rapidly declined until his death at the beginning of December. In his letter, Sam had described how this quintessential farmer had been gently laid to rest in the soil of the farm which had been such a source of joy to him. From what was left unwritten in Sam's letter, Isaac could sense the deep pain his friend felt in not being able to share his father's passionate love for the land. For Sam, the long-anticipated celebration when the Emancipation Proclamation finally took effect on the first of January 1863 was muted and overshadowed by the loss of his father. Ben Johnson had for many years quietly retained a glimmer of hope that his only son would take over the family farm. But now in his father's last hours of life, it was to Sam's great surprise that Ben whispered a distinct and firm "no," when from out of a deep sense of duty and filial devotion, Sam had pledged to maintain the farm after his death. Ben had gone on to tell his son that he was very proud of his scholarship, and he knew that his path must lead elsewhere. "As you advocate for our people, remember the deep and very special connection we have to the land—to *this* land. The unrequited labor of our enslaved ancestors built America. By watering the earth with his blood, sweat, and tears, the Black man has established an unbreakable bond with this country. Now go with my blessing and fight for our people and this soil, which they have made sacred through their suffering!" After his father's death, Sam learned that his sister Hattie and her husband, a local farmer, were quite willing to help his mother take care of the farm. *At least his other sisters, Louisa and Eliza, with Tib and their children, were also able to be there with Ben at the end,* Isaac thought as he reflected on his friend's grief and the inadequate words of condolence he had just written.

Thinking back over the past three months, Isaac could only shake his head in the realization that while his friends and loved ones suffered and died at home far from the battlefield, the Army of the Potomac had essentially done nothing since the catastrophe of December. It wasn't that General Burnside hadn't tried to act; it just seemed that even the elements had conspired against the hapless general. The wry humor of Fr. Corby came to mind when he remembered General Burnside's ill-fated attempt to outflank the Confederates in January—what had come to be known derisively as the *Mud March* by the rank-and-file soldiers. Fortunately, the II Corps, being closest to the enemy, were scheduled to depart last from their positions when the flanking maneuver began on the 20th of January, which spared them the experience. As soon as the march began, the rain came and continued until the roads became a muddy quagmire. The mud was so prevalent that with a twinkle in his eye, the chaplain of the 88th New York related a curious story to Isaac. "A man was going along on the edge of a forest, when, looking out into the so-called road where troops had passed, he saw a hat in a great mudhole. He reached out for it and discovered a head under it. 'Why, what are you doing there?' he cried out. The man in the mud had answered: 'I am looking for my horse; he is somewhere below.'"

Isaac marveled at the good humor of the Irish soldiers. It seemed impossible to keep their spirits down for long, despite the terrible loss of life at Fredericksburg. To be sure, in the days after the battle there was much grieving for their lost comrades. After all, their tremendous losses at Antietam drove the enemy from Maryland, but what had the even more terrible carnage of Fredericksburg accomplished? The two adversaries were in the same positions which they had occupied before the slaughter. Fr. Corby had summed up the despondent mood of the

Irish Brigade, indeed that of the entire Army of the Potomac, in the immediate wake of the battle: "All of us are sad, very sad." What struck Isaac was the palpable change in the soldiers' mood as the Christmas holiday approached. To the surprise of a sober Quaker who did not usually engage in festive activities, the Irish soldiers began to decorate their winter quarters with evergreen boughs woven into the shape of harps, marking a transition to a more hopeful frame of mind. By the time of the *Mud March*, nearly a month later, a healthy sense of humor and irony in the face of the absurd had returned to the men—a most efficacious remedy for soldiers.

Interspersed among the long periods of boredom, there had been some remarkable opportunities for professional growth as a physician. Encountering an ever-increasing variety of wounds had elicited a greater appreciation in Isaac and his colleagues for the healing power of the human body. Unfortunately, he felt constrained by the bounds of decency to avoid describing some of the more fascinating cases he had witnessed in his letters home. He could only contemplate one particular example with continued amazement: the case of Lieutenant O'Brien, who had sustained a gunshot that had passed through the neck and exited near the jugular vein. Instead of succumbing rapidly to what appeared to be a fatal wound, his condition improved sufficiently that he complained of hunger and thirst. Fr. Corby was present to witness the surprise of the lieutenant's surgeons when a piece of gingerbread the wounded officer had imbibed came out the wound in his neck. Isaac and Dr. Reynolds made careful, serial observations of the changes in the lieutenant's wound and the volume of leakage from the fistulous connection between his injured esophagus and neck. They were delighted to see the leakage of both liquid and solid matter gradually diminish over several weeks following the battle. The only intervention either medical officer made was to daily cleanse the wound with water and apply fresh dressings. Isaac smiled to himself, remembering how on the day when no more leakage could be detected from the wound, Dr. Reynolds had expressed the thought of both surgeons at that moment, "I can only think of the dictum of that great French surgeon Amboise Paré: 'I dress their wounds, but God heals them!'"

At the officer's mess that evening, as had been the case for several prior evenings, the main topic of conversation was the coming celebration of St. Patrick's Day on the 17th. Looking across their table at Isaac, Francis Reynolds smiled broadly, no longer able to contain his enthusiasm.

Isaac responded to his colleague's jollity with a mystified expression on his face.

"Isaac, you don't know what a delightful experience awaits you. Just try to imagine the splendor of it all! You will witness some of the best horsemanship the world has ever known, as well as many other displays of Irish manliness." Francis Reynolds went on to describe, almost in ecstatic terms, the many events being planned, including horse races of which the steeplechase was the crown jewel, wrestling, boxing, and marksmanship; all of which, Francis assured Isaac, would manifest the joy of being Irish—all in honor of their national saint. Isaac's look of puzzlement not being fully dispelled by his litany, Francis continued, "And our very own Saint Patrick was himself a slave of the Irish as a young man. Even though he escaped to freedom, the good Lord encouraged him to come back later in his life to those heathenish Irish who had enslaved him to make proper Christians of them!"

Smiling at his colleague's brief hagiographical account of Ireland's patron saint, Isaac replied, "Francis, the story of how an escaped slave comes back to bring the light of Christianity to his former masters is truly inspirational. But I am confused. How are all these dangerous sporting events connected to honoring this great Christian missionary?"

Even the normally ebullient Dr. Reynolds was beginning to feel some frustration with his Quaker colleague. "Isaac, the actual high point of the celebrations will not be any of the sporting events but the Military High Mass, which Fr. Corby will celebrate—a joyous event to behold. Ah, but you Quakers don't approve of such displays, only *silence* for our sober Friends!" Francis added with a tone of mild derision.

Fr. Corby, who had been dining with the officers and quietly listening to this point, interjected: "Now, Francis, silence is a very good and blessed thing but perhaps *not* the only thing pleasing to God. One of the early fathers of the church, Saint Ignatius of Antioch, had much to say about silence. Forgive me, for my memory is imperfect, but I think the good saint says in one of his letters something to the effect that our incarnate Lord Jesus Christ is the Word of God proceeding from *silence*. This implies that the language of Paradise is silence. Can we begrudge the Quakers in their desire to leap over all obstacles and attain to the silence of Paradise in their worship?"

Yet again, Isaac found himself looking at the Catholic chaplain of the Irish Brigade with deep gratitude and could not help but wonder at his insight. *Does he understand the heart of our worship? Has he studied our doctrine?* But Fr. Corby was not finished. "Dr. Burgess, regarding silence, which I firmly believe *is* the language of Paradise, we must also remember that God the Father spoke his Word *from* silence to his children, who live in a world of the senses and symbols. That same great saint, Ignatius of Antioch, who was devoured by lions out of love for Christ, also said about the mass that we must break one bread, which is *the medicine of immortality.* I hope, Isaac, that you will attend the High Mass and search out the silence of Paradise that is present in its symbols and language."

"Sanctus, Sanctus, Sanctus Dominus Deus Sabaoth. Pleni sunt caeli et terra gloria tua. Hosanna in excelsis. Benedictus qui venit in nomine Domini. Hosanna in excelsis." Isaac could only stare transfixed at the military chaplain, who no longer wearing his dusty blue uniform, now stood resplendent in his gold-embroidered vestments as he solemnly intoned the Latin words of the Mass. These were words which the Quaker surgeon, from his study of Scripture and knowledge of Latin, understood but had never heard chanted before, especially in such a context. *Holy, Holy, Holy Lord God of hosts. Heaven and earth are full of your glory. Hosanna in the highest. Blessed is he who comes in the name of the Lord. Hosanna in the highest,* Isaac translated mentally while his full attention was absorbed by the vision of the transfigured chaplain, who stood facing a rustic altar with his back to the assembled congregation of officers and soldiers in their fine dress uniforms. Somehow, even the rude altar in the equally rustic chapel constructed out of felled tree limbs and decorated with evergreen boughs had assumed something of the magnificence of the priestly vestments, which shone in the light of the sun.

Having, until this occasion, assiduously avoided attending any *Romish* services with all their "unnecessary pomp and splendor," Isaac was struck with wonder. *Why am I so affected by what I see and hear?* He smiled at himself in the realization that he had no words with which to describe this experience. *Is this Chaplain Corby's idea of silence—a silence born of awe?* He had to admit that he had been captivated from the beginning of the service, with its incongruous but strangely powerful mix of military ceremony and religious fervor that together were reflected off every surface, whether it be the metal of a bayonet, an officer's saber, or the shiny, clean face of a young Irish private soldier. *But I must resist such notions, so foreign to the simplicity of the Society of Friends. Our silence comes from the still small voice, not the rushing wind, fire, or earthquake!*

Oh, what is he saying and doing now? Isaac, who stood near the altar area, strained to hear the next words spoken softly and slowly with great reverence by Fr. Corby: "Qui pridie quam pateretur, accepit panem in sanctas ac venerabiles manus suas . . . *On the day before he was to suffer, he took bread in his holy and venerable hands* . . . et elevantes oculos in caelum ad te Deum Patrem suum omnipotentem tibi gratias agens, benedixit . . . *and with eyes raised to heaven to you, O God, his almighty Father, giving you thanks, he said the blessing* . . . fregit, deditque discipulis suis, dicens: Accipite, et manducate ex hoc omnes: Hoc est enim Corpus Meum . . . *broke the bread and gave it to his disciples, saying: 'Take this, all of you and eat of it, for this is My Body.'*" Saying this last phrase in a loud voice, Fr. Corby genuflected toward the altar and then raised the host above his head. Isaac was again awestruck, this time by the childlike joy in the faces of battle-hardened veterans standing silently around him. The next moment, Isaac involuntarily dropped to the ground when the loud report of a nearby cannon suddenly interrupted his meditation. Looking around him, he realized that he was the only one present who had dropped to the ground. As he sheepishly rose, red-faced to resume his standing position beside his colleague, Francis Reynolds, he was aware of suppressed sniggering among the other officers and soldiers standing close to him. When Fr. Corby went on to intone: "Hic est enim calix sanguinis mei . . . *For this is the chalice of my blood* . . . Francis gave Isaac a knowing look, as much as to say, "Now be prepared this time, my friend!" Seeing the priest raise the chalice above his head, Isaac braced himself and was not surprised by the second report of the cannon. Francis leaned over and whispered in his ear, "Normally, the consecration of the bread and wine are heralded by the ringing of a bell, but Isaac, this is a *military* mass after all!"

As the reverberations of the cannon blasts dissipated in Isaac's head, his attention returned to Fr. Corby's recitation of the mass. After doing something with the wafer and chalice, which Isaac could not fully see, the chaplain then intoned three times in succession, "Agnus Dei, qui tollis peccata mundi: miserere nobis . . . *Lamb of God, you who take away the sins of the world, have mercy on us.*" Again, Isaac's attention was fully absorbed as he witnessed the priest in his shining vestments reverently commune of the consecrated bread and wine. *Is this really the same unpretentious military chaplain whom I've come to know over the past several months?* Isaac couldn't help but ponder. When Fr. Corby then turned to the assembled officers and soldiers and intoned, "Ecce Agnus Dei, ecce qui tollit peccata mundi . . . *Behold the Lamb of God, behold him who takes away the sins of the world,*" Isaac wasn't prepared for what came next. Without hesitation, as if with a single voice, came the response from all the others present: "Domine non sum dignus, ut intres sub tectum meum: sed tantum dic verbo, et sanabitur anima mea . . . *Lord I am not worthy that you should enter under my roof, but only say the word and my soul shall be healed.*"

Later, reflecting upon what he had witnessed, Isaac realized he couldn't remember the content of the homily given that day, and even the cannon blasts no longer impressed him. It was the childlike joy and devotion shining in the faces of both pastor and his flock that stayed imprinted in Isaac's memory. While the experience still seemed quite foreign to him, Isaac would not soon forget the vision of the transfigured military chaplain who cried out, *Lamb of God, you who take away the sins of the world, have mercy on us.*

Another aspect of that remarkable day in March 1863 also stayed firmly implanted in Isaac's memory. Those same cherubic faces who had cried so fervently, *Lord I am not worthy . . .*, quickly resumed their Celtic ferocity when the various competitive sporting events began as the *heathenish* portion of the Saint Patrick's Day celebration supplanted the sublime. Isaac was astonished by the magnitude of the whole affair. While he had been pursuing the routine of his medical duties over the past several weeks, rank-and-file soldiers and their officers idled by the lull in combat had been making extensive preparations for the big day. The premier event was the steeplechase, in which artificial barriers, ditches, and small streams or creeks were incorporated into the course offering multiple opportunities to demonstrate the skill and mettle of both riders and their horses. Only officers were allowed to compete in the event, apparently hearkening back to some form of ancient chivalry. Isaac was impressed to see the Army of the Potomac's commander, General Hooker, who had replaced Burnside, present with many of his staff for the festivities, as were many others from the entire army; he estimated several thousand spectators. Bracing himself for the many injured riders he expected to treat, he was shocked to discover that the wives of some foreign officers who had volunteered their services to the Union were not only present but also riding with their husbands. Indeed, some of the equestriennes were every bit as accomplished as their male counterparts and came through the race unscathed. Other than a few fractured limbs requiring splinting, many bruises, and several bruised egos, Isaac was surprised there weren't more injuries. Remarking to Francis Reynolds about his sense of relief over the limited number of injuries, his Irish colleague laughed. "Isaac, you should know by now that it takes a lot to kill an Irishman."

When the day's amusements progressed to more prosaic activities like wrestling, boxing, and marksmanship, Isaac saw an opportunity to rest before the next set of injured contestants arrived. As he began to saunter toward his quarters, Francis Reynolds, accompanied by several other officers from the Irish Brigade, caught up with him and asked, "Where are you going, Isaac? Aren't you going to join in the competition? Several of the finest officers of our brigade are hoping to witness your vaunted abilities as a marksman." Eyeing Francis with a mixture of surprise and suspicion, Isaac replied, "Francis, what is the meaning of this? I am a noncombatant medical officer. Why would I enter a marksmanship competition?"

Giving his fellow officers a sly wink, Francis Reynolds expressed feigned confusion. "Why, my dear Dr. Burgess, your friend Samuel Johnson assured me in a conversation before he left us in Maryland that you are a crack marksman. Indeed, sir, he described your many successes in various competitions in your native state of Indiana. Surely, your friend wouldn't prevaricate about such achievements?"

"He might exaggerate a bit for his own amusement, though," Isaac responded with irritation. The other officers present began to laugh, and Lieutenant O'Brien, expressing the thoughts of many, said, "Dr. Reynolds, we all appreciate the medical skill of Dr. Burgess. Indeed, perhaps I can speak to his fine qualities as a physician more than the rest of us, having been the direct beneficiary of his ministrations with my recent wounding. But don't you think it is a bit ridiculous that a pacifist Quaker would also have acquired the skill of marksmanship, especially to the level boasted of by his Negro friend?" All Francis Reynolds could do at this point was to give Isaac a plaintive look and then add, "Well, my friend, as I became better acquainted with Samuel Johnson, I felt confident that I could trust his word when he assured me of your great skill with a musket. Was I wrong to trust him?"

Feeling trapped by the need to defend his friend's honesty and frustrated by the good-natured manipulation of his medical colleague, Isaac thought, *That rascal, Sam Johnson, has had some fun at my expense. I guess the only thing I can do is to make the best of an awkward situation.* Isaac's look of irritation dissipated as a subtle smile developed at the corners of his mouth. "Lieutenant O'Brien is absolutely correct in his assertion. It is inherently absurd that a pacifist Quaker should be highly skilled as a marksman, especially with weapons of war," Isaac noted blandly.

Francis Reynolds, now with a note of anxiety in his voice, said, "Isaac, does this mean that you haven't won several competitions of marksmanship, as Samuel Johnson stated?" Isaac's smile now became a grin as he replied, "Francis, did I not suggest a minute ago that my friend might have exaggerated a bit? What are a few successes in local competitions among farmers in the state of Indiana compared with the level of marksmanship required of a soldier? Whatever skill I developed as a marksman was for the sole purpose of killing game to help my father feed our family."

"Surely, Dr. Burgess, being so modest regarding your skill, you wouldn't want to disappoint your fellow officers by refusing to participate in a friendly competition on Saint Patrick's Day? It would bring us great pleasure to have you participate with us in the festivities in this manner," Lieutenant O'Brien added diplomatically.

"How can I refuse your kind invitation? Of course, I welcome the opportunity to celebrate with you." Then, looking squarely at Francis Reynolds, Isaac added with a slight smirk, "I hope to not disappoint you with the mediocre marksmanship of a Quaker from Indiana."

Lieutenant O'Brien explained the rules for the competition, in which the contestants would fire at the agreed upon targets with the smooth bore muskets favored by the Irish Brigade, first at fifty yards distance and then at increasing distances until one of the contestants failed to hit the mark, at which point a winner would be declared. "Dr. Burgess, we have chosen as your opponent Lieutenant Lynch, since he is generally regarded as one of our best marksmen. Please do not in any way feel intimidated. This is truly intended to be a friendly competition in the truest sense. We are delighted that you are willing to participate and wish you success. With Lieutenant Lynch's agreement, Dr. Burgess, would you care to choose the targets to be used in the competition?" Looking to his opponent, who nodded his assent, Isaac smiling said, "As a mark of my support for the temperance pledges taken by many members of our Brigade, I would like to propose that we use bottles of wine as our targets." This suggestion coming as it did on Saint Patrick's Day, when the alcohol was flowing rather freely, elicited some laughter from the other officers. "Wine bottles will be the targets," Lieutenant O'Brien affirmed with a smile. Isaac then heard a voice behind him mutter, "Hopefully, Lynch will make quick work of the Quaker, so we'll have something left to toast his victory."

Lieutenant O'Brien handed each contestant a musket fully loaded with the standard buck and ball used in battle. Isaac assessed the heft of the musket in his hands, shifting it back and forth, and then nodded to his opponent to go first. The lieutenant had no difficulty in destroying the bottle of wine placed fifty yards away, but neither did Isaac, who after briefly sighting his weapon, held it steady, gently squeezed the trigger, and the second bottle burst after being hit. The officers in attendance began to appreciate that the Indiana-farm-boy-turned-physician might possess some actual skill with firearms. After the polite clapping subsided, the contestants were allowed to reload their weapons, and the action was repeated, but now the wine bottles were placed at a distance of one hundred yards from the contestants. This time, Isaac went first, and another bottle of wine was destroyed with a direct hit. Lieutenant Lynch carefully took aim and pulled the trigger but hit his bottle tangentially, causing it to spin and fall off the tree stump, shattering when it hit the ground. Lieutenant Lynch graciously offered his hand to Isaac, saying, "You hit your bottle dead on; you should be declared the victor." But Isaac responded, "I thought the objective was to destroy the bottle of wine. We both succeeded in accomplishing that. I think your congratulations are premature, Lieutenant. May I suggest we repeat this distance but this time load our muskets with only a single ball." Lieutenant Lynch acquiesced to Isaac's suggestion, realizing that his odds of success had been further diminished by the new conditions.

After loading their muskets, Isaac turned to Lieutenant Lynch and nodded for him to go first. This time, after carefully sighting his weapon and pulling the trigger, Lieutenant Lynch's bottle of wine remained intact, unmolested by the ball, which had gone wide of its mark. Turning toward Isaac, he gave him a wry smile and waited for his shot. After a moment's quiet reflection, Isaac aimed, once again gently pulled the trigger, and dispatched yet another bottle of wine. Francis Reynolds, now delighted by the outcome, started clapping and shouted, "Let's raise a cheer for our Quaker surgeon!" Isaac noticed that there were only a few other officers who joined in the clapping, while several others looked away glumly, and he thought he heard some even curse the outcome. And then something unexpected happened.

A group of enlisted men from another brigade who had been observing the proceedings in the background came forward and expressed their admiration for Isaac's skill. "Doctor, you're a mighty fine shot but we'd like to see how you'd do with a rifled musket. Would you be willin' to compete agin one of our skirmishers?" Now a chorus of voices urged Isaac to accept the challenge. He was surprised to hear such enthusiasm coming from the same glum officers who had been cursing just a few minutes before. *Perhaps they would enjoy seeing me thoroughly humiliated by a private soldier*, he thought. *So be it. I will do my best, but I am certain to be defeated by an experienced veteran. It would be good for me to be humbled—pride goeth before a fall*, he reflected before agreeing to their proposition. As he held an Enfield rifled musket for the first time, he remembered what he had heard and read about the effect of rifling on its behavior. *As the distance from the target increases, there will be a tendency for the Minié ball to follow a downward trajectory when fired. I will have to compensate for that when I fire the weapon*, he thought.

After receiving some basic instructions regarding the loading of the rifled musket, he squared off with his new opponent, a Private Rutherford, who appeared quite eager to get started, and, as Isaac thought, *he is planning to finish me off quickly.* Bottles of wine continued to be the target of choice, but now the starting distance was doubled to two hundred yards. His opponent obliterated his bottle, and—turning to Isaac—grinned at him, awaiting his attempt. After mentally adjusting for the rifling of the musket, Isaac aimed and fired. Thinking he had compensated sufficiently, he was surprised when the Minié ball barely hit the base of the bottle shattering it. *Oh, that was close! I had planned to hit the middle of the bottle*, he thought with some alarm. But when the distance was increased to three hundred and then again to four hundred yards, he had a feeling for the corrections he needed to make and was successful in keeping up with his opponent, whose grin had turned into a look of admiration. When Private Rutherford missed his target at five hundred yards, Isaac smiled at him but shrugged his shoulders as if to say, *It's not likely I will do any better at that distance.* Carefully aiming at his target, Isaac took his time calming himself as much as possible and then pulled the trigger. The Minié ball hit the tree stump near the base of the bottle. To Isaac's amazement, it retained sufficient force to make the bottle wobble and eventually fall on its side and break. Upon the destruction of this last bottle of wine, which had fallen victim to the marksmanship of a temperance man, there was loud clapping and many huzzahs for the "Quaker doctor."

It was now Isaac's turn to protest that since he didn't actually hit the bottle, the contest with Private Rutherford should be declared a draw. Francis Reynolds, speaking for not only the officers but also with the approbation of the private soldiers, declared, "Dr. Burgess, you can't apply different rules to yourself than those you applied to Lieutenant Lynch. You destroyed that bottle at five hundred yards. You have won both challenges, and if my fellow officers do not object, I now declare you an honorary Irishman!"

Even the officers who had cursed his earlier success came up to congratulate Isaac on his great prowess, some suggesting that he might consider seeking a commission as a field officer. Isaac shuddered at the thought, as he remembered something his father had said to him years earlier when he won his first competition back in Indiana: *Isaac, thou hast a gift. How shalt thou use it?*

Heading toward the evening meal, which was to end the day's festivities, as Francis Reynolds walked with Isaac, he mused, "You had me frightened a bit, my Quaker friend with all your modesty." "Why should you be concerned about that?" Isaac asked with increasing curiosity. "Ah, you don't know how much money I had riding upon your success! When that Private Rutherford came along, it was almost an answer to prayer for my poor colleagues, who had bet against you. They more than made up their losses in your second contest with the obliging private," Francis said with growing exuberance. Thunderstruck, his face reddening with anger, Isaac turned to his colleague and indignantly declared, "You have tricked me into participating in a gambling event! Is this how you honor the great missionary to the Irish nation?"

PART TWO

"Those who visit the school are greatly astonished at their progress. Where is there a parallel case among the whites? . . . We cannot find an equal number of whites that will excel them in the avidity with which they try to learn. Old and young come together . . . May we hope . . . that from this small beginning there may be great and important results growing to bless the colored race?"

J. B. ROGERS, CHAPLAIN OF THE 14TH WISCONSIN
VOLUNTEERS, SUPERINTENDENT OF CONTRABAND CAMP
CAIRO, ILLINOIS, DECEMBER 21, 1862

CHAPTER FOURTEEN

"And the fifth angel sounded, and I saw a star fall from heaven unto the earth: and to him was given the key of the bottomless pit. And he opened the bottomless pit; and there arose a smoke out of the pit . . . . And there came out of the smoke locusts upon the earth: and unto them was given power, as the scorpions of the earth have power . . . . And they had a king over them, which is the angel of the bottomless pit, whose name in the Hebrew tongue is Abaddon, but in the Greek tongue hath his name Apollyon."

REVELATION 9:1–11

STANDING TALL IN HIS stirrups, the mounted figure thoughtfully stroked his full goatee, surveying the opportunity that beckoned. Disdaining to shiver as a gust of the chill December wind caressed him, *the angel of the abyss*, otherwise known to his devoted *soldier-locusts* as General Nathan Bedford Forrest of the Confederate States of America, smiled grimly in the direction of the small town of Trenton, Tennessee.

Notwithstanding the challenges of a winter campaign, Forrest was confident in the knowledge that he was where he ought to be—in the saddle and in command—bringing terror and destruction to the Yankee invader. His orders and mission were simple enough. Concerned about the Union Army's threat to Confederate forces in Mississippi, General Braxton Bragg had ordered Forrest into West Tennessee. Securing essential supplies, including firing caps for his troopers' small arms, had been a major concern, since Bragg had not been willing to outfit what he considered to be a collection of partisan guerillas. It wasn't until after completing a rain-soaked crossing of the icy Tennessee River that his

force of two thousand mounted infantry received the necessary implements of war from an individual who had been enlisted for the task by
Forrest. Their primary mission was to disrupt the north-south Mobile
and Ohio Railroad, between Columbus, Kentucky, and northern Mississippi, where it intersected with the east-west Memphis and Charleston
Railroad at Corinth, thereby interrupting a major Union supply line.

Fresh from overwhelming a small Federal force at Lexington, Tennessee, through a combination of his characteristic aggressiveness and
trickery, he was now ready to do some real damage along the targeted
rail line. Using his usual tactics, he had convinced the Union commander
that his force was much larger than its actual size by a demonstration in
his center, rapid thrusts on both Federal flanks, and a bit of theatrics. After determining that Jackson's garrison was too large to engage directly,
he had turned north, to the more manageable target of Trenton. Not one
prone to the contemplative side of life, at least not when there was fighting to be done, Forrest's brief indulgence of a grim smile ended as he
ordered a subordinate to circle around the town and attack the rear of
Trenton's garrison. "Be sure and put on the *skeer*—don't hold back now—
we've got work to do tearing up track all along this line! The sooner we
get these goddam Yankees out of our way the better."

"Yessir, General! Our scouts learned that there's a whole camp of
Negroes in the town. What should we do with them?"

"You be careful with them. They're valuable property that'll be returned to their masters. By now you outta know the policy. But if we
cain't locate their masters, we'll put 'em to work fer us or sell 'em."

"General Forrest, that third volley from our artillery did the job! The
garrison's flying a white flag," was the excited report of a nearby subordinate who had been following the action with his field glasses. One thing
Bedford Forrest did contemplate with particular pleasure was a victory
won with minimal cost. Later, as he rode into the town an officer riding
beside him enumerated the spoils. "Sir, I have the honor to report that we
are now in possession of four hundred prisoners of war, approximately
three hundred Negroes, and a large number of small arms and supplies."

"It's a pity, but we'll have to destroy most of the supplies, since we
don't have the means of transportin' 'em," Forrest replied. Before we
parole the Yankees, let's make sure they know the *true* strength of this
army." It was his subordinate's turn to smile as he reassured his commander that the appropriate demonstrations would be made in which
the Federal prisoners would see large numbers of Rebel troops in motion,

which the paroled Federals would later report to their superiors. By this time, Forrest's troopers were well acquainted with the drill—the same men repeatedly marching or riding by frightened prisoners—the circular motion creating the impression of massive numbers.

Shifting his concern to the *other* spoils of their easy victory, Forrest was beginning to inquire about the Negroes they had captured when angry screams of female distress caught his attention. He was startled to see a young black woman, well dressed in mourning clothes, being held prone with great difficulty by one of his mounted troopers over the pommel of his saddle. The soldier was simultaneously attempting to subdue the young woman, stay mounted, and direct his horse while sustaining a continuous flow of verbal attacks from his struggling prisoner: "Unhand me immediately, you savage! I am no one's property!"

"Soldier, you got yerself a *peculiar* kind o' Negro wench," Forrest observed with a chuckle, which by its rarity startled the officers accompanying him. "Looks like she might be a bit much fer y'all to handle," he drawled, as other soldiers who had been attracted by the noise began to laugh at their comrade's predicament. Before Forrest could ask the soldier what he wanted to do with his prisoner, his attention was suddenly drawn by a young white woman, also dressed in mourning, who came running toward him. Her face flushed, despite the cold, and her luxuriant brown hair in disarray after losing her bonnet, the young white woman's beauty was enhanced by her apparent anguish and distress. His curiosity about the uppity Negro wench was now completely supplanted by the overwhelming impression that here was a woman in need of Southern chivalry. Giving her his full attention, Nathan Bedford Forrest, Southern gentleman warrior, addressed her in a gentle voice far removed from the one he used in battle: "Miss, you appear to be in great distress. I am Nathan Bedford Forrest, the general in command of the Confederate states forces here. How may I be of service to you?"

"Oh sir, please don't allow them to separate me from my best and dearest friend," came the reply in a quavering Southern accent that was not quite familiar to Forrest's ear. "My dear lady, who is this *best and dearest friend*? Pointing to the still-struggling young Negro woman, she replied, "Sir, here she is—the dearest and best friend I have known from my childhood to this very day. This soldier is trying to take her from me. Please don't let him separate us!" And then, adding hesitantly as she burst into tears, "I beg you . . . kind sir."

Turning his attention and growing wrath toward the trooper, who was now beginning to regret his recent acquisition, Forrest's eyes flashed as he began to dress down the hapless soldier. "What is the policy of the Confederate States of America regarding misplaced Negro property?"

"Well . . . sir . . . I believe we're sposed to restore property to the rightful owner."

"You believe? For shame, you *should know* that is without question the policy of our government! And so, why are you brutalizing this young woman's property? Release the Negro wench immediately into the custody of her mistress!" Forrest ordered. As her soldier-captor attempted to assist her dismount, she slipped free of his grasp and slapped him adding a parting benediction: "Don't touch me, you brute!" Perplexed, Forrest looked back and forth between the young *Southern* woman and her *slave*—the well-dressed *slave* glaring at him and the young *Southern slave mistress* giving him only a plaintive look. Finally, directing his remarks to the troublesome *slave's mistress*, he asked, "Are you sure you want yer *best and dearest friend* back? She seems like a whole lot o' trouble to me. She might benefit richly from some discipline."

"Oh no, sir, you needn't worry about her on my behalf. Her bark is much worse than her bite. We really do get along just fine most of the time," was the reply of the young *slave mistress*, who was already showing signs of relief now that her *best and dearest friend* was at her side. Casting a benevolent glance on the young *Southern* woman and her *troublesome property*, Forrest asked her one more question. "Miss, yer accent—I can't place it. It has nothing of our West Tennessee twang. Where did you acquire sech a fine Southern accent?"

After a long pause, the young woman replied, "Why sir, you are indeed very observant. My original home was in North Carolina, but my family has in recent years moved to Kentucky, not far from Columbus. We were on our way back home from a visit to friends in Tennessee when we were caught up in the conflict today. I wish to sincerely thank you, General Forrest, for your kind intervention on our behalf." Removing his hat and bowing in the saddle to the beneficiary of his chivalrous intervention, Forrest said, "Miss, it has been my great pleasure to be of assistance. It would be my distinct honor, Miss . . . I believe we've not been formally introduced . . . to escort you at least to the Kentucky border. These are dangerous times . . . the least we could do would be to extend our protection to keep you safe from any Yankee depredations. Are you and your servant comfortable with traveling on horseback?"

Slowly, with some hesitation, the *young slave mistress* introduced herself. "General Forrest, my name is Rebecca Meredith," and pointing to her *best and dearest friend*, she added, "this is Louisa. The offer of your protection as we journey north to Kentucky is most kind. We are both confident equestriennes and would welcome the opportunity to travel on horseback." Turning to a lieutenant who frequently served both as aide and courier, Forrest motioned for him to come close and then whispered an order: "Go find suitable mounts for the young lady and her slave, and escort them as quickly and safely around Union City to the railway station north of the town, and make sure they are on the next available train heading toward Columbus. They should not be anywhere near Union City tomorrow. Understood?"

"Yessir! I'll make sure they're on that train."

"Miss Meredith, since our Yankee prisoners will not be needing their mounts, we've found a couple of suitable horses that have been outfitted with sidesaddles for you and your servant," Forrest informed Rebecca. By late afternoon, after taking leave of their benefactor and with the lieutenant in the lead, the two mounted ladies headed out of town. As they passed the Union Army prisoners, their commander, Colonel Jacob Fry, noticing the two mounted ladies, gave Rebecca a startled look. She quickly raised a finger to her lips, a gesture unnoticed by her escort but fully apprehended by the captive colonel, who motioned to his men to remain silent as more of them recognized the mounted women.

With only two brief stops for a simple meal and rest, the ladies followed their guide and escort north through the remaining daylight and into the moonlit night, dodging Federal patrols. As the sun was peeping over the eastern horizon, they arrived at the train station in southern Kentucky after circumventing the Federal garrison at Union City. Exhausted and barely awake, Rebecca purchased tickets for a private compartment in what would be the last train departing north from Union City for quite a while. Thanking the taciturn lieutenant, the two women tumbled into their compartment on the train—*an exhausted Southern woman with her servant companion*, duly noted by the train's conductor as he made his rounds.

A little later, that same morning of the twenty-first of December 1862, an elderly matron seething with anger came to lodge a complaint at General Forrest's headquarters north of Trenton. "I must speak to the genrul now!" she exclaimed in a shrill voice. The aide who had been unsuccessfully attempting to shush the noisy harridan so that his commander might have a little more rest before the coming battle later that day at Union City, groaned when Forrest emerged from his room and shouted, "What's the meaning of all this noise?" Pushing aside the general's aide, the old crone crowded up to Forrest and, wagging her finger in his face, scolded, "Why Genrul Forrest, you bin fooled by a dam Yankee abolitionist and her n____r friend! That pair bin down here fer mebbe two days befo' you come and captured the town. They bin bringin' clothin' and other things fer the runaways. Yer boys done requisitioned my two side saddles so's they could escape north! I want compensation fer my losses!"

CHAPTER FIFTEEN

"Come, behold the works of the Lord, what desolations he hath made in the earth. He maketh wars to cease unto the end of the earth; he breaketh the bow, and cutteth the spear in sunder; he burneth the chariot in the fire."

PSALM 46:8–9

AFTER THE CONDUCTOR HAD passed their compartment, the black *servant* gazing at her *mistress* with deep admiration burst into laughter mixed with tears and in a whisper cried, "Rebecca Meredith *Burgess*, you lied! And I thank God you did. Indeed, not to overstate the case, but you are a *very fine* liar."

"Oh Louisa, what else could I do with no clear idea or plan of how to save thee from that Rebel soldier? Truly, I did not lie when I begged General Forrest to intervene on behalf of *my best and dearest friend*. It was not my intent to deceive, but when it became evident that the general was confused about our relationship, it seemed perfectly natural to accentuate the North Carolinian accent that I had acquired from my parents and not disabuse him of his notions. But, allowing one to be deceived and overtly lying—the line was crossed when I became Rebecca Meredith. I have grievously departed from Friends' testimony regarding honesty . . . "

"And in so doing you saved my life," Louisa Johnson finished the thought for her Quaker friend. "Besides, you are Rebecca Meredith; I don't remember the Rebel general explicitly asking for your surname." Giving Rebecca a big hug, she added, "We're both very tired. Let's try and get some rest."

While her friend quickly fell asleep, slumber would not come so readily to Rebecca Burgess as she pondered the recent events that had nearly resulted in the enslavement of Louisa. Her shame in breaking one of the fundamental precepts of the Society of Friends was not so much due to the fact she had lied. After all, if she had not engaged in prevarication, Louisa might well be on her way to slavery in the South, not to mention the possibility of her violation or even torture and murder by her captors. At the thought of these horrors, she involuntarily shuddered. No, she would without hesitation skirt the truth again, if necessary, to save her friend. What disturbed her conscience and would not allow her to rest was the realization that Louisa was right. She was a very fine liar—the lies had come so effortlessly. But worse still, she was proud of having deceived the Rebel general, even now taking pleasure in remembering the details of their encounter. *Oh, how wicked I am! My dear brother, Isaac, is serving honorably as a medical officer, binding wounds, comforting the sick and dying, while I put my dearest friend, as close to my heart as any sister, in harm's way!* With her conscience as her accuser, she reviewed her decisions and actions leading up to their adventure of the previous day.

Happy childhood memories of growing up together in Newport, Indiana, were crowded by recent painful ones as she remembered the decline and death of Louisa's father, Ben Johnson. Newport was a Midwestern town unusual in its mix of free blacks and Quakers, who lived in peaceful proximity. Growing up as playmates on adjacent farms, Rebecca and Louisa, with their brothers Isaac and Samuel, attended the small Quaker school in town. Later, she had followed Isaac and Sam to the abolitionist stronghold of Oberlin College, where Negroes and women could attend, eventually completing the collegiate program and receiving the bachelor's degree. Louisa, who was a year younger than Rebecca, joined them at Oberlin a year later and completed the college's teacher training program.

From childhood, and continuing through their collegiate education, the friends had been actively involved with their families in the Underground Railroad, assisting freedom-seekers on their way to freedom in Canada. Following graduation from Oberlin, they had gained additional experience working as teachers at the Raisin Institute, a school open to students of both genders and all races, founded by the abolitionist firebrand Laura Haviland in Adrian, Michigan. With the dissolution of the Union and the advent of civil war, it became rapidly apparent that the trickle of persons escaping slavery through the Underground Railroad had now become an *above-ground* torrent of refugees.

Rebecca couldn't help but smile at the irony that the first hesitant steps toward emancipation came through a seemingly unlikely source, a Democratic-politician-lawyer-turned-Union-general, Benjamin Butler. When several able-bodied male slaves sought refuge within the Union lines at Fort Monroe, he recognized an opportunity to weaken the Southern war effort. Since in building fortifications and digging trenches, their labor freed white Rebels to fight, directly supporting the Confederate war effort, Butler refused to return them to their masters as mandated by the Fugitive Slave Act of 1850, deeming them *contraband* of war, and the name stuck.

From that time, Rebecca and Louisa followed with great interest the reports in the papers of the growing flood of contrabands, who somehow—through an invisible telegraph all their own—spread the news that refuge from slavery might be sought within the Union Army lines. From correspondence with their old professors and fellow alumni from Oberlin, they learned of plans to send missionaries to *contraband* camps under the protection of the Union Army. Both women were excited by the possibility of assisting the refugees not only as teachers but also directly by bringing food, clothing, and medical supplies. Finding substitutes to take on their teaching duties at the Raisin Institute, they returned briefly to their homes in Newport, Indiana, before assuming new responsibilities as missionaries.

Sam had not been the only Johnson child who had been kept in the dark about their father's declining health. Ben Johnson wanted his accomplished daughter to continue her important work at the Raisin Institute and insisted that his illness be minimized in the family correspondence. Indeed, the secret was so successfully kept that Louisa, arriving only a day before Sam, was shocked by her father's drastically altered appearance, which heralded the close approach of death.

Oh, how blessed I've been, Rebecca thought. *Ben Johnson has been like a second father to me. Indeed, the whole family seemed to adopt Isaac and me—white Quakers with all our peculiarities.* In the aftermath of the funeral, partly to distract Louisa from her grief, Rebecca had told her friend of the plans her uncle Levi Coffin had made to visit the refugee camp at Cairo, Illinois. In a letter to his niece, he had explained his intention of assessing firsthand the needs of the escaped slaves who had sought refuge with the Union Army. Once he had a better sense of the conditions in the *contraband* camp and the specific needs there, he would quickly telegraph the information to the various individuals who had expressed a desire to help, including Rebecca and Louisa. Her uncle had discovered that the War Department was anxious to have the additional support and help from civilian charitable organizations and would provide passes with a military escort on occasion. She recalled his explicit advice at the end of the letter: "If thou commit to direct missionary and relief work, be certain that the places you intend to visit are secured by the Federal forces. Travel nowhere without a military officer acting as escort. Many sincere anti-slavery men are among the officers in the Union Army. Seek out their support and protection." Finally, in her reflections, Rebecca now had a context for appreciating her abolitionist uncle's last admonition. "Do not underestimate the danger for northern Negroes traveling in the South. In addition to the real or imagined risks attendant to travel in country hostile to visitors from the North, thy friends Louisa and Samuel Johnson assume the potential risk of enslavement."

When Louisa had absorbed the full import of what Rebecca had related from her uncle's letter, she said, "It looks like our work is about to begin. I would rather be accomplishing some good, and I think my father would agree, than remain here in Newport a captive to grief. If they need volunteers to accompany and distribute the supplies for the refugees, count me among them! Rebecca, as my friend, you are about to caution me against placing myself, as a colored woman, in danger of enslavement or worse when we travel south. These are dangerous times. I refuse to take the easy and safe path when I have an opportunity to strike a blow for freedom and help my people."

In the wake of his December 5 visit to the contraband camp at Cairo, Levi Coffin's appeal for aid to the refugees was met quickly and generously from multiple quarters. Within a week, a large quantity of warm clothing, blankets, medicines, tinned food, and the necessary military passes had been obtained. Rebecca's mother, Priscilla, was at peace knowing that the plan and process had been endorsed by her ever-resourceful brother, Levi Coffin, who had for several decades been so successful as a leader in the Underground Railroad before the war. *It's essential that my parents continue to have confidence in the inherent safety of the process. The less they know of our adventures, the better. At least, omitting details of our journey is not the same as fabricating false stories—oh no! Rebecca, how thou so easily rationalize deceiving thy parents!*

Louisa and Rebecca had followed Levi Coffin's earlier itinerary by rail across Indiana and then southward in Illinois to Cairo. A backwater at the southern tip of Illinois, the town had acquired strategic significance during the conflict because of its being situated at the confluence of the Ohio and Mississippi Rivers. Besides the fortifications designed to repel attacks from the water, Rebecca and Louisa had been more impressed by the large contraband camp of several thousand colored refugees, mostly women, children, and the elderly, who were housed in the old military barracks. Chaplain Rogers of the fourteenth Wisconsin Volunteers, who had recently been appointed superintendent of the contraband camp, met the women at the train station and gave them a quick tour. Smiling after learning of Rebecca's relationship to Levi Coffin, he startled the two women by stating the current priorities. "Although our refugees here continue to have needs, there is an even greater and *immediate* need south of here. In Trenton, Tennessee, we have a small garrison protecting three hundred contrabands newly arrived within our lines. From the reports we've received, most of these poor souls are in rags, and there is little shelter available to them. Here we are at least blessed with the old army barracks, which we are fitting with stoves. Thankfully, most of our folks by now have received some clothing, even though they will need additional garments as the cold becomes extreme. But that can be addressed with later relief shipments. Captain Reynolds is a strong antislavery officer on leave from his duties at Trenton who will be returning there in a couple of days. If you ladies are willing, he can escort you with your supplies, which we will supplement with tents to help meet the desperate situation facing the contrabands in Trenton." The rail line south from Columbus, Kentucky, all the way to Corinth, Mississippi, has been secured by our troops. Ladies, you should feel safe as you pursue this mission of mercy."

Rebecca remembered the excitement they both felt in the realization that their mission had taken on a more urgent character and that they would be encountering slaves who had only recently escaped from bondage. Even after considering the chaplain's reassurances, they also pondered with some trepidation that they would be traveling into hostile slave states for the very first time in their lives. When Rebecca again expressed misgivings regarding Louisa's safety as a free colored person in the South, her retort had been, "Chaplain Rogers has just reassured us that the rail connections are secure. From the telegraphic reports he has received, it should be clear that our supplies would make the greatest difference to those poor people in Trenton, so I am going." Finally setting aside their anxieties in anticipation of Captain Reynolds's arrival, over the next two days, they spent considerable time observing the contraband school and its students with great interest.

Captain Reynolds, a middle-aged, balding gentleman and former teacher, had been an active proponent of immediate abolition before the war. "It is a singular pleasure for me to meet both of you and especially, Miss Johnson, to meet a colored woman who has attained such an excellent education. Being so well-refined and educated, I fear that you both may be shocked at the degradation to which many of the refugees have been subjected." As they were finishing the meal, the captain smiled and added, "I feel reinvigorated, having been so fortunate to see my wife and three children on leave this past week. I hope you will find our journey to be pleasant and your mission of mercy edifying."

After leaving Cairo, Illinois, by water and disembarking at Columbia, Kentucky, without incident, Captain Reynolds and the women had been able to catch the next train south on the Mobile and Ohio Railroad. He had advised Louisa to stay close to him so that he could prevent any unpleasant encounters with Southerners who might object to the presence of a colored woman in the first-class car. Louisa had responded, with some irony, "Captain, I very much appreciate your chivalrous protection. It's more than I could possibly hope for in my home state of Indiana, where to travel together, my friend Rebecca must ride in the third-class car with me."

Rebecca remembered protesting that she didn't mind at all riding in the third-class car, but Captain Reynolds had interjected, "I am afraid, Miss Johnson, that prejudice against your race is unfortunately present throughout the country. When the end of slavery is finally accomplished through Union victory, it will only represent the beginning of what needs to be done to restore the full humanity and dignity of your race." A shiver went down her spine as Rebecca recalled how as they passed through Union City, Captain Reynolds had blandly observed, "Ladies, we have now entered Tennessee, a state in rebellion against the United States."

Late in the day, arriving in Trenton, the local scenery was notable for the many soldiers in blue uniforms concentrated around the train station, as well as those spread throughout the town. When the overwhelming impression created by the presence of several hundred Federal soldiers in the small town dissipated, the missionaries became aware of a smattering of sullen white faces staring at them. As they closely followed Captain Reynolds on the way to their accommodations in a hotel used by Union officers, an incident that was characteristic of their reception by the local populace occurred. As Louisa and Rebecca passed, an elderly, grizzled white man was leaning against the wall of one of the local businesses, meditatively chewing tobacco. Deciding the moment had come for directing the product of his chewing at the feet of Louisa, he spat, but she was able to dodge the spittle just in time. "Well, I'll be. Cain't she jump an' caper! I bet I could git that n____r to dance even faster with a whip," he sneered. Rebecca grimaced in pain as she heard the old Rebel's verbal attack on Louisa but was deeply impressed by her friend's self-restraint in not responding.

Partly to avoid further antagonizing the townspeople, and for security purposes, the contraband camp at Trenton had been placed on the outskirts of the town and surrounded by earthworks. Rebecca and Louisa had been impressed that a significant portion of the Union garrison's efforts were directed at providing for the basic security of the refugees, not just security against Rebel attack but for *securing* their basic needs, including food, clothing, shelter, and health. From their conversations with the other officers, it became evident that Colonel Fry was also a strong advocate for the refugees who worked well with Captain Reynolds on their behalf.

Louisa and Rebecca were sickened by the horrible condition of the refugees, half-naked and shivering in the December cold. Louisa exclaimed bitterly, "How can one preserve even a shred of humanity under these conditions? But of course, that's the whole point, isn't it? If you treat human beings for generations like livestock, they gradually lose their own sense of humanity. Yet, if through all the efforts of their white masters, they have become nothing more than livestock to be traded, why then do they risk their very existence chasing after this elusive thing called freedom?" All day the two women passed out blankets, articles of clothing, and shoes to the refugees, who were delighted to have something with which to fight the cold.

Both women were impressed by the disproportionate numbers of women, children, and elderly among the refugees. When that evening at supper, they asked Captain Reynolds about it, his response was, "There are several possible explanations that may account for at least some of the disparity. Able-bodied male slaves have often been taken by the Confederate Army to build their fortifications. Some who have escaped to our lines have told us as much. I think that not infrequently, women, children, elderly, and the infirm are intentionally allowed to come into our lines to complicate our management of the towns and forts we must garrison. Perhaps most unfortunate, when the able-bodied male slaves attempt to flee for the Union lines, they become the primary subjects of pursuit. Rebel soldiers will sooner shoot them down than let them escape to provide similar service to the Federal forces."

After dinner, Colonel Fry, the commander of the garrison, thanked the women for their dedicated service and asked them to share their impressions of the contraband camp. Rebecca could still see the animation in Louisa's face as she spoke of her initial horror at witnessing firsthand the degradation of her race, but also the joy she experienced in helping to alleviate at least a small part of their suffering. Perhaps in reference to her unpleasant encounter of the prior day, Louisa further commented, "What is most extraordinary to me is that although degradation has been forced upon them, the refugees have endured danger and severe privation to ameliorate their situation, while it seems that many of their white masters revel in the degraded moral condition which the peculiar institution has nourished within Southern civilization."

"Miss Johnson, you have underscored the essential effect of chattel slavery which degrades *all* who are touched by it—enslaved and master alike," Colonel Fry responded with growing enthusiasm. "But we should not delude ourselves; its poison extends beyond the immediate environment in which it is seen to operate, for our Northern states have also been corrupted by reaping great material benefit from an economy deeply intertwined with the South's peculiar institution. Sadly, it seems this war is a divine judgment on our whole nation . . ." Colonel Fry's speech had been cut short when an aide came up quietly to his side whispering a report.

"Ladies and gentlemen, I have just received an unverified report that a large force of Rebel cavalry coming from the east has taken our garrison at Lexington and may be heading in this direction." With growing anxiety, Rebecca had asked, "Colonel Fry, what dost thou mean by describing the report as *unverified*?"

"So far, what has been reported is *merely* hearsay obtained from a civilian traveling in this direction from Lexington. Not infrequently, local citizens whose sympathies are with the rebellion will spread rumors of imminent Rebel invasion to create confusion and alarm."

"Sir, how would thou *verify* such news?"

"Miss Burgess, when confronted with an unsubstantiated rumor of this kind, military protocol entails communicating telegraphically with the subject of interest, and if this is not possible, then scouts are sent to clarify the situation by direct observation. The report of Lexington remains *unverified* at present because our telegraphic communication in that direction is temporarily inoperative—a not-infrequent phenomenon in a region hostile to an occupying force. Scouts have just been sent out to obtain direct clarification of the situation. Despite the problems with the telegraph, let us be cautiously optimistic that what has been reported is merely rumor. Meanwhile, ladies, may I suggest that you retire early this evening so that you can quickly finish distributing the supplies to the refugees tomorrow morning, in case your evacuation becomes necessary."

Rebecca remembered how the next morning, Colonel Fry had continued to reassure them, even after his scouts had confirmed the presence of a large body of Rebel cavalry in West Tennessee. "Sadly, my scouts were able to confirm the surrender of the garrison at Lexington, but they determined that the enemy's movement has been directed toward Jackson, a town to our south along the Mobile and Ohio Railroad. If you work quickly, I believe you will be able to finish your mission of mercy this morning. As a precaution, I think you should leave the area today, so I have requested that the 10:00 a.m. train scheduled for Union City be delayed for two hours to give you adequate time to finish your work and depart north by noon."

Breakfast had only just finished when loud explosions rocked the center of Trenton, sending porcelain dishes crashing down from their cabinets in the dining room. The Federal commander had not fully appreciated the imminent nature of the danger until it was too late; for having determined that Jackson was too well defended, General Forrest had turned north for easier pickings. Blanching, Colonel Fry had warned Rebecca and Louisa to take cover, since "it is evident, ladies, that we are under attack!" Glancing toward Louisa with concern, he had added, "Try and hide to avoid capture, for if we are forced to surrender, the Rebels may try to enslave you, Miss Johnson." Louisa had responded fiercely, "Whoever attempts to enslave me will regret it!"

Bidding the women a hasty farewell, the colonel had then rushed off to direct the defense of the town. What had followed was a chaotic blur of terrifying explosions, burning buildings, and soldiers, with civilians intermixed, running in all directions. Not knowing what to do, the two friends had stayed in the hotel dining room, huddled together away from the windows and exterior wall during the Rebel artillery barrage. Since the dining room embraced almost the entire first floor of the hotel, it was possible to gain a broad perspective of the town through its windows. During a pause in the bombardment, the women had been horrified to see burning and collapsing buildings in all directions, with large amounts of smoke billowing from the direction of the contraband camp. Two more artillery barrages had driven them back again to the relative safety of the inner wall of the dining room. But when a direct hit during the third barrage had blasted a large hole in the exterior wall at the opposite end of the dining room from where they had been huddled, setting it on fire, they had no choice but to flee. As the women escaped the burning hotel, they were horrified to hear a soldier shouting, "Colonel Fry has surrendered to the Rebs!"

Upon hearing this news, Louisa had cried, "Oh Rebecca, what will become of our poor refugees?" Without thinking, Louisa had begun to run toward the contraband camp moving quickly among the shadows cast by undamaged buildings. Rebecca could only follow with growing anxiety crying, "Louisa, that direction cannot be safe for thee! We must seek a hiding place without delay." But her friend, seemingly oblivious to Rebecca's cries, had kept on running toward the contraband camp as if drawn by a powerful magnet. Turning a corner, Louisa had suddenly drawn back into the shadow of a building where she and Rebecca, who had finally caught up with her witnessed with horror the actions of the Rebel soldiers in the contraband camp.

In a matter of minutes, their charitable labor of the preceding day had been undone by the Rebel soldiers, who like locusts had been stripping the contraband camp bare of anything of value. Their actions had not been limited to inanimate objects, for they had herded the refugees together at gunpoint, stripping warm clothes and shoes off them for their own use. In her memory of the scene, Rebecca was again filled with disgust that nevertheless was mixed with pity at the sight of the ill clad Rebel soldiers, who with delighted grins on their sallow faces had wrapped themselves in warm blankets taken from the refugees, some even cavorting in women's clothing they had taken from their prisoners. Absorbing the scene in all its terrible and even ludicrous qualities, Louisa had turned to Rebecca and whispered, "It seems the Confederates treat their private soldiers not much better than their slaves. Look at those shivering scarecrows, many without coats or shoes—now so pleased to steal Northern charity and warmth from the refugees!"

When one of the refugees resisted the theft of a blanket which covered her baby, the Rebel soldier involved had first cursed and then had begun to beat her with the butt of his musket. Finally, he had wrested the desired blanket from the woman but only after she had collapsed, bleeding from a gash on her forehead, still clutching her baby in her bare arms. In her agitation upon witnessing such cruelty, Louisa had briefly left the protection of the shadows, and before she could retreat to safety, she had caught the attention of a mounted Rebel soldier. Spurring his horse toward the women, he had cried, "What's this . . . a well-dressed n____r wench?" And as Louisa began to run, the Rebel had reached down and grabbing her, lifted her up swiftly, depositing her over the pommel of his saddle. As Louisa had begun to protest vociferously while flailing at her captor, Rebecca remembered hearing a nearby female voice from the gathering crowd of townspeople remarking, "Why, that's the uppity n____r abolitionist from the North who was handing out them clothes yestiday to the runaways! Now our boys'll larn her what her proper place is." It was the panic inspired by this sudden turn of events that enabled Rebecca Burgess to reach deep within herself and deliver a performance that elicited Southern chivalry in Nathan Bedford Forrest and saved her *best and dearest friend.*

Awakened by the conductor's announcement that they would be arriving in Columbus, Kentucky, in an hour, Rebecca realized that she had finally fallen asleep. Sensing that Louisa was looking at her, she opened her eyes and directed a furtive glance toward her friend, which was followed by an exchange of smiles, tearful laughter, and finally hugs. Louisa was the first to speak. "While I thank God and *my* 'best and dearest friend' for my deliverance yesterday, I can only grieve at the fate of the refugees, my African sisters and brothers."

"Oh Louisa, can you ever forgive me for encouraging thee to join such a dangerous mission?" Rebecca exclaimed. Grasping her friend's forearm tightly, Louisa replied, "Please, no more apologies! Didn't God protect us, even in our foolish naïveté? I have never felt so alive as when we were doing the Lord's work—bringing relief to those suffering refugees. Rebecca, through our long friendship, you have very nearly made a Quaker of me, although I'm probably a bit *too fierce* to be an official Friend. And I absolutely refuse to take up plain speech—no *thees* and *thous* for me, except when quoting the Bible! But surely, if even your Baptist friend can sense the clear promptings of the *Inner Light*, how can you as a sincere *Friend* deny the same clarion call to service? Witnessing the subversion of our efforts to assist the refugees by the Rebel Army has only strengthened my resolve to work even more diligently on their behalf.

"Very well, Louisa Johnson, no more apologies, but only on condition that in the future, we continue to travel together as Oberlin missionaries. Furthermore, when and if the occasion demands, please allow me to resume the guise of thy mistress to assure thy safety. Besides, I rather like playing that role . . . oh, there is one more thing."

Louisa, who began to laugh, asked, "And what is that?"

"For the present, I think we should keep our little adventure a secret. It would be distressing for my parents, and I am afraid my uncle Levi, feeling responsible for our safety, might try to block our further activities in the South. Also, I don't want to worry Isaac either, although I suspect he might find our encounter with his *old friend* Forrest rather interesting," Rebecca added with a laugh.

"Agreed." After a thoughtful pause, Louisa declared, "But I think Sam should know. It's essential for free persons of color doing relief work in the South to be fully aware of the risks. He has repeatedly told me of his plan to go south after the Emancipation Proclamation takes effect to help recruit black soldiers for the Union Army, and while occupied with that task, he also hopes to serve the refugees as a teacher or nurse. You know, he quite enjoyed his time working with Isaac at the military hospital in Maryland."

"Is Sam still seeking an officer's commission in the army?"

"Yes, he is the perennial optimist," Louisa answered with a shrug. "Considering how the Ohio Bar rejected him, I seriously doubt that the United States military will embrace him as an officer. Nevertheless, he still hopes that making strenuous efforts to recruit black soldiers will favorably influence the decision regarding his request for an officer's commission in a black regiment."

"How I wish he would be satisfied with serving as a non-combatant. My concerns about Sam serving in the military go beyond the Society of Friends' Testimony Against War. Aren't thou concerned, Louisa, about the virulent language used by the Southern newspapers in describing the preliminary Emancipation Proclamation? They speak of it as inciting *servile insurrection* . . . I am afraid that the sight of black men in Federal uniforms will enrage the Rebel soldiers, who will not respect their humanity, even though they are clothed in Union blue. As you know, before the war, even the mere rumor of a slave conspiracy in the South often resulted in vicious reprisals and the slaughter of innocents. What would Rebel soldiers do to black prisoners of war?"

Louisa sighed. "Of course I'm concerned. But after acquiring first-hand knowledge of the terrible suffering of the refugees, I am even more convinced that Sam and I should help them—and that will entail risks. Rebecca, you know how stubborn we Johnsons can be! I share your fears for Sam's safety, but I also respect his brave commitment to service. By his very nature, he cannot—will not—watch from a place of safety while others suffer and risk serious injury and even death for a cause he holds dearer than his own life. Ultimately, his and our safety will be in the hands of Providence."

Chaplain Rogers was visibly relieved when the women reported to his office upon arrival in Cairo. Minimizing the details of their encounter with Forrest and his Rebel troopers, they begged him to keep silent about the whole affair.

"My most sincere apologies, ladies, for placing you in danger."

"We're none the worse for the adventure and hopefully considerably wiser about how to proceed in the future," Louisa declared in response. "Our greatest regret is to see the refugees stripped of the clothing and other relief materials they so desperately need and then cruelly dragged back into bondage by the Rebels."

"After this harrowing experience, do you intend to pursue more relief work in the South?" the chaplain-superintendent asked with incredulity. "Yes, with better planning and after much prayer," Rebecca replied with a smile. "Our alma mater, Oberlin College, has been recruiting missionaries for the South from among its alumni to teach the refugees."

"As the war progresses and word of the Emancipation Proclamation spreads in the occupied regions of the South, surely the numbers of refugees coming within Union lines will expand rapidly," Louisa added. "Our recent experience has only confirmed our vocation."

Rubbing his forehead as he pondered their temerity, Chaplain Rogers finally replied, "It is clear to me that you are both deeply committed to this holy work—may God bless and protect you both. Your visit to Trenton, Tennessee, will remain a secret, but do exercise more caution in the future than I did in sending you there!"

After hearing Louisa's account of Forrest's raid on Trenton, Tennessee, and her description of Rebecca's role in her rescue from certain enslavement, Sam Johnson gave Rebecca a look of deep admiration. "Thank you, Rebecca; your clever deception saved my sister's life." Then smiling broadly, he added, "If the need should again arise, I hope you would extend your generous offer of once more becoming Louisa's *mistress* to also include me." To Sam's great satisfaction, Rebecca blushed deeply. "Oh Sam, Louisa has greatly exaggerated the importance of my actions in our deliverance."

"I doubt that. If anything, she probably has understated the value of a providential lie coming from the very picture of innocence. In my estimation, only Rebecca Burgess could have summoned forth a serious attempt at *Southern chivalry* from a ruthless raider like Forrest! But regarding your remarkable story, there is one restriction that I must protest. It's unseemly for me to know and treasure such information about you, Rebecca Burgess, while your own dear brother must remain ignorant of his sister's heroism." Blushing again, Rebecca tried to explain. "Sam, I do not regret that in deceiving General Forrest I helped save Louisa, but I am ashamed that I took pride in the act."

"Dear Rebecca, is it a sin to rejoice in a good deed well done? For I would argue that you have mistaken the *joy* of a blessed success for *pride*. Should not your brother also share in that joy, considering the mysterious workings of Providence?"

"Samuel Johnson, it seems thou would be the *self-appointed* advocate before my conscience. Thou hast my promise that I will write to Isaac about our adventure, but I prefer a delay of a few months before I inform him."

CHAPTER SIXTEEN

"The Secretary of War directs that you employ the refugee Negroes as teamsters, laborers, etc., so far as you have use for them, in the Quartermaster's department, on forts, railroads, etc.: also, in picking and removing cotton on account of the Government. So far as possible, subsist them and your army on the Rebel inhabitants of Mississippi."

GEN. HENRY HALLECK TO GEN. ULYSSES S. GRANT, NOVEMBER 16, 1862

Corinth, Mississippi
March 19, 1863

Dear Isaac,

In thy last letter I sensed a note of frustration regarding my brief description of the relief work with which Louisa and I have been engaged over the past several months. As thou canst readily surmise from the address whence this letter has been posted, a fuller account of our activities is long overdue thee. Please forgive me, dear brother, for my only intent has been to avoid causing thee any worry on my account . . . .

FOR SHAME, REBECCA BURGESS, *that's not the entire truth. Now that Louisa and I are in Corinth serving as missionaries, any objections Isaac might have can be of little effect. What is that most useful French expression? Ah yes, it is a fait accompli.* Resuming her letter, she decided to tell the *whole* truth.

Sam thought I should tell thee immediately afterward in late twelfth month, but I was afraid that thou might raise legitimate objections to any further relief activities on our part. To get to the point—Louisa and I have had the opportunity (pleasure

might be an overstatement) to meet thy old acquaintance, Nathan Bedford Forrest . . .

Rebecca read over her account of the December relief mission to
Trenton, Tennessee, including the near enslavement of Louisa and their
seeming miraculous escape, satisfied with the emphasis she had placed
on the prominent role of Providence while minimizing her deception of
Forrest. *I hope Isaac will be satisfied with this and not want further details,*
she thought. With a sense of relief, she continued her letter.

> Since the Emancipation Proclamation took effect at the begin-
> ning of first month, Professor Cowles from Oberlin has in-
> creased his efforts recruiting missionaries among our alumni
> to teach the freedmen in the refugee camps. Louisa and I have
> answered the call and made the journey to Corinth via Missis-
> sippi riverboat, disembarking and resting in Memphis for two
> days before completing the nearly one-hundred-mile train ride
> to Corinth two weeks ago. As thou hast probably learned from
> Sam's correspondence, he plans to follow us soon. Although he
> hopes to help the refugees, his primary mission will be to recruit
> soldiers among the freedmen in the various contraband camps.
> Along with the other missionaries, we received military passes
> for safe conduct and were given a military escort on our voyage
> south. We felt quite safe. . . .

I'd better not mention the times Rebel guerillas fired at our steamboat,
first from the Arkansas and then the Tennessee banks of the Mississippi, she
thought. Resuming her letter:

> Our time in Memphis was well spent. Colonel Eaton, who has
> been authorized by General Grant to organize the care of the
> refugees throughout the Mississippi Valley, is a highly efficient
> leader and compassionate advocate for the freedmen. Before the
> war, he had been superintendent of schools in Toledo. Provi-
> dentially, the administrative skills gained from his prior experi-
> ence are now being employed for an even higher purpose. He is
> most personable, and circumstances permitting has made it his
> policy to meet every missionary arriving from the North. After
> dining with us, he gave an inspiring speech in which he de-
> scribed the multiple needs of the refugees, especially regarding
> their medical care, education, and spiritual nurture. In his final
> remarks, he stated that a major goal of his administration will
> be to help them quickly become *self-sufficient,* for it is the *neces-*
> *sary* policy of the government which in its conduct of the war

must minimize other non-military expenditures. He thanked us repeatedly for our willingness to volunteer and urged us to remind our sponsoring charities, especially the American Missionary Association, that the refugees depend on Northern philanthropy for their very survival.

Only when we personally witnessed the close physical proximity between Union Army fortifications and the refugee camps did we begin to appreciate how the emancipation proclaimed by Mr. Lincoln is utterly dependent on the success of Federal arms. The good colonel was quite enthusiastic when he realized that Louisa and I had been recruited to teach at Corinth. In his view, this camp is a model of the self-sufficiency which he hopes will become a feature of every contraband camp under his jurisdiction. Faced with a flood of contrabands, General Grenville Dodge, the Union commander at Corinth, established the camp in autumn of last year. Shortly afterward, he placed Chaplain James Alexander of the 66th Illinois volunteer infantry in charge of the camp. According to Colonel Eaton, the chaplain proved to be an excellent choice, and in our brief time here, we can also bear witness to his many administrative successes.

From what we have learned, developing the *self-sufficiency* of the contrabands initially involved putting them to work harvesting cotton in the vicinity, which was sold to help the war effort as well as defray the costs of their care. Once this initial harvest was completed, the chaplain encouraged them to also grow crops of vegetables to meet their own needs. In a very short time, this has resulted in a large cooperative farming project adjacent to the camp in which three hundred acres are reserved for cotton and another one hundred acres for vegetables. The intent is for the refugees' cooperative farm to sell their cotton to purchasing agents and sell vegetables to the Union officers and soldiers occupying Corinth. What an incredible thing—to see human beings, many of whom only a few weeks earlier were enslaved property, now acquiring the dignity that can only come from receiving the fruit of their own labor!

Isaac, what is truly extraordinary is how quickly the industry of the refugees has transformed what had initially been a disorganized mass of tents into rows of tidy houses arranged along streets—they have created a village of free persons who in every way demonstrate the right to be called *citizens*. Not only have they built snug homes, but they have also built a hospital, commissary, school buildings, and are working on a church. Chaplain Alexander has extended Colonel Eaton's vision of *self-sufficiency* to another aspect of the refugees' lives.

As thou probably remember from thy time here after the battle of Shiloh, there are extensive fortifications and entrenchments, initially constructed by slave labor for the Rebel forces and later extended by the Federal forces since their occupation of the town. The eastern extent of the fortifications embraces the contraband camp. Anticipating the War Department's efforts, in February the chaplain recruited able-bodied volunteers from among the refugees to serve in a company of sixty colored soldiers assigned to protect the contraband camp. Oh, how Louisa's eyes glistened with tears to see, for the first time, young black men now wearing the blue uniform of the United States. Just imagine seeing them drilling in good order and serving as pickets near the camp!

An almost continuous flood of refugees arrives daily from the surrounding region. Corinth hosts freedmen from southwestern Tennessee, northern Mississippi, and western Alabama. Upon our arrival, Chaplain Alexander warned us that the numbers of refugees coming to Corinth would soon expand further, because General Dodge has begun to send out parties of soldiers from the garrison to gather refugees and liberate any remaining slaves on plantations in the vicinity. The army is specifically looking for able-bodied recruits for the colored regiments they plan to form with the intent to use the colored troops primarily for garrison duty. Not only will this free up more white soldiers for combat, but it seems there is considerable doubt in the government regarding the fitness of the Negro for military service, especially for combat. Louisa is offended by the implication, but I can only hope and pray that garrison duty might be a safer form of service for Sam that he would find acceptable.

After our arrival two weeks ago, it didn't take long before our mission began in earnest. Our primary duties are as teachers, but we also help address the acute needs of the refugees, many of whom arrive in rags, malnourished, and sick. Some of them arrive even bearing severe physical wounds from the malice of their former masters, intent upon the destruction of *human property* that refuses to remain *property*. After breakfast, our days begin with a quick prayer service followed by a morning session of teaching in the tent classroom, which Louisa and I share. Because of the intense heat, even in March teaching does not resume until the evening. Our tent classroom reflects the continual need for more and larger school facilities, but we hope to move into a new school building, perhaps as early as June. Our students are of all ages and apply themselves to learning with an intensity and commitment at which Louisa and I can only marvel. While I continue the same program of teaching basic literacy in the evening session, Louisa has been asked to work evenings with the brightest leaders of the refugee community. Having already acquired basic literacy skills before our arrival, these individuals hope to acquire a much broader education that would support their leadership within the refugee community. Louisa has become a tremendous inspiration to the refugees, who had no idea that such accomplishments could be attained by any member of their race, let alone a colored woman. Louisa occupies a strange position here in Corinth—treated with deep respect, even awe by the refugees, but unfortunately, often with rudeness and the crude derision typical of the prejudices of the local inhabitants and many of the private Northern soldiers. Thankfully, the officers have been uniformly respectful and some quite cordial—the latter behavior typical for those with abolitionist principles. Louisa, with good grace, rises above it all, inspiring me to work harder.

Before I close this letter, I must add an additional anecdote which hopefully may be of especial interest to thee. Four of Louisa's evening students are highly regarded as preachers and religious exhorters among the refugees. One of these colored preachers is an older gentleman named Moses, whose role in the community when not preaching is that of blacksmith. He acknowledges having been a slave on the Magnolias plantation and readily admitted his role in leading his fellow slaves to freedom during the confusion and aftermath of Shiloh. Freedmen from the Magnolias have been following the Federal Army ever since the battle, playing a major role in the foundation of the community here. His preaching continues to inspire, but now he eloquently quotes and reads from a real Bible held in his hand during his sermons, which has replaced the invisible one of thy memories!

So, dear brother, I hope thou canst now visualize our situation here in Corinth. We both feel completely safe and rejoice in the mission that God has given us to fulfill. Please pray for us as we labor to assist the many refugees yearning for a fuller life and acquaintance with the Savior who is delivering them in this great moment of our nation's history.

Ever thy affectionate sister,
Rebecca

Looking up from her writing, Rebecca smiled as Louisa entered the room and declared, "So, you've finally paid your literary debt to your brother. Is your conscience eased a bit?"

"I hope so," was the reply as Rebecca pushed the letter toward Louisa for her approval.

"Well, it is a nice reassuring letter," Louisa smirked at her friend. "Perhaps just a bit too reassuring. Anyway, you really do your brother an injustice. He will read between the lines and understand the true nature of the miracle." Changing the subject, Louisa said, "Rather than discuss the nature of miracles, I came to collect you for our rounds at the hospital. Remember, we have regular nursing duties on Thursday afternoons."

"Yes, of course. Please forgive my distractedness."

Approaching the entrance to the hospital, the two women were met by a stream of refugees arriving in wagons, riding on the backs of mules, or trudging on foot, escorted by mounted Union soldiers. Recognizing the missionaries, a lieutenant who had conducted the raid of two nearby plantations said, "Ladies, most of these folks are in good shape. Their former owners mainly fussed, but in the first wagon you'll find a couple of brothers we picked up on the way back who made their escape from another plantation further south of here. Unfortunately, one of them is shot up badly, and his brother won't leave his side."

"Lieutenant, I'll need some help moving the wounded man into the hospital," Louisa directed while Rebecca began to assess the condition of the other refugees. Once the wounded man was transferred from the wagon, Louisa went in search of a surgeon to examine him.

Shaking his head, the assistant surgeon looked down at the unconscious refugee, whose loud moaning and labored breathing could be heard out in the hallway. Turning to the wounded man's brother, he asked, "How long has it been since he was shot?"

"It's bin 'bout a day, suh."

"How did you escape being shot, yourself?"

"When our massa ketched up to us, I raised mah hands, but mah brother Ned he run and dey shot 'im down. Dey run up to Ned an' said he gonna die fum de wound, an' dey decide to leave 'im right dere to die. I's so upset when I heard dat, I try an' grab de pistol fum de one who shot Ned. De udder two, mah massa an' de oberseer, tried to shoot me, but dey kill de udder man 'stead." Cautiously, instinctively looking behind him, he added in a whisper, "Seein' mah chance, I grabbed de pistol an' shot bof of 'em. I bin carryin' poor Ned mos' all de time since, hopin' to git here when de blue sojers found us. Suh, kin you save Ned?"

"I'm sorry but there's not much we can do for Ned's wound—gunshots to the abdomen are almost always fatal. I doubt that he will live at most more than another day or two. But we will do our best to make him comfortable in his last hours. I admire your courage and devotion to your brother." His voice breaking, Ned's brother thanked the assistant surgeon and added, "Ned alluz said he'd die befo' he'd be a slave agin. At leas' now, he'll die free." Moved by the brother's suffering, Louisa asked him, "Are you a praying sort of man? Is Ned a believer?" Giving Louisa his full attention for the first time, the distraught freedman replied, "Ma'am, Ned an' me, we nebber learn much 'bout de Lord—only dat our massa say dat de Lord want us to be good slaves. But when de war come an' we hear 'bout freedom, we bof decide we want freedom mo' den bein' good slaves. I guess mebbe dat mean we ain't so good at prayin'."

"Mr. Ned's brother, what's *your* name?"

"Ma'am, it's a moufful. Dey gib me de fancy name ob Na-po-le-on, after some genrul, but reglar folks call me Nappy."

"Nappy, may I bring a wonderful preacher to visit you and Ned later this evening?"

"Ma'am, if'n you want to bring a preacher to visit po' Ned an' me, dat be fine wif me. But please jes' don't hab 'im come an' preach fo' us to be good slaves. We's free now."

"Oh, Nappy! The preacher I will bring is a freedman like you. His name is Moses."

"Ain't Moses de man dat brought de slaves outta Egypt?"

"Yes. So, you do know something of religion and the Bible."

"I's afraid dat's 'bout all I knows, ma'am."

"Would you like to know more and learn how to read it yourself?"

Pausing in bewilderment before attempting an answer, Nappy gave Louisa an incredulous look and finally said, "Dey don't 'low slaves to read an' write in Mississippi."

"But Nappy, you just told me that you're free. It's true, you really are free, and that includes even the possibility of learning to read and write!"

"The Spirit of the Lord God is upon me; because the Lord hath anointed me to preach good tidings unto the meek; he hath sent me to bind up the brokenhearted, *to proclaim liberty to the captives . . .*" The tall, lean figure of Moses, sometime blacksmith and slave preacher on the Endicott/Wormeley plantation, was now fully in the service of the Lord. He paused in his reading from the prophet Isaiah to look for any change in Ned's condition as he sat vigil with Nappy and Louisa. Still unconscious, Ned's breathing had become irregular over the past hour, with progressively longer pauses between breaths. Nappy's face, moist with tears, shone in the lantern light as his brother took his last breath. Slowly, with quiet solemnity Moses placed his right hand on Ned's forehead and intoned, "The Lord bless thee and keep thee. The Lord make his face shine upon thee, and be gracious unto thee. The Lord lift up his countenance upon thee, and give thee peace." Then, turning to Nappy, he added, "Son, your brother is finally free . . . maybe not in the way you and he hoped for when you escaped from your master, but he is truly liberated—resting in God's mercy. His dream of freedom in this life, which he was willing to die for must now be united to your own dream; you must live as a freedman not for yourself alone but also for your brother."

"How kin I lib as a freedman fo' de two ob us, when I don' eben know what freedom means?" Nappy cried. Pointing to his Bible, Moses said, "It's all in here, everything you need to know about freedom and how to live a life honoring your brother's memory." Gently placing her hand on Nappy's arm, Louisa added, "Learning is where freedom begins. If you like, I can help you on your way."

"I wud like dat a lot, ma'am."

Rebecca gave Louisa a sideways glance over breakfast the next morning and began her interrogation. "Please tell me about thy vigil last night with Moses and the two brothers. To think that the one brother— Nappy is such an odd name—carried his wounded brother for miles. Such a strong man and quite handsome too, don't thou thinkest?"

"I already gave you an account last night before going to bed. Do you want to hear it again?"

"Yes, I know, but thou didn't tell me of thy *impressions*, only the bare particulars." Louisa paused in the middle of buttering her bread and laughed. "Rebecca, you are being rather inquisitive this morning. Do you want to hear more about the experience of being present at the bedside of a dying person, or are you more interested in my impressions of the dying person's handsome brother?" Blushing, Rebecca retreated to safer ground. "Forgive me. If thou art willing, I would derive much spiritual benefit from thy observations regarding Moses' ministrations during the vigil."

"I must confess it was difficult for me to be there last night . . . It felt as if I was being pulled back to the bedside of my father in his last hours. Such a strange experience—how could the death of a total stranger, tragic as it was, suddenly open the floodgates of grief for my father? Nappy wasn't the only person weeping at the bedside of his dying brother! In his intense grief, I don't think the poor fellow even noticed my silent tears, which I tried unsuccessfully to suppress. Ah, but Moses, he doesn't miss anything! Our pastor back home brought considerable comfort to us when Father died, but last evening Moses brought something more to the dying man's bedside . . . I don't quite know how to describe it. Perhaps the closest I can approximate it in words is to say his was a *presence* filled with a deep, incomprehensible compassion in equal measure to all the suffering that he and Ned had experienced in slavery. While I must acknowledge that his speech and use of Scripture were both eloquent and comforting, it was what Moses communicated beyond words that I will never forget." Tears welling up in her eyes, Louisa paused to recover her composure. "Rebecca, it's so odd—truly incomprehensible. You know me better than anyone else, how insufferably arrogant I can be, and yet in my short acquaintance with Moses I have come to know an unlettered man whose genuine wisdom has put to shame the pretense of an Oberlin graduate.

"Now to my impressions of the handsome brother of a dying man, for I must not disappoint my friend," Louisa's sarcasm had returned. "As you so astutely observed, Rebecca, he is a handsome, powerful specimen of Negro manhood—tall with even features and intelligent eyes. But being a *good* Oberlinite, I am tempted to declare that he is a *tabula rasa*. But no, that's not fair. Locke's notions do not apply here. Nappy may in some sense be closer to Rousseau's *noble savage*, but a *blank slate* he is not! No, I daresay suffering in all its hideous forms has left its indelible mark on this *slate*. The question remains, what can literacy do to excavate the real Nappy buried underneath all that suffering? If he is willing, I mean to assist him in the process of discovery."

If Louisa's task with Nappy was one of excavation, she wasn't the only one doing the digging. Moses, the white-haired patriarch of the community, had an intuitive sense about people. He recognized qualities in Nappy of which the young freedman was largely unaware, since in his former life there was not much opportunity to cultivate or practice introspection. The extraordinary physical endurance, perseverance, and loyalty that were demonstrated by his heroic attempt to save his wounded brother began to be manifest in other ways during his time at Corinth. With Moses's encouragement and Louisa's patient instruction, over the weeks following his brother's death, Nappy applied himself wholeheartedly to his studies. As he made rapid strides engaging in intellectual activities that had been entirely closed to him as a slave, he began to see a way through his grief—becoming literate had been an unattainable dream he shared with Ned that he was now fulfilling for both of them. After his formal studies in the morning with Louisa and Rebecca, his afternoons were consumed with heavy physical labor in the cotton and vegetable fields. Even though exhausted, it was a rare evening that he did not return to his studies, sometimes depending on firelight to read by. With growing mastery of the written word came a similar mastery of the spoken word—he was rapidly shedding the slave dialect and with it, any remaining sense of the servile.

One evening in early May, Moses visited Nappy. Looking around the small but tidy cabin, he smiled and said, "Nappy, you've got a nice place here, but there's one thing missing."

"What's that, sir?"

"Do you remember our conversation the night your brother died?"

"I'll never forget it. You and Miss Louisa were so kind to me."

"We spoke of freedom, a concept you were struggling to understand, if I recall."

"Yes, we did and since that time, I believe I've been catching sight of it here and there. Why I still can't believe I'm learning to read and write—it just seems like a miracle right out of the Bible!"

"Speaking of the Bible, I happen to have one here that Miss Louisa assures me is meant for you." Giving Moses a look of incredulity, Nappy reverently held the Bible in his hands.

"Sir, are you certain that Miss Louisa meant for me to have this?"

"Her distinct words to me were, 'It's high time Nappy move on from the readers.' Nappy, even I wondered whether you're ready, but she insisted, and told me to test you this very night. She's that confident in you! But she gave me the choice of which passage to use for your *test*."

Opening the Bible, Moses pointed with a long finger to the place Nappy should begin reading and said, "Now take your time and sound out any unfamiliar words."

"Bless-ed are the poor in spir-it, for theirs is the king-dom of heaven. . . ." Giving Nappy a broad smile, Moses said, "My friend, you are a mighty quick learner!"

"Thank you, sir. A whole world has been revealed that I didn't know was there until I met you and Miss Louisa."

"Miss Louisa's been doing all the hard work; I just encourage folks as they make the effort—but I must say you didn't need much encouraging."

"Miss Louisa's been an angel sent from God. I had no idea that such beau-ty and in-tel-li-gence could be all mixed together in the same woman—and a colored woman at that! Do you think that she might ever be in-ter-est-ed in a fellow like me?"

"Right now, she's your teacher. Be the best student you can be, and once she can't teach you anything more, then make a commitment to keep learning. I suspect she'll take notice." Smiling, Moses thought to himself, *That young gal has already taken notice of her star pupil. I've seen that look in a girl's eye before.*

CHAPTER SEVENTEEN

*"The want and destitution were appalling, and the provision wherewith
to meet the conditions and ameliorate them was far from adequate.
The situation confronting those of us who had the ordering of the early
camps was really the clashing of the two antagonistic conditions, liberty
and bondage . . . How was the slave to be transformed into a freeman?"*

COLONEL JOHN EATON, GENERAL SUPERINTENDENT OF CONTRA-
BANDS, MISSISSIPPI VALLEY, LATE 1862

"AH, GREENBACKS! IN THESE uncertain times we at least have one thing
upon which we can depend." Chalmers Underwood was warming to
his favorite topic of conversation—money. Prior to the war, Chalmers,
the youngest of Penelope Wormeley's maternal uncles, had been viewed
by his more genteel relations with a mild condescension, for he was a
tradesman. In its apparent fickleness, the wheel of fortune had not only
disrupted the South's social order—parting *loyal* servants from their *benevolent* masters—it had *capriciously* elevated some outside the planter
class who could never properly claim the title of *gentleman*. In happier
times, it had been something of an embarrassment for the family that
Underwood Mercantile of Corinth, Mississippi, even existed. With one
sister deceased and two brothers serving as officers in the Rebel Army,
Chalmers had attained an unusual position in the family. He was the
only one prospering and definitely the only one with greenbacks—lots
of them! A limp, which he had acquired after falling from a horse several years earlier, served to augment a carefully cultivated ingratiating
demeanor when he approached customers. It had also spared him from
military conscription by the Confederate States of America.

"Sometimes it may be necessary for our wellbeing, and of those we love, to do business with the devil himself."

"Is that why you signed the loyalty oath, Uncle?" Penelope Wormeley asked. "Of course that's why he signed," her husband Fitzhugh interjected. "But what of honor—our Southern honor?" Penelope persisted. "Is there no greater act linked to honor than pledging one's word—and here, you have not merely spoken but actually signed with your word of honor, have you not?"

"War, my dear niece—especially civil war—is a nasty business. Someone with all the refinement and sensibilities that you possess as a Southern lady should never have been exposed to such unpleasantness. Please allow me to explicate further my position, which in all sincerity I believe is consistent with the dictates of honor. Certainly, whenever entering formal contracts, or even in less formal undertakings between *gentlemen*, one's word must be one's bond. But we are not dealing with *gentlemen* here. No Penelope, these Yankees are invaders who have dared to tread upon the sacred soil of the South. Seriously, do you think Attila the Hun had a sense of honor? No, my dear, as the saying goes, *all is fair in love and war*. And I would only add that in our present circumstances, love has little to do with it." Quite pleased with himself, Chalmers paused to survey the facial expressions of his audience.

In addition to Penelope and her husband, other recipients of Chalmers's wisdom regarding Southern honor included his wife Letitia, his eldest sibling Flora, and her husband Roderick Henry. Periodically, the adults' conversation was interrupted by the shrill cries of the Wormeley children as they ran in and out of the Underwood parlor. Flushed from the heat on that sultry day in May 1863, Penelope's over nourished Aunt Flora and her husband nevertheless beamed their approval at Chalmers's speech. With a grim smile colored by chronic pain from his wound acquired at Shiloh, Fitzhugh signaled his approval. Almost simultaneously the thought came to Chalmers and his smiling wife, *Finally, we're receiving the proper respect from the family that is our due.* And yet, when Chalmers examined his niece's face, he found neither approbation nor disapproval, only perhaps a fleeting sadness.

Changing the subject, Chalmers smiled as he predicted a bright future. "Let us not fret over the passing challenges of difficult times but rejoice in the brilliance of our generals! We can all take renewed hope from the recent events in Virginia. Wouldn't you all agree that Generals Lee and Jackson have attained their most brilliant victory to date—Chancellorsville will forever be remembered in the annals of warfare! Surely, it will now be only a matter of time before England and France will recognize the Confederate States of America, and we will be rid of this plague of locusts."

"Oh Uncle, a brilliant victory indeed, but at what cost! General Jackson seriously wounded and by our own soldiers—is it a judgment of Providence on the righteousness of our cause? How could such a tragedy happen to one of our most devout Christian generals? If he should not recover, how can Southern arms possibly prevail?"

"Now Penelope, you are altogether too negative in your assessment of the prospects for our country," Aunt Flora answered for her younger brother. "Why if you weren't the Southern patriot that I know you to be, I might suspect you of even harboring treasonous thoughts. Beware, my dear, of surrendering to such despondent thinking."

"But Aunt Flora, any prospect of Southern independence is entirely dependent upon the triumph of our military. The longer the war proceeds, through a process of attrition, we lose irreplaceable leaders and soldiers alike, while the Yankees have a seemingly endless supply of manpower. How can we ignore the painful facts? A major portion of the western Confederacy is occupied, our ports are under blockade, the economy is in shambles to the point of our coveting federal greenbacks, and it is unclear how long the 'Gibraltar of the West,' Vicksburg, can continue to connect us to the trans-Mississippi."

"Penelope, you demonstrate that same disagreeable proclivity for excessive thought and reflection that your late dear father, Jamison, had. Why, he would even express doubts about some of our most cherished Southern institutions. Mind you, nothing good can possibly come from too much thinking. What has been the accepted—indeed the received— wisdom passed down through generations of Southern families, the very bedrock of our civilization, should not require further thought. No, my dear, our tradition only requires respect and reverence. Furthermore, your uncle has taken a very sensible approach to surviving these dangerous times. Unfortunately, as the youngest son, he has been obliged to labor among the trades. And yet, with industry and sagacity, he has shown forth as the true gentleman that he is, and he is now rescuing the family from ruin."

"Chalmers and I are thankful to God, who in his Providence has made it possible for us to help our dear family in this great time of need,"

Aunt Letty responded, glowing with satisfaction as she clasped her husband's hand in triumph.

"Yes . . . yes, Aunt Letty and Uncle Chalmers, Fitz and I cannot begin to thank you enough for your kindness and hospitality to us and our children during this trial. We . . . I will do all I can to be helpful in your business while we are living here."

"Letitia and Chalmers, we are also very grateful for your assistance," Aunt Flora hastened to add. "I still intend to make an appeal tomorrow to the local Yankee commander about our servants. Penelope, you'll be coming with me."

Penelope fanned herself in the oppressive noonday heat as she waited for her aunt. With a look of intense frustration on her face, Aunt Flora appeared at the entrance to General Dodge's headquarters and collected her niece for the next stop on her mission. "Penelope, these Yankees are insufferable," she muttered under her breath as she mopped beads of perspiration from her brow. "Apparently, I must make my appeal to Chaplain Alexander, who has been appointed superintendent of the so-called *freedmen*. I've heard that some of these Yankee military chaplains are among the most fanatical zealots for abolition."

"Aunt Flora, I would not cherish great expectations regarding your servants. It is probably wise to avoid lecturing the superintendent regarding Southern rights. Perhaps, if you emphasize your deep concern for their welfare, which he *undoubtedly* shares . . ."

"Oh Penelope, how can he possibly understand the profound bonds of affection that have persisted over generations—and I believe persist to this very day—between our servants and us?"

As they approached the eastern edge of Corinth, Penelope and her aunt were surprised to see a neat village of small wooden houses arranged in a grid pattern. The Negro inhabitants and the presence of military tents at the periphery of the growing community were the only signs confirming its status as a contraband camp. Penelope noted several public buildings, including a small wooden church. Pointing to one of the larger structures on the main street, she said, "Aunt Flora, this appears to be the superintendent's office."

Superintendent of Freedmen at Corinth and sometime chaplain of the 66th Illinois Volunteer Infantry, James Alexander, looked up from his desk at his visitors as an aide introduced them. Smiling broadly, he advanced to greet them cordially. "Ladies, it is my distinct pleasure to welcome you to the Corinth contraband camp. Mrs. Henry, you may not remember me, but I shall never forget the very kind hospitality that you and your husband extended to my wife and me on two separate occasions several years ago." Aunt Flora, who had come prepared for war, was thoroughly flustered. "Why, Sir . . . I am not certain that I remember . . ."

"Please forgive me. I did not mean to embarrass you. I am a Presbyterian minister with Southern roots and family in Missouri. During the prior decade, my wife and I answered the call to ministry here in Mississippi and served for several years at a parish not too far distant from your plantation. It was your generous support of Christian charities that brought us into contact, although I suspect that we were lost amid the crowd of ministers and laypeople from various denominations that you hosted as part of the charitable campaigns."

"Why, Reverend Alexander, pardon my poor memory, but it is indeed a pleasure to meet you again . . ." Flora Henry hesitated, even more confused, as she stared at the blue uniform of the superintendent of freedmen.

"Mrs. Henry, I see that you are perplexed by the sight of a Southern clergyman in Federal uniform. Ah, where should I begin? To address your perplexity, please allow me to quote the great church father Augustine. In his *Confessions*, he made this remarkable observation about change: '*The extent to which something once was, but no longer is, is the measure of its death; and the extent to which something once was not, but now is, is the measure of its beginning.*' Ladies, we live amid extraordinary change. What my wife and I thought of the South's peculiar institution ten, nay even five years ago, has undergone a dramatic and inexorable change—indeed, we are not the same persons we once were. Just think of it: a Southern man at best indifferent to the issue of chattel slavery for much of his life is now responsible for a large community of newly emancipated persons. But the extent of the transformation has not ended there. Oh, no! This Southerner has recruited and trained a company of sixty Negroes to wear the Federal uniform and provide protection to their community. Why that may be the worst heresy from *Southern orthodoxy* one can imagine—*arming slaves!* From my own personal example, ladies, I think you can appreciate the power of change over time that can transform the lives of individuals. Now, how may I be of service to you?"

"Sir, I can only respond that not all of us are so susceptible of change as you and your wife," Aunt Flora sniffed with growing hostility. "I have come to seek your assistance in finding and returning my servants to me.

When the Federal soldiers came to *liberate*—more accurately *seize*—my servants, it was as if a part of myself had been torn from me. The very hospitality that you and your wife enjoyed in a happier time during your visit to our home depended, still depends, upon the assistance of our servants. Look at my hands, sir; they were not created for manual work. Each member of our society has always had a specific place in it, their unique role to play. How shall we possibly survive without their help and they without our loving guidance and direction?"

"Mrs. Henry, I see that you are in distress. Unfortunately, the inexorable change to which I have referred must, of necessity, be accompanied by varying degrees of pain. As a man under orders, I intend to obey those orders in loyalty to the government and constitution of the United States. My commitment of honor as an officer in the United States Army does not blind me to your suffering, however. My earlier greeting was extended with all sincerity, as was my gratitude for your kind hospitality of the past. Here are the constraints under which I must operate as superintendent. As you must surely be aware, by order of President Lincoln in his recent Emancipation Proclamation, slaves in those portions of the country which are in rebellion against the United States have been emancipated beginning the first of January this year. Notwithstanding any unpleasantness occasioned by the release of slaves from bondage in this region, the soldiers performing this action are fulfilling their duty. Any improper behavior exceeding their orders will be investigated and, if confirmed to have occurred, will be punished.

"Regarding your request to *return* the Negroes which you have referred to as *your servants*, this is what I can offer. As free persons, they are under no obligation to provide service to you or anyone else. In addition to providing adequate food, shelter, medical care, and helping them achieve literacy, it is the policy of our department that the freedmen should be gainfully employed. We believe it is in their best interest and will help them quickly acquire self-sufficiency, the first step toward citizenship. We are in the process of encouraging some of the contrabands here to seek *paid* employment in various trades, as well as in farming. Working with our agents, local citizens who have sworn the oath of loyalty to the government of the United States may be eligible to hire Negroes under contract from this camp, assuming they willingly choose such employment. So, ladies, it may be possible for you to recruit some of your former slaves to work as paid laborers. My staff would be happy to assist you with the details regarding the loyalty oath and the contracting process provided you are able to persuade your *former servants*.

"There is something else I would like to suggest. Several missionaries from the North have been laboring here on behalf of the freedmen—some as teachers and others as ministers to their physical and spiritual needs. I think you might find it edifying to visit our schools, hospital, and church to witness for yourselves the positive effects of change." By now Aunt Flora was seething as she thought, *Positive effects of change—utter nonsense—infernal Yankees have destroyed our civilization!*

"Ladies, please allow me to show you out," the superintendent said, sensing Mrs. Henry's growing furor. Helping the aggrieved Southern matron down the steps from his office, Superintendent Alexander recognized Rebecca Burgess passing by on the other side of the street. Brightening, he called her to come over: "Ladies, I would like to take this opportunity to introduce one of our missionaries to you. Miss Rebecca Burgess, this is Mrs. Flora Henry and Mrs. Penelope Wormeley. Miss Burgess, at a mutually convenient time, would you be willing to give these ladies a tour of our various facilities? They came to me with some concerns regarding the welfare of the freedmen. I think you might be able to allay some of their anxieties."

"Superintendent Alexander, I don't think that will be necessary. Mrs. Wormeley and I have other obligations that will prevent us from accepting your *kind* offer," Flora Henry hissed. *So, the Southern traitor wants to rub salt in our wounds by showing us how he has transformed our servants! Well, I've had enough lecturing on the virtues of change to last a lifetime!* "Penelope, I think we should take our leave, don't you?"

"Aunt Flora, please go on ahead. I'll join you presently after I schedule a time to meet with Miss Burgess, for I would very much like to see what the missionaries are doing here."

"Well . . . I never thought . . ." Flora Henry shrugged her shoulders in dismay, turned, and left. "Don't tarry too long, dear." A look of relief on his face, James Alexander nodded as Penelope thanked him for his time. Returning to his office, he left the two young women to face each other. There was a long, almost uncomfortable pause as they both thought about the serendipity of the encounter and what to say.

CHAPTER EIGHTEEN

"Slavery melts away like snow before the rays of rising civilization."
Francis Lieber, Author of the Union Army Code
of the Laws of War, April 1863

"Miss Burgess, would you by any chance have a brother named Isaac serving as a medical officer in the Union Army?" Penelope broke the silence first.

"Yes, Mrs. Wormeley, Dr. Isaac Burgess is my brother, and he is currently serving in Virginia. Thou must be the same Penelope of whom I heard so much after his southern journey more than a decade ago." Smiling, Rebecca added, "It is a great pleasure for me to finally meet thee; it almost seems providential. When Isaac was transferred to the Army of the Potomac, he expressed a wish that if I ever came south and the opportunity arose, I should seek thee out and inquire after thy health and that of thy husband."

"Perhaps it was another act of Providence that following the battle of Shiloh your brother was my husband's surgeon, for which I am very grateful. From our first meeting so many years ago, I was confident Isaac would make a fine physician."

"Oh, Mrs. Wormeley, in his correspondence after that terrible battle Isaac expressed his joy in meeting thee again after so many years. He was very glad that he could be of some service to thee and thy husband, transcending the differences rending our country. And here's an interesting notion to consider—in his hope of our meeting it is Isaac's opinion that his Southern friend has much in common with his Quaker sister."

"Miss Burgess, I have great respect for your brother's judgment not only as a medical man but also as a judge of persons. If he thinks that we have much in common, who am I to question his judgment? But, if we are to discover the common ground uniting us, you had better call me by my Christian name, Penelope. May I call you Rebecca?"

"Please do, Penelope. I believe that Isaac, in his past correspondence with thee, mentioned his colored friends who attended Oberlin College with us. I will be delighted that thou canst meet my best friend, Louisa Johnson, who is one of the other missionary teachers here. Perhaps thou wilt also meet Samuel, her brother and Isaac's best friend, who will be coming in the next few months to visit Corinth. Oh, forgive my prattle. There is something else that will likely engage thy interest more than all of this. Surely, thou hast not forgotten thy former slave Moses, the black-smith and preacher? Isaac told me of the deep impression Moses had made upon him when he saw him preach. He is Louisa's finest student and one of the spiritual leaders of this community. I am sure he will be pleased to see thee."

Will he be pleased to see me? Now that is a question, the truthful answer of which I am afraid to learn, Penelope thought. Smiling at Rebecca's naïve enthusiasm, she said, "When shall we begin this journey in search of common ground?"

"Penelope Endicott Wormeley, I don't know what to make of your behavior. What would your dearly departed parents think of their daughter consorting with Yankees! Those so-called *missionaries* only want to embarrass and ridicule us and our institutions. I must insist that you cancel your appointment with Miss Burgess tomorrow. Nothing good can come of it." Aunt Flora fumed at the dinner table that evening.

"What's this all about, Penny?" Fitz Wormeley interjected while Uncle Chalmers and Aunt Letty acquired the highly contagious frowns already suffusing the faces of both Henrys. Penelope looked up briefly from the absorbing task of feeding her two-and-a-half-year-old daughter, only to start as Emily gleefully took the opportunity to overturn her bowl, spilling gravy in her mother's lap. Four-year-old Fitzhugh Wormeley II, otherwise known as *Fitzy,* began to laugh loudly at Emily's antics, which was reciprocated by Emily, who then grabbed the upended bowl and crowned herself queen. Forgetting his question, the senior Fitzhugh joined in his children's laughter, which spread faster than the earlier frowns to everyone but Aunt Flora, who resolutely retained a most sincere frown awaiting Penelope's contrition.

"Fitzhugh, Aunt Flora left before I could confirm the most extraordinary coincidence. Miss Burgess is the sister of Dr. Burgess, the Union Army surgeon who cared for you so diligently after Shiloh. It's a shame that a physician of his skill is not readily available here to address the persistent pain in your right arm. His sister told me that Dr. Burgess is now serving with the Army of the Potomac in Virginia." Laughing, Chalmers interjected, "It's a good thing he's there in Virginia. Our boys will keep him busy tending to all those wounded Yankee soldiers."

Directing a look toward her still-frowning aunt, Penelope continued, "The only prospect we have of obtaining the assistance of our *former* servants requires signing the oath of loyalty, as Uncle Chalmers has done, and then negotiating contracts with the superintendent's agents to provide paid employment to the Negroes as agricultural laborers or in other capacities approved by the US military. Fitz and Uncle Roderick, if you decide like Uncle Chalmers to sign the loyalty oath and adhere to all the regulations, you will still need to *persuade* any potential laborers to work for you. It is this last, and perhaps most crucial aspect of such an endeavor that I believe could only benefit from any goodwill and trust that I might generate with the contrabands and missionaries. Who knows, perhaps Aunty Betsy is residing in this camp and might be persuaded to come and cook for us as a *paid* employee." Sighing as she surveyed the chaos created by her youngest child, she added, "She was always very good with children."

"You were always such a clever girl, Penelope, and have analyzed the situation very well. What you learned from the superintendent has confirmed my own discrete inquiries and clarified some of my unresolved questions. Flora, you should thank your niece for her willingness to enter the *lions' den* on behalf of the family," Chalmers stated with admiration. Blushing, Aunt Flora blustered, "Well . . . I do have to admit you had me worried about unseemly fraternizing with the Yankees, but I see the sense of what you have said. Do be careful, my dear."

"Penelope, where should we begin with thy tour? Perhaps it is best to first pay our respects to the newly appointed superintendent of the Corinth Contraband School, the Reverend George Carruthers, who arrived here just a few days ago."

"If he is your immediate superior at the school, it would indeed seem prudent to alert him to the presence of a Southern woman touring his facilities." Penelope then gave Rebecca a mischievous look and added,

"After all, in war spies abound, and even the most innocent-appearing Southern matron should not be above suspicion." Rebecca, flustered by her companion's remark, blushed and then—recovering her composure—replied, "I thank thee, Penelope, for thy sagacious advice, although certainly it is unnecessary to apply it to thyself. Isaac has consistently described thee as a person of the utmost integrity. No, I will introduce thee to Reverend Carruthers in the full confidence that thou wouldst be incapable of any deception." Then, almost under her breath, Rebecca added, "I only wish that I could follow thy example."

Blushing in turn at hearing Isaac Burgess's testimonial regarding her character and her curiosity piqued by Rebecca's strange comment, Penelope said, "Rebecca, such high praise from your brother honors me greatly, more than I could possibly merit. Certainly, you must know that my allegiance is to the South, and yet you trust me completely?"

"Oh, my friend—for I am certain we shall be friends—only by the accident of birth do we find ourselves on opposing sides in this great conflict. Surely, there is something greater here than sectional animosities that can transcend our differences. My brother spoke with great admiration regarding thy vision of preparing thy servants for freedom."

"But I ultimately failed in my task . . . and now it seems that the violence of war will determine their fate," Penelope said with bitterness.

"Thou must not speak of failure, at least not yet, for I am firmly convinced that Providence has brought thee here to Corinth to help in the great work of preparing the Negroes not only for freedom but also to become full citizens. As a member of the Society of Friends, I am greatly distressed by the violence, bloodshed, and suffering occasioned by this terrible civil war. And yet, is it not possible that the gracious Lord in His mercy will make some great good come out of all the evil? Surely, neither of us would have desired to see freedom come to the Negroes through such means, and yet here it is."

"Rebecca, you speak persuasively. Perhaps the gulf that separates us is narrowing. You said something earlier that roused my curiosity. How could you possibly wish to follow my example? Clearly, Isaac has painted his portrait of Penelope Endicott Wormeley a bit too generously."

"Members of the Society of Friends prize honesty as a great virtue, even when there may be fundamental disagreement with the honest person over various issues. Isaac has identified an integrity, a commitment to honesty, in thy life that I can only hope will someday characterize my own. Perhaps, as we come to know one another better, I may someday be able to relate some aspects of my history that I would blush for my dear brother to know. I am confident that thou could give me some helpful counsel . . . but I am too embarrassed to tell thee at present. Shall I now introduce thee to Reverend Carruthers?"

What a curious example of Yankee femininity, Penelope thought as they were waiting for the superintendent of the contraband school. *Surely, she is not representative of most Yankee women. What can possibly account for her delightfully trusting and optimistic nature—her Quaker beliefs, college education, or something else?* As she mused on the distinct differences between Northern and Southern women, George Carruthers emerged from his office. Of average height and bearing a sober mien, the young clergyman/school superintendent's face lit up when he saw Rebecca, while barely noticing her companion. To Penelope, it seemed as if he had been instantaneously transformed into an adoring moth drawn irresistibly to Rebecca's flame. Not being excessively vain but aware of her own charms—the petite Southern blonde possessed of a pale smooth complexion, delicate features, and intensely blue eyes—she was surprised that the *moth* hardly gave her a momentary glance. Greeting Rebecca warmly, George Carruthers asked how he could be of service as he finally directed some of his attention to her companion.

"Reverend Carruthers, please allow me to introduce Mrs. Penelope Wormeley. She is an old friend of my brother, Isaac, whom he met several years ago on a visit to the South. She is very interested in observing our methods of instructing the contrabands."

"Mrs. Wormeley, it is a pleasure to meet you and particularly gratifying to hear of your interest in our work." Laughing, he added, "Any friend of Isaac Burgess is a friend of mine. Isaac and I graduated from the collegiate program at Oberlin in the class of 1858. He went on to medical school in Michigan, while I stayed on at Oberlin for formal training in the ministry, although I am coming to understand that my life's work will likely be in the field of education. So, you see that between Rebecca Burgess, Louisa Johnson, and me, there is a small colony of Oberlin exiles here in Corinth, Mississippi!"

Pausing for a moment, he changed the subject. "On a sad note, we just received the news of General Thomas 'Stonewall' Jackson's death in Virginia. While I can't support the cause for which he fought, his death is a tragic loss that all Americans, both North and South, shall feel deeply. He embodied so many great virtues; he was truly a Christian soldier in the finest sense. As you probably both know, before the war he even personally taught a Sunday school for his slaves." Seeing Penelope's face blanch at the news and concerned that she might faint, George Carruthers said in alarm, "Mrs. Wormeley, surely, this sad news has upset you. Please have a seat. Would you like a glass of water?" *The Southern Confederacy is now most assuredly doomed*, was the inescapable thought suffocating Penelope as she contemplated the full implications of Stonewall Jackson's death.

"George, Mrs. Wormeley had devised a similar educational program of spiritual instruction for her slaves before the war, which had so impressed Isaac when he and my uncle were guests on her family's plantation." Tears in her eyes, Penelope interjected, "It was a small effort, hardly worthy of notice, and certainly not so grand or effective as what General Jackson did for his *people*."

"Mrs. Wormeley, God's grace fills any deficiencies in our labors when they are offered sincerely and with Christian charity. We would be honored to have you observe our educational program for the contrabands and would greatly value any suggestions you might have for its improvement. Perhaps, your schedule permitting, you might even wish to join us in this holy work. I think that Rebecca would agree with me that it is difficult to imagine a labor more blessed than bringing literacy and offering spiritual guidance to those thirsting for knowledge."

Mentally taking stock of the situation, Penelope sadly realized that she had fully expected Jackson's death. *I must not succumb to a cynical pessimism so foreign to my nature*, she thought. *And yet, even an optimist must face facts. Perhaps my optimism will only recover once I pursue a different path.* Recovering her composure, she thanked Superintendent Carruthers for his welcome and kind words of support as she and Rebecca left to visit the contraband school.

"Rebecca, I was struck by the way Reverend Carruthers addressed you, or more precisely *the way he looked at you*. He seemed entirely smitten by you."

"Oh, Penelope, was he staring so intently at me that thou took notice? Isaac is always chiding me for not being aware when men take notice of me. My dear mother, as a faithful Quaker, would hardly ever spend time before a looking glass. She would always say that *a woman's real beauty is to be found in her soul*. Although she tried to teach me the same practice, I must confess that at Oberlin, I would sometimes examine my appearance in a mirror—oh, how vain I am! Perhaps Reverend Carruthers still has some residual admiration for me; he wanted to court me back in college and would pay me all sorts of silly compliments. I just don't understand why he would make such a fuss over a *plain* Quaker girl! And now if what thou perceive is correct, it's most unseemly, for he's a married man. Indeed, he married one of my classmates, who is much prettier than I. Thankfully, she will join him here in Corinth later this month and hopefully consume his full attention in the future."

Her gloomy thoughts banished for the moment by Rebecca's sweet innocence and unaffected grace, Penelope marveled. *Is she truly unaware of her physical beauty, or has she chosen to be unaware of it?*

Entering the rear of the large school room with Rebecca, Penelope was immediately struck by the utter incongruity of the scene before her. Row upon row of benches were fully occupied by Negroes of all ages; jumbled together were those of advanced years sitting next to the very young. Never had she seen white children exhibit the discipline, even reverence, of the colored people as they patiently struggled with their *McGuffey Readers*. Completing her encounter with the incomprehensible, Penelope's attention was then drawn to an even more remarkable figure than that of the attentive colored students. Moving silently among the students and stopping periodically to give a whispered word of encouragement or admonishment was a young, fashionably dressed colored woman. Possessing a sable beauty and dignity, which were enhanced by her above-average height and slender figure, she commanded respect, even awe, among her students. The final piece of décor, which eliminated any remaining doubts about the different world that Penelope had just entered, was the presence of the *stars and stripes* at the front of the room next to the chalkboard.

"Louisa Johnson, may I introduce thee to Mrs. Penelope Wormeley, of whom I spoke?"

Eyeing the Southern matron with a mixture of suspicion, curiosity, and mild scorn, Louisa found it difficult to avoid engaging in mild sarcasm. "Mrs. Wormeley, it is indeed a pleasure to meet you. Isaac had great confidence in your good nature and compassion, although it seems I remember he did express frustration that you couldn't quite comprehend the possibility of an educated Negro. Well, to spare you the expense of visiting the North to see one, I have come south. I hope you won't be disappointed." Laughing, Louisa then offered her hand to Penelope, who hesitated to take it. Intervening, Rebecca explained, "Penelope, thou must not take offense. Louisa has always had a sharp tongue and wit.

Colored people are as likely to be the recipients of her sarcasm as those of a fair complexion."

"Mrs. Wormeley, Rebecca speaks the truth. I am a rather sarcastic creature, but I won't bite," Louisa laughed. "Seriously, I am as curious about you as I suspect you are about me. You left quite an impression on Isaac Burgess and that makes me *very* curious."

"Forgive me. This is all so strange and new to me," Penelope replied, finally shaking Louisa's hand.

CHAPTER NINETEEN

"We are done with hoeing cotton, we are done with hoeing corn;
We are colored Yankee soldiers, as sure as you are born.
When Massa hears us shouting, he will think 'tis Gabriel's horn,
As we go marching on . . ."

SOJOURNER TRUTH

WITH GROWING ENTHUSIASM DURING her tour of the contraband hospital the next day, Penelope was impressed by the clean, spacious, and well-ventilated wards. "All the missionaries have been encouraged to volunteer some of their free time to providing nursing care for the sick," Rebecca noted. "Louisa and I are regularly scheduled to help on Thursday afternoons. Would thou like to join us this next Thursday?" Without hesitation, Penelope replied, "I would like that very much, thank you. Some of my best memories are of nursing our servants in the small hospital at the Magnolias plantation when my parents were still alive."

Both Rebecca and Louisa were quickly impressed by Penelope's practical knowledge and her lack of squeamishness regarding even the most basic aspects of providing nursing care. It did not take long for the assistant surgeon on duty, Dr. Loomis, to take notice of Penelope's competence and energy. As she was helping Rebecca gently reposition an elderly woman with pneumonia, he requested Penelope's help with a difficult dressing change. Following him to another part of the ward, Penelope was surprised to discover that nearly all the male contrabands in that section were recovering from a variety of wounds, including amputations. "Doctor Loomis, having visited a military field hospital after the battle of Shiloh, I am perplexed by the large number of wounded Negroes, which is reminiscent of that experience."

"Ma'am, most of these poor fellows were either shot, bludgeoned, or stabbed with some sharp weapon as they made their escape to the Union lines. It seems that the Rebels have made it a general policy to treat all able-bodied male Negroes who try to escape as slave insurrectionists. When ordered to stop, if they don't readily surrender, they suffer a brutal fate. So, for all practical purposes, in addition to caring for medical illnesses among the contrabands, we do function as the equivalent of a small military field hospital."

"I see . . ." was Penelope's feeble response. *Oh, how this terrible war has unleashed the worst of passions!* she thought with growing horror and shame. Becoming aware of a foul odor, her attention was quickly diverted, and she involuntarily turned aside.

"Ma'am, I see that you have noticed the unpleasant odor that we dread to encounter in our wards. That odor is pathognomonic—sorry for the medical jargon, I meant to say *characteristic*—for hospital gangrene. The contagion can spread rapidly among the patients with almost uniformly fatal results." Whispering to her and pointing discretely to a young contraband in a bed nearby, he added, "This poor Negro required amputation for a gunshot wound below his left knee several days ago, and now, sadly, this complication has developed."

"Is there anything that can be done for his condition?"

"I believe there is, and with your help, he may have a real chance of recovery. It was impossible for me not to observe how bravely you attend to the more noisome tasks that confront our nurses. But as you are a visitor and new volunteer here, please forgive my *pressing* you into service. You may, of course, decline to participate in what will likely be a gruesome wound debridement."

"No Doctor, I am pleased to be of service and am curious to learn more about the treatment you intend to use."

"I have only recently been transferred to Corinth from the Marine Hospital in Louisville, Kentucky, where I worked under the leadership of a truly brilliant physician, Dr. Middleton Goldsmith. He has made hospital gangrene a subject of detailed scientific inquiry. In his research he has found that bromine, a substance used in many hospital wards as a cleaning agent and deodorant, is quite effective as a treatment for hospital gangrene. I have been fortunate to directly observe his work and learn the treatment technique which he has developed. It is critically important to first debride or cut away any devitalized tissues, which in combination with liberal injection of the bromine into the adjacent surrounding tissues, constitute the primary aspects of the therapy. Quite fortuitously, the bromine also promotes hemostasis—oh, sorry—blood clotting, which is another advantage of this remarkable agent. Although Dr. Goldsmith concedes that the precise means by which the contagion spreads in hospital gangrene remains a mystery, I can't help but wonder if the increased emphasis on cleanliness that often accompanies use of bromine may be a factor in determining its efficacy. It will also be prudent for us to isolate the patient during his period of recovery.

"The debridement and bromine administration can be quite painful. Have you ever administered chloroform, ma'am? Well, it is not difficult at all. I will guide you through the steps," the bromine enthusiast declared after seeing Penelope shake her head in the negative.

After completion of the procedure, Penelope asked, "Doctor, when will you know if the treatment has had the desired effect?"

"In the first days after the procedure, I closely observe the patient's general condition, including his state of consciousness, appetite, and overall behavior. Dr. Goldsmith has also emphasized the characteristic odor as an objective sign to watch for assiduously. If it does not return, which has been usually the case in his experience, all will be well. However, its return is a confirmation of the need for further debridement and administration of bromine in the wound."

"May I return tomorrow and observe the effect of your treatment on the patient?"

"Of course, please come anytime. I am very grateful for your assistance, ma'am. Indeed, your ministry of mercy here will greatly benefit the contrabands. Also, if you do come tomorrow, you shall have the opportunity to hear Adjutant General Thomas address the contrabands. It should be quite interesting as he will be giving a recruitment speech. His mission is to create several colored regiments for the Union Army." Joining them at this point in their conversation, Rebecca interjected, "Doctor, Mrs. Wormeley is a Southern woman. The idea of arming slaves is a frightening prospect for most Southerners."

"Oh, ma'am, please forgive me. I did not mean to cause you alarm. General Thomas intends to make disciplined soldiers of the Negroes. You should have no fear of a *servile insurrection*. In fact, from what I have learned, most of the colored regiments will be used for garrison duty at the forts occupied by the Union Army here in the South."

"Doctor, I wish I could share your confidence regarding this latest innovation designed to subjugate the Southern states. Thank you for

informing me. I will attend the general's speech with the desperate interest of one who awaits further knowledge regarding a fatal prognosis."

"Aunt Letty, I can't thank you enough for providing such loving
care to Fitzy and Emily. I was blessed to be of practical assistance to Dr.
Loomis, the assistant surgeon at the contraband hospital this afternoon
in his application of a fascinating new treatment for a dreaded condition known as hospital gangrene. It was developed by a famous physician
from Kentucky."

"It doesn't surprise me in the least that one of our own Southern
medical men would be leading the way," Uncle Chalmers triumphantly
interjected. *I guess I had better not enlighten Uncle Chalmers about Dr.
Goldsmith's color of uniform*, Penelope thought.

Before Uncle Chalmers could continue extolling Southern scientific
achievements, Aunt Letty replied, "My dear, I don't think you realize how
much pleasure, rather I should say *joy*, I receive every day when you allow me to help in the upbringing of your lovely children. When Chalmers and I lost our three children from that retched cholera epidemic so
many years ago, all of them in the bloom of youth, we not only experienced an irreplaceable loss with their deaths, but we were also deprived
of grandchildren."

"Oh, Aunt Letty . . . and Uncle Chalmers, you must consider Emily
and Fitzy to be the grandchildren that were denied you by that tragic loss."

"Penelope, I remember well the wonderful deeds of charity you performed, even as a young girl, on behalf of your servants, particularly the
special regard you had for the sick and infirm servants in the Magnolias
plantation hospital. It seems to me that I see a bit of that old joy from an
earlier, happier time returning to your countenance today. I think you
should continue your charitable work at the Contraband hospital, for it
seems to act upon you like a tonic, while your absence gives me full possession of your darling ones—my tonic!" Fitzhugh nodded his agreement
with Penelope's statement and then added, "Penny, I must admit I never
could see the attraction sick and elderly Negroes held for you. But it's
probably a good thing that you are there to keep an eye on the Yankees."

"Dr. Loomis, your patient looks so much better today . . ." "You
should say 'our patient,'" the assistant surgeon interjected with a smile.
Penelope continued enthusiastically, "He has a ravenous appetite this

morning, is asking to sit up in bed, and is quite voluble—he was so taci-turn yesterday. Oh, and the bad odor is gone."

"Yes, if the present pattern continues over the next several days, we can then be fully confident of success. For the present, we must remain vigilant." As she carried out her assigned duties that morning in the ward for wounded Negroes, Penelope had to admit to herself that she no longer felt suffocated by the death of Stonewall Jackson, or even by the very real possibility that the South could lose the war. Regardless of the outcome of the war, she had found a purpose for her life that did not depend on politics or sectional loyalties. *Just as Rebecca Burgess said, this terrible war will clearly be the instrument in the hands of God to emancipate the slaves. It has also freed me from my old notions of how that emancipation should occur. What I do know is that I must find a way to continue my hospital work among the contrabands,* she thought.

With military precision at the time Dr. Loomis had indicated, a large crowd of mostly Negroes, some Federal soldiers, as well as curious townsfolk had gathered that afternoon to hear Adjutant General Lorenzo Thomas speak. Seeing Rebecca and Louisa, Penelope joined them as the Union officer began to make his appeal.

"Friends, I am here on behalf of President Lincoln to give you his personal greetings. He is the leader of our great country who with the blessing of Almighty God has declared you *forever free*! But that declara-tion of *your* freedom is only words on paper until it is confirmed and brought to full fruition through the success of our arms on the battlefield. This terrible civil war began as a struggle over a state's right to secede from the Union. With the president's declaration, which took effect the first day of January in this year of our Lord, eighteen hundred sixty-three, the war took on a distinctly different purpose, and your fate weighs in the balance. Do you want to see those beautiful words on paper become a reality written indelibly in your lives? If you do, I am here on behalf of the president to request your help in winning that freedom . . . Who among you is willing to join the cause of freedom?"

As General Thomas paused for dramatic effect, someone very fa-miliar to Penelope appeared on the platform next to the Union Adjutant General. It had been over a year since she saw him last, but his tall, thin figure, now with a full head of snow-white hair, commanded her atten-tion and respect even more than in prior years. The general nodded to Moses, who then, in a stentorian voice, added his own remarks to the recruitment speech. "Brothers and sisters, one of our Northern brethren,

Mr. Frederick Douglass, has said that once the Federal uniform is placed
on the Negro—with the eagle on its buttons and "US" on the belt buck-
le—there is no force on the face of the earth that can deny his claim to
manhood and right to citizenship in this great republic. Well, if I ever
have the blessing of meeting Mr. Douglass, I might with all due respect
beg to differ with him *slightly* in his assessment of the Negro. Look at
one another carefully; what do you see? Do we need a uniform to prove
that we are men created in the image of God? I say certainly not. Ah, but
if I ask the question in a different way, perhaps I'm not so far from Mr.
Douglass. For what kind of man would allow others to do all the fighting,
suffering, and dying to achieve his freedom without offering a fair share
of his own blood, sweat, and tears into the mix? Why, he would be no
man at all, only a faint shadow of a man. Ladies, I know some of you are
thinking, 'How will we survive without our men during these difficult
times?' General Thomas's call for service today is as much a call to you
who are also created in the same image of God as your menfolk. This call
today is a call to sacrifice—a sacrifice for future generations in which we
all must share. So now, my friends, what do you say to General Thomas's
request? Who among you are ready to join the cause of freedom?" Loud
cheers followed Moses's appeal.

Motioning for silence, to Penelope's surprise, the Negro preacher
lifted a Bible in his hand and spoke again. "Brothers and sisters, what
must we do this very moment before signing up, before any sad farewells
and last hugs? What is essential and must not be delayed? Ah, I heard one
of the children say it—*out of the mouths of babes and infants thou hast
perfected praise!* Glory hallelujah! Just remember, it's their future you're
fighting for. Well, if I must spell it out for you, the one needful thing,
brothers and sisters, is to pray—pray with all the strength you can muster
for even more strength from the Almighty, because you're going to need
it. Now everyone of you fellows who can read, you must take your Bible
with you—now that's an order from *General* Moses! And the next order
I'll give you is to read that Bible and *pray* in the reading of it, every day.
Now with General Thomas's permission, I will read Psalm 91, a mighty
fine psalm for soldiers to read, maybe even memorize.

> He that dwelleth in the secret place of the most High shall abide
> under the shadow of the Almighty. I will say of the Lord, He is
> my refuge and my fortress: my God; in him will I trust. Surely
> he shall deliver thee from the snare of the fowler, and from the
> noisome pestilence. He shall cover thee with his feathers, and

under his wings shalt thou trust: his truth shall be thy shield and buckler. Thou shalt not be afraid for the terror by night; nor for the arrow that flieth by day; Nor for the pestilence that walketh in darkness; nor for the destruction that wasteth at noonday. A thousand shall fall at thy side, and ten thousand at thy right hand; but it shall not come nigh thee . . .

"Oh Lord, come close to your servants, keep and preserve them from all danger as they offer themselves to the cause of freedom. Fulfill the promise you gave through the psalmist and sustain them in the difficult times ahead . . ." And thus, Moses prayed for his flock, who were about to *directly* enter the conflict from which they had been previously seeking to escape.

After Moses finished his prayer and large numbers of volunteers were signing up for military service, Rebecca turned to Louisa and said, "I can see thy influence on Moses's thinking. You have spoken to him regarding man as *anthropos*, haven't thou?"

"You don't think I would let all your Greek studies go to waste, do you? Of course, I shared with him that *man* in the Bible quite often refers to the human being, or *anthropos*, and not merely the male of the species." Penelope gave the two Oberlin missionaries a questioning look. "Penelope, my friend here not only finished the formal training as a teacher, which I completed; she also obtained the bachelor's degree. Translated, that means she studied Latin and Greek like our brothers, but the one thing she was denied in that enlightened curriculum was the course in rhetoric. The reason for this omission should be perfectly clear to any sensible person."

"Please assume I am not a sensible person. Do tell me why educated Yankee women are not taught rhetoric," Penelope said with curiosity.

"*Yankee women*, as you describe us gals from the North, may obtain a higher education at *some* institutions, but it is still considered quite unseemly for women to give public speeches in mixed or *promiscuous* gatherings and never should they preach from the pulpit, *unless they happen to be Quakers*. We may help a minister husband prepare, perhaps even write, his sermon for him but never deliver it ourselves." Now it was Penelope's turn to laugh at Louisa's sarcastic characterization regarding the condition of educated women in the North. "At least you are allowed to hold and discretely express an opinion. Here in the South, a proper woman does not form an opinion of her own; rather she *inherits* it fully formed from her esteemed ancestors, or it is *bestowed* at the marriage altar." Louisa looked intently at Penelope, and her look was reciprocated, held for a few moments until they both burst out laughing. "Miss Louisa Johnson, you are not the only woman blessed, or shall I say cursed, with sarcastic tendencies," Penelope concluded triumphantly.

Abruptly changing the subject, Penelope remarked, "I am struck by the salutary effect you have exerted on Moses's thought and eloquence— to see him now reading beautifully from a real Bible!" "Penelope, you give me too much credit. Moses was already quite literate, primarily through his own efforts, before we met. I might claim credit for a few subtle refinements, that's all," Louisa demurred.

Penelope smiled at the fundamental paradox embodied by Rebecca Burgess. *Such scholarly brilliance with profound insight, and yet she cannot perceive the meaning behind the stares of male admirers! Perhaps her head has been filled too much with man as anthropos and not enough with man as the male of the species.*

After they retired that night, Penelope watched her husband anxiously reach yet again for the bottle of laudanum on his nightstand. "Fitzhugh, I wish there was something more that could be done to relieve your pain and restore function to that arm. It saddens me to see you so dependent on the laudanum." Since his wounding at Shiloh, he had never fully recovered the use of his right hand and arm due to severe pain. The practical solution for him had been to keep the arm immobilized in a sling, making every effort to avoid jostling it throughout the day. After his prisoner exchange, the Confederate surgeon examining him declared Fitz unfit for duty, advising him to resign his commission. Following his medical retirement from military service, Captain Wormeley had grown progressively morose and withdrawn. With the loss of his enslaved workforce, his plantations no longer generating an income, and—his role in the army gone—he struggled to see any hope of regaining the influence he had enjoyed in Southern society prior to the war. Indeed, Fitz had been at a loss to recognize what remained, if anything, of the old familiar South since the Yankee invasion. But after coming to live with Penelope's uncle and aunt, he could begin to see a way forward. Uncle Chalmers's flexible sense of honor made perfect sense to Fitz, who had no illusions about the Confederacy's long-term prospects. *If we're lucky and our army drives the bastards out of here for good, we can repudiate any commitments we made under duress to feed and clothe our families. On the other hand, if the Yankees prevail, we'll be on the winning side and will be the first to benefit in the new order,* he reasoned. *Signing a loyalty oath and feigning friendship with the devil might be a small price to pay, if I can acquire cheap labor to grow and harvest cotton on my plantations.*

"Penny, I've been giving careful thought to what Uncle Chalmers has said about the loyalty oath. In fact, while you were working at the hospital today, I went with him to speak to the Federal authorities. As great numbers of Negroes arrive here daily, the Yankees are increasingly anxious to find employment for them to pay their own expenses. It is possible that we might be able to quickly hire enough Negroes to plant viable crops on our plantations this season. Uncle Chalmers has promised to invest some of his money in the venture, which will help us get started. Since your name is also on the title to the Magnolias, the Federal officer informed me that even though I signed the loyalty oath, he wants you to also sign it before we will be able to hire Negroes for the Magnolias. Just like Uncle Chalmers said, you shouldn't feel bound by a contract with the enemy."

"Fitzhugh, please understand what you are requesting of me. The Southern sense of honor is for me more than a quaint relic of our culture. Since your wound at Shiloh, I have given considerable thought to it. When I spoke earlier of one's word being one's bond, I meant it. In signing the loyalty oath, I may remain a woman of the South, but you must know that I will *on my honor* pledge my full allegiance to the federal government."

"Suit yourself; I need that signature tomorrow."

CHAPTER TWENTY

"General Jackson is dead! Was a nation's woe ever condensed in so few words—or a people's calamity so far beyond language to express!?"

CAPTAIN EDWARD O. GUERRANT, MAY 15, 1863

REACHING INTO HIS POCKET, Isaac Burgess pulled out the rumpled letter from his sister to read one more time as his horse followed the long line of troops nearing the Commonwealth of Pennsylvania. Wiping sweat from his brow, he perused the letter's contents in search of a temporary distraction from the all-too-familiar horrors toward which he was riding that first day of July 1863.

> 9 June 1863
> Corinth, Mississippi
>
> Dear Isaac,
>   Hearing the news from Virginia, we worry for thy safety and pray that the Army of the Potomac has overcome any despondency caused by the defeat at Chancellorsville. Despite the brilliant nature of the Confederate victory, a persistent gloom has settled over the Southern population here—some even despair for the future of their cause with the loss of Stonewall Jackson. But rumors also abound of a bold stroke that General Lee will implement soon, and that seems to buoy the spirits of some among the more ardent Rebels.
>   In an earlier letter I had mentioned my fortuitous encounter with Penelope Wormeley and related some details of our growing friendship. What she has described as a dormant interest in all things medical has not only revived but has continued to blossom, especially with the confidence the assistant surgeon

here at the contraband hospital has shown in her judgment and skills as a volunteer nurse. He has introduced an innovative and very effective regimen using bromine to treat hospital gangrene and included her as his assistant in the work. Art thou familiar with this groundbreaking work of Dr. Middleton Goldsmith in Louisville, Kentucky? If not, thou may want to familiarize thyself with it soon before the next large battle.

Isaac paused in his reading. *He's the fellow that sent out the circular in March requesting help in his study of hospital gangrene and erysipelas. Dr. Daniel Morgan was doing some interesting work along those same lines in Frederick last autumn. He had to isolate the patients, if I remember correctly, and was quite suspicious that contagion was the cause. Undoubtedly, there will be many more cases to study and report soon.*

Then, resuming his reading:

Louisa and I couldn't understand Penelope's reticence to help teach the contrabands to read and write, especially after seeing how impressed she was by her former slave Moses's excellent diction and reading of the Scriptures during the recruitment speeches for the new colored regiments last month. Louisa finally pressed her about the question. After some hesitation, she explained her qualms, stating that it is illegal to teach slaves to read and write in Tennessee. Louisa bluntly refuted this indicating that Tennessee is one of the *few* Southern states that has not expressly outlawed teaching slaves. To Penelope's further dismay, she observed that after leaving the Magnolias plantation, Moses had acquired his basic skills with the help of a literate contraband from the Nashville area, who had gone to school with his master's permission before the war.

Almost a week later, Penelope approached us and acknowledged the truth of what Louisa had said. When she had confronted her husband to clarify the situation, he apparently shrugged his shoulders and told her he didn't see any value in teaching the slaves to be literate since he had no intention of ever emancipating them. She guessed that to keep peace, her father had also avoided enlightening her about the truth since her mother had never been enthusiastic about emancipation either. Adding to her anger and resentment she confided that she had been pressured by her husband to sign the loyalty oath because of his desire to acquire a contraband workforce for their idled plantations. She assured us that in signing the oath, she *will keep it* as a matter of honor, even though she still has considerable misgivings about Yankees and the Union. With the strain in her family relations, her work at the hospital has increasingly become a refuge from the various conflicts surrounding her. Recently, she expressed a new hopefulness in that her life has now been rededicated to service. In helping the contrabands, I think she has discovered an opportunity to help compensate for her earlier failures as a slaveowner. Most remarkable of all, she has begun to tentatively reestablish a relationship with Moses—consciously struggling against the old master-slave relationship. Indeed, she has approached him cautiously, asking to study the Scriptures with him but only if he is willing to be *her mentor*.

Louisa and I are disappointed that Sam has not yet joined us, although he seems pleased with his work as a recruiter of colored soldiers among the contrabands. He is planning to spend some time in Helena, Arkansas, recruiting soldiers before heading on to Memphis and Corinth. Perhaps thou wilt hear from him before we do. After Adjutant General Thomas's rousing appeal, everyone seems to have caught the war fever here. Chaplain Alexander, who has been such an excellent administrator, has left his role to take command of a colored regiment. The first recruits in his 1st Alabama consist of the sixty colored soldiers he had initially put into uniform as guards of the Corinth contraband camp. Interestingly, his replacement as the new superintendent of contrabands at Corinth is a Captain John Phillips from the 57th Illinois Regiment and a member of the Society of Friends. The military leadership here refers to him approvingly as a *fighting Quaker*. I don't know what to think. So many of our unique testimonies as Friends seem to be bowing down before the altar of war!

One very bright spot amid all these changes has been our uncle Levi Coffin's visit here late last month. It was such a blessing to see him and hear his words of cheer, as well as to receive news from home. I sometimes wonder if my sensibilities have been exposed to chloroform—it was good for me to see our uncle's powerful emotions upon the arrival of a large company of contrabands in rags, hungry, and some barely alive. Perhaps, when we are repeatedly exposed to daily horrors, a type of numbness settles upon our souls. I shudder at the thought, and I thank God for the grace to see, if only briefly, through the eyes of our dear uncle whose heart of compassion only seems to grow larger. As thou knowest, he wastes no time. Taking stock of all the needs he witnessed, he left for the North with a clear plan to acquire additional resources to help the contrabands.

As ever thy affectionate sister,
Rebecca

Rumors of an engagement already underway in a small Pennsylvania college town had been flying through the ranks of the II Corps during the march north that afternoon. Confirmation came with the sad news that General John Reynolds, commander of the I Corps, had been killed. General Meade, the newly appointed commander of the Army of the Potomac, had ordered their own II Corps commander, General Winfield Scott Hancock, to ride on ahead to quickly take command of the situation. *Has General Lee yet again seized the initiative?* Isaac wondered. *It seems we won't be bivouacking in Maryland as we had been told this morning. The men will be thoroughly exhausted by all this heavy marching in such heat.* As he fretted about the potential of an impending disaster, Isaac found comfort in the realization that *at least we are the defending army this time.*

As his horse plodded along in the intense heat and humidity, Isaac's thoughts wandered back over the past several weeks. Although the Irish Brigade had been assigned a supporting role during the battle of Chancellorsville, they nevertheless sustained significant casualties from the Rebel artillery barrage. He shuddered at the memory of the many gruesome injuries that he and Francis Reynolds encountered. Their ministrations were often limited to the completing of near-amputations, dressing of gaping mortal wounds, administration of morphine to relieve the pain of the dying, and the occasional congratulations they could offer to soldiers whose more moderate wounds paid their fare home. However, there was one type of injury he hoped to never again encounter—severely burned soldiers. Some soldiers had even been burned alive after being trapped within a growing inferno as the trees and thickets of the Wilderness surrounding Chancellorsville caught fire during the fighting.

Riding among the veteran Irish soldiers, he sadly acknowledged the painful fact that the famous Irish Brigade, which he had joined at the height of its glory, was now a brigade in name only. Indeed, he estimated that the entire brigade could not have an effective strength of more than about five hundred men—half of a regiment at its full strength! General Meagher had, without success, appealed for a furlough on behalf of his beleaguered men, partly to give them a much-needed rest but also to assist him in recruiting more Irish from New York City to replenish the diminished ranks of the brigade. He had observed the simmering anger as the soldiers began to increasingly murmur against the government, complaining not without some justification, when other regiments were granted furloughs that they were denied. Being overwhelmingly Irish

Catholics and Democrats, they felt as if they were the objects of religious and political discrimination by a Protestant-dominated Republican administration. Frequently, the conversation—whether in the officer's mess or around campfires—would return to a theme distressing many an Irish heart. Was the enormous sacrifice of the flower of Irish youth and their great valor on behalf of their adopted country appreciated—was it worth the terrible loss? Particularly distressing for Isaac, the objections to Lincoln's Emancipation Proclamation that many of the Irish had expressed when it was first announced became increasingly more strident. He would frequently hear officers as well as enlisted men state in often crude terms that they had volunteered "to fight to restore the Union as it was and not to free n____rs!" He could only wonder where such talk would lead. Would emancipation by addition of another cheap competing labor force produce racial conflict in Northern cities? Although many felt regret and some anger when General Meagher resigned his commission in frustration after Chancellorsville, Isaac noted that the remnants of the brigade were quite happy with his replacement, Colonel Patrick Kelly, one of the 88th New York's finest officers.

Isaac's musings were interrupted as Dr. Francis Reynolds joined him and announced, "Isaac, we just received orders to ride on ahead of the troops to help set up the First Division, II Corps hospital in Gettysburg. Our full corps probably won't arrive before the middle of the night, but we must be prepared to deal with casualties as soon as the II Corps arrives, for there is already a fierce fight in progress." In the waning light, Isaac and Francis caught up with their other medical colleagues, who had already selected a farm south of Gettysburg, close behind the front lines, as the site for the field hospital. Quickly taking inventory of the contents from supply wagons that had already arrived, Isaac noted that bandages, medications, and surgical instruments had been delivered, but the food, hospital tents, and other supplies so necessary to the recovery of the wounded were missing.

In search of information regarding the missing supplies, Francis and Isaac rode south on the Taneytown Road and turned into the Spangler farm–XI Corps field hospital, which was now being rapidly transformed into a writhing, moaning mass of human suffering. Navigating the carpet of recumbent wounded, the two surgeons waited until an XI Corps surgeon paused briefly between the myriad amputations he would perform that night. Wearily, he waved his hand in a broad arc to embrace all the wounded occupying nearly every inch of ground surrounding the two-story barn and farmhouse. "Gentlemen, General Meade has made a fateful decision. The instruments of death and destruction—the common currency of war—will always take priority over those kinder elements conducive to survival and recovery, which are their very antithesis . . . I shouldn't complain—at least we have our basic operative equipment and medicines. Unfortunately, the hospital tents, food, and other postoperative supplies were parked in Maryland since they were impeding the movement of soldiers and artillery. I cannot deny the necessity or cruel logic of the decision and, yet the suffering of the wounded, which is already horrific, will only grow worse as they lie hungry and exposed in barnyard filth. It may be several days before those essential supplies arrive, and that assumes a positive outcome for the Army of the Potomac in this current contest. If you will now excuse me, another patient awaits."

Soldiers of the II Corps, exhausted from the intensive marching of the past two days, were sprawled on the ground asleep, many completely oblivious to the preparations for battle going on all around them. After supervising the placement of latrines at the First Division–II Corps hospital that morning of July 2nd, Isaac had taken a break to ride over and see how the barely rested II Corps troops had been placed on the ridge extending south from the town's cemetery. While he was initially pleased by the short distance for transport to the field hospital, he couldn't help but worry that it might be *too* convenient a location. His apprehensions were confirmed later, about three o'clock in the afternoon, when an artillery barrage that signaled the beginning of a Confederate assault on the Union left flank overshot Cemetery Ridge, making the hospital's location unsafe.

Hurriedly, the medical staff abandoned the farm for a nearby schoolhouse that was located on the same property as the XI Corps hospital, to its south. The site was blessed with a stream of fresh, clean water, and a nearby ridge seemed likely to afford protection from any stray shells in the future, although Isaac worried that the new site was even closer to the front line. As he directed the placement of the latrines for the second time that day, a courier from General Hancock's headquarters arrived at the relocated field hospital with orders to make ready the ambulances and prepare to set up aid stations for the First Division troops on Cemetery Ridge. General Hancock had chosen Caldwell's Division, which included the Irish Brigade, to address a growing problem created by a gap in the Union line when General Sickles had ordered the

III Corps forward earlier in the day. According to the courier, the vulnerable, exposed Corps was now the prime objective of an aggressive attack by the Rebel forces to turn the Union's left flank.

Fr. Corby groaned when he heard the courier's report with the others. "More terrible loss of life is about to occur. I must do something beyond the ordinary for our boys—for *all* those who are about to die!" When Isaac heard the chaplain's comment expressed with such intense feeling, he gave Francis Reynolds a questioning look, to which the Irish physician responded with his own shrug of uncertainty. Both officers accompanied the brigade as it moved toward the staging area, their usual logistical concerns now mixed with growing curiosity regarding the chaplain's plan of action.

Just before the Irish Brigade was about to form tight attack columns, Isaac was startled to see Fr. Corby climb up on a large rock in front of the brigade, motioning for silence. The chaplain then began to explain what he was about to do, acknowledging that recent circumstances had prevented the men from attending services, let alone making confession. He then encouraged all those present to make a sincere act of contrition, firmly resolving to confess their sins when the next opportunity should arise. "Be confident of God's mercy and forgiveness as you enter the fray and do your duty as soldiers of this great republic." Fr. Corby paused after his brief address, and Isaac was surprised and deeply moved to see all the men, Catholic and non-Catholic, fall to their knees, their heads bowed. Seeing that even General Hancock, who at times could be quite profane, had removed his hat and bowed his head, Isaac followed suit.

"Dominus noster Jesus Christus vos absolvat, et ego, auctoritate ipsius, vos absolvo ab omni vinculo, excommunicationis interdicti . . . *Our Lord Jesus Christ absolves you, and I, by his authority, absolve you from every bond of interdict of excommunication,* . . . in quantum possum et vos indigetis deinde ego absolvo vos, a peccatis vestris, in nomine Patris, et Filii, et Spiritus Sancti . . . *to the extent that I am able and that you are in need of it, and next I absolve you from your sins in the name of the Father, and of the Son, and of the Holy Spirit,* Amen."

As the chaplain completed reciting the Latin words of absolution, he made the sign of the cross over the soldiers, extending the verbal expression to those beyond hearing through the physical sign.

It was nearly six o'clock in the evening before the Irish Brigade went forward, fully prepared for close quarters combat. While Francis Reynolds returned to the schoolhouse field hospital to make ready the operating tables, Isaac—with several stretcher-bearers—followed behind the advancing soldiers of the First Division and set up an aid station located on the edge of a wheat field. Quickly crossing the field, the soldiers approached a wooded, stony hill on the other side. Soon, Isaac could hear the crackle of musketry and distant yells of the Irish as they charged the Rebel soldiers on the stony hill. At first, it seemed they were making quick work of the enemy, driving them off the hill, but it wasn't long before the surviving Irish were making a fighting withdrawal as their successful assault had exposed them to danger on both flanks. Then, the casualties—which had initially been a trickle—rapidly became a flood, overwhelming the aid station. Isaac realized that he had no choice other than to quickly relocate his aid station to Cemetery Ridge with the retreating remnant of his brigade and other elements of the First Division. As General Hancock sent in more reinforcements, the Federal resistance on Cemetery Ridge stiffened, causing the Rebel advance to sputter out by dark. By the accounts he heard from surviving soldiers, most of their casualties occurred during their retreat across the stony hill and wheat field. With growing frustration, Isaac realized that he and the ambulance teams could not get to many of the wounded and dying because of Rebel control of the wheat field and the growing darkness. Despite this, the field hospital was still swamped with the wounded, and Isaac spent a sleepless night operating with Francis and the other medical staff.

During a lull in the operating as dawn approached on the third of July, and seeing Fr. Corby praying in lantern light with one of the many wounded lying on the ground, Isaac approached respectfully, waiting for the chaplain to finish. "Chaplain, that was a remarkable thing you did before the men went forward into the wheat field yesterday. Even General Hancock joined in that sublime moment of prayer! I am certain it gave many a soldier the peace of mind to go forward resolutely in the face of death. While I was able to understand the Latin used in the prayer, I must confess to not understanding the full meaning of the prayer within your tradition. I was particularly puzzled by the words, *quantum possum et vos indigetis—to the extent that I am able and that you are in need of it.*"

"Dr. Burgess . . . Isaac, in performing this ceremony, my eye covered thousands of officers and men. I noticed that *all*, Catholic and non-Catholic, officers and private soldiers, showed a profound respect, wishing at this fatal crisis to receive every benefit of divine grace that could be imparted through the church ministry. That general absolution was intended for all—in *quantum possum*—not only for our brigade but for all, North or South, who were susceptible of it and who were about to appear before their Judge."

"Chaplain, thank you for such a generous act of Christian charity. I hope that many were *susceptible of it,* as you say, including myself." *For one brief moment, the barriers separating Christians from one another were lifted through the prayer of this humble military chaplain,* Isaac reflected with awe as Fr. Corby smiled in response and moved on to the next recumbent wounded soldier.

Isaac's momentary reflection was suddenly cut short as a cannonade directly to the north of the field hospital began. Sipping a cup of coffee, Francis Reynolds approached and, noting the artillery barrage, said, "Let's hope that we don't have to move the hospital again." An explosion a hundred yards to the right of the schoolhouse field hospital was confirmation that his stated aspiration might not be fulfilled. The Rebel batteries overshot the Federal positions a few more times before the success of the Union attack silenced them.

For Isaac and his medical colleagues, it seemed there would be no rest for the weary. A much-needed nap was abruptly cut short at about one o'clock, when a massive ear-splitting, earth-shaking artillery duel commenced. The entire Confederate line on Seminary Ridge became a sheet of fire as they sought to destroy the Federal defenses and artillery batteries along Cemetery Ridge. This time, the incessant overshooting of the Federal lines by the Confederate batteries could not be ignored by the First Division–II Corps field hospital staff. Indeed, all three II Corps field hospitals were too close to the front lines. Exhausted but now very much awake, Isaac and his colleagues were frantically attempting to evacuate many recumbent wounded soldiers who were exposed and vulnerable to the barrage of shells exploding in their midst. Nervous horses reared in harness, some attempting to bolt in panic down the farm lane near the hospital. Ducking for cover as a shell came screaming down, Isaac could only watch in horror as the horses drawing an ambulance that he had just finished loading with wounded men suddenly bolted out of control, dragging the ambulance wheels over two wounded men awaiting transport. Their stifled cries were the last evidence of two who had briefly been among the hopeful living. After finally stopping the runaway ambulance, one of the young ambulance drivers came running back with tears in his eyes, crying, "We couldn't control the horses!" Isaac, who had just completed a quick examination of both trampled victims, pushed the ambulance driver down as another screaming shell burst in the yard off to their left. "They both died instantly from the crush injury. There is nothing you could have done to prevent it. Go back to your ambulance, and quickly evacuate your patients to safety."

While most of the traffic on the farm lane was directed eastward, as the hospital evacuation continued during the horrific bombardment, Isaac was ordered back to the front line on Cemetery Ridge to set up an aid station, if needed. Ironically, intending to give the exhausted soldiers of the First Division of the II Corps some rest after their heroic exertions of the preceding day, they had been placed in what was considered a *safe* position near the center of Cemetery Ridge, not too far south of a copse of trees. With the whole line along Cemetery Ridge targeted by the Confederate artillery barrage, it became clear that their place of *rest* at the center of the Union line had become the focal point of attack chosen by General Lee. Apparently, the Confederate general was confident that he could finally break the Union line on Cemetery Ridge after inflicting severe damage to both flanks of the Army of the Potomac on the two prior days.

If the Confederate goal had been to destroy the Federal artillery and defenses along Cemetery Ridge, they would soon discover their failure in achieving it. Isaac noted the Federal artillery ceased firing first, which he thought might be a clever ruse. *But is it possible to fool General Lee?* And then something remarkable happened. Out from the trees on Seminary Ridge emerged regiment upon regiment of Rebel soldiers, as if on parade. At first, cheers of admiration erupted from the Federal ranks as they witnessed the maneuvers so expertly executed by the Rebel soldiers forming ranks in perfect order heading resolutely toward the Federal center on Cemetery Ridge. As the Rebel divisions came forward and were now fully exposed, any remaining notions that they had silenced the Federal artillery were now dispelled. Federal batteries opened up and blasted holes in the advancing Rebel regiments, which were closed quickly as they continued to advance toward the Federal line. Some of the Irish soldiers around him began to yell what many were thinking: "Fredericksburg!" Couldn't the great, *invincible* General Lee see that he was sending his finest toward well protected soldiers on high ground? On they came, and even the Quaker doctor could only look with astonishment at the foolhardy bravery of men being willingly sent to their death—the parallels with Fredericksburg, that slaughter pen of the Irish, were too obvious. Before he knew it, he was shouting with the rest, "Fredericksburg, Fredericksburg!" as wave after wave of Southern manhood broke upon Cemetery Ridge.

CHAPTER TWENTY-ONE

"In the midst of life, we are in death . . ."
THE BOOK OF COMMON PRAYER

A VISION OF UTTER loveliness offered to embrace him with its warm caresses. Wildflowers, in their profusion, beckoned: purple coneflowers, red clover, bee balm, milkweed, foxglove, St. John's wort, and many others. Blinking did not make it go away, so he surrendered to it while at the same time struggling to remember where and who he was. Vivid shades of purple, yellow, orange, blue, and white flooded his consciousness, their beauty intermingling yet somehow remaining distinct. And now when it seemed that the vision could not accommodate anything more, butterflies, hummingbirds, and the ubiquitous bees made their presence known. It was as if the horn section in an orchestra had now joined the stringed instruments in picking up a musical theme. And then he came to himself. He could distinctly remember the figure of Fr. Corby making the sign of the cross as he pronounced absolution over him and his fellow soldiers. In a few short minutes they had crossed a wheat field to drive the Rebels from a stony hill. Flanked on both sides, they were forced into a fighting retreat across that same wheat field. At almost point-blank range, he had discharged his musket load of buck and ball into a Reb, who collapsed at his side. And then he remembered the searing pain of a gunshot wound to his abdomen which brought him to his knees . . . *Perhaps there was more, but I just can't remember. No matter*, he thought as he again surrendered to the vision now offering its full embrace. Somewhere in the depths of his being, a growing conviction arose that he must be in Paradise. *What else could it be? I got a mortal wound, and now I must be starin' at heaven itself! But shouldn't one of the saints be here to greet me?* He felt a growing perplexity.

As he pondered the tardiness of the heavenly host, he became acutely aware of an extremely foul odor wafting from somewhere behind him, brought by a slight breeze. He knew that odor . . . where had he encountered it before? The nauseating stench was now unmistakable as he got an even stronger whiff. *That's the smell of death, of rottin' corpses! Am I in purgatory, or is it possible that heaven can be in smelling distance from hell?* he asked himself with growing panic. Realizing that he ought to seek empirical confirmation, he tried to turn over from his left to his right side. Suddenly, sharp pains arising in his abdomen and head forced him to pause. Steeling himself against the pain, he cautiously completed the movement only to shriek in horror as he found himself staring face-to-face at the bloated corpse of the Rebel soldier he had killed. The pacific vision of bees, butterflies, and hummingbirds had now been displaced by myriads of flies, which were avidly swarming in the gaping wound that he had made in the belly of his enemy.

With the Army of Northern Virginia licking its wounds and showing signs of a withdrawal on the country's birthday, Isaac and others had been assigned to search for any survivors from the fight in the wheat field and to direct the burial of the dead. The many corpses of men and horses rapidly decaying in the intense July heat were a source of growing concern to the Army of the Potomac's medical staff. The artillery barrage and Confederate charge on the 3rd of July had prevented a thorough search for survivors from the fighting on the second and delayed the necessary burials. Isaac and his stretcher-bearers were startled to hear a loud shriek coming from among the dead. Running toward the sound, he stopped to witness the incongruity of the scene—the sublime beauty, innocence, and vibrant life of the summer wildflowers contrasted with the profusion of gore, stench, and corruption of death on the battlefield.

Isaac's musings were rudely cut short a moment later, when a Rebel sharpshooter's bullet struck his right temple, the force and pain of impact knocking him down to the ground. Momentarily stunned but realizing that the expected mortal injury had not occurred, he gingerly probed the tender wound, which was profusely bleeding. A stretcher-bearer, shocked by what had just happened and hearing Isaac laugh, exclaimed to his comrades, "Dr. Burgess has been shot in the head and will surely die soon, as he's lost his mind!"

"No, I have neither lost my mind, nor will I die from this wound, although we'd better stay down for the moment, since our friends on the other side of the wheat field seem intent on killing us. It's just that I couldn't help but laugh for joy—to survive such a close encounter with death! The gunshot hit my right temple at a tangent, penetrating deeply into my scalp, but thankfully glanced off my *thick* skull." After wrapping a tight pressure dressing around his head with the stretcher-bearer's help, Isaac then examined his patient as best he could from a crouching position, interposing his body between the rotting Rebel corpse and the Irish Brigade soldier. He quickly noted an entrance wound just below the level of the umbilicus on the right side of the soldier's abdomen, with an exit wound located on the wounded man's left flank. From matted, dried blood on the top of his head and tenderness to touch, he deduced the presence of a blunt injury to the skull and scalp. *Probably the poor fellow had been clubbed over the head for good measure at the time he was shot.* Addressing the wounded man, he asked, "Do you remember what happened to you?"

"I remember shootin' that poor devil behind ye. Almost immediately after that I felt terrible pain from bein' shot meself and then . . . I don't remember anythin' else, except wakin' up here an' thinkin' that I must be in heaven 'til I smelled 'im! Now, I'm so thirsty, I don't understand . . . will I die, Doctor?" Before he could answer, another shot coming from the same direction as the first thudded into the body of the dead Confederate behind Isaac, making him duck down lower.

In a clump of trees about seven hundred yards away, near the Emmetsburg Road, a somewhat different but related conversation was in progress. "What are you trying to do, you fool? Look through that damned telescope on your rifle. Can't you see that fella's green sash? Thankfully, you didn't kill the Yankee doctor the first time you shot him. Why'd you try to shoot him again?"

"They's all fair game as far as I'm concerned—damn Yankees! We're sharpshooters, ain't we? It's our job to kill and terrify the enemy."

"But that doctor's out there looking for wounded soldiers. He might find one of our men and save 'im, if you'd let 'im alone! Besides looking for the wounded who might still have a chance, it seems the only other thing they're up to is buryin' the dead. Shouldn't we leave 'em in peace to do their grim work?"

"You call me a fool. But I havta ask who's the fool here? We've just been through three days of hell—desperate fightin' with nothin' to show for it, except that we must retreat leavin' a lot of *our* dead and wounded behind. We're at war with these devils, but you talk about 'em like they're *people*, somebody I might have as a neighbor. They're never gonna be *my* neighbor. I say kill 'em—kill 'em all!"

"Look here, I'd follow Marse Robert to hell and back, but we always do better in defense of our own soil. Now here we are in a pretty pickle, up in Yankee country, and it's their soil they're defendin'. Maybe this is the way God evens up the odds. I say let's get back to the Old Dominion—*our country*—then God will bless us with more victories."

"Well, I ain't so sure 'bout which side God's on in this war . . . I wonder sometimes if He cares one wit 'bout any of it. But I agree that we need to get back to Ol' Virginny, where we can properly whip these Yankees . . . I'm hungry an' tired. Let's go see if we can find somethin' to eat before we leave this hellhole."

Isaac and his assistants stayed close to the ground for several minutes, waiting for further sniper fire, but when none came even after one of the stretcher-bearers held up his hat on the end of a bayonet to draw their fire, Isaac decided it was time to evacuate their patient. His experienced stretcher-bearers snatched the wounded Irish soldier moving at the double quick to a rhythm accompanied by his groans of pain and only slowing down once they arrived at the ambulance. Finally feeling safe from the threat posed by Rebel sharpshooters, they gently placed their patient in the ambulance. Before he was transported to the First Division–II Corps field hospital that now occupied its *third* location since the beginning of the battle, Isaac finally answered the soldier's question. Looking frightful himself with the blood-soaked bandage encircling his head, he smiled down at the soldier as he said, "Before the Rebel sharpshooter interrupted our conversation, you asked me about your prognosis. I think that you and I are both very fortunate." Showing with his hand the path the bullet took in tangentially striking his head, he said, "I believe that the path followed by your bullet was like mine. In other words, the bullet that struck you entered the abdominal wall on your right side, passed along the planes between the muscles, and exited on the left side without entering the abdominal cavity—something of a miracle! You have some amnesia, loss of memory, probably due to that painful wound on your head, which you likely received from the fellow that shot you. It also explains why you lost a day from being knocked unconscious. Fortunately, I found your skull to be intact. By the way, happy Independence Day!" Then, weakly attempting a grin, Isaac—who was beginning to feel dizzy and lightheaded—added, "You're not the only hardheaded soldier in the Irish Brigade."

Taking one look at his colleague, Francis Reynolds exclaimed, "Isaac Burgess, were you trying to get yourself killed? If your head had been turned just a wee bit more, we'd be asking Fr. Corby to put in a good word with the Almighty for our Quaker heretic friend!" Seeing that his friend was about to faint from blood loss, he desisted from further friendly remonstrances and called for some assistance as he helped Isaac to lay down for a thorough examination of the scalp wound under chloroform anesthesia. Irrigating the wound with water revealed persistent bleeding vessels, which he quickly controlled with ligatures.

To Isaac's surprise and chagrin, he was awakened later by loud crashes of thunder and heavy rainfall outside. He found himself safely ensconced as a patient on his friend's cot inside a farmhouse that now served as the headquarters for their field hospital. As he tried to get up, a young soldier-nurse came up and asked, "Do you need anything, sir?"

"Nothing, private. I should get back to my patients."

"Sir, I'm under orders to keep you at strict bed rest. Dr. Reynolds told me that he would have me court-martialed, if I allowed you to get up."

Beginning about noon, all further attempts to recover any remaining wounded and to bury the dead had been complicated by the violent thunderstorm and torrential downpour that continued throughout the rest of the day. While about half of the hospital supplies, tents, and food had finally arrived from Maryland, many of the wounded were still without shelter during the storm, and their suffering was intensified as they lay in the mud or on damp straw being pelted by the incessant rain. Quick decisions were made, determining who would be so fortunate as to be placed under cover of the tents that had arrived; those who had been operated upon for more serious injuries generally took precedence.

Convalescence did not agree with Isaac Burgess, who chafed at the restrictions imposed upon him as a patient. After two days of bed rest, he was begging Francis Reynolds for his blessing to resume his clinical duties. "Isaac, I think you should spend at least one more day thanking the Almighty for sparing your life, and then I'll consider any proposal you may care to make about returning to lighter duties. I do have some news that ought to bring you some cheer, though. We learned late yesterday that the Rebel Army defending Vicksburg has surrendered—the Mississippi is now fully under Union control, and the Confederacy is split in two!"

"Francis, that is wonderful news—surely, the South will now recognize the folly of pursuing any further bloodshed! Is it too much to hope that we might finally see an end to the madness of this war?"

"Honestly, my friend, it is difficult for me to see how an enemy angry enough to fire upon doctors tending the wounded would be willing to stop fighting any time soon. Usually I'm the optimist, but I fear they will not stop fighting until they have been completely conquered. And then, I doubt that Southern fellows like the one who tried to kill you will ever willingly resume allegiance to the Stars and Stripes."

CHAPTER TWENTY-TWO

"Nothing except a battle lost can be half so melancholy as a battle won."
ARTHUR WELLESLEY, FIRST DUKE OF WELLINGTON

WHILE MANY IN THE North complained about Meade's slow pursuit of Lee's retreating army, his detractors didn't fully appreciate that the old political slogan *to the victor go the spoils* was at best a double-edged sword with respect to war. For in victory, it was true the Army of the Potomac was left in possession of the battlefield, yet its primary *spoils* were the dead of both armies, as well as thousands of sick and wounded Southern soldiers left behind. Thus, Lee's wounded adversary, encumbered by the *spoils* of victory, could only make a half-hearted effort at pursuit.

Reflecting on the nature of war during his brief convalescence, Isaac realized that battles had at least two phases—the first and *glorious* phase being the actual combat, which featured so prominently in newspaper accounts and then another second phase, not so glorious, in which wounds and disease completed the work of combat. After all, war had one ultimate purpose—killing; if artillery, muskets, or hand-to-hand fighting didn't achieve the purpose in the first phase, surely the second phase provided a great likelihood of success. The physicians, nurses, and other medical personnel could only offer their resistance to the inexorable process, and yet amazingly, they sometimes prevailed.

Shortly after returning to duty but still wearing a bandage wrapped tightly around his head, Isaac rode to the XI Corps field hospital in search of some needed supplies. Many of the wounded had been transferred to large well-ventilated tents set up as hospital wards and were for the first time in several days washed and lying on cots in a clean environment. This transformation was in no small part due to the advent of volunteer civilian nurses from the community as well as from the Sanitary and Christian Commissions.

When he was about to leave, one of the XI Corps surgeons took Isaac aside and asked him, "Have you seen much tetanus during your service?"

"I was aware of an outbreak that developed after the Battle of Antietam, but I was not directly involved in the care of the unfortunate patients. One outstanding feature that I remember being discussed was the fact that almost all the wounded soldiers who developed tetanus had been housed in a large barn that had been used as a hospital."

"Well, isn't that interesting. We have several cases here, and every one of the poor fellows was initially placed on the floor of the large barn here. Since the cots and hospital tents had not arrived yet from Maryland, it seemed only appropriate to place the seriously wounded on the floor of the barn rather than exposing them to the elements outside. Now, I wonder about the wisdom of that decision. If you haven't seen tetanus in its various stages, you should come take a look so that you'll recognize it quickly in the future."

"Have you devised a treatment for it?" Isaac asked with growing curiosity as he entered a large hospital tent with the other surgeon. Stopping at the entrance to the tent, Isaac's host spoke in low tones. "Nothing we do seems to make a difference. Once the soldiers begin to show symptoms, they inexorably progress toward a painful, terrifying death. Since the tents and cots have arrived, we have removed all the wounded men from the barn. Indeed, it is our hope that by no longer placing patients there, we will see an end of the outbreak. Perhaps there is some type of miasma present in barns that causes this horrible disease among the wounded."

"I wonder if an approach like Dr. Middleton Goldsmith's use of bromine to treat hospital gangrene might be helpful?" Isaac speculated in a whisper. "Are you thinking something in the soldiers' wounds might produce the disease?" his companion asked with some incredulity.

"I don't know—it's just a thought. I see you have the patients in this tent separated by makeshift curtains."

"Yes. While it is important for you as a physician to see and understand the progression of this dreaded condition, for the sanity of the other wounded soldiers and particularly those who will die of tetanus here, it can only be an act of compassion to keep them isolated and ignorant."

Isaac's guide to the tetanus ward and its horrors proceeded to show him patients at various stages in the progression of the disease. The first soldier they encountered manifested the characteristic *lockjaw* or severe trismus (spasm) of the chewing muscles that was an early sign of the disease, making consumption of food virtually impossible. Another showed extension of the muscle spasms beyond the facial muscles to his extremities, while yet others—in the late stages, prior to death—exhibited extremely painful arching of their backs, coupled with increasing difficulty breathing. The relentless character of the disease process was profoundly disheartening to the medical staff. Having no effective means of treating the disease, they could only bear witness to the great distress of their dying comrades as they eventually succumbed to the agonizing generalized muscle spasms.

"I remember reading about it as a medical student, but now I see that no written description can possibly do justice to the actual suffering," Isaac whispered to his host, horrified by what he had just witnessed. "Would morphine administered by injection relieve at least some of their distress?" he asked.

"It's almost impossible to administer medication to them by mouth; unfortunately, I don't have ready access to a syringe here. We have attempted to anesthetize some of them with chloroform, but when they are in the late stages it's extremely difficult to administer the anesthetic due to the intense spasms. Several of us struggle to hold one afflicted individual down long enough to induce insensibility to pain, and then it only lasts a short time."

"I'm pretty certain that we have at least one syringe at our field hospital," Isaac replied. "If I can locate the syringe, I will send it to you as soon as possible. Thank you for educating me about this dreadful disease."

Isaac marveled at how quickly a sense of order was returning to their medical work as he rounded with Francis Reynolds in the recently established tent wards of the First Division–II Corps field hospital. As with the XI Corps field hospital, it wasn't just the arrival of all the remaining hospital supplies from Maryland that had completed the transformation. Civilian volunteers, some of them wives and mothers who had come looking for wounded loved ones, were cooking, washing clothes and bandages, and preparing lint for dressings. Other women with prior nursing experience also came and were providing a compassionate feminine touch that cheered many a soul in ways soldier-nurses could not. Order, cleanliness, and compassion had finally begun to supplant the medical chaos that reigned during the battle, at least in the field hospitals and their immediate vicinity.

The foul stench from decaying flesh that was already prominent by the 4th of July remained a suffocating presence, threatening the health of the community. Dead soldiers were buried as quickly as possible, mostly in mass graves. Personal effects, when available, were buried with some individuals to facilitate their later identification and reburial. Large numbers of rotting animal carcasses, primarily horses, were burned—the omnipresent stench tormenting the nostrils of the poor citizens of Gettysburg as they tried to reclaim their town.

Resuming his regular duties five days after being wounded, Isaac visited the wounded Irish Brigade soldier he had helped rescue from the wheat field. Sitting up on the edge of his hospital cot, enthusiastically consuming a piece of freshly baked bread, the young soldier was almost unrecognizable to Isaac. "After you finish that piece of bread, I'd like to examine your wounds. It's still hard to believe you survived a gunshot to the abdomen." *It must have traveled in the fascial planes and never entered the peritoneal cavity, like I thought initially,* Isaac concluded as he pondered the apparent miracle. "You seem to enjoy eating. Are you in any pain?"

"Sir, I've been eatin' anythin' they give me, and with pleasure! Me head hurts a bit still. The pain, really, it's just a *soreness* in me belly, ain't so bad. It hurt more before some pus came out yesterday from the hole in front. Now, it feels just fine." Isaac was deeply impressed to see on examination that all the soldier's wounds were healing well. Smiling at his patient, he remarked, "It seems the Rebels haven't been able to kill you."

"I expect they'll likely have more opportunities to try though, with me gettin' better an' all. Will ye be sendin' me back to me regiment soon, sir?"

"I'm afraid there won't be any reason to keep you here much longer."

After stopping to give some orders, Francis Reynolds had rejoined Isaac on rounds. Giving his Quaker colleague a wink, he laughed and said, "Isaac, I had a case very similar to this last fellow. It was before you joined the regiment. One of our officers being shot in the abdomen was brought to me and I did the only sensible thing and gave him the prognosis one normally associates with a lethal injury. And can you imagine the sheer cheek and effrontery of the fellow—he got better! Presumably, I had been mistaken as to the true trajectory of the bullet. Well, you know me, I don't mince words, even with officers. So, when I met him later after his *recovery* from the *fatal* wound, I politely asked him how he felt. The rascal replied, 'I never felt better in my life,' to which I responded, 'Well, you ought to have died to save the honor of my profession.' Unable to wait for Isaac to fully appreciate his droll humor, Francis burst out laughing.

While Isaac was pondering how to respond to his friend's story, a cavalry lieutenant entered the hospital tent and in a loud voice asked, "Is there a Quaker doctor here?"

"Yes. I am a member of the Religious Society of Friends," Isaac answered as he turned toward the lieutenant.

"Sir, I've been given the duty of collecting Rebel prisoners. Some have been wounded and cared for in private homes, and others have been in hiding since the battle. But today has been the first time I ever captured *Rebel Quakers*, four from the same regiment, the 52nd North Carolina from Pettigrew's Brigade. By their report, they were forcibly conscripted into the Confederate Army and were marched north under guard with the invading Rebels because they refused on religious grounds to bear arms. During the chaos of the battle, they were allowed to stay back from the firing line by sympathetic members of their regiment, which made their later escape possible. As we were marching them under guard on the road, Colonel Kelly of the Irish Brigade happened to be riding by, and hearing their odd form of speech, he recognized them as being Quakers. He then told me that he had a Quaker doctor in his brigade and that I should bring the prisoners to you at the field hospital with his compliments for you to interrogate."

Somewhat flabbergasted, Isaac asked, "How much time may I have with the prisoners?"

"Normally, after capture we have been sending prisoners on to Harrisburg, whence they are sent to their assigned prisoner of war camp. They will need to be on their way in the next day or two at the latest. Meanwhile, they can remain with you overnight under guard. They claim to be family—two sets of brothers who are cousins: Thomas and Jacob Hinshaw, Cyrus and Nathan Barker. When we found them, they had been taking refuge for several days in the root cellar of a local Quaker family. The poor fellows are wearing civilian clothes, which are in tatters. When I offered them some Federal issue trousers, they adamantly refused, saying they have a "Testimony Against War" which enjoins them to avoid any form of military involvement. Apparently, that even includes wearing soldier's trousers. It's a good thing we are in the middle of the summer; otherwise, with their scruples they might freeze to death."

Isaac cast an inquisitive glance at Francis, who responded with a wry smile, "I think you'd better get started right away with your *interrogation*. I'll finish up here."

Emerging from the hospital tent, Isaac squinted in the bright sunlight and followed the lieutenant as he approached a cluster of men in their late twenties and early thirties who were dressed in rags. Standing nearby were two Federal privates serving as their guards. The lieutenant was the first to address the prisoners. Pointing to Isaac, he said, "This is Dr. Isaac Burgess, Assistant Surgeon in the Irish Brigade." He then proceeded to introduce each of the prisoners by name to Isaac. "Dr. Burgess will be speaking with you this afternoon. He is a Quaker like yourselves."

The hitherto taciturn Southern Friends now erupted with a strong verbal protest: "He cannot be a member of the Society of Friends, for he is not honoring the Society's Testimony Against War." With a stifled groan, Isaac said, "Thank you, lieutenant, for your kind introduction. You may leave now. I hope to have a friendly chat with the prisoners and then offer them some refreshment, after which they can return to your custody."

"Their two guards will remain on duty for your protection."

"As you wish. I am confident that they will not attempt to escape, and I am quite certain they will harm no one."

As soon as the lieutenant left, the Southern Friends gave Isaac a look of pity as Thomas Hinshaw expressed their thoughts. "We have heard of Friends wearing the uniform of the federal government, some even taking up arms in this terrible war, and now we finally meet such a person! How can thee call thyself a Friend? Perhaps a *former* Friend but not a genuine member of the Society. Look at thee, not only wearing a military uniform—thee also hast a bandage around thy head. Thee must have been wounded in combat. Thee bringest shame upon the Society! Thee hast even abandoned plain speech . . ."

Isaac listened quietly while the Southern Quakers continued their diatribe, listing the many unpardonable sins he had committed. Finally, when there was a slight pause, he asked, "Might thou allow me a word in my defense? Couldst thou possibly be interested in hearing another perspective regarding our Society's Testimony Against War as it relates to this terrible conflict?" The flushed faces of the Southern Quakers appeared to soften, and they remained silent, which Isaac interpreted as permission for him to speak. "First, please allow me to respond to some of thy concerns about me, and then I will speak to the more general issue at hand. I wear the uniform of the US military as a medical officer.

My role is that of a noncombatant physician who cares for all who are sick and suffering from either side, including civilians and refugees from slavery. Did not our Lord say, 'I was sick, and thou visited me?' This word from our Lord has been my primary motivation to serve in the army—where armies go, there great suffering is to be found. The battlefield is a dangerous place, and even noncombatant physicians may become the target of sharpshooters. I received the wound that has been bandaged while treating the wounded on the battlefield. While our plain speech is very meaningful to members of the Society, it greatly complicates communication with those outside our Society. I found it impossible to continue its use serving in the Army."

"Just as thee hast abandoned the Testimony Against War, thee hast found it convenient to abandon plain speech as thee consorts with the world. Abandon one pillar of the faith, and the whole house crashes down. Hast thee been disowned yet?"

"I am not aware of my being disowned, but it is possible. I would deeply regret that happening, but it would not change my commitment to service in this conflict. Canst thou not understand that this war is about ending slavery? Friends have for several generations borne a strong testimony against slavery."

"Of course, slavery is a great evil. We pray daily for its end, for its *peaceful* end. How canst thee justify all the killing, using one very great evil to destroy another evil? It sounds like a devil's bargain to us. No, we'll put our trust in God who will bring peace and justice in *His* time."

"Is it possible that God might expect His creatures to *help* achieve these blessed ends?"

"Not if the *helping* involves violence. Thee may not be aware, but many Southern Friends have suffered greatly for the Testimony Against War. Some have been tortured, others killed, and yet others have been treated as prisoners of war, incarcerated in the harsh military prisons of the Confederacy. We did not support secession, we abhor slavery, but we will not raise a hand against our fellow man. For us, wearing the uniform of either side is unthinkable. So when drafted, we refuse to fight or serve in any capacity—gladly, we accept the penalty of man's law so that we might honor and keep God's law."

CHAPTER TWENTY-THREE

"We are coming, coming, our Union to restore,
We are coming, Father Abraham, three hundred thousand more!"
JAMES S. GIBBONS, 1862

August 14, 1863
Corinth, Mississippi

Dear Isaac,

Please accept my most sincere apologies for being such a tardy correspondent. Also, allow me to convey their warmest greetings to you from Louisa, Rebecca, and a *Southern friend* of yours, Mrs. Penelope Wormeley, along with my own best regards from Corinth, Mississippi. I finally arrived here about a week ago, and anticipating your next question, I do plan to stay put for a while, assuming the war allows. Your letters have caught up with me here, and I must confess how envious I am of you for being a witness to such an historic event as the three-day battle at Gettysburg. It will doubtless acquire a legendary aura as the years pass, and the question will not infrequently be asked with hushed tones, 'Were you at Gettysburg?' And you, my friend, will be able—as hoary old age approaches—to answer in the affirmative, 'Yes and I shall never forget . . .'"

ISAAC COULD NOT HELP but smile as he read these last words. *If it were only the memories of the battle, with all its horrible splendor punctuated by extraordinary bravery, that would be one thing,* he thought. *But how can I ever forget the gore and overwhelming stench of corrupting flesh that persisted, seemingly without end? And the hordes of curiosity-seekers who came after the battle—some merely driven by a macabre fascination with slaughter and others to plunder the dead.*

> In your correspondence you referred obliquely to a "scratch" you received while attending to the wounded on the battlefield. You forget that I have maintained a separate friendly correspondence with your colleague Dr. Reynolds after our time together in Frederick. When I saw "scratch," I thought of something more substantial. Indeed, in a letter written after the battle, he described how you were nearly dispatched by a Rebel sharpshooter and that your scalp wound bled ferociously until he tied off some vessels.

Pausing in his reading, Isaac felt irritated with his medical colleague. *Francis Reynolds, how will sharing these lurid details be helpful?* Resuming his reading, he was reassured by Samuel Johnson's next sentence.

> I thank God you were spared, and rest assured, I will not divulge the seriousness of your "scratch" to anyone without your express permission, although I am sorely tempted—what a great story!
>
> Sadly, it seems that the prejudice and animus toward the Negro, which many in the Irish Brigade expressed so bluntly during my time with you in Frederick, is more universally held among that people. The viciousness of the attacks by the Irish mobs against the colored population in New York City coming on the heels of Gettysburg will forever be a stain on our country's history. I still find it perplexing that an oppressed people such as the Irish would not declare common cause with the Negro. Thank you for sharing with me the many expressions of horror at the wanton violence in New York that many of your colleagues in the Irish Brigade so unequivocally stated. Perhaps it is not unreasonable to hope that among the leadership in the Irish community, wiser heads will eventually prevail. In his correspondence with me, Dr. Reynolds expressed deep regret and chagrin over the behavior of his countrymen. He made one very cogent observation that I wanted to share with you in case he hasn't mentioned it in your conversations. He stated that the Achilles' heel of the democratic form of government lies in the classical Greek etymology of the word "democracy": *dēmos* (people), *kratia* (rule). Since *dēmos* was also used at times by the ancient Greeks to connote a mob, he expressed the fear that during unsettled times, representative democracy will always be in danger of degenerating into mob rule—the tragic New York

draft riots being *prima facie* evidence of this fundamental vulnerability in our form of government.

Enough of political philosophy—I would like to give you a report of my adventures as a recruiter for *Father Abraham's* colored regiments. But before I speak of events in the West, I must pause and proclaim my deep admiration for my brothers of the 54th Massachusetts Volunteer Infantry. If our Northern brethren who possess a paler complexion will read without prejudice the accounts of the fifty-fourth's extraordinary valor during the assault on Fort Wagner, surely they must desist from their ridiculous claims of Negro inferiority. With my own eyes I have witnessed similar valor exhibited by *men* who were considered mere chattel only a few months before.

As you might have predicted, it took longer than anticipated to settle my father's affairs. Thank God for those steady souls who till the soil and preserve hearth and home! My sister Hattie and her husband, Jack, bless their souls, have together become a rock of stability supporting my dear mother in her grief while also preserving my father's agrarian legacy. Louisa and I are strange creatures, the two restless younger members of the Johnson tribe who can appreciate the peace and stability of our childhood home and yet chafe like prisoners if we remain there very long.

I recognized a great opportunity when I received word from my mentor, John Mercer Langston, that the adjutant general, Lorenzo Thomas, had been dispatched on a mission to recruit Negro regiments for the US Army in the Mississippi Valley. As Federal forces penetrate deeper into the South, large numbers of contrabands have sought protection within Union lines. And now there is an active effort by the army to seek out, liberate, and enroll formerly enslaved men of military age into Uncle Sam's service. Possessing the same complexion as those being recruited, it only seemed reasonable that I might be more credible as a recruiter than white soldiers. Furthermore, other positive aspects of this opportunity became evident on additional reflection. My career as a newspaper correspondent might be rejuvenated, my Oberlin training as a teacher might be utilized to good effect among the newly liberated, and finally, I flattered myself that a grateful government might more favorably review my request for an officer's commission.

Ironically, I seem destined to follow in the adjutant general's wake. It was the beginning of May before I could arrive in Helena, Arkansas, and General Thomas had already departed. By all reports, he gave a rousing recruitment speech a few weeks

earlier, resulting in the immediate enrollment of three companies of colored recruits to form the nucleus of the 1st Arkansas
Volunteer Infantry of African Descent. General Prentiss and his
officers welcomed me kindly, and I was even offered a small sti-
pend as a civilian contract employee. My principal duties were
to assist in the recruitment and training of the 2nd Arkansas
Volunteer Infantry, which would be assigned a role in the defense of Helena, the 1st Arkansas Volunteers already having
departed on missions further south.

I would guess, Isaac, that you are probably asking yourself,
What does Sam know about military training? General Prentiss
saw my involvement in their training as primarily focused on
teaching them basic literacy and any other communication
skills that would support military discipline. The general was
also concerned about the moral degradation produced by slavery, so my additional responsibility was to assess and strengthen
their spiritual condition. Just imagine, Samuel Johnson the attorney, now transformed into teacher, preacher, and guardian of
morals!

Curiously, while I looked like my pupils, I found decipher-
ing their slave dialect to be quite difficult at first. Many of the
white Arkansan soldiers in blue would laugh at my mystified
facial expression and then translate for me. Ultimately, the two
worlds—that of an educated Northern Negro and that of illit-
erate refugees from slavery—met over McGuffey Readers. We
learned not only to communicate in the traditional sense but at
a deeper more fundamental level. They introduced me to a reality I thought I knew but only through my intellect. To see and
touch the living, breathing embodiment of untold generations
of suffering—a current of human misery which included my
ancestors—transcends all abstract categories. Theirs has been a
largely voiceless suffering, a cry strangled before finding vocal
expression. But now, black men in blue uniforms are recovering
their collective voice, and they will not be silenced!

As the appointed *guardian* of their morality, I could only
weep for the many stories I heard from husbands or wives,
parents or children separated from one another by the cruel
logic of chattel slavery. Their plaintive refrain could be summed
up in words like these: 'Will I ever find my wife, my husband,
or my dear child again?' Despite the sanctity of marriage and
family relations being trampled repeatedly underfoot by their
Southern masters, their desire for normal family life remains
very strong. I pray that in fostering their hopes of reunion with
loved ones, I have not sinned.

If one doubts the action of the Holy Spirit in the world, ask the refugee from slavery. Almost without exception, the contrabands would confidently tell me that they knew their masters were withholding the fullness of the gospel message from them. When some of them began to read the Scriptures on their own, one of my students came to me and exclaimed, 'It's just as we always thought—*neither Jew nor Greek, neither bond nor free*—God loves the colored folk just like the rest.' But then she paused for a moment, caught up in her thoughts, and added, 'But, maybe He loves them the most of all his children, since they have been up on the cross with his Son for a mighty long time.'

My time was almost entirely consumed with teaching the refugees. Although my formal mandate was to establish basic literacy among the colored soldiers, I could not refuse the same opportunities to their wives and children. When they were not assiduously studying their McGuffey Readers, the new recruits drilled almost with a religious fervor. Daily progress could be observed in their transformation from slaves into disciplined soldiers. General Prentiss and his staff were amazed and pleased by the great, almost natural cohesion among the recruits as they formed the various companies of the 2nd Arkansas Volunteers of African Descent.

By the end of June, rumors of a Confederate attack on Helena began to circulate. At first, General Prentiss seemed to discount them, but after receiving some intelligence confirming the movement of Rebel forces in our direction, he assumed the worst and planned a defensive strategy for the anticipated assault. Although the 2nd Arkansas had not reached its full strength and as a result was not fully mustered into the service, it became quickly apparent that it would soon be given its baptism by fire. It was nothing so grand as Gettysburg or the fall of Vicksburg, but the Battle of Helena was my first exposure to combat and an excellent opportunity to witness firsthand the valor of colored troops.

It seemed that the greatest source of distress for the Federal garrison of Helena was not the anticipation of the coming battle; rather the men were genuinely disappointed that their planned celebration of the nation's birthday was of necessity cancelled. As it turned out, any cancelled pyrotechnics were upstaged by the actual events of the 4th of July as they unfolded in Helena. During the battle, the 2nd Arkansas Volunteer Infantry of African Descent was placed on the far left of the Union line in support of the 1st Missouri Artillery. The men handled their first encounter with combat very well, staying calm and organized as the fight came toward them. Indeed, their commanding officer, Colonel Shelly, noted in his report after the battle that "the 2nd Arkansas [AD] was as prompt as any other regiment in assuming its position."

Several things stand out as I reflect upon my experience at Helena. Refugees from slavery are extremely motivated to better their condition, especially through literacy. Negroes, including former slaves, make good soldiers, exhibiting bravery and retaining discipline under the stress of combat. I believe their willingness to fight and die for their freedom will be decisive in the outcome of the war. Finally, I was very impressed by how effective the expert use of artillery can be.

I remained in Helena after the battle for almost a month, splitting my time between teaching and nursing the wounded from the battle. The experience gained through working with you in the Frederick hospital was invaluable. While my sense of vocation to advocate as an attorney for the dignity and humanity of the Negro remains unshaken, I now realize that nursing the sick and wounded has given me a perspective that no amount of learned or philosophical speculation on human rights could ever match. From now on, let my philosophy be informed by experience—a *practical* philosophy gained through sharing in the privations and suffering of the colored race.

After passing through Memphis briefly, I finally was reunited with Louisa and Rebecca. And what a joyous reunion it was! Along with the other missionaries, our sisters have accomplished so much good among the Corinth contrabands. Louisa seems to have found a second father in the person of a charismatic preacher named Moses, whom I believe you met years ago. His preaching is powerfully emotive and yet intensely practical. He is not satisfied to merely manipulate human emotions, as is so common with many men of the cloth. His rhetoric strives to reform the soul—it searches out the inner man. And well that he does this, because so many of those to whom he ministers will most assuredly die soon enough, whether as soldiers in uniform or through the disease and poverty that chase after the refugees.

Something else has happened to my sister, of which I think she is consciously unaware or in complete denial. Besides her devotion to Moses, she has given special attention to one of the contrabands, a fellow with the curious name of Napoleon— *Nappy* is the diminutive he prefers. Early in their acquaintance, she recognized his intellectual gifts and has poured considerable time and effort into educating the former slave. Interestingly, during this time he has also become attached to Moses, who has been mentoring him as a kind of spiritual son. In the brief time I have been in Corinth, I have also found myself drawn to both persons, who are clearly so important in Louisa's life at present. It's hard to imagine my sister—you may smile at this—succumbing to romantic love, but if it were to happen, heaven help the poor fellow who draws her affection! And yet, there might be something germinating with Nappy. The odd thing is that one would have to be completely blind to not see that Nappy is totally, irredeemably smitten with Louisa, while she gives no evidence that she is even aware of his devotion. While not approaching the topic directly with Moses, he has made it clear to me, by a wink here and a knowing look there, that he is fully aware of the situation. I think he may even be encouraging poor Nappy. Repeated passage through her acid wit to plumb the depths of a great and loving soul would require tremendous courage. Time will tell whether he's up to that Herculean task. Of course, all of this must wait, for Nappy has been enrolled in a colored regiment that currently guards the contraband camp. Through the exigencies of military service, he could be pulled away at any time to some other duty far from Corinth. Circumstances permitting, I hope to develop a friendship with this diligent scholar. His quick wit and passionate commitment to learning, which have helped him progress rapidly with his studies, now add to his already considerable practical knowledge of agriculture. My late father would have loved to speak with him about farming!

I hope that my long letter has made up, at least to some degree, for my earlier neglect as a correspondent.

As always, your devoted friend,

Sam

Isaac's eyes again lingered over the closing salutation in Sam's letter, grateful for this rare communication from his friend that had arrived in the early days of September. Reading and rereading his personal correspondence always elicited a twinge of loneliness as he was reminded of friends and family so far away. Even though months had passed, he was still reeling from the aftermath of Gettysburg. He had seen it all before, but the sheer immensity of the horror had overwhelmed his capacity for rational thought. Of what use was reason in the face of suffering so intense and pervasive that almost every effort to relieve it seemed doomed to failure? Day or night, it seemed his mind might capitulate before sights, sounds, and smells that would come unbidden—ever-enlarging piles of amputated limbs, unrelenting cries of anguish, and the inescapable, suffocating stench of death. He had visited this hell before; Fredericksburg was still a fresh memory. But this time his ability to detach himself from it and carry on had somehow been compromised. Perhaps it was the cumulative exhaustion of resuming his clinical duties too quickly after being wounded. Certainly, Francis Reynolds had said as much and had tried unsuccessfully to make him take more time to recover. "*Physician, heal thyself*"—Francis with his flair for the dramatic had quoted Scripture. Isaac felt a sense of melancholy creep over him as he remembered the Irish physician's kind humor. *When might I see him again?* he wondered, considering his colleague's recent promotion and departure from the Irish Brigade in August. *At least, he will have some breathing space away from the madness for a while.* Francis had approached him before Isaac's departure a week after the battle to rejoin the Army of the Potomac as it finally lurched after the retreating Confederate Army. It appeared that Meade might have an opportunity after all to trap Lee on the northern side of the Potomac and destroy his weakened army. Isaac's services on the battlefield with the ambulance corps would be needed. But Francis, as one of the best operators in the 2nd Corps, had been ordered to stay behind and assist in the transition from the corps field hospitals to the development of a general hospital to be named for Dr. Letterman. "Camp Letterman" would become a site where many of the wounded soldiers would receive longer term care.

Francis, as he explained the changes in his role to Isaac, had tried to soften another aspect of the news he was about to share. "Isaac, you're a fine diagnostician, an excellent operating surgeon, a compassionate caregiver, and one of the most decent chaps with whom I've ever had the privilege to practice medicine. How shall I say this? You have been passed over for a much-deserved promotion to full surgeon. Unfortunately, it seems you have a deficiency of Irish blood, and unlike that fine fellow, Henri IV, King of France, you haven't—so to speak—*accepted the Mass in exchange for Paris.* The good news is that the surgeon who will take my place, Dr. Richard Powell, is a competent doctor and collegial in all his interactions." Isaac remembered denying any personal ambition, but secretly he could now admit that being passed over for the promotion hurt primarily because it was clear confirmation that even after a year of creditable service, he was still not fully accepted in the Irish Brigade. At least, Francis had been correct in his assessment of Dr. Powell. However, it felt a bit odd reporting to a person his own age (and with no more clinical experience) after working so well with Francis Reynolds, a well-regarded veteran surgeon of the Crimean War. Isaac realized that his sense of *befuddlement*, as Francis might have *diagnosed* it, was due to a complex mixture of factors, many of which he hoped would improve with time. *I must be patient, for I am committed to see the Union restored and slavery abolished. That will only occur with the defeat of the Rebel armies. But how long must the madness persist?*

Surprisingly, he had found a growing sense of consolation amid the chaos of war in his relationship with Fr. Corby. The chaplain's indefatigable good humor, unquestioning bravery under fire, and patient optimism had increasingly become an anchor to which Isaac clung as the prolonged nature of the struggle became painfully evident. Unfortunately, the opportunity to destroy the Army of Northern Virginia a week after Gettysburg slipped away when it was delayed by high water at the Potomac crossings. The weeks that followed became all-too-reminiscent of prior marches and countermarches in northern Virginia; wary of a massive engagement, both armies engaged in "cat and mouse" tactics as they maneuvered, hoping to exploit a mistake on the part of their opponent.

It was during this time in motion, back and forth between the Rappahannock River and the twice-cursed battlefield near Manassas junction in the fall of 1863, that Isaac's appreciation for the chaplain's profound humanity deepened, and professional respect evolved into genuine friendship. Looking over at the placid expression on the chaplain's face as they rode together, Isaac was reminded of an incident that he had witnessed earlier on their journey south toward the Rappahannock in pursuit of the Rebel Army. Having marched all night, the soldiers had been given an order to brew some coffee and take a brief rest. Fr. Corby was conferring with acting Brigadier Kelly, the Irish Brigade's commander, under a tree, when suddenly a cannonball came crashing through the top of the tree, dropping limbs all around them. Even though he was not in the immediate path of the surprise Rebel cannonade, Isaac had, with many others, instinctively dropped to the ground. He remembered being astonished at how calmly the chaplain slowly and deliberately made the sign of the cross and then walked away from the tree unharmed. While one of the young officers nearby sarcastically remarked that "it was an insult to call so early, *even before breakfast*," no angry words came from Fr. Corby's lips, even though he had lost his horse, small altar stone, and other articles necessary for serving Mass. To Isaac, the chaplain's imperturbability under fire was a marvel to behold.

Fr. Corby's powers of observation, which served him so well in his ministry to the wounded and dying, also were a source of amazement to Isaac. Rather than become distracted by the Rebel artillery barrage which had so suddenly interrupted their coffee that morning *and nearly killed him*, the chaplain had remained quite sensible of his surroundings throughout the remainder of the day. Noting some movement in the woods off to their flank, he had quietly, almost casually, mentioned his observation to one of the officers, saving them all from a potentially catastrophic ambush by the Confederates. As the troops dug in along a railroad cut awaiting Rebel attack, the chaplain, Dr. Powell, and he had gone in search of a place to set up an aid station with their ambulances in the rear of the brigade. Isaac smiled as he remembered how the humorous would sometimes insist upon making an appearance amid the chaos of war. As darkness was settling over the aid station, their attempt at a supper consisting of roasted ears of corn was interrupted by the arrival of a panicked scout. Breathlessly, he had announced that the ambulances and the medical staff were now cut off from their troops by Rebel cavalry. In the gathering darkness, Fr. Corby, who had been flanked on each side by Isaac and Dr. Powell, was mistaken for a general by the lieutenant in charge of the ambulances, who asked him, "General, where shall I direct the ambulances?" Without hesitation, the chaplain in his *brief promotion*, had given the correct order: "Have them driven to Fairfax!" The more Isaac observed the Irish Brigade's chaplain, the more he became convinced that Fr. Corby possessed a preternatural gift for knowing what to do and say in almost any circumstances. In the gathering dusk, Isaac had barely been able to discern a wink accompanying a quick reply in a low voice to his medical colleagues' unspoken thoughts. "Please, not a word of my temporary promotion to anyone."

"Certainly not, General!" Isaac couldn't help but offer the response as the three broke into laughter before galloping off. They had been on the move through most of that night before feeling confident that they had escaped the Rebel trap. Having slept out in the open, crossing the Occoquan River during the night, their appearance had suffered considerably. After arriving in Fairfax, when Isaac had left Fr. Corby and Dr. Powell to purchase some food at a sutler's tent, the chaplain's temporary promotion had apparently come to an end. A man on horseback dashed up to the same tent and, dismounting quickly, nonchalantly ordered the disheveled chaplain to hold his horse. Isaac chuckled as he remembered how when coming out of the sutler's tent he had quickly understood the situation. To the chagrin and consternation of the anonymous horseman, who was extending the bridle to the disheveled chaplain, Isaac, intent on maintaining the joke, had saluted Fr. Corby, saying, "General, I have a good supply for today." Caught completely by surprise, the cocky horseman's nonchalance drained from his face and was replaced by a sudden pallor as he gave Fr. Corby one more quick glance before darting away. As they rode together silently, Isaac realized how important the humorous interludes were to his sanity—*a medicinal, even blessed levity. It is the extraordinary balance he has achieved between humor and gravitas which is so endearing about Chaplain Corby.*

On October 14, during a counter movement northward away from the Confederates who had hoped to set up a third battle of Manassas, a serendipitous opportunity to strike Lee's Army was presented to Meade. Suffering from too strong a desire *to do unto the Union Army what the Union Army wanted to do unto him*, one of Lee's lieutenants, General A. P. Hill, saw what appeared to be a splendid chance to inflict serious damage at Bristoe Station on the Orange and Alexandria railroad. Not all the retreating bluecoats had yet crossed Broad Run, and Hill intended to prevent them from doing just that. But in his eagerness, he failed to complete a proper reconnaissance. General Gouverneur Warren, who had temporarily assumed command of the II Corps after General Hancock's wounding on the third day of Gettysburg, saw the situation a bit differently and laid a trap for his eager Southern pursuers. As Hill urged his Confederates forward to attack the Federal soldiers south of Broad Run, he failed to appreciate the presence of a large body of II Corps soldiers hidden by the railroad embankment. With horrified fascination, Isaac watched through field glasses as two Rebel brigades were struck by the enfilading fire of three divisions from the Union II Corps hidden by the embankment. The ambush and subsequent slaughter were so *successful* that the Federal soldiers followed up with a brief sortie, during which they captured five pieces of Rebel artillery and 450 soldiers.

That the overwhelming number of casualties were Confederate, 1400 compared to 300 Union, meant a long night of operating on many a Southern boy for Isaac and his colleagues. Fr. Corby was there, cheerfully ministering to every soul—whether friend or foe—children of one God. Warren's *splendid little victory* was costly to Lee, but it, like all the other encounters between Lee's and Meade's armies during the autumn campaign of 1863, seemed like small affairs to Isaac, compared with Gettysburg. Finally, they settled into winter quarters near the Rapidan River in early December. One evening during the officer's mess, he wondered out loud to Fr. Corby about the future. "After all the incredible loss of life, especially during this past year, have we made any real progress toward victory—toward an end to this terrible conflict? After this fall campaign, I am left with the impression that we have reached a stalemate with our adversaries. How could this be possible?"

With a look of profound sadness, Fr. Corby replied, "My friend, I am reminded of something that great French Catholic thinker Blaise Pascal once said. I believe it was in his *Pensées*. He wrote words that have always haunted me, as I have never quite understood their full meaning. But now I am inclined to think him a prophet. For this great and terrible civil war provides the context for his frightening and enigmatic statement that '*Christ is in agony until the end of the world.*'"

PART THREE

*"Well, well, General, bury these poor men
and let us say no more about it."*

<small>ROBERT E. LEE, OCTOBER 14, 1863</small>

*"I tried in all my power to avert this war. I saw it coming, and for
twelve years I worked night and day to prevent it, but I could not.
And now it must go on till the last man of this generation falls in his
tracks, and his children seize his musket and fight his battle, unless
you acknowledge our right to self-government . . . We are fighting for
Independence—and that, or extermination, we will have."*

<small>JEFFERSON DAVIS, IN AN INTERVIEW
WITH J. R. GILMORE, JULY 17, 1864</small>

CHAPTER TWENTY-FOUR

"At last the riot is quelled, but we had four days of great anxiety. Fighting went on constantly in the streets between the military and police and the mob, which was partially armed. The greatest atrocities have been perpetrated . . ."

MARIA LYDIG DALY, DIARY ENTRY FOR JULY 23, 1863, NEW YORK

NEITHER THE FRUIT TREES, with their delicate pink and white blossoms, nor the translucent green of leaves newly unfurled and glowing after a shower in April 1864 could dispel Isaac's sense of melancholy. Through the window of his railway carriage, he stared uncomprehendingly at beauty that struggled to penetrate the gloom which had enveloped him as he reflected on his leave of the past two weeks. Not that the experience had been all that unpleasant—he realized it had been his ambivalence, and this made him feel even more depressed. His last visit home had been on his journey east to join the Irish Brigade back in the summer of 1862.

For the past few months, he had managed to keep busy with the daily routine of sick call, but as increasing numbers of Irish Brigade veterans were given month-long furloughs as rewards for signing up to serve the duration of the war, he could no longer justify staying in winter quarters before the commencement of the spring campaign without taking at least a brief leave himself. After his colleague and senior officer, Dr. Powell, had insisted, he had reluctantly agreed, leaving for his hometown of Newport, Indiana, near the end of March almost two weeks after the St. Patrick's Day festivities of 1864. Somewhat more muted than prior years, the revelry honoring the great saint of Ireland produced fewer injuries and drunkenness than previously.

213

A jumble of images intruded upon his consciousness as he tried to make sense of his recent visit home. He would never forget the shadow of profound sorrow that passed across his elderly mother's face as she first recognized him in his uniform at the train station in Richmond, Indiana. Even though it was quickly replaced with a genuine look of joy at seeing her son safe and sound, the hug which followed was suffused with the quiet suffering of a mother grieving for a son now become a stranger. As she held him close, the warmth of her cheek, moistened by tears, had somehow conjured the unwelcome vision of the Southern Quaker prisoners of war he had met after Gettysburg. *Yes, Isaac you have betrayed the Friends' Testimony Against War.* His mother's tears and his father's muted smile and tentative handshake spoke volumes—a deep chasm had opened between him and all that he had held dear. And yet, he could not stand apart from the conflict that would, by God's Providence, bring freedom to the slaves. Grimly, he remembered the firm intention he had expressed to his friend, Dr. Reynolds, that he would serve for the duration of the war.

Staring with greater intensity out his window through and beyond the beauty that beckoned, he realized that there was something else that had been reflected in his mother's tears. It wasn't just a matter of betraying the Friends' Testimony Against War, as bad as that was. Indeed, he had to acknowledge his fear that the Inner Light might be receding from him. He had witnessed the momentary fervor of soldiers caught up in the religious revivals that would move like a storm through the army, but it was a rare thing to see a steady commitment to the higher things. In his musings, an image of Fr. Corby's kind face, tired but always faithful, appeared, forcing him to consider the difference between evanescent religious fervor and devotion to duty.

Another image pushed its way into his thoughts. Throughout his visit to Newport, he had been trailed by a younger cousin, Ezekiel Burgess, the eldest grandson of his father's brother. At eighteen, in the prior autumn, Ezekiel had matriculated at Earlham College, a recently founded Quaker College in Richmond, Indiana. From an early age he had admired his cousin Isaac, and now he declared an interest in entering the medical profession in emulation of Isaac's commitment. Grateful for his cousin's interest in his profession but also concerned to the point of irritation by his persistent questions about medical care in the Union Army, Isaac had tried to discourage further questioning, counseling Ezekiel to concentrate on finishing his collegiate education in preparation for medical school and avoid distractions related to the war, especially since Ezekiel's father could afford to pay for a substitute if the draft became an issue. However, Ezekiel had ideas of his own and peppered Isaac with questions about the presence of volunteer nurses and stretcher-bearers in the Army of the Potomac. Briefly, a slight smile was reflected in the window as Isaac remembered his final firm admonition to Ezekiel about staying in school. *At least I kept him from making a bad choice that would cause great distress at home*, he thought with relief.

Resolving to bury for the moment his concerns about his spiritual state with the reassuring thought that the local Friends' meeting in Newport had deferred any final decisions about the status of Quakers serving in the Union Army, Isaac realized that his train was approaching Washington. Beginning to resume his military demeanor, a voice at the door of his railway compartment exploded whatever calm he had been able to collect from the chaos of his thoughts. "Cousin Isaac, I am sorry that I lied to thee," came the plaintive words of Ezekiel Burgess. "Surely, thou must understand, I cannot stand by when great deeds are being done. I hope thou wilt forgive me, but I must come and help thee in thy work."

Groaning inwardly, Isaac stared at his young cousin, who had secretly followed him on to the eastbound train. Recognizing himself reflected in Ezekiel's enthusiasm and determined expression, Isaac paused, searching for the appropriate words to chastise and send him back to Newport, but gave up and, much to his own surprise, began to laugh. "Oh Ezekiel, what is to be done with thee! I cannot guarantee thy safety. If thou shouldst die, it would break many hearts back home, and I would be responsible."

"But Cousin, I left a letter explaining everything. I take full responsibility for my actions, and my ultimate safety is in God's hands. Thou needn't worry at all. Oh, I also took a leave of absence from Earlham College. I still plan on becoming a doctor, but right now I must help those who are suffering the best I can."

Now reluctantly reconciled to his cousin's presence, for the remainder of the journey back to camp, Isaac first instructed and then relentlessly drilled Ezekiel in the rudiments of being a stretcher-bearer and military nurse. Whereas he had earlier demurred when Ezekiel had asked for details of his medical work in the army, now Isaac—as if to test his cousin's resolve—presented one anecdote after another emphasizing the dangerous and gruesome aspects of the work. Cheerfully absorbing everything Isaac offered, no matter how horrific, Ezekiel began to win over his older cousin.

"Ezekiel, I hope thou dost understand that thy life and the lives of the wounded soldiers under thy care will depend on remembering everything I have taught thee and that thou must obey the other, more experienced soldier-nurses and stretcher-bearers without question. Since as a volunteer thou wilt not be in uniform, thy duties *must* be limited to nursing and transporting wounded soldiers in the *rear* of the army. Dost thou understand this? Thou must stay back from the battlefront."

"Yes, Cousin."

Also, our plain speech is an impediment in the army—I will not be using it when we return to camp, and I recommend that thou not use it either. Thou must no longer address me as 'Cousin' or 'Isaac' but use either 'sir' or 'Dr. Burgess,' once we are in camp."

"Yes, Dr. Burgess." Ezekiel grinned and added, "I am at *your* service, sir."

"Fine, Mr. Burgess. You seem to be a quick learner, but we'll see how you can apply in practice the theoretical knowledge you have just acquired," Isaac said, smiling at his cousin's naïve enthusiasm.

Isaac and Ezekiel arrived at camp as the sun was setting on a warm afternoon in early spring. Two topics were dominating the conversations among enlisted men and officers alike. First, much speculation abounded regarding the appointment of General Grant as overall commander of the Union Armies, especially when it was learned that he had made the Army of the Potomac his *headquarters in the field* while retaining General Meade as its titular head. Remembering Grant's near-fatal delay on the first day of Shiloh, Isaac kept his counsel, while others noted that the hero of Vicksburg and Missionary Ridge had yet to encounter the likes of *Marse Robert*.

Second, disturbing reports were circulating of the wanton massacre of black soldiers *after* their surrender at Fort Pillow in Tennessee by Rebel soldiers under the command of General Nathan Bedford Forrest. It appeared that the Confederate authorities intended to make good on their threats to treat black soldiers in Federal uniform as slave insurrectionists. Already, there were calls for a congressional investigation of the alleged atrocity and demands for revenge in the Northern press. *How wrong I was so many years ago in my original impression of Forrest as a kinder sort of slave-dealer*, Isaac thought as sleep initially evaded him. *Perhaps he had better intentions at one time—but the business of trading in human beings can only corrupt one. . . . Of course, war has hardened all of us. But, still to give no quarter to surrendering soldiers in uniform and then to hunt the survivors down to torture and slaughter them! What monsters these Confederates are! It should be obvious that their cause is lost, and yet they fight more tenaciously and with such viciousness. I wonder what Sam thinks about the sorry business.*

After breakfast the next morning, Isaac's further ruminations were cut short by an orderly who entered his tent and handed him an order. Quickly scanning its contents, Isaac turned pale and hesitated before responding to the orderly. "Please, report to the colonel commanding that I will join him presently." Turning to his cousin, who was sitting in the tent with him, Isaac cryptically said, "Ezekiel, I must attend to a medical duty this morning. You must remain here while I am gone."

Ezekiel protested, "Can't I be of some assistance with your work?" Frowning, Isaac replied, *"Not this kind of work.* I must go now; I will explain later."

Apparently, Isaac had returned to his duties at a most inopportune moment. He was aware of prodigious efforts by recruiters to replenish the ranks of the severely depleted Irish Brigade. Indeed, Colonel Kelly, the brigade's commander, was still away in New York on a recruiting mission. Not everyone who answered the call to service answered from the highest motives. Some individuals had become quite adept at claiming the bounties offered for signing up and then quickly absconding, only to repeat the process, pocketing a handsome profit. One fellow who had not stayed far enough ahead of the authorities had been caught and was now facing the penalty for desertion. Military protocol required the presence of a physician at such events to confirm the outcome. Having just returned from leave and being immediately available, Isaac was ripe for the opportunity to serve as the medical officer responsible for witnessing the proceedings.

The dogwood trees were late in blooming that spring. Mounted beside Colonel Smyth, the temporary commander of the Irish Brigade, Isaac was drawn to the delicate beauty of the blossoms which shimmered in the early morning sunlight, filtering through a copse of trees yet untouched by the horrors of war. In their purity, the white cruciform blossoms evoked a paradoxical sweetness, seemingly heedless of the task at hand. Responding to the same vision, Colonel Smyth turned to Isaac and, pointing to the nearest dogwood, exclaimed, "How extraordinary! Just think of it, doctor—beauty and crucifixion united in a humble flower. What a lovely day for an execution!" Before the startled Isaac could think of a response, Fr. Corby cantered up to join them on their journey to a large, open field a mile in the rear of the brigade.

"Fr. Corby, is the prisoner ready?" Hesitating for a moment, the chaplain tentatively answered, "Colonel, I hope and pray that he is ready, if anyone can be, for this special liturgy of death." Sensing the chaplain's distress, Isaac asked, "Are you well, sir?"

"Oh, I'm well enough, Dr. Burgess. Thank you for your concern. It's our business this morning that makes me tremble," Fr. Corby answered grimly as his mind was drawn back to his intense encounter with the condemned on the previous night. In reality, the *man* to be executed was hardly more than a boy, barely twenty years of age. Realizing that a Catholic chaplain stood before him, even in his shackles, the young Irish tough from the Five Points neighborhood in lower Manhattan had assumed a swagger. "*I s'pose you've come to hear me confession, Father.*" Giving Fr. Corby a knowing wink followed by a leering grin, one of Five Points' *finest* proceeded to *confess*.

"I shan't disappoint ye, Father. I bin doin' some mighty big sinnin' since me days as an altar boy." He proceeded to brag how in his mid-teens, he had joined one of the Irish American gangs that terrorized the seamier parts of New York City. Indeed, as Fr. Corby listened to the youth, it wasn't at all clear how many of the evil deeds being *confessed* had actually occurred or were being offered merely to shock a Catholic priest. Eventually, the condemned youth began to describe his recent activities leading to his court-martial. His tone changed ever so slightly, and his swagger dropped briefly as he related his involvement in the draft riots that had brought so much destruction to his city during the prior July. It seemed to Fr. Corby that a shadow tinged with horror briefly passed over his face while speaking of his participation in the lynching of a Negro who had the misfortune of being captured by the rampaging mob. His features hardened again as he described the pleasure derived from bounty jumping. He and his comrades thought it great fun to fool Uncle Sam while receiving the $300 bounty each time they enlisted, only to desert and show up at another recruiter's office to repeat the game. Seeing the sad expression on the Catholic chaplain's face, he declared, "*Father, I'd do it all agin, if I could escape. Why I must have at least $3000 I haven't spent hidden away.*"

"*But my son, have you considered the fact that you won't escape? You do understand that tomorrow you will be executed by firing squad, don't you? You are only hours away from a dishonorable and shameful death.*"

The condemned youth's face was drained momentarily of its defiance, revealing the terrified child within. Turning away, unable to tolerate Fr. Corby's compassionate gaze, he protested, *"I have nothin' to be sorry for. There ain't no way I'd die to free the darkies, an' besides, the draft ain't fair. Bounty jumpin' is me way o' protestin' this injustice agin us poor Irish."*

"Would you trample thus on the honor of your Irish brothers, who voluntarily, without receiving any bounty, have been suffering and dying to preserve this Union? My son, does anything stand out in your memories of your service at the altar?"

"Well . . . I remember the large crucifix—the sufferin' Jesus scared me as a boy."

"What kind of death did He suffer?"

"Weren't He killed the way they killed criminals in those days?"

"Ah, so you did learn something of the faith during your service at the altar. Was anyone else crucified with Him?"

"Two thieves, I think . . . yes that's right, one on either side of Him."

"So, the Lord of Glory voluntarily died as a common criminal with two others, sharing their dishonorable, shameful death."

"But Jesus weren't no criminal," the former altar boy protested, his eyes glistening. *"The other two fellas they deserved what they got but not Him. In fact, didn't one of 'em say as much while t'other only cussed and complained?"*

"Yes. Do you remember the rest of the conversation He had with the good thief?"

"The good thief asked to be remembered when Jesus would come into His Kingdom, and then Jesus told the feller he would be with Him that very day in heaven."

"Do you see any similarity between the two thieves crucified with Jesus and your own predicament?"

"You're tryin' to get me to repent for me sins, Father. You just about tricked me into doin' it—remindin' me of what I was taught as a boy!"

"It seems to me, my son, that there is one question you need to ask yourself as honestly as you can. Are you even a wee bit sorry for what you've done? If you admit that you are, and I believe you are indeed sorry (if you can only stop being proud of your sins for a moment), then why not be sorry for everything? What do you have to offer God in these last moments of your life other than your death—a dishonorable death to be sure—but also an honest repentant death like that of the good thief? Could you not also

offer your dishonorable death on behalf of your Irish brothers so that their deaths may be honorable?"

And thus had Fr. Corby left the condemned bounty-jumper, worrying that he had either pushed too hard or not hard enough in his efforts to bring him to repentance. But now, his attention and that of his companions was drawn to a scene that would be indelibly inscribed in the memory of every person present that morning.

Not only the Irish Brigade but almost the entire division of which they were a part had been called out to witness the execution of the bounty jumper. A large, open field had been chosen for the event, and according to protocol, the troops were lined up in ranks, forming three sides of a large square, with the fourth side left open to accommodate the condemned man and the firing squad. Silence descended upon the ranks when the somber notes of the "Dead March" could be heard as the provost marshal's entourage approached with musicians in the lead playing fife and drums. Twelve men chosen at random from the ranks to serve as the firing squad followed the musicians. Each had received a loaded musket, one of which had only a blank, creating a blessed uncertainty regarding the source of the fatal shot. Next in line, the condemned youth walked slowly and disconsolately behind a wagon carrying his coffin. The provost marshal and his assistants made up the rear. The procession continued until the wagon carrying the coffin arrived before a freshly dug grave, in front of which the coffin was unloaded. The bounty-jumper was then escorted to the coffin and directed to sit upon the coffin facing the assembled soldiers.

The youth blanched as the provost marshal first read the charge against him and then the sentence—*death by firing squad.* Turning to the condemned, the provost marshal offered him the privilege of addressing those assembled. Fr. Corby, who had seemed distracted to that point, started when he heard the provost marshal's invitation to the condemned youth to speak. His hands securely tied behind him, the youth struggled to his feet and paused for a moment, standing before the wooden box that would soon house his earthly remains in an unmarked grave. His face shining and moist from tears, his eyes sought out Fr. Corby. Seeing the chaplain, who returned his gaze, the youth's face lit up with a smile, now devoid of any swagger, and he began to speak. "I'm not much for makin' speeches but I'm grateful that I can say a few words. Everythin' the provost marshal has accused me of doin' I did. You see me here standin' before you a condemned man. I am now ashamed to say that I took pleasure in stealin' and every kind of violence. I stole more than $3000 by me bounty jumpin'. How will a dead man enjoy his stolen money? I brought shame on me Irish brothers. I hope that God may forgive me, and the example of me shameful death will help every one of you to avoid me crimes and to die honorable deaths when your time comes."

Before his blindfold was applied, Fr. Corby approached the youth, who now had resumed his seat on the coffin after finishing his confession. "Father, you were right. I was a wee bit sorry for me sins." Directing a shy glance toward the crucifix in Fr. Corby's hands, the youth paused and took a deep breath, his whole frame trembling, as he asked, "Can I kiss Him?" Fr. Corby, with tears in his eyes, offered the crucifix to the youth, who kissed it as reverently as the most pious of faithful parishioners. Isaac could barely hear Fr. Corby, after making the sign of the cross, intone, ". . . ego te absolvo a peccatis tuis in nomine Patris, et Filii, et Spiritus Sancti. Amen." With the blindfold in place, the chaplain quickly retreated while the provost marshal called the firing squad to attention, and then, "ready, aim, fire!"

When Isaac examined the condemned youth to confirm the execution, he was met by a serenity in death he had rarely seen in life.

CHAPTER TWENTY-FIVE

"Put a United States uniform on his back and the chattel is a man."
UNION OFFICER OF A NEGRO REGIMENT

FINALLY ABLE TO EXAMINE his mail after attending the execution of the bounty-jumper, Isaac was delighted to find a rare letter from Sam Johnson, who was even less faithful than Isaac in his correspondence.

March 28, 1864
Memphis, Tennessee

Dear Isaac,

Although I know that you have received more consistent news from Rebecca of the many changes that have engulfed the Corinth contraband camp, it is long overdue for me to give you a brief personal sketch of my impressions arising from the activities of the past several months. But where to begin? You are already aware of the demise of the camp—that glorious experiment in freedmen's self-sufficiency—precipitated by General Sherman's orders at the end of last year. Of course, military necessity will always take precedence. Without the triumph of Union arms, there will be very few freedmen indeed, but it is still painful to see the fate of the contraband camps so utterly dependent on the military situation. Something quite extraordinary was accomplished at Corinth through the goodwill and dedicated efforts of so many people. Seizing an unprecedented opportunity, refugees from slavery, in a matter of months, became—to a great degree—self-governing citizens. Previously, I had expressed to you my great admiration for the valor of Negro soldiers fighting for the Union. In no way is that admiration diminished when I confess an equal if not greater reverence for the enormous sacrifices made by their mothers, wives, sweethearts, grandparents, and children, which will ever remain unsung as monuments are erected to honor those slain in battle.

Imagine a thriving village organized into four wards, tidy well-built homes, straight streets free of garbage, as safe and secure as any *proper* town in Ohio or Indiana—the only difference being that this community was comprised entirely of dark-skinned humanity, who only weeks and months before, could be bought and sold! Miracles do happen, my friend. Unfortunately, only a few are blessed to witness them before they disappear and become faint memories to be eclipsed by other, *greater* events. But I ask you, what could be truly greater than the full recovery of one's dignity as a member of the human race?

It is impossible for me to do justice to the agricultural achievements of Corinth. You know how tone-deaf I am with respect to farming. However, I believe that Rebecca's letters have given you at least some idea of the refugees' productivity in that arena—for several months prior to its closure, the community had been generating a substantial income for Uncle Sam, in addition to providing amply for its own nutritional needs. As my practical talents lie in different endeavors, more in nursing and education, I will confine most of my observations to that aspect of life at Corinth, adding a discussion of my newest avocation at the end of this letter.

Shortly after my arrival, I offered my services as a volunteer nurse in the contraband hospital. Again, I remain extremely grateful for the wealth of knowledge and experience I gained through my work with you and Dr. Reynolds at the General Hospital in Frederick, Maryland. As an educated free Negro from the North, to be able to apply that knowledge for the direct benefit and succor of refugees from slavery has been an extraordinary blessing to me. I am truly at a loss for words to describe the transformation in my perspective. (I can almost hear your laugh, Isaac, as surely the thought must come unbidden, *Sam at a loss for words!*) It began with my experience at Helena and has only been confirmed and strengthened by the additional work at Corinth. Strangely enough, your old acquaintance Mrs. Penelope Wormeley has had a hand in it as well. Perhaps some vignettes from the hospital work may help give you a sense of my meaning.

Missus Penny, as she is known to her patients, was, to say the least, quite an enigma to me when first we met. I suspect she viewed me in similar terms. From my first visit to the contraband hospital, it seemed that wherever the most unpleasant, noisome, or demanding tasks were to be found, without hesitation, *Missus Penny* was there ministering to the suffering. I was unable to detect the least bit of condescension in the care she offered to refugees from the peculiar institution that had sustained Southern civilization, indeed, the only way of life she had known, until the advent of the Yankee invaders. When I introduced myself as a friend and Oberlin classmate of the esteemed Dr. Burgess, she paused briefly to look me over and then, resuming her dressing change, said, 'Could you go fetch some clean water and more bandages, please?'

When I promptly complied with her request and brought the requested materials, I must have passed the test, for she immediately gave me another task. Such was our relationship for nearly a month—very little conversation other than what was essential to completing the task at hand. To keep up with her pace of work, I would arrive at dawn and work into the evening, spending increasing amounts of time working side-by-side with this Southern matron and former slaveowner. And then a curious thing happened one morning, when we were fortunate to have a short break in our work. After taking a sip of coffee, *Missus Penny*, turning suddenly, met and held my gaze for several moments and then laughed! Giving me a big smile, she explained, 'Here I am, a white Southern matron working shoulder-to-shoulder with a Northern Negro, who is far better educated than I. We make quite a pair, don't you think? I daresay *my people* would be as scandalized as *your people* by our professional association, and yet we work well together. You must tell me about your education at Oberlin College. I suspect it may have been more enlightening than what I learned from my governess.'

Gradually, over the following weeks, we became both the students and teachers of one another. She confessed that she had not believed your earlier declarations about educated Negroes. It just seemed impossible within the universe of her experience, and yet here were two undeniable living examples in the Johnson siblings. For my part, I had a view of the Southerner formed in large part from a reading of the abolitionist literature, in which willful ignorance, unyielding prejudice, and violent cruelty were the defining characteristics. Although born and bred within that milieu, Penelope Wormeley had shown a remarkable willingness, even hunger, for learning and understanding that had previously been beyond her ken. I now see why you had expressed such admiration for the youthful Penelope. You clearly recognized the potential locked within this beautiful Southern soul.

Sadly, too many of her fellow Southerners fit all too well their image as portrayed in the abolitionist literature, including the poor woman's husband, a disgruntled ex-Confederate officer, disabled by a wound received at Shiloh. Ah, but you know much more about that. In any event, he did not take kindly to his wife's professional collaboration with an 'uppity Yankee n____r' once the Southern ladies' gossip society had reported on the unseemly 'fraternizing' involving his wife's work at the contraband hospital. Not long after, I was nonplussed to encounter Mrs. Wormeley walking with a limp and bearing a bruise on her cheek that no amount of rouge could hide. When with indignation I asked her, 'Who did this to you?' she turned away with silent tears, attempting to focus on her duties. Foolishly, I pressed her, even insisting on my honor that I would thrash anyone who would assault her. Finally, she turned her swollen, bruised face toward me and said, "Mr. Johnson, I believe you are indeed a man of honor, and now I beg you to not persist in being my champion. It is enough for me to know that you are willing. Sacred bonds tie me to another who has a very *different sense of honor.*"

So, Isaac, thus abruptly ended my professional association (but hopefully not my friendship) with one of the most remarkable persons I have ever met. I cannot bear the thought that she should suffer because of her association with me. Through your dear sister, I was reassured that my Southern friend's torments ended with my departure from duties at the contraband hospital. Most importantly to me, Penelope Wormeley did confide to her how much she valued our friendship and that she could not sufficiently express her gratitude to her Negro mentor for enlightening her about a world hitherto unknown to her.

In my earlier correspondence I had indicated my intention to become better acquainted with the former slave, Napoleon, who is known by his nickname of Nappy. Now effectively banished from the contraband hospital, I focused my energies on assisting Rebecca and Louisa in their educational endeavors, primarily serving as a tutor to their most gifted and motivated students, including Nappy. The only time available in Nappy's very busy schedule for additional study was in the evenings, for his days were occupied either with assisting and overseeing the farming activities of the community or in military duties. Like most of the able-bodied men among the refugees who had not been hired to work on nearby plantations, Nappy had been recruited by Chaplain Alexander to join a thousand-man strong Negro regiment, the *First Alabama*, to provide security for the community and surrounding outposts. I am thankful that Nappy's duties kept him at the Corinth contraband camp; otherwise, the opportunity of his friendship would likely have been denied me. Apart from my own selfish considerations, I am also glad he was spared the indignity of having to work for Southerners, many of whom had perjured themselves, signing the loyalty oath for purely pecuniary reasons—their newfound loyalty to the *stars and stripes* in truth actuated by an intense interest in *greenbacks*. My blood boils when I think about that scoundrel, Wormeley, who—because I enjoyed the protection of the Union Army—would display his hatred for me by beating his wife. He was one of the most obsequious hypocrites professing his undying loyalty to *Uncle Sam*, so he could qualify to hire contraband labor to work his idled plantations.

Before I came to know Nappy, he had already acquired the extraordinary gift of basic literacy with Louisa's assistance. Transformed from an ignorant slave into a man of the spoken and written word, he could now give eloquent expression to what had only been vague, wordless hopes and aspirations in his prior life of servitude. No matter how seemingly trivial, there wasn't a fact or observation that could be expressed with words which did not capture his interest. Although the initial evenings we spent together were often focused on discussing the latest book he had devoured, our encounters quickly changed to conversations in which it seemed like every spare piece of knowledge I possessed was surrendered to his probing questions. However, not all our time together was spent in the transfer of knowledge from teacher to student. As our friendship grew, the burly former fieldhand cautiously began to reveal a contemplative aspect of his personality—a deeply profound sensibility that he had previously shared only with his spiritual mentor, Moses. He would refer with great reverence to the Scriptures, which had only been recently opened to him. For all my formal theological education at Oberlin, I must confess hòw often he has astonished me with his novel insights into the meaning and application of passages that I thought I knew so well. Repeatedly, he would demonstrate his gift for applying biblical truths directly to current need, while at the same time grounding his insights within the context of the tremendous suffering from which he and so many others in the Corinth Contraband Camp had recently escaped.

To give you a better idea of the remarkable character of my new friend, I must share one anecdote. During the process of enlistment in the Union Army, the former slaves are required to give their full name, both their given name and surname. In practice, this typically has resulted in the Negro recruit randomly choosing a surname that might catch his fancy or, assuming the surname of his former master, often in the hope that this latter choice might assist in a future reunion with enslaved loved ones. Knowing the tragic history of how his brother had been killed, I expressed my surprise when Nappy signed up for the Union blue choosing the surname of his former master. Sadness suffusing his face, Napoleon Heyward paused and, giving me a look that penetrated to the depths of my soul, replied, 'Sam, there has not been a day since my master, James Heyward, killed my dear brother that I have not been haunted by the scene—my brother receiving his mortal wound as I watched, helpless to prevent it, and then my own desperate action in a few seconds, filled with rage that resulted in the deaths of my old master and his overseer. Our Lord, the only *true* Master, has insisted that we must forgive our enemies, even *love* them. My enemy has shed the blood of one dearer to me than my own life and I, in turn, have shed his blood. As I see it, Sam, I am bound by ties of blood to my former master. By taking his name, I hope to forgive and redeem him as I seek God's forgiveness for the violence that I have committed.'

Isaac, I must confess my past skepticism regarding the notion of a vocation to ministry. Perhaps it is because of my legal training and acquaintance in that context, with the many varieties of hypocrite who inhabit the pulpit. So many seem enamored of the prestige and authority inherent in the ministry but with little true devotion motivating their service. Not so with Napoleon Heyward, who I believe has a true vocation to Christ's ministry in this distressed world. In the several months of his close acquaintance with the preacher Moses, he has found a mentor, spiritual guide, and adopted father. His love for Moses (and his secret devotion to Louisa) overflow in every encounter he has with his fellow contrabands, from small acts of kindness to words of encouragement. He has begun to manifest a talent for exhortation not unlike his mentor. Although his diffidence prevents him from exercising bolder oratory, nevertheless, the authentic man, full of compassion for his fellows, shines forth in his humble speech. I feel it is not my place to intervene in relationships of the heart, but I have confided to Rebecca my hope that Louisa and Napoleon will come to a mutual understanding and that the war will not prevent their eventual union.

Earlier in this missive, I alluded to a revelation about my own future. As the war has inexorably ground on, and having witnessed the recruitment and organization of many Negro regiments, I have come to the realization that it is highly unlikely that as a Negro, I will receive an officer's commission. Apparently, Uncle Sam is quite content to have men of African descent stop bullets and be torn apart by shrapnel, but he is wary of placing the black man in a position of leadership. Thus, the standard organizational structure for colored regiments excludes Negroes from the ranks of commissioned officers. Observing the humble devotion of Nappy and many others who are willing to lay down their lives as private soldiers to assure the end of slavery and restoration of the Union, I realize that my first duty is to serve in whatever capacity I can—personal ambition has only been a snare and delusion for me.

Pausing in his reading, Isaac thought, *Oh no! Sam has joined up. I had so hoped he would sit out the conflict.* Anxiously, he returned to the letter.

You probably remember from my earlier correspondence how the efficient use of artillery made such a crucial difference in the Battle of Helena. Here was a form of the military art that employed an understanding of mathematics and the natural sciences, which was attractive to both the intellect and one's martial spirit. Later last year, in addition to the First Alabama Infantry Regiment, a regiment of heavy artillery was recruited in Corinth, the 6th United States Colored Heavy Artillery (6th USCHA). With my encouragement, Nappy requested a transfer as I joined the newly formed artillery regiment where we have both been assigned to the same company. After several weeks of drills and training, I was promoted to sergeant, and a short time after, Nappy was promoted to corporal. So, you see, Isaac, your friend's ambitions have been realized—perhaps not in the grandiose fashion I had imagined but in a very real practical sense. I have come to know and care deeply for each of the men who directly report to me only as a non-commissioned officer can. We are fortunate to have a commanding officer, Major Lionel Booth, who is fair, an excellent instructor in the artillerist's art, and most importantly, treats the men with respect. He does not seem to be afflicted with the prejudices against the Negro which are so common among many of the white officers.

Forgive me for keeping this from you for so long. Rebecca and Louisa both fervently urged me against this decision, spreading before me all the compelling arguments against potentially sacrificing a future life of service, enriched and informed by all the educational benefits I have been so blessed to receive. But my future is *now*—I cannot stand back from the fray. More importantly, I must fully share in the suffering of my people. I am not quite certain that Louisa and Rebecca have forgiven me for insisting on remaining silent about my enlistment and that only I should inform you at the appropriate time. One very gratifying byproduct of this decision, mitigating some of the pain I have caused for those I love, has been to realize that Louisa's tears were not shed for me alone. I now rest assured, by subtle but unmistakable signs, that my sister's sarcastic wit could not completely hide her profound regard for Napoleon Heyward. She might not be ready to consciously acknowledge it, but when it comes, Louisa's expression of love for her former student will be unambiguous and complete. I smile when I recall the expression on Nappy's face after I told him a few days ago, "As your senior officer, I expect you not only to do your duty, but you must survive whatever may come, because I am absolutely certain that *someone* will be waiting anxiously for you—and you know who I mean!"

In reviewing what I have just written, I am a bit ashamed of its melodramatic quality. The painful reality is that the destiny for most US Colored Regiments foreseen by the War Department seems primarily to be one of guard and garrison duty on the fringes of the action. It seems likely that there will only be a dull, uneventful future marked by boredom awaiting the colored soldiers of the 6th USCHA. Indeed, our greatest danger will probably be from disease. Hopefully, my experience nursing the sick will be helpful, if needed. Anyway, today we have orders to leave for garrison duty at a little backwater, a fort north of Memphis on the Mississippi—I doubt you've ever heard of it— Fort Pillow.

Your devoted friend,
Sam

CHAPTER TWENTY-SIX

"Hard work, dirt, and death everywhere."

CIVIL WAR NURSE, FREDERICKSBURG, VIRGINIA, MAY 19, 1864

"FORT PILLOW!" EXPLODED FROM Isaac's lips as he reread the end of Sam's letter in disbelief. Suffocating within a dense fog of fear, rage, and despair, he was initially oblivious to the anxious inquiry of his startled cousin Ezekiel.

"You look terrible, Cousin. Is there bad news?"

"It's . . . it's Sam Johnson. He joined the 6th US Colored Heavy Artillery and was ordered to Fort Pillow at the end of March. Did he arrive there in time for Forrest's attack and the massacre?"

"Oh, Isaac . . . Sam was your best friend . . . " "*is* my best friend!" Isaac corrected Ezekiel with a vehemence that frightened them both. "Forgive me, Ezekiel, for my anger—the thought of Sam killed, possibly tortured and mutilated by the Rebels is more than I can bear. He *must* be alive. He couldn't have been there at the time of the attack. It's unthinkable. I won't believe he is dead until I hear directly from Louisa and Rebecca as to his fate." His repeated verbal denials bringing him little solace, Isaac realized that he must seek objective confirmation by writing immediately to both women. Uncertain of their exact whereabouts, he wrote each of them separate short letters in care of Chaplain John Eaton, the General Superintendent of Contrabands for the Department of the Tennessee in Memphis, Tennessee. "Now we can only wait and live with the terrible uncertainty."

Although the *terrible uncertainty* hovered like a dark cloud over him, Isaac had little time to brood about it. From the increasing bustle within camp, it became clear that Generals Meade and Grant were on the verge of setting the Army of the Potomac in motion. Working closely with his colleague, Dr. Richard Powell, Isaac took refuge in preparing for the casualties that would inevitably be coming very soon. Pausing from recording inventories of medical supplies in the sultry heat, Dr. Powell remarked to Isaac, "The stretcher-bearers and soldier-nurses have all remarked how much they appreciate your cousin's help. In the coming action, I hope you have encouraged him to stay back from the front line. You know the boys'll take advantage of a generous and good-hearted fellow like Ezekiel. It would just not be right to see a volunteer put in harm's way unnecessarily. Besides, look at him! He's even taller than you and would make a good target for some angry Rebel sharpshooter."

"Thank you, Richard, for your thoughts about Ezekiel; he has been a quick study. I have repeatedly warned him to stay back from the front line, but he is eager to help the wounded wherever he can—perhaps *too eager*. His parents would pay for a substitute if he were to be conscripted, and yet here he is, serving as a non-combatant volunteer against their wishes. Although I have done all in my power to discourage him from pursuing this course of action, our family will not see it that way, especially if he were injured or killed."

Orders to cross the Rapidan River came the next day; their march would begin the night of May 3rd. Isaac felt a deep sense of foreboding when he learned that the II Corps would be making their camp at Chancellorsville. What kind of welcoming reception would General Lee offer the Army of the Potomac? Like so many of his comrades, he could only hope that they would not tarry too long in the Wilderness, a region that had been so distinctly hostile to soldiers in blue.

Crossing the Rapidan without incident, on the bright, sunny morning of May 4, 1864, the men's anxieties receded as bands struck up patriotic airs and they set their faces south toward Richmond. Even Isaac's premonition of woe and nagging fears about his friend's fate were briefly held at bay as he was caught up in the wave of optimism that flowed over the column. It did not take long for the sense of impending doom to return, however. Arriving late morning at Chancellorsville, both new recruits as well as veterans of that earlier campaign could not ignore the presence of myriad reminders from the contest fought there a year ago. Numerous partially exposed skeletons emerging from shallow graves offered the soldiers a silent welcome, assuring their guests that there was plenty of room for more.

After the ambulances had been parked, Ezekiel Burgess, his face drained of color, approached his cousin who had arrived earlier near the head of the column. "What do you think, Cousin?" Isaac asked, making a sweeping gesture toward the macabre souvenirs of an earlier battle.

"I'm not certain of what to *think*, but I *see* many a grieving father, mother, wife, sweetheart, brother, sister, and child reflected in the bones lying here."

Isaac nodded silently with a sad smile. *Ezekiel will be a fine physician. He can still see beyond the gruesome relics of a military defeat, but have I lost the capacity to comprehend the larger human tragedy?*

After a night's rest, the men of the II Corps were up early and had resumed their march south on the fifth. Isaac shared the hope of many that they might quickly leave the Wilderness. There had even been speculation that their corps would play a decisive role in turning Lee's flank . . . but only if they could escape entanglement in this infernal region and find open country, better suited to large scale military maneuver and action. When nearly free of the Wilderness, the order came for a countermarch toward the distant sound of musketry. *Lee means to trap us again in this evil place.* Reluctantly, Isaac turned back with the other medical staff to the rear of the column, preparing for the casualties that were sure to come.

Embracing Union Cavalry Commander General Phil Sheridan's very simple strategy of getting at Lee's army wherever it might be and *smashing it up*, Grant and Meade had gotten bogged down in fighting on the fifth, which intensified tremendously on the sixth. Narrow country roads flanked by deep thickets made assembling large numbers of troops in line of battle nearly impossible. Thus, the two-one numerical advantage of the Union Army was largely neutralized, giving the Confederates a distinct advantage. Nonetheless, a Union breakthrough—a genuine *smashing up*—of the Rebel Army nearly occurred on the sixth, only to be prevented when Longstreet's Corps arrived just in time for a fierce counterattack. Worse yet, the Rebel counterattack also took advantage of an unfinished railroad cut, turning the Federal left flank and forcing a loss of their earlier gains. Ironically, Longstreet's success, like Stonewall Jackson's a year earlier at Chancellorsville, came at a great price. While personally directing an extension of the successful flanking movement, he was seriously wounded in the neck, and a young general at his side was killed by an accidental volley from their own men.

Several aspects of the fighting on the fifth and sixth challenged Isaac and his assistants as they sought to care for the wounded. Dense smoke accumulating from repeated volleys of musketry further reduced the limited visibility of the terrain. As a result, units quickly became disoriented, sometimes heading in the wrong direction and in the confusion, firing on their comrades. Perhaps most horrific of all, sparks from the gunfire started random fires among the dead leaves of the previous year, making it nearly impossible to reach some of the wounded trapped by the flames. As the flames engulfed them, the screams of the dying were mingled with the staccato explosion of cartridges in their cartridge boxes, producing additional hazards to those seeking to rescue them.

Tormented by a growing sense of impotence, Isaac attended with mechanical regularity to the grisly business of examining wounded soldiers fortunate enough to be retrieved from the maelstrom. *Here we are once again, attending to endless slaughter in a place of Lee's choosing—a truly fitting anniversary celebration for his great victory a year ago!* His bitter reflections were interrupted by the loud cries of a stretcher-bearer who was stumbling toward the aid station. With tears marking small channels in the soot and grime coating his cheeks, he wailed repeatedly, "I killed him, I killed him! Oh Lord, I'm damned fer sure, I killed him!"

Shocked by the hysterics, Isaac quickly finished applying a splint to the leg of a wounded soldier whose face began to reflect the contagion of panic. Motioning to two other assistants to transport the wounded soldier to the ambulances in the rear, Isaac turned and addressed the distraught stretcher-bearer who was now visibly shaking as he continued the refrain, "I killed him."

"Edward, what's the matter with you? You are a stretcher-bearer, not a killer. How could you kill anyone?" Finally, to get his attention, Isaac grabbed his shoulders and shouted at him, "Look me in the eye, soldier, what's this all about?"

Still shaking uncontrollably, Edward slowly gave Isaac an account of his actions. "Sir . . . I wa . . . was looking for wounded in the thickets and heard some screamin' off to me left. It was hard to see fer all the smoke, but I'd know me best friend Tommy's voice anywhere. An' there he was, wounded awful bad, lyin' on the ground, and surrounded by flames—I couldn't get close to 'im. When he saw me, I tried to speak some words o' comfort to 'im, but he said, 'Eddie, ye wouldn't let yer best friend burn to death, would ye? I can bear most any kind o' death, but not burning . . . Please, I beg ye, shoot me!' He could see I was cryin' an' unwillin' to do it.

But, as the flames were startin' to heat up his feet, he continued to beg in the mos' pitiful way, 'Please Eddie . . . God'll forgive ye . . . Ye must do it . . . Do it fer the love of yer best friend . . . Remember, how we bin friends since we were young'uns in Ireland.'

"At that moment I saw a feller with a wounded leg limpin' along a hundred yards from where I was standin'. I ran over to him and directed him to head your way, sir, and then told him I had need of his musket and cartridge pouch. He gave me a queer look, but I insisted that he hand them over. He looked back once over his shoulder as I loaded that instrument of death and then hurried on his way. By this time, me friend Tommy was screamin' in pain, for his legs were beginnin' to burn. Seein' that I had returned and come closer, Tommy cried out, 'Do it Eddie, lad!'

"Well, sir, I *did it*, I shot me best friend in the head, and I even thanked God that I didn't miss. Oh, I am damned fer certain—thankin' God in the act of killin'! What will I ever tell his family?"

It was Isaac's turn to be shaken. *Has it come to this? Must we now offer compassion in the form of a Minié ball?* And then for a moment, the carefully constructed barriers restraining thoughts of Sam's fate collapsed in the face of the collective madness and ruthless logic of war. Surrendering to the deep despair that had been growing within him, he cried out in silence, *Is there an Inner Light? Where is God? Has He abandoned us?* Terrified by this self-revelation, he quickly retreated to the safety of addressing the problem at hand.

"Edward, you will tell no one about what you did, except Fr. Corby. Officially, if anyone asks me, I will say that seeing all the suffering today, your nerves momentarily got the better of you. To your friends, you can honestly say that seeing and hearing soldiers die in the burning underbrush unnerved you and leave it at that. Later, if you can give me the address for Tommy's family, I will write a letter to them, explaining how their son died a heroic death to preserve the Union," Isaac said, rationalizing that the immediate cause of the unfortunate soldier's demise was not so important to share, since his death was indeed as heroic as it was unavoidable. "Edward, you must understand that you did not have any good choice in that terrible situation. But now you must be focused on the work at hand. You couldn't save Tommy, but there will be others whom you can help save. When the fighting settles down, I think you'll feel better if you can talk with Fr. Corby."

"Yes, sir," came Edward's reply with audible relief in his voice.

Later under lantern light, Isaac, Richard Powell, and the other operating surgeons of the First Division of the II Corps spent most of the night performing amputations, wound explorations, and debridement under chloroform anesthesia—a familiar rhythm that would define many of the nights to come. Isaac was surprised at how confident and adept Ezekiel was in assisting at the operating table, especially with the anesthesia. With a modest smile, Ezekiel responded to Richard Powell's compliment regarding his skill. "Dr. Powell, I have been blessed to work with the same mentor that Dr. Burgess had when he was learning the medical art. Dr. Henry Way, a physician member of the Society of Friends in our community, has always been willing to share from the extensive fund of his knowledge and experience." Looking up at Isaac across the makeshift operating table, Richard Powell replied, "Dr. Way must be an exceptionally good teacher."

"He is, Richard, indeed, he is," Isaac warmly affirmed, briefly recalling happier times. "Clearly, two members of the Burgess family have benefited greatly from his wisdom. One thing he would always emphasize to me, was that a surgeon can never have enough light . . . and here we are operating by lantern light!"

As the fighting of the 5th and 6th of May 1864 abated, Isaac and his colleagues did not yet realize that it was just the beginning of almost forty days of continuous warfare. Constant skirmishing, punctuated by large scale combat and the maneuvering of the two behemoths, would translate into many nights with minimal sleep for soldiers of all ranks—but especially the medical staff of both armies. Many expected Grant and Meade to retreat due to the massive losses of wounded, killed, or captured that were nearly twice those of their Confederate foe. Surprisingly, the Army of the Potomac began another southward flanking movement toward Spotsylvania Courthouse to catch Lee off guard. With his uncanny ability to read his opponent's mind, the Rebel commander anticipated the move and beat Grant in the race, setting up the next confrontation.

Grant's motion to the southeast necessitated a change in his base of supply to Fredericksburg on the Rappahannock, which also meant less distance to transport wounded soldiers to more stable medical care, or so it seemed. Unfortunately, because of poor coordination between the army and naval transports, wounded men from the fighting in the Wilderness who had already been sent via ambulance further north for transport from Belle Plain were now ordered back on the evening of May 7 to Fredericksburg. Consequently, many critically injured soldiers spent another twenty-four hours without food and water being jostled on the hot, dusty roads of Virginia before arriving at Fredericksburg, with many dying along the way. It became increasingly evident that no one in the Army of the Potomac had anticipated the magnitude of the need for medical transport that developed with the nearly continuous fighting. With so many ambulances in motion carrying wounded toward the new base of operations, there was an acute shortage of ambulances available for transport at the frontline. As a result, Isaac and his colleagues began to commandeer regular army wagons and any available conveyances to transport the wounded from the battlefield. Without the spring suspensions and other modifications of the ambulances designed to smooth the ride over bumpy roads, transport of wounded soldiers in conventional wagons could be quite traumatic, with some wounded soldiers even dying from exsanguinating hemorrhage following disruption of amputation wounds.

The next major rendezvous between the Army of the Potomac and the Army of Northern Virginia was at a peculiarly shaped salient in the Rebel defenses at Spotsylvania, nicknamed the "Mule Shoe," that jutted out toward the north. Initial attempts in the afternoon of the tenth to storm the defensive works were repulsed with great loss. After the intrepid tactics of a young officer, Colonel Upton, showed promise of success, Grant and Meade decided to make another assault on the Mule Shoe, but with greater numbers of assaulting soldiers and better coordination of effort. A cool rain brought relief from the sultry heat but turned dust into mud, slowing movement of troops and equipment. The assault, scheduled to begin at 4 a.m. on the 12th, was delayed a half-hour due to dense fog.

A deep-throated cheer rumbled back to Isaac at his aid station as soldiers in blue surmounted the outer defenses, engaging in desperate hand-to-hand combat with the surprised defenders as they fanned out to left and right. Within a very short time, the triumphant attackers had captured, wounded, or killed several Rebel generals as well as large numbers of panicked Rebel soldiers, the remainder being driven back in chaos toward their secondary defenses. The victorious Union soldiers had quickly taken possession of nearly a mile of the defensive line in the Confederate center. Unfortunately, succeeding waves of assault columns began to pile up in the crowded trenches, slowing the initial momentum of the assault, which gave much needed time to Lee as he struggled to fill the growing and potentially fatal hole in his center.

As wounded soldiers began to arrive at Isaac's aid station, their initial elation upon the success of the breakthrough was infectious. Joyful exclamations like "this may be the end of Lee's army!" competed with the cries of pain from the wounded, often coming from the same lips. Isaac's mood rose with that of the wounded soldiers. The roar of artillery sending screaming shells over the heads of the attacking Federal troops into the fleeing mass of Rebel soldiers even lost some of its ominous character. One of the wounded noted the sound and said with satisfaction, "I like the sound of that music." Isaac smiled grimly. *I will heartily endorse his sentiments if I never have to hear such "music" again.*

Between the delays occasioned by the increasing congestion of arriving Federal troops in the captured trenches and the rapid response of Lee and his generals, fresh Rebel soldiers rushed to reclaim the lost salient. As the rain continued to fall, vicious close-quarter fighting developed along the line where Federal and Rebel soldiers in the trenches were separated by only a few feet. Possessed of a manic fury, they proceeded to kill each other by thrusting bayonets over or through gaps in the defenses, firing muskets or revolvers at point-blank range, or the more primitive but effective use of their muskets as clubs, or by simple bare-knuckled brawling.

With morning turning to afternoon and the violence continuing unabated, stretcher-bearers struggled to efficiently remove dead and wounded soldiers from the Union's *prize* to make way for fresh soldiers to finish what their fallen comrades had begun. As the hours passed with no break in the fighting, the initial optimism had given way to a mad determination. More than once, wounded soldiers reported seeing their comrades fighting with such intensity that they had lost all sense of fear and concern for self-preservation. During Isaac's examination of what appeared to be a superficial stab wound to the upper abdomen, the wounded soldier exclaimed, "Doc, you wouldn't believe what some of our boys were doin'! Most of us were happy to stick our bayonets through any hole we could find, hopin' we'd make some Reb squeal. An' of course, they were doin' the same, as you can tell by the looks of me. But that weren't enough for some of our boys. One feller, only a few feet from me, jumped up on the parapet and started shoutin' down at the Rebs, cussin' them sumthin' fierce. What I couldn't figger was that they just cussed him back fer the longest time 'til I guess they got tired of it and finally shot the poor feller."

By early evening, still with no break in the fighting after more than twelve hours, Isaac wondered if it would ever end. But then, as if the clouds had parted, an epiphany came to him. *The last vestiges of the so-called rules of engagement for this "civilized" means by which human beings resolve their differences have finally been suspended today. All pretense at being 'civilized' has been dropped, and the true nature of the business is fully manifest. Malice, pure and simple, reigns supreme; the Rebels prefer to die to the last man to preserve their "rights in property" and will never yield in their hatred for the Yankee. For their part, the Yanks clearly reciprocate their foe's sentiments, and now when the Rebels should, in all decency, yield and admit their defeat and yet fail to do so, there is neither grand strategy nor elegant tactics—only 'lex talionis'—an eye for an eye and a tooth for a tooth. And it seems that elaborate weapons of war are no longer necessary to achieve this end; bare hands are more than sufficient for the task! The only brake on this wholesale slaughter seems to be the time required to empty the dead from the trenches so that the living can take their place.*

Only by midnight did the feverish fighting gradually die down, succumbing to physical exhaustion. Reporting to Dr. Powell, who with the assistance of Ezekiel was operating on one of the many wounded, Isaac was struck by the stark contrast between the madness he had been witnessing for nearly the past twenty hours and the quiet, sober demeanor of his cousin as he calmly went about his voluntary duties. *How can I protect him from the contagion of war? He is still pure and undefiled by all this evil. His patience, sense of duty, and compassion have been tonics for the medical staff and brought great credit to the Society of Friends.*

Mired in the Virginia mud, which seemed to have conspired with the rain to favor the Confederate Army, maneuvering by the Army of the Potomac was sufficiently hampered in the coming days as to thwart any gains from the struggle at the Mule Shoe. Sealing the near fatal wound to the Army of Northern Virginia, Lee's soldiers, under cover of darkness in the early morning hours of the 13th, had constructed a new line of trenches and earthworks, which effectively closed off the salient that had been taken at such terrible cost. Not yet willing to acknowledge that they had reached a stalemate with the Rebels, Grant and Meade attempted an abortive flank attack on the Rebel right and then, several days later, returned to have one more go at the now infamous Mule Shoe. The rain and mud, strong Southern allies, eliminated the element of surprise, and Lee was able to effectively anticipate the Federal movements.

Isaac surrendered to a growing sense of futility as he foresaw the imminent slaughter before the assault columns were ordered forward on the morning of the eighteenth. A depressing sense of *déjà vu* was augmented by the nauseating stench of the unburied dead that lay directly in the path of the attacking units. For nearly a week, the decomposing corpses had offered a pungent witness to the foolishness of a repeated assault in that quarter. Even so, Isaac was impressed at how well new Irish reinforcements from the Corcoran Legion acquitted themselves. *They bravely stop Rebel Minié balls just as well as any veteran of the II Corps. Will the stalemate ever end? Are we to remain in constant motion, moving from one venue of death to another until no one is left to kill or be killed?*

After the unsuccessful assault was called off later that morning, the Quaker assistant surgeon mounted his horse and accompanied the ambulances filled with the wounded as they headed to the rear for more definitive medical care. Approaching the division field hospital, his mood lifted briefly as he witnessed his cousin Ezekiel, confidently and efficiently moving among the arriving ambulances, gently assisting in the transfer of the wounded. Dismounting from his horse, Isaac was approached by a noncommissioned officer, who startled him with the words "Dr. Burgess, you have a letter."

Isaac accepted the letter, but with growing anxiety as to its nature, he carefully avoided looking at it until he had entered his tent and could sit down on his camp stool. His hands trembling, he turned the envelope over and immediately recognized the handwriting of Louisa Johnson but was perplexed by the return address, *Mound City General Hospital, Illinois*. He hesitated, afraid to open it. *Where is Mound City, Illinois? Is it possible that Sam was wounded and taken to a military hospital?* Paralyzed by fear regarding his friend's fate, at the very moment of revelation he held back, terrified of the contents in that small envelope.

CHAPTER TWENTY-SEVEN

*"I hope I may never see a Negro soldier,
or I cannot be . . . a Christian soldier."*

CONFEDERATE SOLDIER

THE AUTHOR OF THE missive which Isaac Burgess so dreaded to read had experienced her own journey of uncertainty, denial, and self-revelation on the way to its creation. It was impossible to forestall the transition from brilliant orange to the more somber purple of the setting sun on the evening of April 15, 1864. Louisa Johnson searched the gathering gloom on the western horizon in vain for some ray of hope as she stood on the upper deck of a US naval transport heading north on the Mississippi River. A wry smile inadvertently came to her lips as she remembered how her students had often asked her to repeat the Biblical story of Joshua making the sun stand still. *It really was about stopping time,* she thought. *If only such miracles could occur in these terrible times. I would have gone into that fort and dragged my foolish brother and pupil out of that madness. Why wouldn't Sam listen to reason?* Tears flooded her eyes as she stared into the deepening dusk. *Did he . . . they survive?*

Rumors of the catastrophe at Fort Pillow had spread like a plague through Memphis early on the 13th of April. The emerging facts were rapidly transmuted to suit the prejudices of the audience. As Louisa and Rebecca were walking that morning to the contraband hospital near Fort Pickering, where they shared nursing duties with Penelope Wormeley, she could not help but notice the surly looks of triumph on many faces they encountered in the street. As they passed an aging belle of Memphis, whose charms had diminished with time and her growing corpulence, she haughtily observed, "Our General Forrest has clearly demonstrated the utter incapacity of Negroes for soldiering." And then, focusing her venom directly at Louisa, "Now mark my words. Our fair city will be liberated soon from *uppity* Negroes and every form of Yankee filth!" Sensing that Louisa was about to erupt with a withering response, Rebecca had gently placed her hand on her friend's arm but to no avail. For Louisa was in no mood to appease the sensibilities of Southern *gentility*. "Madam, there is filth that can be washed away with soap and water, and sadly, there is another filth that is not so easily cleansed. If you take pleasure in the Confederate policy to give no quarter to the Negro in Federal uniform, and if the rumors of this policy being carried out at Fort Pillow in yesterday's battle are true, may heaven help you! For 'he, which is filthy, let him be filthy still . . .'" Rebecca was relieved that they had reached their destination and could disappear into the contraband hospital before the now-irate woman could summon a crowd to *defend* her *honor* from the *impertinence* of an *uppity* Negro.

When news of the arrival of the hospital ship *USS Red Rover* carrying survivors from Fort Pillow reached the women, they rushed to the docks, only to be disappointed when neither Sam nor Nappy were among the wounded. Compounding their distress, descriptions from eyewitnesses confirmed initial reports of a terrible atrocity in which surrendering Negro soldiers were given no quarter after the battle. In despair, a distraught Louisa begged the ship's captain for any information about other survivors. After checking telegraphic dispatches, he came back and said, "Miss, there was another ship, the *Platte Valley*, which picked up some of the wounded before the *Red Rover* arrived. It went upriver—I believe its destination is the US General Hospital at Mound City, Illinois. You might inquire there." Without further reflection, Louisa decided to head upriver as soon as she could book passage on a military transport to look for Sam and Nappy among the wounded Negro soldiers at Mound City.

Early on the 15th she had boarded a northern-bound stern wheel transport, the *New Madrid*. Louisa ignored the mixture of curious stares and leering gestures of some of the white passengers, who couldn't help but observe the apparent incongruity of a fashionably dressed, dignified black woman, which conflicted with their expectations of an amalgam of plain homespun and servility. Notwithstanding her ability *and willingness* to stare down potential adversaries, she found that the military pass she carried from *Colonel Eaton, General Superintendent of Contrabands*, removed most barriers she encountered on the voyage. Later that day, as they approached the still smoldering ruin of Fort Pillow, the captain had sent out a warning to the passengers to clear the decks because of reports of Rebel soldiers lingering in the area who seemed to have a predilection for taking potshots at passing Yankee vessels.

Despite the captain's warning, Fort Pillow had exerted a magnetic attraction for Louisa. Perhaps if she strained her vision sufficiently in the direction whence arose all her anxieties, she might divine the truth of what had happened to Sam and Nappy. As she stared up at the bluff upon which the ill-fated fort stood, her imagination was rife with images of the chaos and mayhem that had reigned there only two days before. Caught up as she was in her thoughts, she failed to notice the first—and even the second—whistle and thud of Minié balls that, passing close to her head, became embedded in the wall of the steamboat behind her. A sailor who was safely hidden behind a barrier nearby shouted at her, "Get away from the railing and seek cover!" At the same moment she heard the sailor, Louisa, to her consternation, could see the source of her close encounter with death. Grinning with triumph, a mounted Rebel soldier apparently felt sufficiently confident of his own safety to leave the cover of the woods near the base of the bluff and fire upon the transport. Ducking for cover, Louisa watched with horrified fascination as the young Rebel boldly capered about on horseback in full view of the transport. She jumped involuntarily as a rifled musket was discharged a few feet from her. The bold capering of the young Rebel trooper suddenly ceased as he dropped from his saddle. The same voice which had peremptorily ordered Louisa to seek cover had then expressed a deep satisfaction. "Damned Rebel! It's bad enough that they slaughter our soldiers without mercy, but then to taunt us after the act." Now as the last vestiges of the sunset faded in the west, Louisa was haunted by the image of the young Rebel trooper's face, at one moment marked by an ugly grin and then in the next, transformed into the startle of a sinner about to meet his Maker.

A tidal wave of suffering had engulfed many lives because of General William Tecumseh Sherman's order to abandon Corinth in December 1863. Its effects extending into the winter of 1864 upended the lives of the contrabands as well as the aid workers and teachers committed to their education and support. Louisa Johnson, Rebecca Burgess, and Penelope Wormeley, each from their own perspectives, could appreciate its destructive implications. Their work which had already borne so much fruit was now threatened and potentially in jeopardy. In a conversation shortly after learning of Sherman's intentions, Louisa placed their fears for the future and their frustration at the sudden turn of events within a larger context. "It seems that our work here has been strangled in its infancy by the whim of a military commander. But notwithstanding our own bitter disappointment, what is to be the fate of the contrabands, who so recently have tasted many of the joys of citizenship with their own homes and hopes for the future—has it been no more than an ephemeral dream?"

Louisa remembered how, in consequence of Sherman's precipitous order to abandon Corinth, even the local inhabitants were left in a quandary. She still marveled at the unlikely friendship that the two Yankee missionaries had developed with Penelope Wormeley. In witnessing the respectful working relationship, indeed friendship, that had developed between her brother and the Southern matron, she was especially struck by the steadfast character of Penelope's commitment to her voluntary nursing duties, despite the vicious way her husband had treated her in response to the town gossips' groundless assertions regarding her *scandalous* collaboration with a *n____r* from the North. She smiled to think that greed had made it possible for Penelope to continue her service among the contrabands—specifically, Penelope's uncle's greed. Regardless of their professed political sympathies, Corinth's merchants had acquired a decided taste for Yankee greenbacks, and Penelope's uncle was no exception. Realizing that opportunity was moving away from Corinth toward Memphis, Chalmers Endicott had decided to move his business accordingly. Between this fortuitous decision and the fact that her husband had managed to hire contraband labor for his plantations and had departed to supervise their work, Penelope was free to move with her uncle and aunt to Memphis. Her aunt continued to delight in caring for the Wormeley children, while Penelope was again free to volunteer in a contraband hospital, but now one in Memphis.

Louisa realized that since Sam's work with Penelope, Rebecca was no longer needed to play the role of mediator between Penelope and herself. *If I never encounter another honest, loving white Southern soul, I can truly say that I have known one whom I can respect and without hesitation call my friend.* As soon as the thought came, she realized how important Penelope had become to her. *There is at least one Southerner who would never countenance the barbarities perpetrated at Fort Pillow, and one who will grieve for my brother, if he is no more.* Again, the tears came, and this time she gave full freedom to her fears. *Oh, how could it be possible that either of them survived such horrors!*

The *New Madrid* turned up the Ohio River on the 16th, arriving at Mound City late that evening. Louisa, with Colonel Eaton's pass in hand, headed directly for the naval hospital. Struck by the general cleanliness and sense of order, she made a remark in passing to one of the hospital's nurses, who replied with a smile, "You should have seen this place before Mother Bickerdyke took it in hand."

With growing trepidation, Louisa approached the office of the Medical Director of Mound City General Hospital, Surgeon Horace Wardner, to seek permission to search for Sam and Nappy among the wounded. After listening to Louisa explain her mission and reading the pass from Colonel Eaton, Dr. Wardner, who had been scratching away at a report by the light of a kerosene lamp, without looking up, said, "Well, Miss, I'm sorry, but it may require quite a search on your part. We have survivors scattered and isolated throughout our many wards to prevent an outbreak of erysipelas." Discerning from her speech and her fine dress that she must be a woman of refined sensibilities, the busy surgeon added, "The extreme condition of the poor unfortunates who arrived from Fort Pillow has greatly disturbed all of us who are seasoned medical staff. Perhaps it would be better for you to leave the names of your loved ones with our hospital steward, so that we can make a thorough search for them in the morning and then notify you of their presence and condition."

Not to be put off by such genteel concerns, Louisa placed her gloved hand on the surgeon's desk and said, "Sir, I cannot wait until morning. I have nursed wounded soldiers. Please, permit me to begin a search immediately." Finally, looking up at this persistent female who would not leave him in peace to complete the pile of paperwork on his desk, he was startled to see that Louisa possessed a darker complexion than expected from her speech and dress. His face acquiring a slight smirk, he said, "Well, in your case, the search might be easier to complete. He got up and left the office briefly and returned with a middle-aged nurse. Gesturing toward Louisa, he told the nurse, "Miss . . ." "Miss Louisa Johnson," Louisa interjected. "Yes. Miss Johnson would like to search for her loved ones this evening. Since you are responsible for Ward N, I think you might be able to help her complete her search this evening."

Louisa followed the nurse, who led her through one ward after another filled with convalescing soldiers to a remote ward at the back of the hospital. Before crossing the threshold, she turned to the middle-aged white woman who was on duty that night and asked, "Ward N? This seems to be a rather crowded ward. I recall Surgeon Wardner saying that the wounded from Fort Pillow had been spread out among many wards to prevent an outbreak of erysipelas."

"Yes, Miss Johnson. As you have just witnessed there are many wards in this hospital that are each identified by a letter of the alphabet. Ward N is for the colored soldiers. There weren't many of them that arrived on the Platte Valley, and the ones that did make the journey were in a sorry condition when they arrived. Two died on the way north and one after disembarking."

"Ward N—how very convenient. Of course, the letter *N* is for Negroes, which entitles them to one ward all their own. So much for erysipelas precautions!" Louisa's bitter sarcasm collapsed as she fully appreciated the sad, bewildered expression on the nurse's face who had accompanied her to the ward. Her voice now breaking with emotion, Louisa asked, "Do y— . . . you know if there is a Sergeant Samuel Johnson or a Corporal Napoleon Heyward among the patients here?"

"I'm sorry Miss, but most of them have been too weak to communicate much with the staff, and it appears that anything of value—including personal items that might help identify them—was taken by the Rebel soldiers. Only a few have been able to tell us their names and the units in which they served. If the sergeant or the corporal are present among the wounded here, they have not yet been identified. But come with me as I make my rounds. It will be a balm to their spirits to see one of their own women come and speak a few words of comfort to them. I must warn you that several of the poor fellows don't quite seem right in the head. They often cry out in their sleep, apparently reliving the massacre in their dreams. Even though several are swathed in bandages so that the most disfiguring wounds are covered, you may still find their appearance disturbing."

"In addition to my teaching responsibilities, I have served as a nurse . . ." Her guide interrupted her, ". . . of extreme combat casualties? Not only were these soldiers wounded severely, but they bear the marks of torture." Swallowing hard as a tear rolled down her cheek, Louisa responded in a low steady tone, "No, only a few gunshot wounds, mostly hospitalized patients with pneumonia, diarrhea, typhoid . . . But I *must* see each of them."

The nurse gently placed her hand on Louisa's forearm and, looking directly into her eyes, said with an unexpected vehemence, "I'm a widow. My only child is languishing in a Southern prison, somewhere in Georgia—he was captured at Chickamauga, fighting to end slavery. I volunteered to serve as a nurse in this terrible war because I share his firm opposition to that wicked peculiar institution of the South. What the Rebels have done to these poor unfortunate men is the most terrible and compelling evidence that I have ever witnessed of the evil nature of slavery—its unspeakable cruelty to the Negro and the depth of spiritual degradation to which those who would enslave their fellow man have fallen. The Rebels who committed this violence have descended to the level of wild beasts." Pausing, her face flushed with emotion, the nurse grasped Louisa's hands in her own and said in a gentler tone, "Let's go visit some suffering souls in need of healing. I hope you can find your loved ones and that they have somehow miraculously escaped this great tragedy."

"Nurse . . . I don't know your name."

"Nurse Johnson, Mrs. Rachel Johnson. It seems we not only share a revulsion for slavery but also our surnames."

"Mrs. Johnson, please forgive my bitter outburst about Ward N."

"You needn't apologize to me. It's entirely unjust to treat colored soldiers in such a prejudicial manner. Sadly, many of the white soldiers would loudly object and even mistreat the colored soldiers if we attempted to mix them. Dr. Wardner has assured me that he will assemble additional tent wards to provide adequate isolation, if it appears that the colored soldiers begin to develop erysipelas or some other form of contagion."

When she was faced with the actual prospect of crossing the threshold into Ward N, Louisa hesitated. Rachel Johnson, who had walked on ahead, was about to introduce Louisa to the first patient when she realized that her guest had not yet entered the ward. With a smile that contained a full measure of compassion acquired through her own suffering, she gently motioned to Louisa, who now—thoroughly embarrassed and flustered—quickly joined her.

"I apologize for my hesitation."

"My dear Miss Johnson, I should be quite surprised if you were not at least a bit hesitant."

Wiping her moist cheeks with a handkerchief, Louisa gave Rachel Johnson a profound look of gratitude before turning to greet the first wounded soldier. To her utter surprise, the barely recognizable human form who was nearly buried beneath a mass of bandages extending from head to toe, cried out in joy, "Why it's Miss Louisa—an angel has come to visit us!" Other wounded soldiers nearby cast looks of incredulity toward the voice buried in bandages while Louisa struggled to identify the owner of the voice.

"Oh, Miss Louisa, it's Ransom . . . Ransom Anderson. You taught me to read and write back in Corinth."

"Of course, Ransom Anderson, one of my better students; thank God you're alive! By the number of bandages you've acquired, it looks like the Rebels hurt you badly. Are you suffering a lot, my friend?"

"Well, Miss Louisa, I must confess to hurtin' in many places, but then the pain reminds me that I'm alive. We learned that the Rebel soldiers don't take kindly to Negro soldiers fightin' them, so when we surrendered, they wouldn't give us quarter. Dr. Black, my surgeon, says that I'm the very first patient he's ever had who has been wounded by both gunshots and saber cuts." Pointing to his chest, Ransom added with a laugh, "Dr. Black thinks I might survive the wound here, since I'm still breathing. Oh! I shouldn't have laughed—it does make it hurt so. Anyway, he thinks I'm somethin' special, with all my wounds and such. I told him I'd just as soon not be so special if I could've missed that fight."

"Ransom, do you know what happened to my brother Sam or my friend Nappy in the battle?" Louisa asked, trying to suppress her emotions. The tone of the voice buried in bandages changed from jocular to somber as Ransom slowly responded to Louisa's question. "Miss Louisa, I wasn't in the same company with Sam and Nappy. But during the fight, our artillery pieces were close to each other in the fort. Both those fellas were in the thick of the fightin' and gave the Rebels hell! Oh, pardon me for usin' bad language—I got excited rememberin' the fight. What I meant to say is that you would be mighty proud of them. They were a real credit to our people. During the truce, the Rebels cheated and snuck up right close to our defenses. After the truce ended, they swarmed over our breastworks, and we had no choice but to surrender. Since they wouldn't give us quarter, we had to run for our lives. Durin' all that commotion I lost sight of Sam and Nappy. I'm sorry Miss, I don't rightly know what happened to 'em after the Rebels took the fort."

As they moved on to the next wounded soldier, Rachel Johnson, turning to Louisa, remarked with admiration, "I've read in the newspapers of the extraordinary work done at Corinth with the contrabands. I never thought I would meet one of the brave souls who accomplished so much in such a short time. It is an honor to meet you, Miss Johnson. I only wish it were under happier circumstances."

"Please address me by my given name of Louisa."

"Only if you will address me as Rachel."

"Rachel, I am surprised that news of the Corinth Contraband Camp made its way north. Considering the present situation, it seems as if it were nothing more than a passing dream—a dream become nightmare. I had many students like Ransom, so eager to learn but ultimately subject to the whims of generals and the exigencies of war."

Louisa's presence and kind words brought comfort to many of Ransom's comrades who were sufficiently conscious to respond. But she experienced a growing frustration as she encountered many others who were either incoherent because of delirium or remained unconscious due to their severe injuries. After passing by each patient in the ward and not recognizing Sam or Nappy, Louisa grasped Rachel's hand and plaintively said, "There must be more colored soldiers here." Reciprocating Louisa's grasp, Rachel Johnson shook her head. "No, my dear, I'm so sorry. We have passed the bed of every colored survivor of the massacre that is in this hospital." Fighting off a sense of complete despair, Louisa replied, "Then I must go back and carefully examine each of the soldiers who did not respond to me whom I could not identify."

"But Louisa, that leaves us with only the most severely wounded men, many of whom have faces and heads covered in bandages. Those are the poor souls who have been either delirious or unconscious since they arrived here."

"Perhaps if I call for them by name . . ." Louisa's voice broke as tears began to again flow down her cheeks. Suddenly, she turned and rushed back to a cluster of heavily bandaged recumbent wounded soldiers crying, "Sam . . . Samuel Johnson, are you here? Nappy . . . Napoleon Heyward, are you here?" Repeating her call a second time, she looked anxiously around her, hoping to see some sign of recognition, and yet there was nothing. Rachel Johnson quietly approached Louisa and, gently taking her arm, said, "Let's go rest for now, and if you wish, we can come again tomorrow morning." Now frantic, tearing free from Rachel Johnson's benevolent grasp, Louisa summoned her most imperious schoolmarm voice and almost shouted, "Samuel Johnson, Napoleon Heyward, speak to me! It's Louisa."

Out of the corner of her eye, Louisa noticed a slight movement coming from one of the wounded to her left. Not unlike her former student Ransom, the wounded individual's head was also swathed in bandages but even more so, since his left eye was completely covered. Being propped up on his right side, initially Louisa could not see any facial features until the wounded man slowly, and with evident pain, attempted to turn in her direction. In concert with the movement, a faint murmur, no more distinct than water in an eddy, came from the wounded man. Encouraged even by this incoherence, Louisa moved toward him and emphatically repeated, "It's Louisa Johnson, I'm here!" And almost as if it were a faint echo, came the tentative reply, "Miss Louisa . . . here?"

At the very moment she heard her name spoken by that familiar voice, Louisa Johnson, the imperious and ofttimes sarcastic schoolmarm, discovered a deep truth hidden within her soul. The owner of the voice that echoed her name was dearer to her than her own life. This time, crying out with a mixture of joy and relief—"Nappy, you're alive!"—she managed to awaken the few remaining wounded who had still been sleeping in that part of *Ward N*. Before she could pounce on him, Rachel Johnson placed a restraining hand on Louisa's shoulder and whispered, "I am so happy for you, Louisa. Please take care regarding his wounds to avoid causing him more pain."

Now assuming her companion's whisper, Louisa replied, "Rachel, thank you for warning me. Reason nearly left me for the joy of finding him alive. Where are his wounds?"

"From the doctor's examination, he is missing his left eye, there is a gunshot wound extending through the palm of his left hand, another has traveled through the muscle of his right shoulder, and finally, he has another wound in his right thigh. It seems a miracle that none of the gunshot wounds touched bone. Other than his eye, all his wounds have entrance and exit sites—amazingly, the bullets passed through his tissues. The surgeon could find no evidence of retained bullets or their fragments, while some of the wounds exhibited powder burns. He thinks these features may reflect the likelihood that the wounds were received at close range. Regardless, your friend lost considerable blood, and even the whiskey we gave him for the shock exerted minimal, if any, benefit. This is the first coherent speech I have heard from him. His doctor has expressed concern for his survival. Louisa, your presence may be what is necessary to bring him back to the land of the living."

Pulling up a stool on the opposite side of Nappy's cot, Louisa cautiously placed her hand on his right forearm and began to gently stroke his skin. After what appeared to be a considerable effort, his right eye fluttered opened for a moment in which he once more murmured, "Miss Louisa" and then sank back into unconsciousness. After Louisa had kept vigil for more than two hours at Nappy's side, Rachel Johnson returned after attending to the other patients' needs on Ward N. "Louisa, it is past two o'clock in the morning. Please come and get some rest. You can share my room with me. There is another bed that is not claimed. The nurses' apartments are adjacent to the hospital. You won't be of any assistance to your friend if you don't get some sleep."

Louisa's voice rose in protest, "But I must stay with him. Perhaps he will awaken and tell me of Sam's fate. I'm not sure I could sleep anyway without knowing what happened to Sam!" After a second, more vociferous declaration of her brother's name, both Louisa and Rachel noticed that Nappy's brow furrowed, and after a long pause, an answer of sorts came as a solitary tear emerged from his right eye and, overflowing its source, traveled slowly down his cheek.

CHAPTER TWENTY-EIGHT

" . . . in all my operations since the war began,
I have conducted the war on civilized principles."

GENERAL NATHAN BEDFORD FORREST, JUNE 1864

SLEEP ELUDED LOUISA AS she reclined on the extra cot in Rachel Johnson's quarters. *All I have is a solitary tear for an answer from a man who is more dead than alive, and yet it speaks volumes regarding Sam's fate,* she thought, stifling a sob. *Perhaps I'm reading too much into it. Tears are associated with pain—surely, Nappy is in pain, and it signifies nothing else.* But no matter how she attempted to rationalize that teardrop, she could not escape from an overwhelming sense that her brother was no longer among the living. Finally, she drifted off into a fitful sleep . . . there was Sam's face smiling down at her as she lay on the cot. *"Samuel Johnson, you gave me quite a fright! I thought you were gone. So, what do you have to say for yourself?"* Such an infuriating brother—only smiling! *"I want answers, Sam. Speak to me!"* But Sam only continued to smile as he reached down to wipe the tears from his sister's face. Louisa awakened with a start to Rachel Johnson's gentle touch as she wiped her cheeks and forehead with a damp cloth.

"Louisa, you've been quite agitated in your sleep this past half-hour. Were you having a nightmare, my dear? I was beginning to worry that you might be developing a fever, so I began to apply moist compresses to your face. Only now did you finally awaken."

"Oh, Rachel, I saw my brother Sam. As I lay here, he was smiling down at me with such a kind, loving expression. But he wouldn't speak to me. He was so vivid—and then I awakened to see and feel you ministering to me."

"Louisa, is it possible that his smile was the answer? What a blessing you were given to see him one more time! I had a similar experience after my husband died, which I will always cherish. Perhaps the dead are sometimes permitted a final encounter to bring comfort to those who will miss them the most."

As her tears flowed freely, Louisa nodded. "Last night, I refused to accept the meaning of my friend Napoleon Heyward's solitary tear, even though I *knew* in my marrow what it meant. To see my brother once more, and with such a smile on his face—God's mercy comes unexpectedly and unbidden! Oh, how I still wish it weren't so, and yet I thank God for that smile. My brother's at peace in a better place."

Later that morning, Louisa sent the following telegram to her family in Indiana and to Rebecca in Memphis:

> April 17, 1864. Arrived safely in Mound City, IL. Thorough search of colored ward at general hospital made and Napoleon Heyward located. He is critically wounded and unconscious— outcome uncertain. Sam not located yet. Will remain here to nurse Napoleon while awaiting more news of Sam. Louisa

Although I am certain of Sam's fate, I will await further confirmation before dashing the remaining hope of my family. Coming so soon after losing Father, this will be devastating to Mother. I cannot hold back from Rebecca, though. She will suspect there is more than what is conveyed in the telegram. But I better not write anything to Isaac until I am absolutely certain. He doesn't need this blow right now, as he faces all the suffering of the spring campaigning.

With trembling hands, Louisa assisted Rachel Johnson with Nappy's dressing changes. Nappy groaned but did not fully awaken while they gently manipulated his limbs. Rachel Johnson, anticipating Louisa's question, said, "For painful wound care we usually use chloroform anesthesia. Dr. Wardner has advised against it for the present with Nappy because he is concerned that his heart might not sustain any adverse effects from the drug." Feeling Nappy's pulse at the wrist, Louisa marveled, "His heart rate is quite rapid, but at least it is not irregular. I hope it does not portend a serious fever."

"I see that you have had significant experience as a nurse," Rachel commented with admiration as they began to remove the dressing from

252

Nappy's left hand. Seeing Nappy grimace from pain as the dressing was being removed, Louisa offered some soothing words as they continued. She gasped upon examining the wound and hole that extended through the palm of her friend's hand. "I've never seen such marks around a gunshot wound!"

"Neither had any of us, here at Mound City. These are powder burns from a weapon discharged at extremely close range."

"Oh, I see some movement in the wound—maggots!"

"Does their presence distress you, Louisa?" Rachel asked sympathetically.

"I guess it is impossible to not be disgusted by them, but this is not the first time I have seen them. My first encounter with our little wriggly friends was as a child when I saw them in the gunshot wound of a runaway slave my family cared for back in Indiana. It looks like they have been doing a nice job of cleaning up the deeper part of this wound. How I wish we could find a means of relieving at least some of the pain in his wounds!"

When they shifted their focus to the bandage over Nappy's left eye, Rachel offered to do the wound care herself, since the wound might be particularly distressing. Louisa insisted on helping but nearly fainted when she was confronted by the hollow eye socket where there once had been an organ of sight. In a horrified whisper, she said, "It looks as if his eye was gouged out! Thank God, there are no maggots in this wound. I'm not sure I could bear seeing them here."

"Eyewitnesses have reported that most of the wounds were received after our soldiers surrendered. They appear to have been inflicted by an enemy intent on murder . . ." ". . . and torture!" Louisa interjected, tears welling up in her eyes. "What kind of monsters could perpetrate such acts on soldiers who have surrendered?"

"Only those who refuse to recognize their humanity. Louisa, some of our wounded who have been able to speak of the massacre report that the Rebel soldiers repeatedly shouted, 'No quarter for n_____rs,' insisting that the colored soldiers in Federal uniforms were slave insurrectionists and would be dealt with as such."

As they were speaking, a medical officer had quietly approached and was observing Louisa with interest as she assisted Rachel with Nappy's wound care. "Miss, you seem to be quite familiar with dressing wounds. It looks like Rachel has found an excellent assistant." Looking up from their task, Rachel smiled and said, "Dr. Gordon, please allow me to introduce Miss Louisa Johnson, a missionary teacher and volunteer nurse from Oberlin College. She is a close friend of this patient, whose name, it turns out, is Napoleon Heyward, otherwise known by his nickname of *Nappy*. Miss Johnson is also hoping to find her brother, Samuel, or some news regarding his fate. He also fought in the battle at Fort Pillow, but sadly, he is not among the survivors on Ward N."

"I am very pleased to meet you, Miss Johnson. My full name is Dr. Stewart Gordon, and I am an acting assistant surgeon, US Army, currently serving as the medical officer in charge of this ward. As you may have already learned from Mrs. Johnson, most of us who are assigned to Ward N consider it a privilege to serve the wounded Negro soldiers from this tragedy. Like Mrs. Johnson, I am a committed abolitionist. If there is anything I can do to assist you during this distressing time, please do not hesitate to ask." As he was about to move on, Dr. Gordon turned back and, motioning to Louisa, drew her aside and spoke to her in low tones. "Your friend has been through a very difficult experience at the hands of the Rebels—truly beyond the comprehension of decent folk. Before he lapsed into unconsciousness shortly after his arrival here, he told us that in addition to his horrific wounds inflicted by the Rebels, they had buried him alive. I think you can appreciate that his survival thus far is nothing short of miraculous. If he regains his faculties, it might be advisable to not press him for details of the battle, his wounding, and the horrific treatment he received from the Rebel soldiers until he initiates that conversation."

Stunned by this revelation, Louisa was speechless. But as Dr. Gordon began to move on to the next patient, recovering her composure, she grasped his sleeve and said, "Thank you, Dr. Gordon, for sharing this information with me. I will exercise due caution, for I truly do not want to add to his suffering or impede his recovery. There is one request I would like to make, if possible."

"Please, tell me."

"I understand the hesitation to use chloroform for the dressing changes because of his tenuous condition, but he clearly winces and groans in pain during wound care. From a friend who is an assistant surgeon in the Army of the Potomac, I have learned that it is common practice to place morphine powder in combat wounds at aid stations near the frontline for acute pain relief. Would it be possible to try sprinkling morphine powder in my friend's wounds during dressing changes? It might help reduce some of his pain without posing the risk of chloroform."

"Miss Johnson, that is an interesting suggestion. I will check our inventory of morphine. If there is enough to meet the other needs of our patients, I will gladly help you apply it to his wounds. It would be quite interesting to determine its efficacy for pain relief later in wound care."

"Thank you, Dr. Gordon, for considering my request. The powder burn on his left hand seems to be particularly painful. Perhaps we could start there."

On the following day, Dr. Gordon appeared for the dressing change. Witnessing Nappy's distress as the bandage was removed, he observed, "It is not clear how application of the morphine powder will address this pain."

"No sir, my hope is that it will reduce his pain during the *next* dressing change," Louisa replied, thanking him for his willingness to make the trial. Both Louisa and Dr. Gordon were gratified to see less wincing and hear almost no groaning during subsequent dressing changes. "It's rather curious, and my eyes may deceive me, but the wound looks better after several days of applying the morphine powder," Dr. Gordon enthused.

Realizing how tenuous Nappy's condition was, Louisa also pressed the hospital cooks for milk punch, beef broth, and eggnog, which she administered to Nappy over the next several days, first coaxing him to cautiously taste and swallow increasing amounts of the fluid nutrition. She realized that her first attempts were too aggressive when he coughed violently after partly aspirating a rather large swallow. After the rough start, she established a rhythm of small feedings administered with a spoon every one to two hours but graduating to larger volumes after the second day. Each day she could see a steady improvement in Nappy's condition and his ability to participate in his care. His pulse slowed, the dressing changes caused less pain, initial fears of fever and contagion were unfounded, and Louisa reluctantly had to admit that even the maggots had done their bit to help. Early the fifth day, after beginning her aggressive nursing regime, she sat at Nappy's bedside pondering the terror of being buried alive as she stroked his arm, when she felt a hand gently touch her left hand. Shifting her gaze toward her patient, she was overjoyed to see Nappy's face suffused with the warmth of a smile while his remaining eye glowed with recognition. "Miss Louisa, my angel! Where am I? Is this all a dream? But you feel very real to me."

"Napoleon Heyward, I assure you this is the real flesh and blood Louisa Johnson sitting beside you stroking your arm. I thank God you're alive, my love."

"My love . . . ?"

"Pardon me, Miss Johnson for intruding on your conversation. I see that your excellent nursing has significantly moved our patient along the road to recovery. Corporal Heyward, I am your doctor, Acting Assistant Surgeon Dr. Stewart Gordon. Do you remember anything of your journey here?"

"Only snatches here and there, sir."

"You are a patient on Ward N of the general hospital here in Mound City, Illinois. We're just upriver from Cairo. Do you remember what brought you here?"

Involuntarily shuddering, Nappy nodded. "Yes, sir. I was wounded at Fort Pillow." At this turn in the conversation, Louisa grasped Dr. Gordon's sleeve and, pulling him away from Nappy's bedside, said, "Please excuse us for a moment, Nappy."

"Dr. Gordon, didn't you advise me just a few days ago to not interrogate Napoleon about his travail because it might impede, even harm his recovery?"

"Miss Johnson, forgive me. I did give you that advice, and now I am under orders to disregard my own medical advice. There is a congressional delegation here to investigate the atrocities committed at Fort Pillow. Specifically, senior members of the Committee on the Conduct of the War are here to take sworn testimony from survivors. Napoleon has made remarkable progress under your care. I am certain the committee members will want to hear his testimony, especially since Dr. Wardner has already told them that we have a wounded soldier who had been buried alive. I was about to ask Napoleon if he would be willing to give testimony—I would never force him."

"Of course he will not refuse to testify. He's not the sort of man to refuse such a request; he will see it as his duty as a soldier. I abhor what the Rebels have done at Fort Pillow, but to make Nappy relive that experience now—you may be opening a wound that was finally beginning to heal!"

When Louisa and Dr. Gordon returned to his bedside, Nappy could see distress written in their faces, and—partially divining the issue at hand—he said, "Dr. Gordon, if you want to know more about the battle and how I was injured, I am willing to tell you about my experience." Looking directly at Louisa, he added slowly with sadness, "I have information of a sorrowful nature that I must share with Miss Johnson, as well."

Dr. Gordon, pleased by Nappy's willingness, quickly explained that representatives from the Congressional Committee on the Conduct of the War were in the building and would momentarily be coming to his bedside to take his sworn testimony. Shifting his gaze back and forth between Louisa and Dr. Gordon, Nappy suddenly surprised them both as he laughed, "My best friend, Sam . . . I mean, Sergeant Johnson, liked to say, 'Most regular people don't mind waiting a bit, but you must never, ever keep a politician waiting!' Well, Dr. Gordon, here I am. I'm not going anywhere."

"Your name is . . . ?"

"Corporal Napoleon Heyward of Company C, 6th US Colored Heavy Artillery. My friends call me Nappy."

"Do you swear to tell the truth, the whole truth, and nothing but the truth, so help you God?"

"Yes, sir."

"Where were you raised?"

"In Mississippi, sir."

"Have you been a slave?"

"Yes, sir."

"Were you in Fort Pillow at the time it was captured by the Rebels?"

"Yes, sir."

"When were you wounded?"

"I was wounded after we all surrendered, not before."

"At what time?"

"They shot me when we came up the hill from down by the river."

"Why did you go up the hill?"

"They called me up."

"Did you see who shot you?"

"Yes, sir; I did not know him."

"One of the Rebels?"

"Yes, sir."

"How near was he to you?"

"I was right at him; I had my hand on the end of his gun."

"What did he say to you?"

"He said, 'Whose gun are you holding?' I said, 'Nobody's.' He said, 'God damn you; I will shoot you,' and then he shot me. I let go, and then another one shot me."

"Were many shot at the same time?"

"Yes, sir, lots of them, lying all 'round like hogs."

"Did you see anyone burned?"

"No, sir."

"Did you see anybody buried alive?"

"Nobody but me."

"Were you buried alive?"

"Yes, sir; they thought they had killed me. I lay there till about sundown, when they threw us in a hollow and commenced throwing dirt on us."

"Did you say anything?"

"No, sir; I did not want to speak to them. I knew if I said anything they would kill me. They covered me up in a hole; they covered me up, all but one side of my head. I heard someone else say they ought not to bury a man who was alive. I commenced working the dirt away, and one of the secesh made a young one dig me out. They dug me out, and I was carried not far off to a fire."

"How long did you stay there?"

"I stayed there that night and until the next morning, and then I slipped off. I heard them say the n____rs had to go away from there before the gunboat came, and that they would kill the n____rs. The gunboat commenced shelling up there, and they commenced moving off. I heard them up there shooting. They wanted me to go with them, but I would not go. I turned around and came down to the riverbank and got on the gunboat."

"How did you lose your eye?"

"They knocked me down with a carbine, and then they jabbed it out."

"Was that before you were shot?"

"Yes, sir."

"After you had surrendered?"

"Yes, sir; I was going up the hill, a man came down and met me; he had his gun in his hand and whirled it around and knocked me down, and then took the end of his carbine and jabbed it in my eye and shot me."

"Were any Rebel officers around when the Rebels were killing our men?"

"Yes, sir; lots of them."

"Did they try to keep their men from killing our men?"

"I never heard them say so. I know General Forrest rode his horse over me three or four times. I did not know him until I heard his men call his name. He said to some Negro men there that he knew them, that they had been in his *n____r* yard in Memphis. He said he was not worth five dollars when he started and had got rich trading in Negroes."

"Were any white men buried with you?"

"Yes, sir."

"Were any buried alive?"

"I heard that one white man was buried alive; I did not see him."

"Who said that?"

"A young man; he said they ought not to have done it. He stayed in there all night; I do not know as he ever got out."

At this point in his testimony, Nappy was showing clear signs of exhaustion. The honorable member of Congress Daniel Gooch, satisfied with the wealth of detail and its graphic character, thanked Nappy for his testimony and moved on to the next survivor. Tears streaming down her face, Louisa urged him to rest. Offering a wan smile, Nappy responded, "But my angel, I have more to tell you . . ." and then he drifted off into a fitful sleep for several hours. Unwilling to leave his side, Louisa gently rested her head against his right arm, at once angry that Nappy had been put through the ordeal of testifying just as he was beginning to recover while at the same time drawn by a horrified fascination to want to know more, especially regarding Sam's fate. *I must be patient—poor Nappy, the horrors to which he has been subjected!* Gradually, she drifted off to sleep herself but was later awakened by Nappy's growing agitation. It began with restless motion of his arms and legs, quickly followed by inarticulate moaning, and then suddenly a very clear and piercing cry—"Sam!"—that caused Louisa to jump.

Realizing that Nappy was still very much asleep, trapped within the terror of an all-too-vivid nightmare, she began to lightly dab his face and neck with a moist cloth, hoping by this means to calm him. *As I witness his suffering, it becomes clear to me how much the demons love to attack innocent souls,* Louisa reflected as she continued to mop the sweat from Nappy's face. *For those unfortunate defenders of Fort Pillow, there was no need to make the descent into the nether regions. Hell opened wide its mouth, and Forrest with his legions came forth to torment the living!* She trembled as she remembered her own close encounter with Forrest and his troopers. No longer able to summon her usual sarcasm, she could only express profound gratitude to God for Rebecca's inspired prevarication, which saved her from certain enslavement or death so many months before. *I wonder which is the worse fate: to die and find peace in the bosom of Abraham or to survive and live on with memories*

*that haunt every waking moment and transform dreams into nightmares.
Oh, Sam, I pray that you are indeed resting in that kind patriarch's bosom!*

Pausing in her reflections, she felt warmth come to her cheeks as she
suddenly realized that Nappy was now awake, a tender smile on his face,
looking intently at her. "Miss Louisa, I dreamt just now that *my angel* had
come to drive away the darkness, and here you are!"

"Nappy, weren't you having a nightmare? You seemed very agitated
and even called for Sam in your sleep."

"Yes. It was a nightmare—I fear that Fort Pillow will be my companion for the rest of my days. I can't begin to thank *my angel* enough for her
presence. You light up all the dark corners of my soul. Before I fell asleep,
I said that I had more to tell you . . . and it is high time you heard of your
brave brother's fate. But before I begin, would it be too much to ask for
some of that wonderful eggnog or milk punch that you have been feeding
me? It has been so helpful in restoring my strength."

"Back in the Corinth days, Moses always emphasized to me the
Lord's saying that *there is no greater love than this, that a man lay down
his life for his friends.* Sam had that kind of love for all of us who served
under him. I don't know how the newspapers have reported it, but we
put up a good fight against the Rebels and might have held them off for
a much longer time until reinforcements could come. Unfortunately,
Major Booth was killed early during the battle. He was an able and fair-
minded officer. When Major Bradford assumed command, he did not
carry out Major Booth's order to destroy the buildings on the edge of the
fort. Eventually, the Rebels got control of them, and their sharpshooters
used that shelter to wreak havoc on us in the fort. Still, our situation was
not hopeless. The rebel general, Forrest, cleverly called a truce to demand our surrender. During all the back and forth between Major Bradford and General Forrest, the Rebels took undue advantage, and their
forces slipped up very close to our fortifications. When Major Bradford
refused to surrender, the Rebel assault forces were in position to quickly
overwhelm us. Sam could see the treacherous behavior of the Rebels during the truce, but sadly all he could do was to prepare us as best he could
for what would come.

"For some reason known only to Major Bradford, he distributed
barrels of spiritous liquor to the troops during the truce. Sam refused it
for our battery, dumping the barrel's contents on the ground. He told us
of his concerns about Rebel treachery and then said, 'Men, we all may

be about to meet our Maker. Being drunk is not the way to prepare for that encounter. If the enemy gets the better of us, our very survival will depend on us having all our wits about us. But if we are to die, let us die honorably, with a prayer on our lips.' Sure enough, as soon as Major Bradford had rejected General Forrest's terms and the truce was over, a horde of Rebel soldiers swarmed over our battlements. Our artillery was now useless; only close-quarters combat was possible. Sam and I got off a few rounds with our revolvers but with little effect. Within just a few minutes, we were surrounded by angry Rebel soldiers bent on our destruction. Sam had just shot one Rebel when I saw him take a gunshot to his right chest from a few yards away, which spun him around and threw him to the ground facing toward the edge of the hill behind us and the river beyond. Somehow, he managed to shout an order for the members of our battery to surrender with the other troops in the fort. I could see his look of horror when the slaughter began—it became immediately clear that the Rebels had no intention of giving us quarter. In fact, there were shouts of 'no quarter for the n____rs' coming from all directions. In the next instant, he shouted at me, 'Nappy, make a run for the river. Remember my order: you must survive, for *someone* is waiting for you! Goodbye, my friend.'" Napoleon paused, choking with emotion, and Louisa, grasping his arm, said, "Nappy, would you like to rest awhile?"

"No, thank you, Miss Louisa; I should finish telling you everything. I'm afraid some of the information I gave Mr. Gooch may have gotten muddled a bit. It happened much like I told Mr. Gooch, but it was hard to describe our terror as the secesh soldiers came at us from all directions, clubbing some, stabbing others, and shooting many at point-blank range. The urge to get to the river was overpowering as many of us tumbled over the edge of the hill trying to reach the water. But the water wasn't much protection because many of us couldn't swim, and they started to rain bullets down on the men in the river. It looked like boiling water at one point, there were so many bullets coming from all sides into the water. For those of us who hadn't yet sought refuge in the water, the Rebel soldiers above ordered us to come back up the hill. That's when I lost my eye. As I was coming up, a Rebel knocked me down with the butt of his carbine and then turned it around and gouged my eye out. For a few minutes I became crazy with the pain. That Rebel didn't shoot me. He only laughed, apparently thinking it great sport and went on to shoot the fellow next to me in the chest. All I could do was stagger up the slope, where they were waiting to finish us off. From the stabbing pain where my eye had been, I was certain that I would die very soon. In fact, I must confess that I wished for death, it hurt so bad."

Louisa couldn't help but interrupt, "Is that why you grabbed the end of that other Rebel's gun? Were you hoping he would shoot you? Why did you answer him the way you did when he asked you if you knew whose gun you were holding?"

"Miss Louisa, it's hard to explain. Yes, the pain was crying out for an end, but there was something even deeper than the pain that moved me to act and speak as I did when I told him that he was *nobody*. You must understand, at that moment I fully expected to die by his hand. He wanted me to beg, to plead with him, 'Please spare me, massa!' In that instant I chose instead to declare my humanity—I would die as a soldier wearing the uniform of the United States. Sadly, through his full embrace of cruelty, his lack of mercy, he had lost his humanity—he had become *nobody*.

"Enraged that I declared his true identity, he shot me through my left hand at point-blank range. That explains the powder burn that's there with the gunshot wound. Since it was at point-blank range, the bullet went all the way through my hand and produced the second wound in my right shoulder, because of the way my body was turned toward him when he shot me. One of the other secesh soldiers standing with him decided I had also offended him, and that's how I received the additional wound through my right thigh. But enough about my wounds; they're of little interest. What was truly amazing, a gift from the Lord, was to discover, after I had fallen to the ground, that I could see and hear Sam. God decided that I should come all the way back up that hill to be close to Sam as he died. The Rebels had done me a great service!

"On more than one occasion, Sam had spoken about his—your—wonderful father. He would speak of your father's deep respect and love for the land while lamenting his own limited interest and gift for farming. Even though he was confident of your father's love, Sam felt his choice of career had been a disappointment to him. You can understand my surprise when I could distinctly hear Sam speak in short bursts between gasps for air to his unseen father: 'Is that you father? You need help plowing the back field? I'm coming father, I'll be right there!'

"Unfortunately . . ." Nappy paused again as his emotions rose and Louisa gently brushed her hand against his cheek. "At that moment, another voice broke in interrupting the conversation between father and son. 'Why, dis ere *n____r's* still alive. He's callin' fer his pappy.' 'Well, private, what're you waitin' fer. Send 'im to his pappy!'

"Miss Louisa, you will probably read many accounts of the massacre in the newspapers, including some describing how many of our men were dispatched by a revolver shot to the head, but I can assure you that your noble brother was already in a better place before that secesh pulled the trigger. At the moment of your brother's murder, I felt a pain far greater than that coming from my physical wounds, for I had to play possum to avoid attracting their attention. But from the depths of my soul, I wanted to cry out, with all the strength left in me, 'Murderers!' In Sam I had found another brother to replace the one I had lost, and now both were lost to me.

"I have little to add to the account of my burial alive and miraculous survival, including the escape when the gunboat came, except to acknowledge the power of the human conscience. I had occasionally experienced acts of human kindness from white folk during my time as a slave. The fact that the secesh soldier's conscience could not be silenced when he noticed my slight movement in the mass grave is a reminder that God moves in the hearts of every person. I don't even know his name, and yet I owe my life to his conscience and the mercy of God."

Sometime after their tears had dried and they had remained in silence together, Louisa's curiosity got the better of her. "Nappy, you said something about an order that Sam gave you to stay alive because *someone* was waiting for you. I wonder who this *someone* could be?" Louisa asked, a slight smile forming at the corners of her mouth. "Could this order my brother gave you have influenced your will to survive such horrific trials?"

"Before I answer your question, Miss Louisa . . ."

"Napoleon Heyward, 'Louisa' is quite sufficient—please stop calling me 'Miss Louisa'!" Louisa interrupted. As a cautious smile formed on Nappy's lips, he tried once more. "Louisa, I thought I heard you say 'my love' in my presence. Now, I could have been delirious, but I thought I heard you even say it more than once. Who were you speaking to when you said that?"

"Of course, I was speaking to you, Napoleon!" Louisa exclaimed with mock indignation. "And which *angel* were you referring to when I heard you repeatedly say 'my angel'? Your nurse, Rachel Johnson, has certainly been an angel to you." Grinning, Nappy replied, "She has definitely been an angel, no question about that, but not *my angel*—there is only one woman who could ever be *my angel*!"

"Nappy, forgive me, silly woman that I am. I had to nearly lose you before I could admit that I have always loved you."

"But Miss Louisa . . . sorry, Louisa, I'm all shot up—wounded inside and out. Besides, with only one eye, I must be a terrible sight, only good for frightening small children. How could you possibly want a sorry mess like me. You deserve much better."

"Enough of such talk, Napoleon Heyward, unless . . . you don't reciprocate my feelings for you."

"Oh Louisa, how could I not love you? I have cherished a small hope from the very first moment we met. Moses gave me some encouragement to hope—he said that you loved me, just didn't know it yet—so my hope began to grow. I worked hard at my studies, hoping that you might think better of me, an ex-slave. And then I discovered how much I loved learning, which made me love you, my beautiful teacher, even more. When I acquired a new friend, really a new brother, your brother Sam, he put some extra logs on the fire. It was after one of our military drills, when he told me that he knew you better than you knew yourself; in fact, he said it with that hearty laugh of his, you know, the one coming from deep inside. Then he looked me in the eye and said, 'Napoleon Heyward as your senior officer, I expect you to survive this war, and that's an order, because there's *someone* who is waiting for you even though she doesn't know it quite yet.'"

"Indeed, it seems all these men have known me better than I knew myself," Louisa couldn't help musing out loud. "Well, who am I to argue with the wisdom of Moses or my dear brother? Napoleon Heyward, you have conquered my heart, which I daresay is the best soldiering you have ever done! If only Sam was here to rejoice with us!"

CHAPTER TWENTY-NINE

"A man likes to get the worth of his life if he gives it."

Anonymous, Union Army, May 1864

Ezekiel Burgess sat quietly on a camp stool in his cousin's tent while Isaac was completely absorbed in reading the letter from Louisa Johnson. Since the beginning of the spring campaign, he had observed changes in his cousin's demeanor that to him seemed out of character and were frankly disturbing to the quiet Quaker youth. He had always known Isaac to be a calm person, not prone to emotional outbursts. Although his cousin continued, for the most part, to evince this same familiar persona during individual patient encounters and surgical operations, an emotional fraying began to manifest itself outside of his professional work.

He was very much aware of the powerful bond that existed between Isaac and his friend Samuel Johnson. In fact, within the family and the larger community of Friends in their hometown of Newport, Indiana, the friendship between Isaac and Sam had been extolled as a model of ideal Christian brotherly love transcending racial boundaries. It was yet one more reason why Ezekiel so much admired his cousin. Notwithstanding the controversies arising from the advent of war and the apparent abandonment of the Testimony Against War by many young male members of the Society of Friends who joined up to fight against slavery, Isaac's choice to serve as a noncombatant medical officer had been respected by many as a principled compromise. Even Dr. Way, a revered mentor to both cousins, had in his own manner expressed his support for Isaac's choice. Not a man to waste words or offer an unsolicited opinion, he nevertheless had, on more than one occasion during Friends' meetings, asked for prayers "for our young men serving in this war to end slavery, that they be spared, if possible, from committing violence." Then, mentioning Isaac by name, he would add, "And especially for those like Dr. Isaac Burgess, who minister to the suffering and wounded in noncombatant roles."

As each day passed since the seemingly endless, continuous fighting began, Ezekiel had noted a growing agitation in Isaac, especially as more news reached the army regarding the details of the atrocities committed by the Rebel forces at Fort Pillow. It was difficult to separate fact from fiction in the embellished reports of newspapers eager to capitalize on the sensational nature of the news. But what concerned Ezekiel was Isaac's insatiable appetite for more news, regardless of its quality. While Isaac clearly waited anxiously for a letter from Louisa Johnson or his sister Rebecca with definitive information about Sam's fate, his face would often betray a sense of relief when that letter did not arrive with the daily mail.

Ezekiel was acutely aware of his cousin's deteriorating sleep pattern. It was hard enough that on some nights, due to the extensive casualties, they were completely deprived of sleep, but when the opportunity for rest came, it was clear to Ezekiel that his cousin was struggling with insomnia. He had learned to avoid interrupting Isaac when he was ruminating over yet another newspaper account of what had become known as the Fort Pillow massacre. Invariably, when he would be cross and snap at Ezekiel, Isaac would immediately apologize with deep remorse but then repeat the behavior all over again a short time later to his great distress.

Only a few days earlier, a recent edition of the *New York Times* had arrived which contained the reports of the Joint Committee on the Conduct of the War concerning both the Fort Pillow Massacre and medical examinations of Union prisoners of war recently released from Confederate prisons. After another exhausting day, Isaac had pored over the report into the wee hours of the night, looking for any information that might enlighten him regarding Sam's fate. While learning nothing specific regarding Sam's condition, he was horrified by the detailed firsthand accounts of the egregious acts committed by the Rebels after the surrender at Fort Pillow. Reading of the horrible conditions endured by Union prisoners of war in Rebel prisons only added to his anger. At the next morning's officer's mess, he abandoned his usual reticence and bluntly stated with vehemence that "the Rebels—the entire Confederacy—are barbarians, no longer fit to be considered members of the human race!"

Still on tenterhooks, Ezekiel almost fell off his seat when Isaac abruptly ceased reading and groaned deeply. With tears streaming down his face, Isaac said, "Louisa's letter confirms that Sam *is* dead—one of those wretched Rebels put a bullet through his brain!" Uncertain what to say, slowly Ezekiel got up and, silently approaching his distraught cousin, placed his hand on Isaac's shoulder. Grateful for the silent company, Isaac mumbled through his tears, "Louisa says in her letter that a close friend from his regiment witnessed Sam's death and said that he died in peace. Apparently, before Sam was killed, he even heard him speak to his dead father, saying, 'I'm coming!' Oh Sam, if only I could find your peace—all I see is darkness, a deep limitless void!

"Ezekiel, I am very sorry to cast such a dark shadow over you. I'm not fit company right now. When I tried earlier to dissuade you from volunteering your services, I couldn't adequately express my reasons. But now, I think you can begin to see why I was concerned—not just for your physical safety. You have had an opportunity to closely observe what regular exposure to the horrors of war can do to a person. It must be obvious to you that your cousin is not the same person you knew before the war. I've gradually become numb to the suffering around me. Oddly, I can still perform my medical duties, but increasingly it's as if whatever compassion I did have has drained away into one of those puddles of blood that surround our operating tables. Forgive me, Cousin, for I never wanted to contaminate you with the contagion of despair, and now, with the hate that consumes me." Then, as if he were cloaking himself from the elements, Isaac drew back into a deep, impenetrable silence.

In the ensuing minutes, Ezekiel struggled with the silence, for it seemed to insist on being filled with something, anything, that might relieve Isaac's unbearable pain. But he remained quiet as he remembered a profound moment of tension during a Friends' silent meeting wherein silence, not the spoken word, had ultimately prevailed. Who was he to speak, and what could he possibly say at such a time? It almost seemed a blasphemy against the Inner Light for him to attempt to fill a void that only *Someone* else could fill. Rather than speak, Ezekiel gently squeezed his cousin's shoulder in an effort to express his sympathy.

After what seemed an eternity, Isaac rose and their eyes met. What could not be spoken was now expressed wordlessly by a momentary glance—*yes, Isaac I share thy grief and would apply a healing balm if I could.* Returning his glance with an intensity that caused Ezekiel to shudder and turn away inadvertently, Isaac said, "I *must* keep you safe, Cousin—I can bear no more losses."

While the evening's operating was certainly not a tonic, it did serve as a welcome distraction from Isaac's grief. Even Ezekiel's anxieties for his cousin were allayed somewhat as Isaac seemed to fully embrace the familiar rhythm of caring for the wounded from the latest misadventure at the Mule Shoe salient. In a short break between procedures, Ezekiel quietly approached Dr. Powell and informed him that his cousin had received some very bad news, which he had been anxiously awaiting for some time.

"Ezekiel, thank you for telling me. Wherever I can, I will try to lighten his load a bit in the coming days." When a lull in the operating developed shortly after midnight, Dr. Powell took the opportunity to send an exhausted Isaac to bed, saying, "Ezekiel and I have it all in hand, why don't you get some rest?" After making a feeble protest, Isaac willingly acquiesced. As he lay down on his cot, he felt a strange sense of relief in knowing Sam's fate—an unexpected emotional release—that permitted a deep sleep to envelop him.

The morning of the 19th of May dawned, promising to be another hot Virginia day, but for Isaac—who slept well—it also held the promise that he would somehow cope with his grief. *I will stay busy and keep my thoughts directed toward the immediate needs of the sick or wounded soldier in front of me*, he thought. Word quickly spread of yet another movement by the II Corps planned for later that day. It seemed that the peripatetic corps was to serve once more as the spearhead of another thrust, this time around Lee's right toward the Confederate rear, with the grand goal of drawing the Rebels out of their entrenchments into open ground, so that Grant and Meade could finally crush them. As the II Corps was being prepared for a night march around Lee's right flank, Isaac and other medical staff were assigned the duty of escorting their wounded via ambulance train in the opposite direction to temporary hospitals in Fredericksburg before their naval transport to hospitals in the North.

After a quick farewell to Ezekiel, who left ahead of him with the ambulance train, Isaac felt relief that his cousin was moving away from the direction of combat. He was also glad to have a respite from aid stations near the frontline. *If only I could escape these endless inventories and reports!* But, after a moment's reflection, he had to acknowledge that even the bureaucratic aspects of his work provided a helpful distraction, shoring up the mental wall he had constructed to contain his grief.

Nearly an hour after his cousin had departed, Isaac directed his horse north along the Fredericksburg Road. The wagon train was moving slowly because of the sticky mud, a residual effect of the recent rains. It was sometime after 5 p.m. when Isaac caught up to familiar elements of the II Corps ambulance train as it slowly headed north, passing new reinforcements coming south from Washington to join the Army of the Potomac. The new troops, who had acquired the nickname of "the Heavies," were drawn from heavy artillery units, which had been part of the capital's defenses. The Heavies, who had not yet seen combat, drew snide comments regarding their capacity to fight from some of the wounded veterans in the ambulances as they passed. But Isaac could only wonder, *How many of these green troops will soon come under my knife?*

His musings were rudely interrupted by the sharp clatter of musketry about a mile ahead. Dread seized him as he spurred his horse ahead, realizing that the Rebels must have managed a flanking movement and got into the Union rear to attack their supply trains. *Ezekiel is somewhere up ahead—he could be caught up in the fight!*

Isaac was not the only one rushing toward the sounds of battle—the Heavies did not shirk their baptism of fire. Ignoring the increasing proximity of the fighting, Isaac's attention was directed toward the ambulance train, which had halted—the ambulance attendants torn between the call to assist the newly wounded as well as protect those already under their care. Finally, seeing some of the ambulance attendants with whom Ezekiel had departed earlier that afternoon guarding the wounded in their ambulance, Isaac shouted to them, "Where is Ezekiel Burgess?"

Nodding in the direction of the fighting, one replied, "Dr. Burgess, he went with t'other stretcher-bearer."

"How long ago?"

"It couldn't a bin more'n four, mebbe five minute ago."

Securing his horse's reins to the ambulance, Isaac plunged through the field adjacent to the road in search of his cousin. Moving forward rapidly toward the fighting, in less than a minute he found himself surrounded by retreating soldiers in blue. It was at that moment that he caught sight of Ezekiel and the stretcher-bearer about 300–400 yards ahead to his right. They had not joined the retreating Federal forces in time and were now dangerously exposed. Isaac's shouts could not reach them above the din of battle. His fears for Ezekiel rose as he realized that his cousin, being dressed as a civilian, did not bear the green and yellow chevron on his sleeve that would identify him as a stretcher-bearer. He panicked as he thought, *He's a perfect target for either side! But how can I get him out of there?*

And then, to his great horror, Isaac watched helplessly as Ezekiel fell, apparently hit by a Rebel Minié ball. For a moment transfixed to the spot, Isaac witnessed a Rebel soldier occupy the place where Ezekiel had stood, apparently hovering over his victim. Reaching his breaking point, Isaac surrendered fully to a rage that could no longer be contained. Looking to his right and to his left, the Quaker pacifist began to wave his forager's cap and shout, "Forward, boys! Let's end it right here! Who will follow me?" As he moved forward, other individuals nearby began to turn, small units regrouping and coalescing, so that in a matter of seconds, a blue wave had formed. With a deep-throated cheer, they charged at the double-quick toward the gray line, which began to waver. Seeing the Rebel soldier still standing where Ezekiel had fallen, his anger now in full flower, Isaac turned to a corporal who was moving at the double-quick beside him and asked, "Soldier, is your musket loaded?"

"Yes, sir."

"Hand it here." Grabbing the rifled musket, Isaac stopped, remembering the last time he fired one—on St. Patrick's Day more than a year previously—and, sighting his target, aimed but then hesitated when he distinctly heard his father's voice. Just as happened many years earlier, he once more heard the paternal counsel, "*Isaac, thou hast a gift; how wilt thou use it?*"

Taking a deep breath, he shifted his aim from the Rebel soldier's chest to his leg and calmly pulled the trigger. The Rebel soldier cried out in pain and fell as the Minié ball found its mark. Handing back the musket to the corporal, he again raised his cap, shouting, "Forward, boys!" The Federal counterattack continued to surge forward and drove the gray line back sufficiently, so that Isaac could make his way to his cousin. Rushing up to Ezekiel, he found him to be in pain and bleeding from a flesh wound located below his right knee in the back of his leg.

Turning to examine the *enemy*, whom he had spared at the last moment, he only saw a small boy, who could not be more than fifteen or sixteen years of age, lying very close to Ezekiel and moaning softly. Isaac's shot had destroyed the Rebel youth's left knee. *Could this really be the bloodthirsty Rebel soldier who I saw gloating over Ezekiel?* With growing distress, Isaac examined the young Rebel soldier's musket. The barrel was cold. He had shot the wrong man—a young boy at that! Concerned by the large pool of blood that was rapidly forming at the base of the wounded knee, Isaac placed the only tourniquet he had with him around the young Rebel's thigh. Painfully attempting to raise himself up, the boy in gray said, "Thank you, Doctor! You saved my life."

Shifting his attention back to his cousin, Isaac examined Ezekiel's leg and wound more closely. Confident that there was no injury to bone, Isaac apologized. "I'm sorry Ezekiel, I only had one tourniquet with me, but thankfully your wound is less serious, and the bleeding can be controlled by placing pressure directly on the wound."

"Isaac . . . Dr. Burgess, it hurts terribly, but I should be able to apply the pressure myself," Ezekiel replied. And then, adding with admiration, "Was that you I saw leading the counterattack?"

"I didn't know how else I could get you out of trouble. Both of you were nearly surrounded." And then Isaac, in an irritated tone of voice, turned and spoke to the uninjured stretcher-bearer: "You do know that you need to follow the ebb and flow of our forces during a battle—the last to go out with the tide and the first to recede when it goes in—don't you?"

"I'm sorry, sir. This is the first action I've seen. I'm one of the replacements that just joined the II Corps from Washington."

His anger ebbing away with his sarcasm, Isaac quickly apologized. "I'm sorry. Now, please run back to the ambulance and recruit three other stretcher-bearers to come back with you as soon as possible. You'll need another stretcher, since there are two wounded who need to be evacuated. If you find a field medical kit, bring it to me as well."

While the stretcher-bearer was off getting help, Isaac was able to appreciate that the Heavies were doing a thorough job of thrashing the Rebels from Ewell's Corps. Indeed, *the tide was way out*, as the Heavies had proven their detractors wrong.

The soft moans of the wounded Rebel youth shifted Isaac's attention back to him. A bitter sense of failure nearly incapacitated him as he recalled his victim's words of thanks. *Thanking me for saving his life, the one who nearly killed him! I have become what I have despised, a murderer like Forrest and his troopers. Oh father, I heard thy voice but would not heed it fully.* But could his father's words have an additional meaning? *He could just as easily have been speaking of another gift, the gift of healing as a physician—not just my skill with a rifled musket.* Thankful that he had not killed the Rebel youth outright, he would now devote all his energies to saving him and Ezekiel.

With this resolution forming in his mind, the stretcher-bearers arrived, and he returned with them to the ad hoc field hospital being quickly assembled just east of the Fredericksburg Road. As he trudged along, a captain from the regiment that he had helped rally during the counterattack came up and, saluting, congratulated Isaac on his contribution to the success of the engagement. "I didn't know medical officers could lead men in combat so well as you did this afternoon."

"Neither did I," was Isaac's rueful answer.

"I assure you, your bravery and leadership will be mentioned in my dispatches."

CHAPTER THIRTY

"Save me, O God; for the waters are come in unto my soul. I sink in deep mire, where there is no standing: I am come into deep waters, where the floods overflow me."

PSALM 69:1–2

BEGINNING WITH THE VICTIM of his marksmanship, Isaac's attention had been occupied by nearly continuous operating the night following the encounter with Ewell's Corps. Surveying the extensive damage to blood vessels caused by his well-placed shot, Isaac realized that without the tourniquet, the Rebel youth would have exsanguinated very rapidly. As it was, the considerable blood loss he did sustain produced a profound pallor, rapid pulse, and restlessness in the boy. In Isaac's professional assessment, the poor fellow was even more malnourished than most wounded Rebel soldiers he had treated. As he quickly proceeded to an amputation of the injured leg above the knee, he missed Ezekiel's capable assistance, having to rely instead on one of the stretcher-bearers who struggled to follow his explicit instructions. Ezekiel did offer invaluable service in one respect. He patiently held pressure, controlling the bleeding from his wound until Isaac could attend to him. Fortunately for the young Quaker, the path of his gunshot wound avoided the bones in his leg completely, with entrance and exit wounds located behind the bones. Isaac used chloroform anesthesia to examine his cousin's wound, irrigating it with fresh water obtained from a nearby stream and gently debriding away nonviable tissue. He found it necessary to ligate two smaller arteries that began to bleed again during the wound exploration; otherwise, he did not encounter any other surprises in the wound. Applying a clean dressing, he was quite hopeful that his cousin would make a full recovery.

Early the next morning, Isaac made his rounds in the makeshift hospital that had been created from several large tents assembled in series. His first visit was to check on the young Rebel he had shot and was now desperately trying to save. Pulling up a camp stool near the wounded boy's cot, Isaac sat for a moment, observing him closely. Somehow sensing he was being watched, the youth opened his eyes and, seeing that it was his doctor, smiled faintly.

"Doctor, you had to take my leg off, didn't you?"

"Yes, I'm sorry, but the damage was too extensive—your kneecap, the bones and blood vessels underneath were all destroyed. The rest of your leg was barely attached. What's your name?"

"Jimmy Thornton . . . I guess I ought to say, Private James Thornton, Ewell's Corps, Army of Northern Virginia."

"How old are you, Jimmy?"

"Sixteen, sir. But I'll be seventeen next October."

"How long have you been a soldier?"

"Only a couple of months; some fellows came by our farm down near Danville and told my ma that they needed another soldier. I was out in the field plowing when they came. She wasn't so happy about it. You see, I'm the only one she has left. My pa and older brother, they joined up a couple of years ago, and they're both gone now—my brother at Second Manassas and my pa at Gettysburg."

"Do you like soldiering?"

"No, sir. I know my ma needs me at home. How's she going to get through the next winter without me? That's been on my mind a lot. Besides, I hate killing. Even when I hunt rabbits and other critters to put food on the table, I always feel bad about harming God's creatures. My ma would always tell me, 'Jimmy, you're an odd one, seeing beauty in the strangest places.' Yes, she would say, 'You're too soft, you need to toughen up like your old pap and brother.'"

"And now you're a wounded prisoner of war."

"If the good Lord wants me to serve, even die, as a soldier, I accept his will."

"If there wasn't a war, what would you do with your life?"

Jimmy's face brightened as he replied, "Oh, I always hoped to be a preacher, to encourage others in the faith. My ma is probably right about me being an odd one. I have been blessed to see beauty where others see ugliness. God has been very kind to James Thornton; yes, sir, very kind. Take, for example, this here Yankee hospital. Everyone has been so generous, even though we're supposed to be enemies at war with one another. Why, Doctor, I know you've done your very best to save my life—but whatever God wills."

"Jimmy, I need to visit my other patients, but I will be back soon to chat some more."

As he moved on to check Ezekiel's wounds, Isaac's head was swimming. His cousin, who was awake, greeted him with a smile that quickly changed to a look of concern. In a low tone, he whispered, "Isaac, you look awful. Is it just exhaustion from last night's labor or something more?" Isaac's persistent look of despair confirmed Ezekiel's anxiety about his cousin's mental state.

"Ezekiel, I have done a terrible thing—a great sin!" Quickly completing Ezekiel's dressing change, the distraught assistant surgeon grabbed a stool and, sitting close to his cousin, proceeded to tell him the full story. After hearing Isaac's account, in his agitation Ezekiel reverted to his Quaker plain speech and whispered, "Isaac, it is entirely my fault. I should never have left the ambulance train; I disobeyed the explicit instructions thou gave me after I joined thee."

"No, Ezekiel. It was I who chose to grab the musket from the soldier; it was I who aimed and pulled the trigger. I have betrayed our Society's Testimony Against War. In my rage, I barely acknowledged my conscience, speaking through the voice of my father. I shot an innocent sixteen-year-old boy who, if given his preference, would never have been a soldier. He just finished telling me that his only desire has been to preach God's word! Ezekiel, I thought in my arrogance that I would magnanimously spare him, my supposed enemy, by shooting him in the leg. He has lost a lot of blood, and his constitution is not strong—I fear he will not survive the next two or three days, despite my best efforts as a surgeon.

"Ezekiel, the Minié ball spared your bones but tore a chunk out of the gastrocnemius muscle at the back of your leg. You're otherwise quite healthy and should make a full recovery, but you will likely limp for some time after it heals and will need to use crutches in the meantime. Your adventure with the Army of the Potomac is coming to an end. I expect you've gained much valuable practical experience that will inform your medical practice in the future. You have the heart and hands for this kind of work. Now, my primary concern is for you to return safely home, where I know Dr. Way will be able to supervise your full recovery. I will send a brief telegram to your parents, notifying them of your injury and that you will be heading home soon via Washington.

"You should inform Hannah Way and the other ministers at Newport Friends' Meeting of my sin. Please let them know that I submit fully to their judgment—I am not worthy to remain a member of the Society . . . " Interrupting, Ezekiel protested, "Isaac, doesn't the fact that thou saved my life mean anything? Thou must allow me to explain the full circumstances and thy state of mind at the time of this tragedy to Hannah Way and the others. She is a very wise and compassionate minister, a true *Mother in Israel*—she will not make any decision to disown thee in haste." Isaac did not object but only nodded sadly and then added, "I cannot bear to contemplate the pain this will cause my parents and the whole family. Uncle Levi always warned of the dangers of putting on a military uniform, and here I am, living proof of his concerns."

With growing dread, Isaac returned to Jimmy Thornton's bedside that evening. He could not put it off any longer. Pulling up a camp stool, Isaac contemplated the innocent face of the sleeping youth. *He seems entirely at peace, despite what I have done to him.* Gently touching his shoulder, on awakening, Jimmy asked, "Doctor, do you think I will live? I know you and the others are doing all you can to help me, and I'm truly grateful, but I can't help feeling that my time is short."

Struck by the youth's presentiment, Isaac paused and took a deep breath before answering. "Jimmy, I am worried about your recovery. You lost a lot of blood, and you're quite scrawny. It seems you have not had enough to eat."

"The soldiers in my regiment are hungry most all the time, and food is hard to come by back home. It doesn't seem right for me to take food away from the others, since I'm just a new fellow, and most of them are veterans. I've been grateful for what comes my way." *Which isn't much,* Isaac thought. "Jimmy, I would prefer to keep you here for a few more days, if possible, to give you some nourishment while I monitor your wound.

"But there is something else I must tell you, and I'm not sure how to begin." As Isaac proceeded to tell his patient that his doctor was the one who had wounded him, the Rebel youth's eyes grew wide and alert. To Isaac's distress, the Southern boy interrupted him and said, "Sir, you were only doing your duty. When I was wounded there on the ground, I heard you talking to your stretcher-bearers. One of them was wounded right there beside me. Why, you were only trying to rescue your own men. You probably thought I shot the fellow that was on the ground beside me."

"But you didn't . . ."

"No, I didn't, but you didn't know that."

"I'm sorry, Jimmy, I am not explaining myself clearly. I am a medical officer and a member of the Society of Friends." Giving Isaac a puzzled look, Jimmy said, "I'm not sure I understand, Doctor—you're a friend . . . or do you want to be my friend? I can't think of anything better than for us to be friends, even though we're in opposing armies." A smile mixed with profound sadness suffusing his face, Isaac tried again. "I'm a Quaker—we abhor violence and advocate peace. I joined up as a doctor to care for the wounded of *both* armies, but in a moment of anger I shot you. Please forgive me—can you forgive me? You have every reason to hate me, rather than be my friend."

"Doctor . . ." "Burgess, Isaac Burgess."

"Dr. Burgess, I hold to what I said before. You were doing your duty when you shot me, and now you're doing your duty by being my doctor. Don't you see—there's something beautiful in this—your anger turning into mercy! I expect there's a sermon in that, something about God's mercy always overcoming his righteous anger."

"I'm afraid there was nothing righteous about *my* anger," Isaac groaned.

"Maybe not, but there certainly is God's mercy in what you've done for me since."

"Can you ever forgive me?"

"Of course, I can and I do with my whole heart. Isn't that what being a Christian is all about? But if you don't mind, I like the idea of that society of friends you belong to. Would you mind ever so much counting me among your friends? Now that I'm your prisoner, we're not at war anymore, you and me." His eyes glistening, Isaac nodded. "I am not worthy, but I would be deeply honored to be your friend."

Having finished his first homily, James Thornton, would-be preacher of the good news, smiled at his doctor and said, "Now that we're no longer enemies but are friends, I hope that I've lifted a burden from your soul." Afraid of his emotions, Isaac could only nod with a gratitude beyond words as he squeezed his patient's hand. After a period of silence, the young Rebel spoke up again. "Dr. Burgess, if I die, would you write to my mother and let her know that I tried to do my duty as best I could, that I love her, and that my faith in God and His mercy have never wavered?"

"Of course, I will, but I hope that I won't have to convey that message. Where is your home? Is there a specific address?"

"Oh, it's quite simple really. Our farm is about a mile outside Danville, on the road to Greensboro, North Carolina. If you were to address the letter to Mrs. Hazel Thornton, near Danville, Virginia, on the Greensboro Road, I think it should reach her."

"My parents were raised near Greensboro, North Carolina, before they emigrated to Indiana."

"Well, Dr. Burgess, that practically makes us neighbors—all the more reason to be friends!"

Early the next morning, while Isaac was exploring another soldier's amputation wound that had begun to bleed, an orderly briefly interrupted the procedure, announcing that orders had come to immediately dismantle the temporary field hospital and transport all patients north to Washington via Fredericksburg. Irritated, Isaac responded, "Please convey my greetings to the officer commanding. There are wounded soldiers, including the one on the operating table before you, that cannot, or at least should not, be moved until they are more stable. I would appreciate very much a delay in carrying out this order until I can determine which patients can withstand the rigors of the journey."

"Yes, sir."

To Isaac's dismay, after completing the revision of the amputation and two additional wound debridements under chloroform anesthesia, he discovered that not only had his request been ignored, but with unusual efficiency, more than half of the patients had already been evacuated from the field hospital. Searching through the remains of the tent hospital, which was being rapidly dismantled, he could find neither his cousin nor Jimmy Thornton—both were already on the road north to Fredericksburg.

Most ambulances had been diverted south to the main army to address the ongoing shortage, so that Isaac encountered almost every other kind of conveyance besides proper ambulance wagons on his ride to catch up with his patients. Cries and groans coming from the wounded as they were jostled and bounced in wagons without any suspension became a continuous cacophony, providing background music for Isaac's ride. He had to pick his way carefully around the congestion caused by the many wagons on the narrow road. Eventually, he encountered familiar faces among the teamsters driving the wagons and began to look in earnest for his cousin and Jimmy Thornton among the passengers. After several frustrating minutes of searching among wagons that were moving at a snail's pace, Isaac caught sight of his cousin, whose eyes were closed but with a look of distress on his face. Riding up alongside the wagon, he called to Ezekiel, who, opening his eyes, grimaced in pain and said in a low voice, "Isaac, thy Rebel patient died, and the wagon driver just dumped him at the side of the road. I begged him not to, but he insisted, saying, 'He's just a traitor. I don't need him weighing down the wagon.' I'm so sorry."

His face flushing with anger, Isaac asked, "How long ago did it happen?"

"I can't be certain, but I don't think more than half an hour has passed since he was dropped out of the wagon."

Moving up alongside the teamster, Isaac asked him if he had a shovel on board. Receiving an affirmative reply, Isaac asked him to hand it over. The teamster, who was a civilian contractor reeking of alcohol, replied in a surly voice, "Why should I give it to you? I might 'ave need of it."

"You dumped one of my deceased patients from your wagon. I plan to bury him properly." The teamster, eyeing Isaac with contempt, spat on the ground and replied, "Oh, you mean that damn Reb. He ain't o' no account. Let his body rot fer all I care." Raising his voice and glowering at the intoxicated teamster, Isaac threatened, "You can either willingly hand me the shovel, or I will compel you." Realizing that the officer was in earnest, the drunk settled on a more peaceful approach. "Now, let's not get hasty. It's right here." Pulling a serviceable shovel from under his seat, he handed it to Isaac. Riding back, Isaac told Ezekiel he would rejoin him as soon as he had found and buried Jimmy Thornton.

As he revisited the ground over which he had just ridden coming north, Isaac realized that he had not been paying much attention to the ditches at the side of the road. He now began to make frequent stops to examine the dead who had been unceremoniously dumped on the way to Fredericksburg by earlier ambulance trains on prior days. Although some had been obscured by tall grass, he was chagrined that he had not noticed the many corpses in varying states of decomposition by the side of the road. It was only when he had begun to look for a specific corpse that the *invisible* became *visible*. *Has the ubiquity of death rendered me insensible to its presence?*

Finally, his diligence was rewarded, as he found his *new friend*, James Thornton, lately of Danville, Virginia, lying at rest on God's green earth beside the Fredericksburg Road. Jimmy was on his back, his eyes partly open, with a gentle smile still on his lips. Tears coming to his eyes, Isaac thought, *Jimmy Thornton, you are indeed an odd one—even beautiful in death!* Gently closing Jimmy's eyes and moving him away from the road, Isaac found a spot near a spreading oak tree to dig his grave, marking the location in his mind and carving *J. T. May 20, 1864* into the tree trunk with his pocketknife. Before placing him in the grave, Isaac realized that he should probably examine the dead youth's clothing for any artifact that might eventually be returned to his mother as a keepsake. He hesitated as he remembered with revulsion all the times that he had witnessed others robbing the dead on the battlefield. *I must do this for his mother's sake. He would want me to save anything that might be meaningful to her.* His search yielded a small New Testament in an inside pocket. As he leafed quickly through its pages, it became clear that Jimmy had spent much time studying its contents. Carefully underlined portions and small notes in the back were ample evidence of the young Rebel's faith and devotion. Isaac reverently placed the relic in his own pocket and then laid Jimmy to rest in the grave he had dug. Fashioning a crude wooden cross from some loose branches he found nearby, Isaac placed it at the head of the grave, sensing Jimmy would want that. And then he paused, not certain how a Baptist preacher would want to be offered back to God. The bulge in his pocket prompted him, and out came the New Testament for another quick look. Opening it at random, here were the words on a well-worn page reverently underlined by the deceased: "I am the resurrection and the life: he that believeth in me, though he were dead, yet shall he live . . ."

Isaac silently read the entire chapter from the Gospel of John describing the raising of Lazarus and then spoke the underlined portion out loud over the grave. He was struck by the immense irony that here he was, laying to rest an enemy combatant whom he had mortally wounded in a fit of rage and then desperately tried to save without success. In reading the account of a dead person brought back to life by the mercy of God, he could not help but sense that his young Rebel friend in death had offered him one last homily—one of great hope. By an inexplicable miracle, the one he could not save was saving him.

CHAPTER THIRTY-ONE

"'Tis the gift to be simple, 'tis the gift to be free,
'Tis the gift to come down where we ought to be,
And when we find ourselves in the place just right,
'Twill be in the valley of love and delight.
When true simplicity is gain'd,
To bow and to bend we will not be asham'd,
To turn, turn will be our delight,
Till by turning, turning we come round right."

SHAKER HYMN, 1848

Isaac caught up with the wagon carrying his cousin and several other wounded as it arrived in Fredericksburg. Helping the wounded off the wagon, Isaac was frustrated to see that Ezekiel had not been given crutches before being hustled north. "You should be cautious about using the wounded leg for at least another week. I don't want to risk any bleeding from the wound before it has fully granulated. At least don't bear your full weight upon it during that time. Please lean on me for the present, until I can find some crutches," Isaac instructed as he helped his cousin. "It's a wonder that between the rough conditions on the road and a wagon with no suspension, your wound did not begin to bleed."

"It's because of the excellent care I received," Ezekiel said, trying to smile but still wincing from the pain of the journey.

Isaac found himself struggling to navigate the chaos of a poorly organized, temporary medical system spread out across a hostile town that elicited painful memories of the disastrous battle one and a half years earlier. He was fortunate to find temporary lodging with a local widow.

Although suspicious of the Yankee physician and his patient, she was relieved that housing the pair protected her from more demands upon her small domicile and limited resources. While searching for crutches, Isaac also acquired cans of food and other staples to help provide for the widow's future needs. Being satisfied that Ezekiel was competent in the use of his crutches, he shepherded his cousin on to a light-draught steamer on the Rappahannock leaving for Washington on the 22nd of May. Worrying over details of the ship-to-ship and then ship-to-rail transfers that his injured cousin would have to navigate, he realized that his fussing was beginning to annoy Ezekiel.

"Forgive me, Ezekiel, I know you are very capable of managing your travel. Because of everything that has transpired, I just want to make sure that you will arrive home safe and sound. Please send me word of your safe arrival as soon as possible, and give my chastened greetings to everyone there. While I was searching for your crutches, I sent a telegram to your parents alerting them of your impending travel. I just received orders to rejoin the Army of the Potomac, so I must be in the saddle as soon as you depart."

"Isaac, I thank thee again for saving my life and for enough memories of medical care in this great civil war to share with several generations of Burgesses. Thou wilt be in my prayers for safety from shot and shell but most especially from despair. God will help thee through this travail of grief, I am certain of it."

"Thank you, Ezekiel. I may not have always shown it during our time together, but I am deeply grateful for our fellowship. You will be a very fine physician. Now go home, finish your studies at Earlham College, and then give serious consideration to attending my alma mater in Ann Arbor, Michigan, for your medical studies. I would be proud to have you follow in my footsteps there."

Isaac had mixed feelings as he retraced his journey toward the Army of the Potomac along the Fredericksburg Road. It was easy enough to discern from his orders that Grant and Meade must again be in motion, probably moving yet once more around Lee's right flank. *It seems that hope springs eternal in the minds of generals. Perhaps this will be the time they finally draw Lee out in to the open on a field of their choosing, although it seems highly unlikely.* As he approached the large oak tree marking the site of Jimmy Thornton's grave, Isaac stopped, dismounted, and led his horse over to the side of the grave. Standing in silence, he was grateful that the traffic along the road had abated and was now barely a trickle.

As he stood by the primitive cross at the head of the grave, Isaac was engulfed by a deep sense of wonder as he pondered his short-lived relationship with Jimmy Thornton. While feeling almost unbearable shame, he was unexpectedly flooded with an inexpressible joy that he had never known. It seemed clear to him that he could not claim the latter without embracing the former, and they would be forever linked within his soul. He knew that he had crossed a threshold, but the path ahead remained a mystery.

"Farewell, my friend. I will write to your mother, informing her of your death, and give her the message that you entrusted to me, but I must make my confession to her in person. So, I pledge to you, James Thornton, that I will preserve and protect this New Testament that I hold close to my heart, presenting it to her after this terrible conflict has ended."

The next confrontation between the two great armies was at the North Anna River. Anticipating Grant yet again, Lee had placed his troops in an excellent defensive position behind the river. The Rebels' compact defense allowed Lee to move reinforcements quickly to any point under attack. Bends in the same river effectively isolated the different Union Corps. To reinforce each other during an attack, they would have to cross the river, making each Corps vulnerable to separate, piecemeal destruction by Lee. A sharp attack by the Rebels was repulsed by the II Corps on the 24th of May, Lee missing the opportunity to take full advantage of his unique position. Further probing and maneuvering by the Army of the Potomac revealed that the Confederate position was essentially impregnable.

During a lull in the action on the next day, Isaac joined several of the medical officers for an evening meal. A familiar voice drew his attention away from his plate of food, and he looked up to see a smiling Fr. Corby standing beside him. "May I join your fellowship this evening, gentlemen?" Several voices joined in a chorus of invitation. Isaac quickly made room for the chaplain to sit next to him at the table. As officers began to leave the table at the end of the meal, Fr. Corby, lingering behind, touched Isaac's arm and in a whisper asked, "How have you been, my friend? I have heard some extraordinary rumors about the martial exploits of a certain Quaker assistant surgeon I know and wondered if you knew anything about the stories. I've even heard from a reliable source of a citation for bravery and an offer of a commission as a field officer."

His face reddening, Isaac suggested continuing their discussion in his tent. "Chaplain, I am extremely embarrassed . . . I should say, sincerely ashamed of my recent behavior. A citation for bravery and the offer of a battlefield commission are incontrovertible evidence of how far I have fallen away from the Friends' Testimony Against War. At the beginning of this conflict, I made a conscious commitment to serve in a noncombatant role, which in a moment of rage I abandoned, tearing to shreds a life dedicated to peace. I am no longer certain who I am."

"With the constant motion of the army and the unprecedented number of casualties, Dr. Burgess, I regret that we have not had an opportunity to chat for some time. In the brief encounters we have had in the field hospitals, I have sensed that your usual equanimity has been undergoing an intense strain. I should have approached you earlier to offer at least a word of encouragement, if nothing else, amid all the chaos; please forgive me."

"Chaplain, your primary duty has always been to the suffering soldiers, especially those with serious and mortal wounds," Isaac protested.

"If I'm not mistaken, you are wearing the uniform of a soldier, and I would have to be blind not to see that you are suffering, my friend. I might also hazard to add that not all serious wounds are physical. I cannot believe that the life you have dedicated to peace is completely in tatters, no matter what you have done. Would you be willing to share your story with a sympathetic friend? I have broad shoulders; perhaps I can help bear some of your burden."

Surprising himself with his eagerness, as if he had only been waiting for the invitation, Isaac's story poured forth as Fr. Corby listened. Beginning first with his anxieties about his cousin's safety, he went on to tell of his devastation over Sam's fate and how it had grown into an all-consuming anger and rage. Even though he altered his aim upon hearing his father's voice, the rage still reigned and he pulled the trigger. "I knew in the depths of my being that I was running toward a precipice, but I could not stop. It is as if the Inner Light has departed from me—I feel abandoned by God."

Finally, with profound awe, Isaac described the extraordinary faith of the young Rebel who, refusing to hate or condemn Isaac, freely forgave him. When he tried to describe his friendship with the youth that began before and now continued even after death, Isaac's voice broke with emotion, ending his tale.

"Dr. Burgess . . . Isaac, from our past discussions about Quaker beliefs and practice, is it safe to say that the Inner Light is the distinguishing mark, the *sine qua non*, of Quaker belief, or should I say life as a Quaker?"

"Yes, our Society has always taught that God is within us, as the light of Christ illumining every man."

"I remember being struck by the beauty of this doctrine. This intimate experience of God has been sought diligently by all the great Christian mystics. It was very encouraging to make the discovery that at least one group of Protestants have discovered this truth.

"Isaac, as you reflect on what you have done, at what moment would you say that you sinned?"

"Clearly, when I pulled the trigger and shot James Thornton."

"Are you certain that was the crucial moment? Perhaps a more pertinent question might be this: when did you begin to *hate* the Rebels? Is it possible that you could name one or more individuals in the Rebel Army that you already hated, even despised as less than human, well before General Ewell decided to attack the rear of our army?"

Isaac, slowly nodding his head, looked at Fr. Corby with a mixture of surprise and awe. "Of course, you're right—my progressive fatigue with a seemingly endless war has transitioned from a growing impatience with the stubborn resistance of the Rebels to anger and finally, to a fully mature hatred and malice. After the massacre at Fort Pillow and the loss of my best friend, I directed that hatred at Nathan Bedford Forrest. He has become for me the very embodiment of evil and was the focus of the intense loathing that was burning within me when I rallied the troops to rescue Ezekiel. But rescue was not enough: I saw the figure of the young Rebel standing over my cousin, and malice took full control of me. I can only give thanks that my conscience prevented me from killing him outright."

"It seems so strange to me when I hear some Christians these days claim that the age of miracles ended long ago. I daresay that by the grace of God, your guardian angel stayed your hand, so that you could come to know James Thornton. Earlier, you said something quite remarkable about the Quaker doctrine of the Inner Light; it is the light of Christ illumining every man. Just think about that for a moment—*every* man. Does your doctrine extend to Southern slaveholders, Confederate soldiers, even to Nathan Bedford Forrest, the scourge of Fort Pillow, who should have many souls on his conscience? Is it possible that in some dark corner of Forrest's soul, the light of Christ is present, now only sputtering but waiting for a gust of the Spirit to burst into flame?"

Isaac responded with a groan, "Chaplain, will you deny me the one *legitimate* target of my hatred?"

"Isaac, did you not say that when you shot James Thornton, you realized that you had become the very *thing* you despised, a murderer like Forrest and his men, ruled by the same passions that motivated their actions? Before God, you are a murderer; before men, you are a hero worthy of citations and promotions. God has brought you, Isaac Burgess, to a crossroads. Crossroads are places where travelers often meet. Who did you meet but a young Rebel soldier, an *enemy* filled with the light of Christ to a degree that would be the envy of the saints.

"You're a scholar of Greek, from your time at Oberlin. Do you remember the meaning of the word *metanoia*?"

"'Repentance' is usually how it is translated."

"Yes, but what is its more fundamental meaning?"

"If my memory serves, it means to turn around, to change one's direction."

"Precisely. Which direction was young Jimmy Thornton urging you to take? What direction would your friend Samuel Johnson wish you to choose? I think I should share some of my own travails with you. Do you remember the moment on the second day at Gettysburg when I got up on the rock and pronounced an absolution for all, North or South, who might be susceptible of it?"

"Yes, it was a very generous gesture."

"It was an essential act, both for the soldiers and this unworthy priest. I was moving down a path not unlike that which you have traveled recently. If the Inner Light of Christ illumines every man, I realized that I must not regard the Rebel soldiers as somehow unworthy of God's mercy—that's for Him to decide, not me. Unfortunately, we spend much of our lives as Christians knowing things *about* God and only rarely knowing God through experience. God has taken you, Isaac, through this extraordinary experience from an abstract knowledge of the doctrine of the Inner Light to a real vivifying experience of it—He who was the ultimate Victim has revealed Himself to you in the person of your victim. He did not abandon you; you turned away from Him, distracted by your anger and hate. All you need to do is turn back toward Him. If you truly desire to turn around and change from being the person that you hate, start praying for him by name."

"Are you saying that I should pray for Nathan Bedford Forrest?"

"Exactly. Try something very simple, like 'Lord, have mercy on Nathan Bedford Forrest,' followed by 'Lord, have mercy on me.' It seems to me that your life and that of the Confederate general are intertwined both in this life and in the age to come. At the beginning of our conversation, you had stated that you no longer know who you are. I suspect your journey of self-knowledge has only just begun. With patient persistence, as you pray for your enemy, I believe you will discover who you truly are.

"And I have one more practical piece of advice. Recently, I have learned that many of the new colored regiments are without competent medical officers. You are overdue for a promotion to full surgeon. From what I know of your friend Sam, I think he would be very pleased if you were caring for his people in one of their regiments. Please consider honoring him in this manner."

His eyes glistening, without thinking, Isaac said, "Thank you, Fr. Corby." Blushing at the involuntary slip of his tongue and departure from his usual *Chaplain Corby*, Isaac, nevertheless, got up as the chaplain was leaving his tent and repeated, "Fr. Corby, thank you!"

As Fr. Corby walked slowly back to his own tent, he smiled at Isaac's slip—*I wish I could have given him absolution.*

CHAPTER THIRTY-TWO

"Behind all this was constantly present to our eyes and mind the scene of a great stream, a procession . . . of human souls on their way to eternity."

FR. WILLIAM CORBY, CHAPLAIN, IRISH BRIGADE

IN A BREAK FROM the constant motion of the past several days, Isaac paused to reread once more the voluminous correspondence he had received from persons and a place so dear to him yet so remote. Staring at the written material before him, his mind was able to shut out the bustle of soldiers preparing for combat the next day. First, there was the telegram from Ezekiel's parents confirming his safe arrival and containing the terse assessment from Dr. Way: "Thy patient doing well—should make full recovery." Reading the telegram had become a source of hope. To his surprise and delight, he had received more correspondence in the week following its arrival than he would typically receive in three months. Since the confirmation of Sam's death, the news from loved ones steadily improved. Louisa was now a woman on a mission, as only a woman deeply in love could be. He was amazed by Sam's accurate intuition of his sister's incipient feelings for the former slave, Napoleon Heyward. Isaac smiled in the realization that neither Louisa's complexion nor her female sex had inhibited her from taking on the military bureaucracy on behalf of her man.

In a series of letters, which miraculously arrived in the same sequence as they were sent, Louisa first described Nappy's medical and psychological condition in detail, along with her intention of moving him to Newport, Indiana, so that he could recover in her mother's home. Somehow, through constant importuning of Dr. Wardner, the medical director at Mound City Hospital, and a flurry of telegrams back and forth between the hospital and Memphis, she had lobbied successfully for this plan. Because of her service at the Corinth contraband camp, she was able to obtain the crucial support of Colonel Eaton, Superintendent of Contrabands in the Mississippi Valley. She was hopeful that Nappy would be given at least four weeks' leave for further recovery in Newport before having to return to active duty.

In her second missive, she told of the young couple's intention to be married during Nappy's convalescence, even though it might be unseemly to marry during the formal period of mourning for Sam. In defending the decision not to delay their upcoming nuptials, Louisa declared, "In a short passage of time, I've lost both father and brother; I have no intention of losing Nappy! I am quite certain that Sam and my dear father would bless our expeditious union, considering the circumstances." She then explained to Isaac that she had also been lobbying for Nappy's transfer away from garrison duty at Fort Pickering in Memphis, where survivors of Fort Pillow were being assigned. "I don't think it will be healthy, mentally or spiritually, for Nappy to be immersed in constant reminders of the massacre. He has had a growing sense of vocation to serve as a Christian pastor after the war and has expressed a deep horror of more killing. Recently, he asked me to read the Beatitudes to him. He raised a hand for me to pause when I came to '*Blessed are the peacemakers, for they shall be called the children of God.*' With great emotion, he told me, 'Louisa, I only want to be a peaceable child of God. I pray that I may never again kill anyone. Is there another way I can serve in the army without killing?'" She went on to express her interest in the Army of the James commanded by General Benjamin Butler. "He is one of the strongest supporters of the Negro in the US Army and has formed an entire division of colored soldiers. General Butler has also established excellent programs in support of the educational and social needs of all the refugees, including women and children. I am confident that I would be able to use my educational and nursing skills to best advantage there."

Returning to a discussion of Nappy's disabilities, Louisa expressed the idea that because of the loss of an eye, he could serve better in the capacity of an ambulance driver, stretcher-bearer, or army nurse, rather than in frontline combat. She hoped that she had not abused her connection with Colonel Eaton by asking for too much assistance but was convinced of the absolute necessity of a change in Nappy's military duties. She expressed disappointment that Isaac would not be present for her wedding but assured him that full details of the event would be related later by his sister. Rebecca, who already on her way to Newport, had received a short leave from her nursing and teaching duties at Fort Pickering. Ending with a slice of her humor, Louisa wrote, "Even though you will not be able to attend our wedding, perhaps I will be able to introduce you to my wonderful husband on our *honeymoon*, if it takes us to the Army of the James! I understand it is not too far from where you are in Virginia." When Isaac had first read this letter, he was struck by the serendipity of Louisa's schemes to transfer Nappy (and herself) to the Army of the James and the fact that he had applied for two openings in colored regiments of the same army for the position of regimental surgeon.

The serendipity acquired a providential character when he received a third letter from Louisa in which she excitedly reported Napoleon Heyward's transfer to the 22nd United States Colored Troops (USCT) in the 3rd Division of the XVIII Corps, Army of the James. A caveat was included: "While recognizing that his physical disabilities may limit his effectiveness as a soldier in combat, any final determination of Corporal Heyward's fitness for duty and the nature of that duty would be determined by his regimental surgeon." One day earlier, Isaac had received offers of a commission as full surgeon with the rank of major in either the 5th or the 22nd USCT; promptly accepting the commission in the 22nd USCT, he would be part of the newlyweds' *honeymoon* experience after all! Corporal Heyward was ordered to report for duty on June 10th, 1864. Isaac's transfer would take effect on the 8th of June.

As Isaac sat in his tent marveling at the miracle documented in the papers laid out on his desk, his heart was drawn away by the plaintive voice of one of the Irish Brigade's finest tenors:

> *"Oh brother Green, do come to me,*
> *For I am shot and bleeding,*
> *And I must die, no more to see,*
> *My wife and my dear children.*
>
> *The Southern foe has laid me low,*
> *On this cold ground to suffer,*
> *Dear brother stay and put me away,*
> *And write my wife a letter.*
>
> *Tell her I know she's prayed for me,*
> *And now her prayers are answered,*
> *That I might be prepared to die,*
> *If I should fall in battle.*

Go tell my wife she must not grieve,
Go kiss my little children,
For I am going to heaven to live,
To see my dear old mother.

I have one brother in this wide world,
He's fighting for the Union,
But oh dear wife, I've lost my life,
To put down this rebellion.

Go tell my wife she must not grieve,
And kiss the little children,
For they will call their pa in vain,
When he is up in heaven.

My little babes, I love them well,
Oh could I once more see them,
That I might bid a long farewell,
And meet them all in heaven."

Leaving his correspondence for a moment, Isaac stood outside his tent while the words and melody of the ballad washed over him. Grant's latest flanking movement had resulted in a race between the Northern and Southern armies to reach the crossroads of Cold Harbor, where there was a direct road to Richmond, only nine miles distant. Initially, the Army of the Potomac won the race, but in planning a large-scale assault, Grant wanted Hancock's II Corps, including the Irish Brigade, to be brought up from the rear as part of the attacking force. Isaac remembered the confusion of the past twenty-four hours as the II Corps got lost on a *shortcut* and had only arrived at noon, much later than planned. Reluctantly, Grant delayed the assault until early the next morning on June 3rd. Meanwhile, more Rebel troops were arriving hourly and forming elaborate defensive works to oppose the coming assault.

Like Isaac, most of the soldiers nearby had quietly shifted their attention toward the singer during his sorrowful song. As the last notes and words faded away, they became absorbed in a common activity which he couldn't quite make out. Curious, he walked among the soldiers, who appeared at first glance to be repairing their uniforms. But as he came closer, he realized that the soldiers were not using needle and thread to close holes in fabric; they were sewing pieces of paper into their uniforms with their names and home addresses on them to help identify their corpses after the battle. One young Irishman, looking up from his task, asked, "Doc, have ye seen the fine work of our *friends* across the way? We're to be in the first wave tomorrow." Not knowing what to say in the face of such practical wisdom, Isaac could only nod sadly in reply and move on.

His excitement in anticipating the opportunity to see Louisa and meet her husband, whom Sam had held in such high regard, was tempered by a flood of poignant memories of his time with the Irish Brigade. *Will this be my last battle with the brave Irish? Did the delay imposed by our corps' late arrival give Lee the time needed to prepare his defenses? It seems our soldiers already know the answer. I hope they are wrong but I doubt it.*

At 4:30 a.m. on the 3rd of June, the morning stillness was broken by the sudden deep-throated cheer raised by many thousands of Union soldiers from three corps surging forward toward the Confederate defenses. The emotive force of the human voice was rapidly supplanted by a cacophony of musketry and artillery fire as the two armies brought their deadly technology to the encounter. Lee's boys had been busy preparing a *memorable* greeting for their Northern cousins. In a short-lived moment of glory, some of Hancock's troops broke through the Rebel defenses. But the earthworks, with their concave design repeated along the Rebel line, made them a death trap—the closer a soldier in blue progressed toward the enemy, the greater the number of Rebel soldiers drawing a bead on him. Unfortunately, the no-man's-land between the opposing armies did not have many obstacles or depressions in the terrain to provide shelter from the hail of Rebel bullets. Horrified, Isaac could only watch as his worst fears were realized. While the assault was deadly, the journey back to their own lines for the retreating soldiers in blue was treacherous in the extreme. Initiating the mayhem was a quick affair—the assault was over in less than an hour. Officiousness and military protocol brought it to full fruition for the many unfortunate wounded left on the field to suffer in the intense heat and humidity.

Because of the proximity of the two armies, Rebel sharpshooters could sweep the field, making it extremely dangerous for stretcher-bearers to safely retrieve the wounded. Many of the wounded had little choice but to draw the bodies of dead comrades around themselves, piling them up to provide some protection from the snipers' bullets. Despite the Rebel sharpshooters, Isaac and his colleagues were still flooded with casualties—those fortunate enough to have made it back to Union lines under their own power and others brought in through the bravery of stretcher-bearers who had run the gauntlet of Rebel Minié balls to save the wounded.

As the attack sputtered out, distraught stretcher-bearers came to Isaac at his aid station, expressing great frustration at the apparent relish Rebel snipers seemed to take in making it nearly impossible to reach the wounded. The cries of the wounded, who suffered greatly from thirst as the hot Virginia sun beat down on them, became a torment for their comrades, who kept vigil out of sharpshooter range. Isaac and other medical officers pressed their brigade commanders for a truce to attend the wounded. It wasn't until the 7th of June that a truce could finally be arranged, at which point much of the suffering on the field had been relieved by death.

During his rounds in the division field hospital, Isaac ran into Fr. Corby, who had just given last rites to a dying soldier. The chaplain got up from his seat by the dying man's cot and offered his hand to Isaac. "Isaac, it is a pleasure to see you. I heard some good news about you. Is it true that you've received a promotion?"

After confirming the news of his promotion, Isaac added, "I leave for the new assignment tomorrow with mixed feelings. Perhaps you know more than anyone that my time with the Irish Brigade has been filled with many personal challenges. But I cherish the many professional associations and friendships formed during my service with the brigade, and especially my friendship with you."

"Well, hopefully there will be nothing to prevent us from continuing that friendship, which I also value greatly. It's not every day that a Catholic priest has a chance to learn the fine points of Quaker doctrine," Fr. Corby said with a wink, giving Isaac another hearty handshake.

Having finished his rounds in the field hospital, Isaac approached his aid station behind the front line to check on his stretcher-bearers, still hoping they might somehow find a few survivors. "Sorry sir, but we haven't found any more survivors; the burial details have been quite busy, though. One of the fellows found something I thought you might want to see. It came from one of the many bodies that were so black and swollen they could not be readily identified."

Isaac cautiously opened the small, blood-stained diary, which bore the name of the tenor who sang so beautifully the evening before the battle. The entry for June 3, 1864, read: *'I died today.'*

PART FOUR

"*I have given the subject of arming the Negro my hearty support. This, with the emancipation of the Negro, is the heaviest blow yet given to the Confederacy. . . . By arming the Negro, we have added a powerful ally. They will make good soldiers and taking them from the enemy weakens him in the same proportion they strengthen us.*"

GEN. ULYSSES S. GRANT

"*You say you will not fight to free Negroes. Some of them seem willing to fight for you . . . . There will be some black men who can remember with silent tongue, and clenched teeth, and steady eye, and well-poised bayonet, they have helped mankind on to this great consummation; while, I fear, there will be some white ones, unable to forget that, with malignant heart, and deceitful speech, they have strove to hinder it.*"

ABRAHAM LINCOLN

"*I prayed on the battlefield some of the best prayers I ever prayed in my life. Why? Sometimes it looked like the war was about to cut my ears off. I would lay stretched out on the ground and bullets would fly over my head . . . I made God some of the finest promises that ever were made.*"

BLACK SOLDIER, UNION ARMY

CHAPTER THIRTY-THREE

"Oh, freedom!
Oh, freedom!
Oh, freedom over me!
And before I'd be a slave
I'll be buried in my grave
And go home to my Lord and be free."

Negro Spiritual

BECAUSE OF UNANTICIPATED DELAYS, Isaac's departure by steamer from White House Landing on the Pamunkey River did not occur until the afternoon on June 8. Major Burgess, the newly appointed Surgeon of the 22nd US Colored Infantry was not about to complain; finally, the military bureaucracy had worked in his favor. Just before embarking, he received the much-anticipated letter from his sister Rebecca. Standing on the deck of the steamer, Isaac perused the familiar calligraphy, pausing at times to reflect while surveying the Virginia landscape that was evolving before his eyes.

May 25, 1864, Newport, Indiana

Dear Isaac,

I write with haste in the knowledge that thou must hunger greatly for news of Louisa's wedding to Napoleon Heyward. Before I begin my tale of happiness mingled with sorrow, I want to confirm that our cousin Ezekiel arrived safely earlier today, and his wound appears to be healing well. I know that his parents sent thee a telegram to the same effect, but I wanted to also acknowledge that privately, Ezekiel shared with me some disturbing details of his wounding and thy role in his rescue. He became quite excited as he related the particulars of the incident, expressing concerns about thy state of mind. It all became quite confusing—something about thy shooting a Rebel soldier who later died despite thy best efforts to save him! He went on to describe thy great remorse and that thou wilt submit to the judgment of our community regarding being disowned. Finally, he was emphatic in his support for thee and intends to speak on thy behalf to Hannah Way and the other ministers. I know that thou wilt inform me and our parents regarding the incident when thou art ready, but I felt it necessary to tell thee of my conversation with Ezekiel. As thou can guess, the rumors will be flying soon enough!

Looking up from the letter, Isaac paused and swallowed hard as he considered how the news would affect his parents. Likely, his own account of Ezekiel's wounding and his role in the death of the young Rebel soldier would soon be in their hands, if it had not already arrived. Resuming his reading:

Please be assured, dear brother, that my prayers, indeed the prayers of our parents and of many others, are continually for thy safety as thou art confronted by the physical and spiritual perils of war. To return to the subject of Louisa's marriage, all the details of the blessed event are fresh in my memory, since it happened only yesterday. Forgive me for being so scattered, but I must give thee some antecedent history to set the context.

All that has happened since the tragedy of Fort Pillow has become a great blur in my mind. I can hardly think of our dear Sam without tears coming to my eyes. I must confess that I have derived great consolation from witnessing Louisa's love for Nappy—Napoleon Heyward. In some strange and inexplicable manner, I sensed Sam's presence and blessing at their nuptials. Oh, Isaac, if thou could only come to know Nappy!

But sister, I will come to know him very soon, Isaac smiled as he observed a seagull landing near him on the ship's railing. Addressing the seagull, who was edging closer to him with a quizzical look on its face, Isaac said, "I expect I'll meet many more of your kind as we approach Fort Monroe. It is most kind of you to come such a distance to welcome me in advance of your fellows." As Isaac doffed his forager's cap to his feathered visitor, two sailors passing by gave him odd looks, and he could hear one mutter to the other, "Army officers talkin' to birds! I count myself fortunate indeed to serve in the Navy. You can see what fightin' on land does to men. It makes 'em crazy!" Isaac laughed and spoke again to his feathered companion. "I think yonder sailor is an astute diagnostician—do you care to share an opinion as well?" Not offering a reply, the gull edged closer, and Isaac returned to Rebecca's letter.

I only arrived in Newport five days ago. It was impossible to leave my duties at Fort Pickering any earlier. As it was, Penelope Wormeley generously assumed the additional burden of my nursing duties when I left. Her aunt's love for Penelope's children has freed much of her time for service to the sick, and yet, I could perceive the increasing strain it placed upon her as a loving mother. To compensate for her absence during the day, her evenings are taken up with the children; as a result, she's afraid she may be spoiling them. Thankfully, her estranged husband has focused his time and energies away from Memphis. He seems determined to collect as many greenbacks as possible by ingratiating himself with the "Yankees" wherever he can gain an advantage, whether it be in obtaining cheap labor for his plantations or other financial schemes he has concocted. As details of the horrors inflicted by the Rebel soldiers at Fort Pillow emerged, and when we finally received confirmation of Sam's death, Penelope shed many a tear with me. Even though her friendship with Sam was of short duration, it was genuine and defined by a profound mutual respect. More than once she has told me how mistaken she had been about the capacities of Negroes. After becoming personally acquainted with Sam and Louisa she realized that thou had not exaggerated thy claims about educated Negroes. Before I boarded the northbound transport, she raised a concern that I feel compelled to share with thee. She is confident that Fort Pillow will not be the last time that Rebel soldiers commit atrocities against Negroes in blue uniforms and the white soldiers serving with them. Grasping my hands in hers, she said, "While the addition of colored men in uniform may appear to Northerners as the final element comprising an army of liberation, for most white Southerners it will confirm their worst fears of Yankees inciting servile insurrection. If Louisa's husband is required to return to duty, I fear greatly for his safety."

It is a strange fact that occasions of sorrow and joy must occur to draw together families and reunite loved ones, but I found myself at such a gathering in which sorrow was so fully intermingled with joy that the two elements could not be disentangled. Perhaps it has always been this way for any profound encounter among members of the human family—sorrow and joy held together in a tight embrace. Mary Johnson warmed quickly to Napoleon Heyward despite the ongoing grief of losing her husband, which was now compounded by the fresh wound of her son's tragic death. Recognizing in Nappy traits that would have endeared him to her husband Ben, while also appreciating his blossoming intellectual gifts and vocation for the Christian ministry, she is determined that he must survive his wounds and has focused all her energies to that end.

Poor Nappy, he must contend with the expectations of others seeking in him a replacement for their profound losses while at the same time discovering his own identity as a free man. On one occasion, I was with Mary Johnson as she began to gently admonish Louisa to spare her *intended* the usual sarcasm and caustic wit for which she is famous in the family and among her friends and acquaintances. Louisa accepted her mother's counsel without a murmur. Indeed, after listening respectfully, her response surprised both of us. Quietly weeping, Louisa expressed her chagrin that she had to almost lose Nappy to realize the depth of her love for him. She went on to say that her well of sarcasm had just about dried up. But the Louisa we know and love then added, "If it requires all my energies, this man whom I love will—he *must*—survive the war. To anyone who would dare harm him or thwart his recovery from the terrible wounds he has received, I can only say *beware*—you will have to answer to Louisa Johnson Heyward!"

I cannot begin to express my delight in seeing Eliza, Tib, and their family, who came from Canada for the wedding. The children have grown so much! Tib surprised us with an exciting announcement. He and his brother, Cicero, have been recruited to teach at Wilberforce University in Ohio; Tib will teach classics and history, while Cicero will teach science and mathematics. Thou may recall that the university had closed when the war began. With new leadership and financial support, Bishop Daniel Payne of the African Methodist Episcopal Church reopened the institution last year.

Hattie, the only member of the Johnson family to stay in Newport, has, with her husband, been an enormous support to her mother. The tension between grief and joy was palpable in the Johnson household. Mary Johnson bustled about with many tasks, stopping to hug a grandchild or worry over Hattie's increasing fatigue (she's in her eighth month) but always coming back to check on her future son-in-law multiple times throughout the day.

Now I must turn to a description of Napoleon Heyward's condition after his harrowing trial. In earlier correspondence thou may remember how I described him. He was and continues to be a handsome man. His dark complexion matches that of the Johnsons, and characteristically, he has always exhibited a thoughtful, quiet demeanor which has never prevented a winsome smile from frequently illuminating his face. While all of what I have just written about Nappy is still true, it also misses the mark completely. How can one survive a journey to hell, and more than one face-to-face encounter with Death, without being altered by the experience? The most obvious change in his physical appearance is the black patch he now wears to cover the absence of his left eye. When Eliza and Tib's youngest approached Nappy with some trepidation and asked, "Are you a pirate, sir?" his smile as he answered, "I hope I'm a good pirate" showed some of the old Nappy but with an admixture of deep sadness. It's very difficult to hold back my tears as I describe it for thee. Before Fort Pillow, Nappy was quite muscular, stockier in build than Sam, although a bit shorter; with time and good nutrition, he may regain his earlier physique. But I must confess that I gasped upon seeing him quietly resting on the same couch in the Johnson parlor which had been host to the young runaway, Tib, so many years ago. When Louisa saw my reaction to his appearance—a mere shadow of his former self—she responded with irony, "You should have seen him in the hospital at Mound City." She went on to describe how he had made rapid progress, now walking only with the assistance of a cane, his right leg wound still causing him to limp. But she acknowledged that it would take some time for him to recover his former physical strength. The additional respite time in Newport would likely not have occurred without her persistence and the support of Colonel Eaton. Nappy's wounds involving the right shoulder and thigh are hidden by clothes. The wound in his left hand has been the slowest to heal and continues to give him pain, even more than the one involving his left eye. He has found that wearing a thick leather glove is helpful in providing some protection from the frequent inadvertent, often trivial injuries that nevertheless exacerbate the pain.

I hope, dear brother, that I have given thee sufficient context to now describe the saddest and most joyful wedding I shall ever attend. Pastor Ebenezer Jones, who has presided over earlier Johnson family weddings, is moving more slowly these days.

He claims it's not for a lack of spirit—just rheumatism. While he has never been at a loss for words, and I think that both of us can attest to his powerful exhortations, the old gentleman seemed quite subdued as he began the marriage ceremony of Napoleon Heyward and Louisa Johnson. As thou might imagine, the whole community of Newport, both Friends and Negro Baptists, came out for the service to see a survivor of the infamous massacre be married to one of their own. Even though it was crowded beyond its capacity, silence dominated the Baptist church, as silent as the most reverent of Friends' meetings. Perhaps it was an unspoken recognition by all those present that something more than the Christian rite of holy matrimony was to be celebrated that day. In his homily, Pastor Jones began slowly, warming to his subject with time. "Marriage is a great mystery, as the apostle Paul declares in his letter to the Ephesians, a Scripture passage I have quoted so often over the years on similar occasions. And yet, brothers and sisters, I think you would agree with me that we are being called to reflect upon a deeper, more profound sense of that mystery today. Paul speaks of a man and woman uniting to become one flesh, which he then identifies with the mystery of Christ and his church . . ."

As Corporal Napoleon Heyward stood in his best uniform of Union blue—leaning on his cane, facing Louisa—the suffering etched deeply into his features was mirrored in his bride's face. All of us who were present could only gaze briefly at the couple before involuntarily tearing up and looking away—their combined suffering was so intense, it burned like fire. And yet, all of us also realized we were privileged to witness a miracle. Pastor Jones, who stood close to the couple and by the nature of his duty could not look away, could only stop frequently to choke back his sobs before attempting to proceed further. "Marriages are happy occasions, or at least they're supposed to be. But *happy* as a description is a bit threadbare for what we are witnessing today. There's just too much pain, sorrow, and suffering to be banished by such a tepid word. No, my friends, I'm looking for something more solid. *Joyous* comes much closer to my meaning. But what is the nature of this joy? Brothers and sisters . . ." and here again, Pastor Jones involuntarily paused, with tears streaming down his face, "this can only be the joy of the resurrection! We grieve for those who are absent . . . and yet Napoleon Heyward is here standing before us as a promissory note from God, a foretaste of that resurrection joy when we will embrace Samuel, Louisa's father, and all our loved ones, especially those who have lost their lives in this struggle for freedom. In another place, the apostle urges us to *"bear one another's burdens and so fulfill the law of Christ."* Pausing again, the old preacher sobbed aloud, "I cannot begin to conceive of the horrors this young man has endured, first as a slave and then more recently, as a soldier offering his life on behalf of freedom. But there is another brave, God-loving soul standing here, with a faith and courage only few possess, who with her whole being has offered to share his burden and halve his grief . . ."

Isaac paused as he realized that the drops moistening Rebecca's letter were his own tears. As he had been reading, the seagull had boldly advanced along the railing and was now less than a foot from him, still scrutinizing the young medical officer with great interest. Having no more words for his feathered companion, Isaac resumed reading the letter.

Before finishing his homily and the exchange of vows, Pastor Jones went on to extol the combined virtues of the couple. He was especially thrilled to speak of Nappy's nascent vocation to serve in the Christian ministry and how it would truly be a shared ministry with his talented wife. And because of this, he expressed his firm belief that God would protect the young couple through the end of the conflict.

Louisa asked Tib and me to sing a duet at the close of the wedding, much like we had done years before when I was a child, but all I could think of was the many subsequent duets that Sam and I had sung together as students at Oberlin. Louisa reassured me, "Rebecca, you know Sam would want you to do this for me *and for him*." As always, Tib brought his wise and calming presence to bear and made a wonderful suggestion. I assume thou must know the lyrics of the following Negro spiritual, but I record some of the words for thee to emphasize the healing power contained therein.

How lost was my condition,
Till Jesus made me whole;
There is but one Physician
Can cure a sin-sick soul.

There is balm in Gilead,
To make the wounded whole;
There's power enough in heaven,
To cure a sin-sick soul.

It was a quieter, most solemn piece to offer as a benediction on the union of our dear friend and sister, Louisa with her Nappy, returned like a modern-day Lazarus from the dead. Many tears were shed, but as Pastor Jones declared, it was a joyous wedding, an unforgettable event and blessing for those who attended.

Louisa shared one extraordinary bit of news with me after the ceremony; a telegram had arrived during the service indicating that Nappy's transfer away from Memphis is official. He will be coming thy direction to the Army of the James to serve in the 22nd US Colored Troops. Louisa will be overjoyed to introduce thee to her husband. She hopes to find teaching and nursing duties there. As thou can understand, she has no intention of being separated from him, hoping I think, to be an additional guardian angel for her *Lazarus*.

Dear Brother, my prayers continue for thy peace of mind and healing of thy wounds. Please pray for the work that Penelope and I continue to do among the suffering Negro soldiers and contrabands at Fort Pickering.

Ever thy loving sister,
Rebecca

CHAPTER THIRTY-FOUR

"During both my army and university experiences, there have been occasions when I was tempted to exclaim, 'Yes, a white man is as worthy as a colored man—provided he behaves himself as well.'"

DR. BURT WILDER, SURGEON 55TH MASSACHUSETTS INFANTRY (COLORED) AND LATER PROFESSOR OF NEUROLOGY AND VERTEBRATE ZOOLOGY, CORNELL UNIVERSITY

PRESSED ON ALL SIDES, the pungent odor of human sweat and blood choked and nauseated him. A dim awareness dawned that he was pinioned by arms, legs, torsos, and even by a head or two. He wanted desperately to move, just a little, but realized that he was nearly immobilized. *It's so hard to breathe; why are they crowding me so?* And then suddenly, a shovel full of dirt hit him in the face. To his surprise and great relief, one of his hands was near his face, and he found he could use it to partially shield himself from the soil raining down on him. He could hear voices coming from somewhere nearby.

"Something moved in there!"

"Ah, yer jus' seein' things."

"No, I swear, there's someone alive in there."

"So, what if there is. It's jus' a *n____r.*"

"It ain't right to bury someone alive."

Yes, it isn't right to bury someone alive. Why, they must be speaking about me! He tried to scream, but not a word would come from his mouth as he clawed at the soil surrounding his face.

"Nappy darling, it's me, Louisa! You're safe, no one will hurt you." Louisa Johnson Heyward tried to calm and reassure her husband as he awakened from his nightmare.

"Oh Louisa, I'm so sorry. Did I hurt you?"

"No, my dear; I'm quite agile. I was already awake before you started to push with your hand. Was it the same nightmare you've had before?"

"Yes. I found myself back in that mass grave. I just don't understand. I haven't had the nightmare for some time now. I was so hopeful that the joy of married life would banish such terrors from me."

"My darling, you forgot one small complication—you're still a soldier in the Union Army, now returning to duty under new, unfamiliar circumstances with all the attendant anxieties." Surveying their tiny, cramped cabin in the faint light of dawn, Louisa smiled. "There could be no more spacious and charming venue for our honeymoon voyage than this, our very own private nook on a Union Navy transport, don't you think?" *And this only through the kindness of a ship's captain with abolitionist sentiments,* Louisa thought as she tried to keep her native sarcasm in check.

Gently stroking her hair, Napoleon Heyward made his own survey of their diminutive quarters and perceived something very different. "Louisa, not so long ago, your husband's notion of domestic comfort was a dirt floor, surrounded by drafty wooden walls and covered with a leaky roof. In the quarters, privacy was a concept yet to be defined, for it was certainly never experienced. For me, to be here alone, in company with the one creature dearest to me in the entire creation, is a miracle transforming this large closet into a palace."

Chastened somewhat, Louisa responded, "Well, my dear husband, shall we rise and leave our palatial surroundings to see where our *royal yacht* is taking us?"

Standing together on the deck of the transport, the rising sun embracing them with its warmth, Louisa and Nappy were struck by the beauty of the Virginia countryside as seen from the James River. Mansions, fields, and gardens—apparently oblivious to the apocalyptic forces at work only a few miles distant—still managed to exude a mixture of charm and Rebel defiance. Irked by what she saw, Louisa remarked, "Such beauty—extracted through the sweat and suffering of slave labor! It has a devilish quality about it."

"Oh Louisa, don't say *devilish*. Beauty cannot be evil. The *beauty* of these grand homes, lovely gardens, and fields has been *created* by the labor of slaves. My own labor as a slave was sometimes *extracted* with the lash—and that was a devilish thing—but I also took great joy in *creating* beauty. No amount of cajoling, threats, or whipping can create beauty.

My master may have owned his mansion, land, livestock, and *even* his slaves, but he did not own the *beauty* that was created through our suffering. It was ours as much as it was anyone's. The good Lord helped us create a beauty that the master could only dimly see."

The young couple's attention was diverted from a discussion on the nature of beauty as the rapidly narrowing James began to twist and turn while their transport proceeded further upstream. To their right, on the northern side of the river, a wharf under a bluff came into view. A sailor called out, "Wilson's Wharf ahead!" After unloading some cargo and personnel, the transport rounded a bend, and a fortification came into view on the southern side of the river. A shiver went down Nappy's spine as he was reminded of another Federal fort on the Mississippi River. Approaching a Negro sailor, he asked, "What's the name of that fortress?"

"Oh, that's Fort Powhatan. Wilson's Wharf and Fort Powhatan were built by colored troops, mostly from the 22nd USCT Regiment," he declared with evident pride. "My brother's serving in that unit. We're Jersey boys, as are many of the others, while the rest are mostly from Pennsylvania. I joined up earlier when the US Navy was the only option for a black man. Corporal, what regiment are you in?"

"I'm on my way to join the 22nd USCT today. My orders are to report to Bermuda Hundred for a medical examination."

Scrutinizing Nappy more closely, the sailor said, "You look like you've already seen a bit of hell. Shouldn't you be reporting to the Invalid Corps instead of a regular regiment?"

"I was ordered to join the 22nd USCT and here I am."

"Where are you from? From your accent, you don't sound like anyone I know from New Jersey."

"No. I'm from Mississippi."

"You were a slave? I can't believe it. You don't talk like a contraband."

"Thanks to this lovely woman at my side, I have learned to read, write, and speak without the slave dialect." Turning his attention to Louisa, the sailor exclaimed, "You must be some kind of miracle worker!"

"No, I'm no miracle worker, my husband is just a very good student."

Returning a few minutes later, the sailor, with some hesitation, asked Nappy, "Do you mind my asking where you received those wounds?"

"It was at a place far from here. You might have heard something about it in the papers—Fort Pillow in Tennessee, on the Mississippi River."

"Why, you're a survivor of the massacre at Fort Pillow! May I shake your hand, sir? My brother and all his comrades in the 22nd USCT have declared that they will give no quarter to Rebel soldiers. When they hear the Rebel yell, they'll respond with 'Remember Fort Pillow!'"

Nappy slowly shook his head and groaned. "Now I begin to understand why God has sent me to Virginia. My comrades and I suffered greatly at Fort Pillow on that terrible day, but colored soldiers must not descend to the depths of depravity to which our foe has fallen. Slaveowners in the South have regularly proclaimed that we children of Africa are less than human as justification for making us slaves. But Fort Pillow is proof of what the institution of slavery has wrought in the souls of the white masters. It has turned them into the very beasts they claim us to be. Seeking revenge will only reduce us to their level; we must do better . . ." Seeing Nappy's increasing agitation, the black sailor quickly apologized. "I didn't mean to upset you, sir. Would you mind very much if I brought some of my comrades to pay their respects? I promise that they won't mention anything about giving 'no quarter' to the Rebs."

A few minutes later, Louisa was surprised to see a long queue of Negro sailors form to diffidently pay their respects to the "hero" of Fort Pillow. Embarrassed, Nappy graciously greeted each sailor, saying little of his personal experience other than to express his gratitude to God for sparing his life. By the time Nappy had shaken the hand of the last sailor in the queue, they heard, "City Point just ahead" as the transport was rapidly approaching the bluff overlooking the confluence of the Appomattox and James Rivers. City Point was their last stop before arriving at Bermuda Hundred, a short trip further up the James.

After disembarking, Louisa bustled about as she directed several stevedores who unloaded multiple trunks of books and other teaching materials that had been donated by old friends from Oberlin for *their missionary* to the Army of the James. Nappy, who stood by admiring his wife's initiative, was also rather dazed by the flurry of activity. After the sailor's grim appraisal of his fitness for duty, he had hastily decided to give up use of a cane, stating to Louisa, "You taught me an expression—I believe it is something like 'putting one's best foot forward.' I don't want to appear helpless after all when I meet the medical officer." Shaking her head, Louisa retorted, "My dear, if you fall, it won't be putting your best foot forward!"

Satisfied that all the trunks including their own small trunk had been accounted for, Louisa turned to Nappy and laid out her strategy for the remainder of the day. "Let's go find the medical officer for the 22nd USCT to discover your fate and then secure our lodging. If there is more time this afternoon, I will seek an audience with General Butler to report my safe arrival with the educational materials intact and my availability to begin teaching contrabands as soon as possible."

The former corporal of the 6th US Colored Heavy Artillery hesitated as he stood outside one of the ubiquitous tents at the headquarters of the Army of the James, the only feature distinguishing its medical character being the yellow flag flying close beside it. Finally, with some trepidation and after casting a plaintive look back toward his bride, who was waiting in the shade of a tree, he approached the entrance and inquired if he might enter. He heard a voice from within state in a brusque tone, "Please enter and state your complaint."

Raising the tent flap, he saw a tall, thin figure with neatly trimmed brown hair and a full beard hunched over a crude desk, scribbling away at what appeared to be a mountain of paperwork. The white officer wore the green sash of a physician and shoulder straps indicating the rank of major. As Nappy hesitated on the threshold of his tent, without look-ing up, the officer repeated his invitation to enter but now with some impatience.

"Sir, I am reporting for an examination to determine my fitness for duty in the 22nd Regiment USCT." The officer slowed the furious pace of his scribbling and asked, "Have you been transferred to this regiment?"

"Yes, sir."

"Please state your name and the unit from which you are being transferred."

"Corporal Napoleon Heyward, the 6th US Colored Heavy Artil-lery . . ." Barely had Nappy spoken his name when in an instant every-thing changed. The white officer gasped, dropped his pen, and turned his full attention to the corporal standing before him. The white doctor, who at first had seemed indifferent, now stared with intense interest at the thoroughly disconcerted colored corporal. Suddenly, before he knew what was happening, the doctor's face lit up, and—his eyes glis-tening—he rose and rushed forward to Nappy, hugging him tightly. Frozen with fear and his mind numb, Nappy went limp in the arms of his *white assailant* and crumpled to his knees.

As he came to himself, he was startled by the tears running down the face of the white officer in front of him. "Please forgive me for causing you such a fright—a white man in uniform dashing toward you must have brought back some terrible memories. I completely forgot all decorum when I realized that you were the last person to see my best friend alive! I am Dr. Isaac Burgess, and I hope despite my poor introduction we shall be good friends, Napoleon Heyward. But where is your bride, Louisa?"

Stepping back, Isaac noted the grimace of pain that still permeated Nappy's features. "Oh, I am terribly sorry, in addition to giving you a great fright, I have hurt you in my exuberance!"

"Sir, really it is nothing . . . just some tender spots that are still healing. Louisa is waiting nearby in the shade of a tree for my interview with you to end. We had no idea that you would be the surgeon of the 22nd USCT."

"Neither did I until very recently. I need to examine you carefully, but please forgive me if I congratulate your bride first."

Corporal Heyward's surprise and confusion reached new heights as he watched the tall white medical officer quickly exit the tent and sweep a startled Louisa up in his arms, lifting her above him as she screamed in shock and delight. With all that had just transpired, he was amazed at how in a matter of seconds Louisa had regained her native wit. "Why, Isaac Burgess what are you doing here? Have you abandoned your Irish *friends* for the *darkies*?"

"Mrs. Heyward, I have indeed abandoned them. You know I have a decided preference for the company of the darker complected members of the human race."

"Isaac, you may put me down now." Stepping back as if to gain a better perspective, she scrutinized her old friend. "The uniform suits you— the shoulder straps of a major, no less! You didn't transfer to a colored regiment out of raw ambition, did you? You're still handsome but too thin. It appears that Uncle Sam has not been feeding you properly. And what about your speech—definitely a deficiency of *thee* and *thou*. What will *thy* parents say?" Louisa smirked and then burst out laughing, but it was laughter mingled with tears as she hugged Isaac.

As he reciprocated her tight embrace, tears ran down Isaac's cheeks. "Oh Louisa, I've lost more than the Friend's plain speech during my service in the army. There is much more in my military record to grieve the hearts of my dear parents than abandoning peculiar forms of speech." Looking steadily into his eyes, Louisa smiled. "Rumors were abounding back in Newport after your cousin Ezekiel returned from his adventure.

Isaac the military hero didn't quite set well with *Isaac of the Friends' Testimony Against War.* It is strange how we grieve for those whom we love and have lost. I daresay, Dr. Isaac Burgess, that grief for my brother was inextricably bound up with your actions. And for that love, manifested in a very un-Quakerly manner, I honor you, my dear friend."

Her attention was drawn back to her husband, who was staring with a mixture of fascination and profound discomfort at the scene of a young black woman—his wife—held in the tight embrace of a white man in uniform. "Napoleon Heyward, why are you looking at us with such an expression on your face? Isaac and I have been friends since childhood. Indeed, a black brother and sister have been neighbors, playmates, and best friends with a white brother and sister as long as we can remember."

Nappy hesitated about how to respond; *We have certainly come together from two very different worlds.* "Dear Louisa, I could not help but contemplate the reverse situation. For I also grew up with my master's white children, who were for a time my playmates and friends. But after my master's daughter was no longer a girl, if I had merely touched her, I would surely receive a whipping, but lifting her in the air would be my death."

"And yet, a white master lifting up a black woman in his arms might not have been so unusual a sight . . ." Isaac finished the comparison and verbalized Nappy's unspoken thought. "Napoleon . . . Nappy, please forgive my thoughtless presumption. I'm afraid that in the North, you might not fare much better in that regard. The friendship that my sister and I have enjoyed with Sam and Louisa, disregarding skin color, is a rare phenomenon in this land."

As he examined Nappy, cataloguing his physical wounds, Isaac could not help but exclaim, "More than once have I recommended discharge from active military service for soldiers with less severe physical injuries than yours. I shudder to contemplate the full extent of the hidden ones! And yet here you are, dutifully reporting for service to a country that does not even recognize you as a citizen. Corporal Heyward, by all rights, I should recommend your medical discharge."

"Please, sir, don't recommend that. I want to serve, only—I beg you—not in combat. I've seen and done enough killing for several lifetimes. The good Lord said, 'Blessed are the peacemakers, for they shall be called the children of God.' About the time I came to know Louisa back in Corinth, Mississippi, I also met a remarkable man, a colored preacher named Moses. He taught me all about God's mercy and love—even for contrabands. Since meeting him, I've felt something deep inside, calling me to a different kind of service. I'm sure Moses would correct me and say, 'Some*one*, not some*thing*.' I hope with all my heart that it is so. How can I be the Lord's child and serve Him as a minister of the gospel of peace while I'm killing others?"

A succession of images flashed through Isaac's mind as he heard the former contraband speak the name Moses. Time and distance fell away as he once more saw that very same Moses preaching with great fervor to slaves and their owners more than a decade earlier, during his travels in the South with his uncle, Levi Coffin. Snippets from his clandestine efforts when a medical student to support slaves escaping to Canada returned, only to be supplanted by, the relentless slaughter of a civil war that seemed endless. Just as these memories mingled to form a powerful eddy, they in turn were swallowed up in the innocent forgiving smile of a young Rebel soldier—a smile which alternated with memories of the deep sadness engraved in the faces of his parents, searching in vain for the pacific son they had lost to war.

"Dr. Burgess? Sir?"

"What . . . oh, I'm sorry, corporal. You said something just now that struck me to the core. You mentioned your intense desire to serve the Lord's gospel of peace. Having been among Quakers while you were in Newport, Indiana, you probably heard about our Testimony Against War."

"Yes, sir. Louisa told me about it and how you are serving as a doctor to help instead of killing people. I want to serve in a similar manner, if I can still be useful without having formal training."

"Even though I started out with that firm commitment to peace, I killed one of the Rebel soldiers."

"Sir, I know a little about your story from Louisa, and perhaps you heard something of my story. It seems that the violence we have committed should all the more firmly bind us to that gospel of peace. We've both stumbled, but here we are with another chance to do better. Sometime, I would be honored if you heard my story . . ."

". . . and I would likewise be honored if you would hear mine," Isaac interrupted.

"Well, sir, do you think there is some peaceable duty I could perform for the regiment?"

"At present, I will declare you fit for service as an ambulance driver. I worry about that wound in your left hand; it may trouble you for a long time. Something seems to make it fester, while your other wounds have healed well. Do you think you will be able to hold reins and handle skittish horses during battle?"

"Yes, sir. In my previous line of work, I drove teams of horses and mules among my other chores on the plantation. Some of those animals were none too friendly from poor treatment, but with some gentle words and handling, they would calm right down."

"Your primary duty will be the ambulance, but there may be occasions when you will have to help the stretcher-bearers. I worry about your ability to carry heavy weights, not to mention the pain it may cause in your left hand and right shoulder. Later, as you do recover strength, you may be able to work as a nurse in our field hospital. I cannot guarantee that in a tough spot during battle, you would not be called upon to assist in combat, especially considering your skills with heavy artillery. But you have my pledge that I will do everything within my power to protect you from that possibility."

"Thank you, sir."

CHAPTER THIRTY-FIVE

"Woman should take to her soul a strong purpose, and then make circumstances conform to that purpose."

SUSAN B. ANTHONY

"You cannot make soldiers of slaves, or slaves of soldiers. The day you make a soldier of them is the beginning of the end of the revolution. And if slaves seem good soldiers, then our whole theory of slavery is wrong."

HOWELL COBB, CONFEDERATE GENERAL AND POLITICIAN

SEATED IN THE HEADQUARTERS of the Army of the James, Louisa quickly took in the modest interior, but it was the strange being sitting at the desk opposite her on that hot day in June 1864 that like a magnet irresistibly drew her full attention. Beads of sweat lining up in rows across a balding pate like soldiers on parade compelled her to stare more than was polite. Regaining perspective, she was able to place the large sweaty head into the much broader context of a man sitting before her but could not avoid the impression that she was in the presence of a large toad—to be sure, a very intelligent and industrious toad—who was intently perusing the documents she had offered him. Even though he was a large man, his head seemed disproportionately large in relation to the rest of his bulk. As he was reading, he would periodically pause and look up at her, apparently attempting to smile, but the odd squint of his beady eyes would lend a disconcerting quality to the gesture that transmogrified it into a smirk.

So, this is General Benjamin Butler, the same man who so cleverly coined the term "contraband of war," setting in motion the events leading to the Emancipation Proclamation, she thought. *Oh, if only Sam could be here to witness this interview. He thought it such a very lawyerly stroke of brilliance on Butler's part—placing the Negro squarely in the middle of the conflict. And this coming from a politician who had nominated Jeff Davis for President of the United States in 1860; how times and people change! Not only has he become the strongest and most vocal advocate for the martial qualities of the black man, but his advocacy for the welfare and education of all refugees from slavery has been extraordinary. If the strongest champion for colored persons among our generals happens to be a large toad, so be it! The ways of God are not as our ways . . .* Louisa's musings were suddenly interrupted as she became acutely aware that the *toad* was directing his cross-eyed gaze in her direction.

"Hmm, Oberlin graduate among many other accomplishments . . . Mrs. Heyward, Colonel Eaton speaks very highly of your work among the contrabands in the Department of the Mississippi. I have followed the experiment at Corinth, Mississippi, with great interest, and I am very pleased that you are bringing the wisdom gained from that experience to the eastern theater of the war.

"Please accept my sincere condolences on the death of your brother in that horrific affair at Fort Pillow. I can assure you that the colored troops here in the Army of the James have every intention of avenging that atrocity. I am delighted that your brave husband can find a place here to serve his country, away from the source of so many painful memories."

"Sir, we are both grateful for this opportunity."

"In his letter, Colonel Eaton indicates that your husband has advanced far beyond simple literacy through your efforts."

"I appreciate the colonel's kind words, but it was through his *own* diligent efforts and intellectual gifts that my husband has achieved so much in such a short time . . . and as his duties permit, he hopes to continue his quest for knowledge. From my experience teaching contrabands, I have witnessed an unparalleled thirst for knowledge. Certainly, some individuals are naturally more gifted intellectually than others, but I would dare say that it would be difficult, if not impossible, to find the same level of commitment to learning and self-improvement among the white population." Realizing that in her enthusiasm she might have offended General Butler by her comparison of colored with white students, Louisa stopped to see the general's reaction.

When the general's response was to smile, Louisa began to warm to that odd squinty-eyed smirk. "Mrs. Heyward, I can only confirm the veracity of your observations. You probably know something of my history as a Northern War Democrat. The scales of prejudice against the Negro quickly fell from my eyes when I was fortunate enough to personally witness the plight but also the initiative of the contrabands, first at Fortress Monroe and then later during my administration of the city of New Orleans. It is my intention to help all those who desire to become literate not only achieve this basic skill but also, with the assistance of competent teachers like yourself, to prepare them for full citizenship in this republic. The Confederates have attempted to dignify their rebellion by calling it a revolution. Well, they are right to call it a revolution, but it has become an entirely different revolution from the one they had envisaged. Just think of it—armed Negroes in the uniform of the United States Army—what could more effectively strike terror into Southern hearts? I intend to complete the sacred work of John Brown. His crucial idea was to arm the black man, and it is precisely in the fulfillment of his vision that slavery will be abolished and this terrible rebellion will be crushed. Mrs. Heyward, you won't have to look very far to see that Brown's vision is being fulfilled here in the Army of the James!

"My priorities for you, if I may be so bold, are first to help oversee and assist personally, in the efforts already underway, to achieve basic literacy for all the colored soldiers in the Army of the James, and second, to further develop these same efforts among the contrabands. Oberlin's commitment to train missionaries is well known. I would specifically encourage you to use that training to elevate the moral and religious spirit of our contraband communities. My assistant will prepare passes to facilitate your safe passage without hindrance among the different contraband communities here, as well as among the colored regiments in the Army of the James. I look forward to periodic reports from you, not only of successes but also regarding any challenges, especially where I might be able to help."

Colonel Joseph Kiddoo looked up from the map laid out on the table, where he and the other officers of the 22nd USCT had just finished dining the evening of June 14, 1864, and smiled. "Gentlemen, early tomorrow morning, colored troops—including the 22nd USCT—will act in concert with their white brethren recently returned from Cold Harbor as the XVIII Corps attacks the defenses of Petersburg. It will be a glorious opportunity to demonstrate what we know the Negro soldier can accomplish beyond building fortifications and garrisoning forts." Isaac

Burgess marveled to hear senior white officers so strongly supportive of black soldiers and thought, *I made the right decision to seek a commission in a colored regiment.*

While he had participated in the frenetic preparations of the Army of the James since his transfer, the larger plan had only become apparent to officers at his level during the prior twenty-four hours. His thoughts whirled between the new army he had joined and the realization that his old comrades from the Army of the Potomac were in motion, executing an incredibly ambitious maneuver to give General Lee the slip, crossing the James River with the intention to capture the railroads supplying the Army of Northern Virginia and ultimately take the Confederate capital from the rear. What seemed particularly astounding was the apparent element of surprise favoring the planned assault. From a recent reconnaissance in force, as well as intelligence gathered from observation towers that had been constructed at General Butler's orders, there was a paucity of Confederate forces defending Petersburg south of Richmond. It just might be possible to break through the lightly manned defensive works which protected the city and the rail lines, so critical to survival of the Confederacy. Could it be true that Grant had finally caught the ever-canny Lee unawares?

In the predawn gray, Isaac moved at a deliberate pace among the ambulance units under his command, offering a word of encouragement or counsel to as many of his men as possible before what he sensed would be a day of carnage. Carrying a kerosene lantern to guide his path, he smiled at the thought that he might be a latter-day Diogenes in search of an honest man. It did not take long for him to find his man, for as Isaac lifted his lantern to examine the next ambulance in line, the sad benevolence of Napoleon Heyward's remaining eye met and held Isaac's gaze as a slight smile slowly framed his lips.

"Are you ready, Corporal Heyward?"

"Only God knows, sir. I hope that when I come face-to-face with my Lord, I will truly be ready." Taken aback by Nappy's response, Isaac paused. "I'm not certain that I can recall in all my experience of this terrible war, ever receiving such a response to a simple question. Forgive me, Corporal, for clearly your reflections are directed toward the sublime, toward ultimate things, while your commanding officer's thoughts run toward the mundane. While I inquire about the status of your supplies, equipment, and horses, you offer me a report on the state of your soul."

"I'm sorry, sir." Patting the rumps of his two horses, Nappy's subtle smile broadened to a grin. "The last time I was in combat, I very nearly met my Maker, so my thoughts have been drifting along in that direction, considering today's activities. My animal friends and the fine ambulance wagon which have been entrusted to my care are all in excellent order. The two soldier stretcher-bearers should return soon with a few more supplies."

"Perhaps there is a place between the sublimity of your response and the banality of my intent. How is your courage, corporal?"

"Sir, you have known my dear wife longer than I. She has enough courage for both of us; I am strengthened by her confidence and prayers."

In the early morning light, after the troops had been transported across the Appomattox River near City Point, the ambulance train took up its place at the rear of the two brigades comprising General Hinks's 3rd Division of the XVIII Corps. Riding ahead with Colonel Kiddoo, Isaac was struck by the extraordinary spectacle. Never had he seen a solid host of black soldiers, rank-on-rank, marching in close order with rifled muskets gripped by hands that were ready to claim the full rights of humanity and citizenship long denied. Turning toward Isaac, Colonel Kiddoo said, "Dr. Burgess, we are blessed to witness history being recorded today, writ large in *black* letters—living . . . and dying letters—intermittently punctuated by white officers."

Resting their horses by the side of the road, the two mounted officers quietly saluted the standard-bearers at the head of each regiment as they passed. Suddenly, the commanding officer of the 22nd USCT was unable to suppress a cry of excitement upon seeing the unique standard of his regiment carried proudly aloft in company with the Stars and Stripes. Having heard something about it beforehand, Isaac still gaped upon his first sight of the remarkable image portrayed on the regimental flag. A victorious colored soldier in Union blue was depicted as he was about to thrust his bayonet into the stomach of a defeated Rebel officer who had fallen backward to the ground. An inscription in Latin, *Sic semper tyrannis*, was the crowning glory turning the motto of the Commonwealth of Virginia on its head—*Thus always to tyrants!* But there was something more in the image. In addition to the sword falling from his right hand, the doomed Rebel officer had also dropped what appeared to be a white flag from his left.

"Such an extraordinary regimental standard! I've seen nothing like it, even the motto emblazoned on the standard of the Irish Brigade in which I served, *Riamh nár dhruid ó spairn lann*, or *Who never retreated from the clash of spears*, pales in comparison with the powerful irony expressed by the 22nd USCT's appropriation of this Southern motto. But colonel, what is the meaning of the white flag in the image?"

"Dr. Burgess, there may be a bit of intentional ambiguity in the image, but I think that considering how colored soldiers have been treated recently by their Rebel captors, the ambiguity fades, a clear message remains, and it could be expressed thus: *Remember Fort Pillow! No quarter!* Our colored troops have no illusions about their service in Uncle Sam's army. With the threat of torture and immediate execution, or at best, enslavement if they surrender in battle, the flag's meaning is clear enough. They have no intention of surrendering. I expect that they will fight with the desperation and ferocity of condemned men." At these words, Samuel Johnson's smiling face appeared before Isaac's inner eye, and he gulped hard. "Colonel, I guess we will learn soon enough the full meaning of what is depicted on their flag."

"Our flag, Doctor, *our* flag. The Rebels don't care much for us 'n____r' officers of colored regiments, whom they consider to be traitors to the white race. If I'm captured by the Rebels, I don't expect or desire any different treatment than that received by our enlisted men."

Approaching a place known locally as Baylor's Farm, where a Rebel defensive outpost had been established, the two brigades of colored troops formed in line of battle. For the day's fighting, the 22nd USCT was assigned to Colonel Samuel Duncan's brigade, which, of the two, had the more experienced soldiers. Colonel John Holman's brigade consisting of dismounted colored cavalry (the 5th Massachusetts) and the 1st USCT were placed behind Duncan's four regiments, which were deployed with the 6th, 4th, 22nd, and 5th USCT from left to right in a single line of battle. Two artillery batteries followed behind the infantry and dismounted cavalry with the medical staff and ambulances in the rear.

A patch of swampy woods slowed the soldiers' advance. Emerging from the tangle of trees, mud, and fetid water, they encountered a Rebel cavalry brigade and battery which were quietly waiting to *greet* them across several hundred yards of open plain. Fragmentary details of what happened next were learned by Isaac and the other medical staff as they were inundated with a sudden and massive influx of casualties making their way to the aid stations in the rear. Before Colonel Duncan could fully organize a coordinated plan of attack, elements from the 4th USCT, in their enthusiasm, surged forward without orders and were hit very hard by Rebel fire. To make things worse, the dismounted men of the 5th Mass. Cavalry that were stationed behind the 4th USCT panicked and fired at their comrades in the 4th USCT before heading for the rear. Colonel Kiddoo, who had significant prior experience under fire, managed to steady the 22nd and 5th USCT, averting disaster, and led the two regiments on to a coordinated attack, routing the Rebels and even taking a twelve-pound howitzer as a prize.

Nearly swamped by the initial flood of wounded soldiers, Isaac and a medical cadet recently arrived from Philadelphia worked with medical staff from the other regiments to impose some order amid the chaos as they assessed and transported casualties back to City Point. Isaac felt fortunate to have the additional assistance even though his young colleague, Gideon Barnes, was not a fully qualified physician. While ambitious men with abolitionist sentiments sought opportunities for advancement as the white officers of colored regiments, there was generally less interest on the part of physicians to provide medical care for black soldiers. Young medical students eager to see a bit of the action as well as gain invaluable experience were given intensive training as medical cadets and could then potentially serve as assistant surgeons in regiments with chronic medical staff vacancies, especially colored regiments.

Returning to City Point with the first wave of wounded soldiers from the encounter at Baylor's Farm, Isaac and the other medical officers from Hink's Division quickly discovered that the hospital facilities were not equally available to all the wounded. After some tense words were exchanged with medical staff from other divisions, it became clear that far fewer hospital tents were available for the care of the colored soldiers than he and his colleagues had initially thought. Suppressing his anger, Isaac motioned to Gideon, who silently helped him organize and move their operating equipment and supplies to a tent on the far side of the hospital complex, furthest away from the battlefront. While they were hastening to reestablish a functional operating tent, the lieutenant in charge of the ambulance train rushed off to find more tents for what would become the foundation of a fully segregated hospital for the colored soldiers. Before dismissing Gideon to return to the regimental aid station at the front, Isaac could no longer suppress his anger. "Even in the Army of the James under the command of General Butler, who has not hidden his strong support for the Negro, we have such prejudicial attitudes toward colored soldiers. They are the first to be wounded in today's action, and the medical leadership, even in this *enlightened* branch of the US Military, withhold essential facilities and delay access to life-saving care because of their supposed inferiority! They say, 'Oh, we must preserve our supplies and facilities for the white veterans who have just returned from Cold Harbor.' Well, I say that the blood draining away from their black bodies is as red as yours or mine!"

The young, bespectacled medical cadet, who also happened to be a Philadelphia Quaker, gave Isaac a pained look in response to his angry, sarcastic words. Rather than say anything, he anxiously mopped the beads of sweat from his forehead, where an already-receding and wispy blond hairline prematurely aged him beyond his twenty-two years. Seeing his confusion, Isaac laughed. "During our short acquaintance, we've not discussed our common heritage in the Society of Friends. As you might guess, my military experience has had a corrupting influence on me. Now hurry and go tend the wounded, and send them back here for their operations. Maybe sometime I will tell you a story about a Quaker who lost the Testimony Against War."

Napoleon Heyward adjusted his eye patch as he tried to make sense of what was unfolding before his remaining eye. Heat from an angry Virginia sun beat down upon the ambulance driver and his horses as the day wore on. Returning to the regiment after ferrying the wounded from the fight at Baylor's Farm back to City Point, he had witnessed the rapid forward progress of Hink's Division to the extensive defensive fortifications outside Petersburg known as the Dimmock Line, only to see the advance stall. He couldn't understand why their victorious soldiers weren't attacking the Rebel defenses. The interminable delay extended from mid-morning until late afternoon. Rumors spread among the ambulance drivers that General Smith, who was in command of the overall assault, was checking the Rebel defenses from every imaginable angle before committing his troops to a potential disaster—no more Cold Harbors!

He wondered how the troops on the frontline could stand the suspense of waiting and remembered with a shudder the anticipation mixed with dread that he and Sam Johnson had experienced during the ill-fated truce in the Rebel attack on Fort Pillow. But this was no Fort Pillow; that was in the past. Here, colored soldiers in great numbers were on the offensive. That Southern atrocity had been seared into the collective memory of every soldier of African descent. Indeed, it was precisely because of this transformation that he was not surprised when he could hear the distant strains of "Joshua Fit the Battle of Jericho" wafting back to him from the soldiers as they waited impatiently for the order to go forward.

> Up to the walls of Jericho
> They marched with spears in hand
> "Come blow them ram horns," Joshua said
> "'Cause the battle is in my hand."
>
> Joshua fit the battle of Jericho, Jericho, Jericho
> Joshua fit the battle of Jericho
> and the walls came tumbling down . . .

But finally, as the sun was beginning to set in the west, the order was given, and the colored regiments went into motion with a shout that rolled up and crashed against the vaunted Rebel defenses, striking terror into many a Southern heart as the distinct words could be heard: "Remember Fort Pillow!"

In the diminishing light, Nappy could clearly apprehend that the sounds of battle were moving away from him, and then soon enough, his stretcher-bearers came bearing extraordinary news, along with the wounded soldiers in their care. "They've punched a big hole in the Dimmock Line; on to Petersburg!" One enthusiastic private wounded in the leg who arrived a little later by stretcher declared, "This could be the end of it all—just think of it—and we had a part in the glorious end!" Alas, it was not the end, only the beginning of the end—the beginning of a long siege.

After an exhausting night of operating, the next morning over coffee, Isaac could only groan to hear from Colonel Kiddoo how close the end had been. "Doctor, we had taken batteries three through eleven, more than a mile and a half of the Dimmock Line. I am confident we could have marched right into Petersburg, and then inexplicably, General Smith called a halt. Apparently, he was uncertain of the promised support from General Hancock. For once General Lee had been fooled, but with the hesitation and delays yesterday, followed by the failure to press the attack after dark last night . . . well, if you ride up to the front now, you will see the Rebs hard at work creating a new defensive line. We missed the greatest opportunity of the war last night." But Colonel Kiddoo wasn't quite finished with his tale and commentary. "The colored troops fought magnificently, and I had the signal honor of commanding some of them. Who can justly deny their claim to full manhood and rights of citizenship in these United States?"

Observing the omnipresent clouds of dust raised by the constant motion of ambulances bringing the wounded from the Petersburg front to the overextended hospital facilities at City Point, Isaac could not shake off an oppressive feeling. Realistically, the combination of extreme heat, with temperatures in excess of 100 degrees Fahrenheit, the inescapable filth, and collective misery of so many wounded soldiers subjected to intolerable conditions, should more than account for it, and yet there was something more that he couldn't articulate. It came to him as his attention turned to his conscientious assistant, the medical cadet Gideon Barnes, who was laboring over the last patient of that afternoon's sick call. The clouds of dust thrown up in the air by the wagon wheels brought to mind a vivid image from a memorable lesson in his Quaker youth. As an act of profound repentance in response to Jonah's prophecy of doom, the king and citizens of the ancient city of Nineveh were throwing dust and ashes up in the air over their heads. He smiled as he remembered his youthful disgust at the thought that becoming so filthy would in some way please God. *Well, here we are, just like the Ninevites covered in filth, but where is our repentance? Are we pleasing to God? So much misery, and now it must be prolonged as a siege. If only we could at least obtain the necessary supplies and facilities to care for the sick, wounded, and dying.*

While those in the chain of command, like Major Isaac Burgess, might be frustrated by the military bureaucracy, others freed from the constraints of uniform and empowered by an authority gained through experience and personal relationships were able to outflank the obstructions imposed by red tape and personality. To Isaac's great surprise and joy, over the next week large numbers of supplies designated for the proper construction and equipping of a hospital for the colored troops began to inexplicably arrive at the City Point wharves. When he made quiet inquiries about the dramatic about-face in the prioritization of the hospital for colored troops at the divisional headquarters, he was told by a staff officer, "It's all due to a woman's influence. Some gal from Massachusetts has been collaborating with the Sanitary Commission, helping with the wounded on the battlefield and in the field hospitals since the Peninsular Campaign, and as a result, she has General Burnside's confidence. Apparently, she heard that the colored soldiers weren't getting the care they deserved and made it her mission to seek help from Burnside . . ." At this point, the staff officer gave Isaac a suspicious look, to which Isaac responded, "I only wish I could take credit for informing her."

"Well, now you can take satisfaction in the fact that she has managed to overturn the normal procedures upon which a large army depends, and so now your precious Negroes will have their hospital ahead of many others."

"May God bless her!" Isaac exclaimed. "What's her name? I hope I may have the honor to meet her and thank her personally."

"That shouldn't be a problem—you'll be working with her. She has been given charge of the hospital's administration and will oversee the nursing staff. Her name is Helen Gilson from Chelsea, Massachusetts."

CHAPTER THIRTY-SIX

"The more this experience comes to me, the more I am lifted into the upper ether of peace and rest; I am stronger in soul and healthier in body; yet, I have never worked harder in my life."

HELEN GILSON

"There is not a man in our regiment, who would not lay down his life for Miss Gilson."

UNION SOLDIER

BEFORE OPENING A LETTER that had just arrived from Rebecca, Isaac paused to read a passage from Jimmy Thornton's New Testament. Whenever he had a moment's respite from his medical duties, he would often pore over this treasured relic of the dead Confederate. Although quite familiar with the Scriptures, he drew comfort from each reading, at least in part due to his discovery of extensive notes, reverently written with a pencil in a small but confident script on blank pages in the back of the Testament. Turning to the eleventh chapter of Matthew's Gospel, he read verse twelve: "And from the days of John the Baptist until now the kingdom of heaven suffereth violence, and the violent take it by force."

Never having heard a clear explanation of this enigmatic passage, he was pleased to see that Jimmy Thornton had written a note about it. *The regimental chaplain said that this passage should be taken as an exhortation for us to fight as hard as we can to preserve the Confederacy. He says it's just like heaven suffering violence when Lucifer rebelled and became the Devil. He insists we must take it back by force from the Yankees, and to do so, that means we must be violent. But I wonder if that is really what the Lord is saying here. When John the Baptist came, he preached repentance. And what about the kingdom of heaven suffering violence, didn't Christ also say that 'the kingdom of God is within you'? It seems to me that all the violence must be directed inside each of us, where the kingdom of God should be. If I'm supposed to be violent, it's all about making some real change inside, not outside. O Lord, help me make it through this war without being violent toward anyone except my own inner man. If it be thy will, preserve me from killing anyone. Amen.*

Forgetting himself, Isaac spoke aloud, "Now, that's a real Testimony Against War!" At that very moment, in need of a signature, Gideon Barnes entered Isaac's quarters. Reddening, he murmured, "Excuse me, sir. I am sorry to intrude."

"Gideon, you are not intruding at all." After signing the requisition, Isaac offered a camp stool to Gideon. "If you have a few minutes, for many weeks I have owed you a story about a Quaker who lost the Testimony Against War. But first let me begin that story by quoting a difficult passage of Scripture, which I believe has been brilliantly interpreted by a friend of mine." After reading the Scripture passage and the young Confederate's interpretation to his startled assistant surgeon, Isaac laughed. "I suppose you would like to know how I came to possess a Confederate soldier's New Testament; that's precisely how I lost the *Testimony*."

After Isaac finished his tale, he paused to observe his subordinate's reaction. The normally taciturn medical cadet slowly removed his spectacles, rubbed his eyes, and—hesitating a moment—cleared his throat and said, "Sir, I'm not sure you ever lost the Testimony Against War. It seems you may have misplaced it for a while, like so many of us do with the real treasures of life, but you certainly have rediscovered it, and in a most unexpected place."

> August 28, 1864
> Contraband Camp, Fort Pickering
> Memphis, Tennessee
>
> Dear Isaac,
>   It was with great relief that I received thy letter of August 15 confirming thy safety after the terrible explosion at the City Point wharf—to think it was no more than a mile from thy hospital! From the accounts in the newspapers, I cannot escape the conclusion that Providence spared General Grant for a higher

purpose since his headquarters was deluged with fragments from the explosion that injured and killed some of his subordinates. I remain grateful to that same gracious Providence who spared thee as well as Louisa and Nappy from injury and death. The official reports call it a terrible accident—I wonder. Coming so soon after the disastrous Battle of the Crater on July 30, it seems not unreasonable to speculate that Rebel saboteurs might have been seeking a form of retribution with the explosion of the ammunition barge at the City Point wharf. Regardless, whether there is any truth to such speculation, the fact that colored laborers represented the largest group of victims only adds to the poignant reality that the suffering of the Negro is at the heart of this horrible conflict.

At Rebecca's reference to the Battle of the Crater, Isaac paused, and his consciousness was flooded with the successive sounds, sights, and even smells of that day. Poor Ambrose Burnside—a brave, intelligent, and patriotic general, and yet his best laid plans would inevitably fail in execution. Isaac remembered the delay in delivery of pontoons that changed Fredericksburg from an opportunity to a death trap back in December 1862. He then reflected on Burnside's recent willingness to entertain and support the innovative idea of constructing a tunnel under the Rebel works at Petersburg, packing it with explosives and then blowing a large hole in the Rebel defenses that might permit a rapid breakthrough for Union forces. Like most of his fellow soldiers, Isaac's first awareness of the audacious plan was the very loud explosion coming from the direction of the Petersburg trenches early on July 30. Rumors about what was afoot had quickly spread at the colored hospital, which by that time had acquired the more dignified title of the Corps d'Afrique hospital. It wasn't long before urgent orders were received to send all available ambulance staff to the front to collect the growing numbers of wounded soldiers and to prepare for massive casualties at the City Point Hospitals. Only later would Isaac learn that the plan of attack had been changed and that originally, colored troops under General Ferrero's command in the Fourth Division of Burnside's Ninth Corps were to lead the effort. Apparently, personal conflicts, racial prejudice, and possibly drunken incompetence among some of the general officers won out over careful planning, so that unprepared units of white soldiers were thrust into the gap created by the explosion rather than skirting the defect at the moment of greatest Rebel surprise and confusion, which had been the original instructions and training given to the colored troops. In the debacle, increasing numbers of hapless soldiers were thrust into the crater. Unable to scale the sides of the crater, they now became extremely vulnerable targets for the Rebels, who had quickly recovered from the initial chaos caused by the explosion. To cap the folly, the Negro units, who in the reorganized plan had been placed at the rear of the attack force, were now ordered forward to be further crowded within the crater-turned-tomb, over the protests of their direct commander.

Over the ensuing hours, trains from the front had continuously transported large numbers of severely wounded soldiers the eight miles to City Point, keeping Isaac and the other operating surgeons busy all day. It was only during a break at the end of the day that he could fully appreciate the horrific futility of the battle when he heard the ambulance driver's account. Nappy had just brought in some of the few remaining wounded, colored soldiers who had avoided capture by the Rebels. Shaking continuously, and with a steady stream of tears flowing from his remaining eye, he was initially unable to speak in his deep distress, but finally a torrent of words came like a dam that had burst. "Sir, it was Fort Pillow all over again! Our boys were trapped in that crater with no way out. The Rebs were taking the white soldiers who surrendered as prisoners, but the colored soldiers who tried to surrender they shot down like dogs, shouting 'kill the damn n____rs!' Some of us volunteered to go in and try to rescue as many of our wounded as possible." At this point Isaac had interrupted Nappy: "Surely, you didn't go into that maelstrom, did you, corporal?"

"I had to, sir. I wouldn't be able to live with myself if I hadn't at least tried to help."

"But you must have been under continuous fire from the Rebels!"

"Not so much, sir. The Rebs were mostly preoccupied with the soldiers trying to surrender."

"Were these wounded you just brought in part of that effort?"

"Yes, but it was only a small number we could rescue. The worst of it was that as we got closer to the Rebels, I could see that some of them were offering to take our colored soldiers as prisoners of war, but it was only a trick! As soon as they pulled them up out of the crater, they began to torture them, cursing, beating, and bayoneting them without mercy!" Isaac remembered the horror written on the face of one who, in witnessing these fresh Rebel atrocities, was clearly reliving the massacre at Fort Pillow. At that moment Isaac had made a decision which in retrospect he should have made earlier. He wrote out a forty-eight hour leave for

Nappy with a short note of explanation to Louisa, apologizing for her husband's re-exposure to Rebel atrocities. Handing them to Nappy, he told him to report back for his new hospital duties at the Corps d'Afrique hospital at the end of the leave.

His thoughts gradually returning to Rebecca's letter, he silently agreed with her. *Yes, Rebecca, "the suffering of the Negro is at the heart of this conflict."*

> I assume, Isaac, that by the time thou will read this letter, the news of the recent events here in Memphis will have reached thee and may even be "old" news. But I must share with thee my perspective on Forrest's raid and the profound impact it has had on me. I won't dwell on the incompetence of the military leadership here; certainly, the newspapers have already had quite a lot to say in that regard. Neither will I express much concern about my personal safety during the raid, although I must admit being initially frightened when I was awakened from a sound sleep in the early morning hours to the sounds of gunfire and screams of "Rebels!" and "Memphis is under attack!" Later it became evident that Forrest's audacious ride into his hometown was more an attempt to boost Southern morale than anything like a real military threat, although some Union generals who were the targets for kidnapping by his troopers might feel differently! Indeed, he was successful in causing Union forces to pull back and abandon their positions in Northern Mississippi for a time. But none of these aspects of the incident are more than interesting anecdotes to share with my grandchildren someday. (If I should ever be blessed with marriage and children, let alone grandchildren, only a kind Providence knows!)
>
> For me, the profound impact of his raid came as the culmination of the long litany of Nathan Bedford Forrest's depredations. How could I reconcile the cheers of the populace in Memphis for their "chivalrous" hero as he "put the Yankees in their place" with the continuing atrocities committed by his soldiers against our brave colored troops since Fort Pillow? The sheer arrogance and bravado of the raid at this late stage in the war makes me ill. Dear brother, I do not doubt the ultimate victory of the North but I fear what will come after the South surrenders and all its bastions are occupied by the Northern conqueror. Will repentance and brotherly love reign supreme, or will the festering hatred for the "inferior race" erupt in acts of violence that will make the massacre at Fort Pillow seem commonplace?

It isn't only Southern resentment and violence I fear—I fear myself. Oh, Isaac, I must confess how sinful I have been toward thee and before God; please forgive me—I hope God will eventually forgive me. I was initially horrified to learn of thy action in wounding the young Rebel soldier who later died. In my Pharisaical attitude, I assumed that I would never entertain such angry, hateful thoughts, let alone act on them. But now I confess that Forrest's raid exposed my hypocrisy and brought all my hidden anger to the surface. Along with the Federal wounded, severely wounded Rebel soldiers left behind by Forrest were also brought to Fort Pickering for medical care. When called upon to care for them, all I could think was "these are the same men who mercilessly carried out the massacre at Fort Pillow and, boasting of their heinous actions, have gone on to commit further atrocities against the colored soldiers following the battle at Brice's Crossroads." Would I be relieving the thirst, dressing the wounds, and offering comfort to the very monsters who killed Sam and tortured and maimed Nappy? My grief for Sam came rushing back to me, but now it was transmuted into rage! Penelope could perceive my agitation and distress at the prospect of caring for the wounded Rebel soldiers and offered to take the primary responsibility for their care, hoping to spare me any direct contact with them. But in my self-righteousness, I insisted that it was *my duty* to care for all the wounded, regardless of their uniform and allegiance.

Remembering with incredulity how thou hast drawn some peace from the counsel given thee by Chaplain Corby to pray for mercy on Forrest and thyself *together*, I refused to contemplate such an approach in my relations with the wounded Rebels under my care. As thou might suspect, many of the Rebel soldiers had received mortal wounds. When I reflect on my actions, it is with great shame I confess that I not only treated the Rebels with brusqueness, providing only for their most basic needs in the most peremptory manner, but I began to take secret delight in seeing them suffer. No kind word or smile from my lips was I willing to offer to those who were about to encounter eternity, ignoring their pitiful cries for a mother, sister, or sweetheart. In my arrogance, I had already done God's work of judging the wicked for Him—I was fully confident of the eternal fate awaiting each of these *goats*. Thou might rightly wonder whether I had forgotten the Lord's commandment to love our enemies. Indeed, I have never allowed alcoholic spirits to pass my lips, but I was fully intoxicated by something far more potent and dangerous than alcohol—*hate*. I thank God that Penelope intervened before I caused more undue suffering, this time insisting that she would take on the responsibility for nursing the Rebel soldiers. In her great kindness and sensitivity, she attempted to divert my thoughts in a more constructive direction.

As thou might guess, her interest in all things medical has continued to blossom in the variety and sophistication of the hospitals that have been established here in Memphis by Dr. Bernard Irwin, whom thou came to know after the battle of Shiloh. His innovative approach to the development of division field hospitals has extended to the expansion of the size, number, and character of hospitals here once the city came into Federal hands in late 1862. Further arousing Penelope's interest, he has even authorized development of a hospital devoted solely to the treatment of soldiers suffering from gangrene, based on the scientific work with bromine of Dr. Middleton Goldsmith of Louisville, Kentucky, of which she was already familiar. At the same time, Mother Bickerdyke has undertaken the task of improving the diets and general cleanliness of the military hospitals under Dr. Irwin's authority. Together, their efforts are bearing much fruit. I think it safe to say that both the suffering and mortality of soldiers cared for in these facilities has been significantly mitigated in 1864 compared to the early days of the war.

Thou art probably wondering about my extensive digression, but hopefully thou will understand its necessity in what I will relate next. I must also confess, dear brother, my growing anxieties regarding the spiritual dangers of thy friendship with Chaplain Corby and thy increasing reliance on his spiritual counsel during thy service in the Irish Brigade. Clearly, thou must remember well how we were taught to be wary of "Papists" during our college years at Oberlin, not to mention our Society's testimony regarding unnecessary religious pomp and ritual that has defined the form of worship among Friends. Well, here I finally arrive at the *gentle* lesson that Penelope taught me, caught as I have been in a web of profound malice and Pharisaism. Touring the many other Memphis military hospitals, she hoped to learn as much as she could that might be of practical help to the refugees and soldiers treated in the colored hospital. In the process, she encountered two separate orders of Catholic nuns, Dominicans and Sisters of Mercy, who have been nursing wounded and sick soldiers since the war began, regardless of uniform or color of skin. Curious as to their loyalties, she wondered if they, like her, had become disillusioned with the Southern cause. When she asked one of the sisters about this possibility, she was met with a puzzled stare, followed by this response: "Oh dear . . . it's not that at all. When we are given the great privilege of touching one of these suffering ones, we are blessed to care for our Crucified Lord Himself, who comes to us in many guises."

After quoting the Catholic sister, Penelope looked at me and said, "Rebecca, I suspect it has been difficult for you to see our Crucified Lord in Nathan Bedford Forrest, his troopers, or any Rebel soldiers for that matter. It certainly has been increasingly difficult for me, a once-staunch Southern patriot. And yet, I am certain these Catholic sisters would not hesitate to care for the worst scoundrel, Yankee or Confederate, recognizing in the wounded person before them only the image of their suffering and Crucified Lord."

Oh, Isaac, I wept bitter tears . . . the purity of the love motivating the Catholic sisters . . . but all I could offer was pure, unmitigated hate. Where was my sunny confidence, always ready to share the Friends' Testimony Against War? God in His mercy has shamed me, exposing my hypocrisy through the love and compassion of Catholics!"

Isaac paused and recalled with gratitude his own experience working with the Sisters of Mercy in their hospital in Detroit during his medical training before the war. Resuming his perusal of her letter, he groaned silently as he began to realize the direction it was taking.

Penelope Wormeley's friendship has been an enormous comfort, helping greatly to steady me during this time in which I have been tested and found wanting. But how I miss Louisa's company! Her marriage and departure to the east has left a gaping hole in my soul. Every letter from her uplifts my spirit, and in her present circumstances she has been able to provide me with a perspective on thy activities that is not only highly informative and at times amusing but also causes me some concern on thy behalf. Before I write more about my concerns for thee, I must answer thy question about my social relations here in Memphis. There really is little to say. Several officers from the garrison here at Fort Pickering have shown interest in me, but I have not been able to reciprocate their interest. For the most part they have behaved as gentlemen, following a well-worn path at social events: first, there is the interminable hovering like bees around flowers; second, one bolder than the rest offers a silly compliment about my appearance that is typically awkward; and third, when an attempt at conversation is initiated, it almost always ends even more awkwardly than the compliment preceding it. I suppose that I am to blame as much as the officers. The painful truth is that they are boring. If I try to discuss some intelligent subject from history, literature, the arts, or even the events of the day, they almost invariably acquire a blank expression on their face that confesses without words their ignorance of said subject. In summary, they bore me and I bore them. Thy sister may end her days a spinster, too educated for her own good.

In her last two letters, Louisa has expressed growing admiration for a young woman from the Boston area named Helen Gilson. From thy correspondence in late June, I remember thou had expressed great frustration with the state of the hospital facilities available for the colored troops who had been wounded during the failed attempts to breach the Petersburg defenses. Inexplicably, there was no mention in thy next letter, only a few weeks later, whether thy frustration with those same hospital facilities had been resolved. Louisa lifted the veil on the mystery when she explained that Miss Gilson, who has extensive prior experience with hospital and battlefield nursing, and who is well known to General Burnside, offered her services to organize a proper hospital for the colored troops. Louisa has given a glowing account of the quiet efficiency and excellent diplomatic skills of the young lady from Chelsea, Massachusetts. According to Louisa, in a matter of a few weeks, her leadership and efforts have led to the establishment of the Corps d'Afrique hospital as the model for all others to emulate at City Point.

Here, Isaac paused to reflect on the truly remarkable transformation which Helen Gilson had wrought in such a short time—*nothing short of miraculous*, he thought. Before she arrived, the hospital for the colored troops had been nothing more than a roof, dirt, and bugs. He still remembered her exact words at his first meeting with her when she succinctly summed up the dreadful conditions, fanning herself in the hundred-degree Fahrenheit heat. "The dust is intolerable . . . No roses here, nothing of beauty, only a parched and arid plain, a mile square of hospital tents, filled with sick and wounded men." Turning to him, she had quietly declared, "I can't ignore this suffering, I must do something for these soldiers." Isaac had marveled how with the greatest tact and negotiating skills, she had proceeded to create a healing environment marked by cleanliness, wholesome food, compassion, and especially beauty. *How often does one single individual materially improve the lives of so many? Miss Gilson, with her combination of humble persistence, true philanthropy, and natural charm has accomplished what the entire military chain of command was incapable of doing.* Other recent memories came to mind as he pondered Helen Gilson's work. Many a night he had seen her making her rounds by candlelight through the different wards, speaking a word of comfort here or gently adjusting a bandage there. He smiled as he recalled the first time he had heard her sing a hymn to a rapt audience of wounded soldiers. Her soprano voice rivalled Rebecca's in its clarity and poignance of expression. With a wistful sigh, Isaac returned to his sister's missive.

> Louisa has also shared her observations about thy relationship with Miss Gilson, about which thou hast been remarkably silent in thy correspondence with me. Louisa doesn't mince words, as thou knowest. She thinks that thou art quite smitten with Miss Gilson. She went on to enumerate all her physical charms and beauty, as well as extolling her virtuous character. Before thou leap into the unknown of romance with this woman from New England, has it not occurred to thee that she is almost assur-edly a Unitarian? While our Oberlin professors warned us of the dangers of Papist traditions, they were even more concerned to protect us from the Arian heresy of their Unitarian cousins who have departed from sound Congregationalist doctrine, even de-nying the divinity of Christ. Surely as an orthodox Friend these doctrinal deviations should be of equal concern to thee.

Isaac paused again and scratched his beard. *Oh, Rebecca, Rebecca, how shall I respond to your concerns? I never spoke to Helen about doctrine, but what I have witnessed is a beautiful woman singing Christian hymns with great feeling to comfort the faint-hearted and dying. What shall I say of her feeding the hungry, clothing the naked, visiting the sick, and even those in our military prison? For indeed, she daily commits such acts of Christian love and more. Her doctrine may be unsound for all I know, but her soul is pure and, I daresay, pleasing to God. All her selfless service on behalf of the suffering soldiers at the Corps d'Afrique hospital has brought her exhaustion and malaria, which has nearly taken her life. One of the greatest blessings of my entire life has been the privilege to keep vigil at her bedside during the worst of her illness. The memories of mopping her forehead during her delirium I will always treasure. She has become the epitome of the feminine for me. But, Rebecca, you need not worry about your brother marrying a heretic, at least not yet, because to my great sorrow Helen is promised to another—the most fortunate of men!* Coming to him-self, Isaac said out loud, "Better not write anything about it to Rebecca.

I'll let Louisa tell her the *good news.*" Then, turning back to the last lines of the letter, he laughed when he read his sister's final admonishment.

> Hast thou inquired whether thy medical cadet is an orthodox Friend, or is he of the Hicksite separation?

Well, finally something about which I can reassure my dear sister. I will give her the good news of his orthodoxy personally in my next letter, after I calm down from reading this one.

CHAPTER THIRTY-SEVEN

"The man who says the Negro will not fight is a coward.... His soul is blacker than the dead faces of these dead Negroes, upturned to heaven in solemn protest against him and his prejudices."

GEN. BENJAMIN BUTLER

AS AN ARDENT ABOLITIONIST and Protestant minister from the North, the Reverend Christopher Burrows had eagerly sought a commission as a chaplain in one of the newly formed colored regiments and was extremely pleased when his appointment as chaplain of the 22nd USCT came through in May 1864. It was one thing to preach abolition and preservation of the Union from the pulpit; it was quite another to be personally present with the troops, encouraging them in the good fight.

Although his primary responsibility was to address the spiritual needs of the black soldiers in his regiment, Chaplain Burrow's duties rapidly expanded to embrace not only soldiers but also civilian refugees, including service as a teacher. His revulsion for the South's peculiar institution and strong belief in the equality of all men did not prepare him fully for the reality of the situation he encountered when he began his ministry in earnest at City Point among the diverse population of colored persons. His own regiment, the 22nd USCT, was something of an anomaly, comprised largely of Northern Negroes, a majority of whom already enjoyed at least a rudimentary literacy. On the other hand, most of the colored people whom he met at City Point or in the Corps d'Afrique hospital were recently enslaved persons who, in escaping to Union lines, had become contrabands. Depending on the success of Northern arms, they were now in an uncertain transitional state awaiting the full realization of Lincoln's Emancipation Proclamation. It was this vast sea of refugees that was the source of many recruits to the newly formed and forming colored regiments. With the able-bodied refugees from slavery also came the elderly, infirm, women, and children. Uncle Sam had become one vast employer, so that many refugees found employment in and around City Point in a variety of capacities as cooks, laundresses, stevedores at the busy wharf, and teamsters, among other occupations.

Farsighted leaders like General Benjamin Butler realized that this was the time to not only address the immediate needs of the refugees but also to prepare them for citizenship after the war. It wasn't long before he realized that his literacy program must expand beyond the colored troops to embrace as many of these new refugees as possible. The Massachusetts-politician-turned-general might have had his limitations as a military tactician, but his astute political instincts were never asleep; he recognized the great importance of transforming the former *contraband of war* into educated, politically engaged citizens who would be crucial agents of change in the rebirth of an American society and culture freed from the taint of slavery. Volunteer educators like Louisa Heyward coming from the American Missionary Society and other benevolent Northern organizations became valued partners in his grand scheme. The refugees' educational curriculum included not only reading, writing, spelling, grammar, geography, and history, but also very practical subjects like arithmetic, sewing, and even in some instances, gymnastics. In the teaching, there was a balance between an emphasis on transforming former slaves into citizens and their moral improvement. While a variety of contemporary textbooks were used, the overwhelming favorite among the refugees was the Bible. Eventually, regimental chaplains were given increasing responsibility to achieve Butler's educational goals. But for individuals like Chaplain Burrows, whose naïveté and good intentions were challenged by a culture so foreign to him, it was Negro educators, especially those not far removed from an enslaved past like Napoleon Heyward, who would become the bridge.

Chaplain Burrows's first encounter with Nappy had been near the middle of August, while he was making rounds among the wounded soldiers at the Corps d'Afrique hospital. Entering a ward, he was surprised to see how nearly all the colored soldiers were giving their rapt attention to a striking figure in blue with the two chevrons of a corporal on his sleeve standing in their midst. As the black man turned, revealing his profile, the chaplain was struck by the confident muscular form of the Negro who was now addressing a contingent of survivors from the Battle of the Crater. Initially, disconcerted by the speaker's eye patch, he realized that in this company, it only added authority to his speech; it was immediately evident to all that this man spoke from personal experience.

"Brothers, I know you burn with the desire for revenge against the Rebs, but hear what the apostle Paul says in his letter to the Romans: 'Avenge not yourselves . . . for it is written, *Vengeance is mine; I will repay, saith the Lord.*' Don't misunderstand me. What the Rebel soldiers did to our brothers at Fort Pillow and now have repeated here at the Crater cries out for vengeance, but for the just retribution that can *only* be administered by the *only* truly Just One, our Lord Jesus Christ. Who among us is so righteous to be the judge over our fellow man? And yes, the Rebs are our fellow men, even though they would treat us like animals to be bought, sold, and even worked to death at their pleasure. I beg all of you, do not descend to their level of depravity. Many times, have I cried out to God in my own suffering, 'O Lord, shake Jeff Davis over the mouth of hell, *but O Lord don't drop him in!*' Why such a prayer, you might ask? What is better, for Rebs who committed these terrible atrocities to rot in hell or for them to repent and be saved? Mind you, it would be by *the skin of their teeth*. I don't know about you folks, but I already have enough on my conscience to answer for—I don't want to pretend I can do the Lord's work for Him. But I'll end by suggesting this as a path you all might take. I have found more peace praying for the fellows who tortured and nearly killed me at Fort Pillow to repent than dreaming about their damnation."

There was complete silence for some moments on the ward after Nappy finished his short homily and then someone spoke up and said, "Corpr'l yours is de right path to be sure, yes, it is, but oh, so hard! I don' know if'n de hate kin eber git outta my heart. Will you pray fer dis sinner?" The answer came swiftly, "Of course, I will but you must pray for me too!" At this exchange, from all corners of the ward came loud amens, and the chaplain could sense there were few present whose eyes did not glisten, including his own, as they pondered the corporal's words. From that moment, Chaplain Burroughs sought Nappy's help and advice, but in his humility, the Negro corporal would repeatedly demur, declaring that he wanted rather to learn from the chaplain, who had been properly trained for the Lord's ministry. Gradually, over the coming weeks and months, they formed an enduring friendship based on mutual respect—Nappy's profound respect for the formal theological training of the chaplain and the chaplain's respect and awe for a faith and piety that he regarded as nothing less than miraculous in the former slave.

Pacing back and forth with a rate hastening to keep up with the passionate enthusiasm of his speech, General Benjamin Butler captivated Louisa with his personal account of the battle of New Market Heights that had occurred at the end of the previous month of September. "Mrs. Heyward, you should have seen them—the colored troops, how they sustained a withering fire from some of the finest Texas units of Lee's army, and yet they kept advancing! My respect for the courage and manhood of your Negro brethren reached its crowning moment when they took those Heights. Through their valor and sacrifice, Lee's defensive line protecting Richmond has been weakened, forcing him to retrench and divert essential troops from Petersburg who were protecting the rail line that feeds his army. General Grant's patient strategy of extending his left to threaten the Rebels' right flank and supply lines will sooner or later pay great dividends. I want you to know that several of the Negro soldiers fought with such valor that I have recommended they be recognized for their individual exploits with the highest honor this nation can bestow—the Congressional Medal of Honor. But there is more: I want to personally honor all those brave Negro soldiers who took part in this recent action, as well as those who in future engagements during this siege demonstrate a similar spirit in combat. Therefore, I have designed a medal to be struck that I hope will in somewise recognize the courage which they have demonstrated in this crucible of war. What do you think of the following inscription for the medal? 'US Colored Troops . . . Distinguished for Courage, Campaign before Richmond.'" Benjamin Butler abruptly stopped pacing and squinted at Louisa, awaiting her response.

"Sir, everything you have said is deeply heartening to me, as I know it would be to all freedom-loving Negroes in these perilous times. My heart swells with joy to think of how you intend to honor our brave soldiers."

"Mrs. Heyward, I have reviewed your thorough report on the condition of colored education in the Army of the James and among the contrabands under its protection; I must congratulate you on work well done. Negro education has been a crucial element underlying our recent success on the battlefield. Without basic literacy, it is nearly impossible to maintain military discipline and achieve the coordination of action so essential to survival, let alone success, in the heat of combat. I am especially pleased to see confirmation in your report that nearly every regiment of US Colored Troops in the Army of the James now has its own dedicated school. You indicate that the educational curriculum is remarkably standardized, of very high quality, and that there are adequate educational supplies and books. But what would you say is the element of their education they appreciate the most?"

"General, most of the troops have a copy of either the Bible, or at least the New Testament. I can personally testify from repeated observation that the sacred Scriptures are being read by the soldier-students as their preferred textbook par excellence, not only in school but in their spare time."

"Mrs. Heyward, in your report you also mentioned that many of the regimental chaplains are voluntarily teaching the Negroes in the evenings after completing their regular duties. Knowing this, it seems reasonable to make the education of colored soldiers and refugees a formal responsibility of the chaplains in *every* colored regiment. With the colored soldiers' enthusiasm for the Scriptures as a foundation, the chaplains should make great strides in nurturing their moral advancement."

"Sir, enlisting *every* chaplain in the effort will also help fill existing gaps in the overall educational program, which can only benefit the colored refugees. Success breeds success: many benevolent aid organizations from the North, recognizing your remarkable achievements here, have responded by generously increasing their support for the education and welfare of the colored refugees which is felt in all quarters."

"Yes, Mrs. Heyward, it has been my goal to provide the best possible support to the Negro in his struggle to achieve freedom and the full rights of citizenship in the United States. It is for this reason that I have petitioned General Grant to transfer the colored troops from the IX Corps to the Army of the James. After suffering so terribly during the Battle of the Crater, they deserve a better opportunity for healing and rehabilitation than I think they are receiving in the Army of the Potomac. With their transfer, I intend to offer their family members the same benefits that colored soldiers' families receive in the Army of the James. One grave injustice weighs heavily on my soul—the unequal pay that colored troops have received from the beginning of their service. I still hope to see justice done, with their full pay restored in arrears."

As the summer gave way to the chill of autumn with the threat of a severe winter, it became evident to Isaac that his transfer of Corporal Heyward to the Corps d'Afrique hospital had been one of the best decisions he had made with his expanded authority. Louisa was extremely grateful, not only for her husband's increased safety but also that his nightmares had begun to dissipate after being relieved of his frontline ambulance duties. A never-ending flux of serious gunshot wounds inflicted by sharpshooters alternating with ghastly wounds from bursting shells arriving daily at the Corps d'Afrique hospital defined the rhythm of trench warfare. For Nappy, being at a distance from the explosions and firing line made a profound difference. To be sure, he still could not escape the blood, gore, and screams of soldiers in agonizing pain arriving at the hospital. But Helen Gilson, in her calm, quiet way, had created a clean, healing environment that mitigated much of the horror. In caring for the sick and wounded soldiers, he experienced a joy unlike any previous he had felt. As he learned his duties, whether it was assisting in wound care, gently feeding those too weak to feed themselves, gathering medicines and supplies for the hospital steward, or increasingly assisting Chaplain Burrows in the spiritual care, he found the work energizing.

Discovering that the corporal was literate, the hospital steward began to increasingly rely on Nappy to help with recording the large inventories of drugs, supplies, food, and equipment that were essential to the hospital's function. Helen Gilson and the hospital steward came separately to Isaac in late November and asked him why he had not sought the promotion of "our indispensable corporal." Having been concerned about the appearance of favoritism, he was relieved by these unsolicited endorsements. Chaplain Burrows even came forward with an unsolicited letter of support, stating that "Corporal Heyward's literacy and deep piety have been invaluable to my ministry among the colored soldiers and their families."

"Now hold your horses, Sergeant Napoleon Heyward! You can't have your shirt yet. I'm not finished sewing the additional chevron on the sleeve. Allow me to gently remind you, Sergeant, that I will always outrank you," Louisa declared in the most pompous tone she could muster and then burst out laughing. Ever modest, Nappy smiled broadly and replied, "Of course you outrank me, my darling. You are my queen, my joy, and now the expectant mother of our child."

Stepping back, Louisa slowly scrutinized her husband from all angles after he had donned the shirt. "Well, well . . . I must say it suits you. Yes, indeed, my handsome man is now a sergeant in the Union Army." Hugging Nappy tightly, she added, "I am honored to be your wife and the mother of your child; I love you, Sergeant Heyward."

As he made his rounds that cold December day through the different wards, invariably at least one of the patients would notice the three chevrons and remark upon it with good natured teasing, often embarrassing Nappy, who would have preferred to not be the center of attention. "Someone, find the doctor! I musn't be seein' straight. Are those three stripes on the corporal's sleeve?" Then loud laughter would follow with a resounding "three cheers for Sergeant Heyward!"

Wondering whether being promoted was more a curse than a blessing, Sergeant Heyward maintained as quiet a presence as possible throughout the rest of his rounds, hoping not to draw more attention to himself. By late afternoon, he had high hopes that the notoriety of his newly exalted state was beginning to abate when Chaplain Burrows approached, loudly congratulating him. "Sergeant Heyward, your promotion could not have come to a better man or at a better time for that matter." Nappy gave the chaplain a look of curiosity, hoping for an explanation of what *at a better time* could mean. The explanation came quickly.

"Sergeant, with increased authority comes increased responsibility. I can declare with the utmost enthusiasm how pleased I am to be able to *share* with you a new and important responsibility. Having been charged by our commanding general with the responsibility of encouraging cleanliness and order in the personal appearance of each of the colored soldiers in our regiment, I have determined after careful consideration that there is no better person than yourself to identify through careful inspection that soldier who exemplifies the highest standards of personal hygiene. What an opportunity to instill the best values in our soldiers; after all, *cleanliness is next to Godliness*. This task can only increase the great respect and regard for you among the men," the chaplain enthused. "Once you have made your determinations, the cleanest man of each guard detail will be excused from the detail and given a three-hour pass. A full day's pass will be given to the cleanest man at each company's morning inspection. In addition, the cleanest man in the periodic corps reviews will receive a twenty-day furlough, and the two cleanest men in each division will receive fifteen-day furloughs. As you can see, these latter categories will encourage *friendly* competition in cleanliness between the men of our regiment and their counterparts throughout our newly formed XXV Corps."

Thanking Chaplain Burrows for this unexpected opportunity, a subdued Sergeant Heyward returned to the queen of his life, who—noticing the absence of his earlier ebullience—asked, "What happened to my happy sergeant?"

"I learned that with increased authority comes increased responsibility."

CHAPTER THIRTY-EIGHT

"The natural selection of races leads to the survival of the more cerebrally-developed, while the less cerebrally-developed disappear."
HERBERT SPENCER, *THE PRINCIPLES OF BIOLOGY, VOLUME I*, 1864

IMPERCEPTIBLY, THE CLEAR CRISPNESS of a bright January morning had surrendered to a gray cloud cover which had embraced the barren landscape pockmarked by war. Sleet, quickly turning to snow, began to pelt and then blanket the two travelers, one on horseback and the other driving a pair of mules pulling a military ambulance. Both men, absorbed in their own thoughts, unconsciously struggled to resist the omnipresent gloom which the weather seemed determined to foist upon them.

"Ah, finally . . ." Isaac Burgess declared as they arrived at their destination, one of the field hospitals of the II Corps. "Now, we can get out of this miserable weather for a bit." Napoleon Heyward, who was driving the ambulance, quietly nodded his relief.

"Sergeant, I have said very little during our journey because I was afraid of what I might say regarding this whole business, which I consider to be a fool's errand. In fact, I have dragged my feet as long as possible, but after receiving direct orders from my superiors, I couldn't hold up *progress* any longer. But you're likely to hear a lot from me, maybe more than you'd ever want to hear, about the purpose of our mission on the return trip to City Point. I'll need to speak with one of the medical officers about the equipment, receive some basic instructions in its use, and then I will recruit some men to help us load all of it on to the ambulance before we leave. Meanwhile, let's find a warm dry place for you to eat and drink something while you wait."

"Major Burgess, I cannot begin to tell you how gratifying it has been for me to be a part of this important medical research; I'm certain you will feel the same once you get started," exclaimed the young assistant surgeon from the 20th Massachusetts, a regiment originally comprised of many students from Harvard. "The collection of thorough statistics from over seven thousand Caucasian soldiers will certainly be highly informative, even crucial for comparative purposes, but the crowning achievement will be when you and your colleagues complete the work on the Negro soldiers. Just think of it, this will be the largest and most comprehensive statistical study of man to date—no more speculation, *only facts*! The army has been conducting similar studies on white soldiers, but it is the US Sanitary Commission that has taken the lead in developing these crucial comparative studies between races. How otherwise will we know what to expect regarding the fate of the freedmen after the war or the relative effectiveness of the Negro as a soldier in comparison with white soldiers?"

Now nearly in raptures, the assistant surgeon of the "Harvard Regiment" went on to explain in detail the various anthropometric measurements that could be performed with the large apparatus and ancillary equipment. Isaac had no choice but to take copious notes regarding the many measurements and answers to questions to be recorded on a special form for colored troops, Form EE, as distinct from Form E for white soldiers. First, he was introduced to the andrometer, a nearly seven-foot-tall wooden post with multiple attached calipers for measuring standing height, limb length, and trunk width. Other calipers facilitated additional measurements, including the *facial angle*, or the angle created by a horizontal line from the ear to the nose, and a vertical line from the jaw to the forehead. Second, he learned the intricacies of a spirometer, a wooden box with a tube attached, into which soldiers would exhale to determine their lung's vital capacity.

Remembering a lecture he had heard Dr. Samuel Augustus Cartwright give more than ten years earlier at Memphis Medical College, he began to bristle at the implications of the study. Cartwright, a professor of medicine from New Orleans at the time, had claimed without empirical evidence that Negro slaves' lungs and other organs functioned inefficiently and, in a manner, distinctly different and inferior to Caucasians. With horror, Isaac realized that the study would require detailed, even intimate measurements of the soldiers. He was reminded of the slave auction he had witnessed in antebellum Memphis, where potential buyers would poke and prod the naked bodies of Negroes, treating them like so much horse flesh. *Many of these men will be forced to relive some of the most degrading moments of their lives as slaves—all in the name of science,* he fumed.

Form EE included questions about social status and ancestry. Examiners were to determine whether the individual was a "full-blooded" Negro or of mixed race. Isaac realized there was no way to indicate any gradation in racial mixing; thus, either the soldier would be rated as full-blooded Negro or mixed-race mulatto, regardless of a mixed status that could range from half-white to as little as an eighth African ancestry.

In his excitement, the assistant surgeon-lieutenant went on, "The anthropometric measurements we have been discussing are only part of a larger whole. Preliminary autopsy studies examining differences in cranial volume and brain weight among races have already yielded important findings. A colleague has shared with me some of his data showing smaller cranial volumes and lower brain weights in Negroes compared to Caucasian soldiers. For many years, there has been a tacit assumption that fundamental differences between the races of mankind exist—the proponents of enslaving Negroes in the South justified their cruel system upon this assumption. But now we are finally acquiring solid empirical evidence upon which to establish a rational science of race, and sadly for the Negro, it seems to confirm his inferior status. When one considers Charles Darwin's profound insight regarding *natural selection*, what Herbert Spencer has recently described as *survival of the fittest*, the freedmen's evident inferiority does not bode well for their future survival here in the United States."

"Lieutenant, I appreciate your enthusiasm for scientific inquiry, but how do you know that all the careful anthropometric measurements have any relevance to the *survival of the fittest*, or for that matter whether they measure what you claim they measure? Please allow me to be more specific. Inferring the mental capacity and character of an individual by examining the contour of one's head, in a word, *phrenology*, has been discredited for the fraud it is. Why should we assume that measures of cranial volume or brain weight are necessarily better than phrenology? Or let's assume that you are correct that a larger brain is correlated with higher function. Does the large brain, by its own impulses, create education, civilization, and refinement, or do education, civilization, and refinement create the large brain? It seems to me that the methods and evidence suit the prejudices and assumptions of the investigators rather than answer fundamental questions; therefore, they may only condemn the freedmen to greater misery. Have you ever asked yourself what your intellectual condition might be if you and your ancestors had experienced successive generations of slavery?"

"Sir, you make some interesting points, but clearly you can't be serious. Are you not acquainted with evolutionary theory? Have you not read Darwin, Spencer, Wallace, and the others? Surely there is already a clear consensus among the best scientists regarding the extraordinary process in which more primitive forms of life have steadily progressed toward greater complexity through evolution over the eons. Thus, it is only reasonable to recognize that the emergence of human beings from human-like anthropoid ancestors has been characterized by increasing cranial capacity and brain size. If the preliminary data is confirmed with further observation, then the larger brains of Caucasians provide compelling evidence that is consistent with the theories of these great scientists. I must add that I don't find it particularly helpful to engage in the oxymoronic exercise of imagining myself and my ancestors as slaves—generations of the best New England stock—*slaves*, how utterly ridiculous!

"As I understand them, these are the facts we must consider. Slavery has been a great evil and stain on our Republic since its founding. I am personally committed to assist in its destruction. Will Negroes, who have left no great civilization, be able to adapt and survive, even flourish, as freedmen in a superior civilization? The studies we have been asked to conduct will help answer these questions. As a Harvard-educated Unitarian committed to the pursuit of truth, I must accept the best available scholarship and scientific evidence. I will not be trapped by the superstitions of the past. I started out in this regiment believing in the fundamental equality of all men. However, fine sentiments must ultimately yield to hard empirical evidence. A recognition of Caucasian superiority in the struggle for existence will likely be the only realistic foundation upon which to develop a rational and truly compassionate policy regarding the Negro question. We must honestly face the very real possibility that in liberating the Negro from slavery, we may have sealed his doom."

Trying in vain to suppress his indignation, Isaac curtly thanked the assistant surgeon and offered a last parting word. "To deny the effect of two and a half centuries of chattel slavery, with its attendant horrors and deprivation, on the ability of a group of people to survive the vicissitudes of life after their immediate liberation is sheer hubris and folly. If the outcome of this research is already foreordained, then may heaven help the poor Negro, and shame on us who contribute to such a fiction!"

"But . . ."

"Goodbye, lieutenant, I won't detain you any longer. I will follow my orders, but just as you enthusiastically embrace them, I will question them every time I reluctantly perform the measurements."

Napoleon Heyward looked up from reading his Bible to see Isaac Burgess approaching, his face flushed, muttering to himself. When their eyes met, Isaac, noticing the sergeant's look of concern, broke into laughter. "Well, sergeant, what did I tell you on our journey here this morning?"

"Sir, I believe you said something about possibly becoming upset."

"You didn't know that I had the gift of prophecy, did you?"

"Forgive me, sir, but perhaps it is only that you know well enough what will anger you."

"Yes, of course. Let's get some help loading all the equipment, and then I will tell you all about what made me angry."

On the return journey to City Point, the snow had abated, and there were even fainthearted attempts by the sun to break through the clouds. It was at one of these moments of brief sunshine when Isaac finished his description of the research, its purported purpose, and his irritating encounter with the medical officer from the Harvard Regiment. When the two friends were alone, they would revert to familiar speech. "Nappy, what do you think of all this nonsense?"

Nappy paused, carefully choosing his words. "Well, Isaac, I appreciate your great regard for the Negro, but I am alarmed that you were nearly reprimanded for not beginning the measurements sooner. We Negroes should not be afraid of the truth. If the research accurately shows that our brains are smaller than the brains of white folks, so be it. But without a better way to measure intelligence than brain size, it will be nearly impossible for any Negro, however smart he or she may be, to refute such *scientific evidence*. Besides, we Negroes fit well in their evolutionary scheme, *tucked in nicely somewhere between orangutans and you white folks.*

"I wonder if the real question the scientists should be asking is what ultimately makes us human. To me, their definition doesn't appear to be about that at all; they seem to be mainly worried about who is superior. So, they define the *value* of different races of men by what they make or create. How can I argue against the tremendous creativity of the

European peoples? If technology and artistic achievement are weighed in the balance, we Negroes will fall short compared to white folks. But are cleverness and inventiveness the best measures of what it means to be a human being created in the image and likeness of God? The great contraband preacher Moses once told me that the Devil and his hosts of evil angels are more intelligent and cleverer than any human beings. Since God humbled himself to become a servant, it seems to me that the colored folks might have an advantage in that regard compared to our white brothers. Don't get me wrong. I greatly value *my intellect* and want to learn all I can, but ultimately, I must follow my Lord's example of humility if I want to be truly human. Otherwise, I might find myself in a competition to become the cleverest devil of all! I guess what I am trying to say is I think one's character has more to do with defining our human-ity than intelligence. Also, there might even be something to be said for wisdom acquired through experience—book learning isn't everything, and you know how I love books!

"Once this terrible war is over, we will certainly appreciate any help-ing hand offered by our white brothers. But from your conversation with the scientist, it seems we'll be largely on our own. Although they may have already made up their minds that we are a doomed race, I know that Louisa and I aren't the only colored folks who will do their best to prove them wrong, even if our brains aren't as *thick* as theirs!"

After all the anthropometric equipment had been unloaded and catalogued, Isaac rushed off in search of Helen Gilson. Agitated from his quick search through many wards, he finally came upon her softly singing a hymn at the bedside of a dying Negro soldier. His feelings for her unchanged, he blushed as he stood to the side awkwardly waiting for the *angel* of the Corps d'Afrique hospital to finish escorting one more soul through the portal of death. *Is it possible that this perfect creature holds the same faith as that disciple of science whose highest principle is the "survival of the fittest"?*

Observing that her patient had breathed his last in cadence with the last notes of the hymn, Helen silently offered a prayer. Rising to leave, she noticed Isaac standing quietly nearby.

"Major Burgess, I didn't realize you were there waiting for me. I hope that I have not delayed some important ministry to our suffering soldiers by tarrying here."

"Miss Gilson, there could be no more important ministry than what you have just provided." Smiling and perceiving Isaac's agitation, she asked, "Sir, what can I do for you? You seem distressed."

"May I speak with you in your office? I had a disturbing experience earlier today."

Helen Gilson sat quietly, a grave expression on her face, as Isaac described in excruciating detail his encounter with the assistant surgeon from the 20th Massachusetts Regiment. "Forgive me, Miss Gilson, for taking so much of your precious time, but I could not reconcile your Christian ministry of mercy with this physician's cold 'scientific' assessment of the value of a human being based on one's intelligence and ability to survive."

"Major . . ." "Please, Miss Gilson, call me by my given name, Isaac, for are we not friends?"

"Only if you will call me Helen. Isaac, I'm not sure I understand how this physician and I are connected. You have had many opportunities to observe my attitude to our colored patients here at the Corps d'Afrique hospital. Clearly, I do not subscribe to such degrading ideas. If scientists provide compelling proof someday of Negro inferiority, it would be our greatest duty to do all that we can to help them ascend. I could never stand by and passively watch the decline and disappearance of their race just because scientists have predicted such a fate for them."

"Helen, in our discussion, he went on to assert that for him as a Unitarian, all belief, including religious faith, must submit to the best scholarship and scientific evidence. Consequently, he doesn't believe in the doctrine of the Trinity or in miracles and indicated that he will likely modify his belief in the equality of all human beings with further 'scientific' evidence of Negro inferiority. Are you not a Unitarian as well?"

"Oh dear! Now I see, my friend, why you are so upset. Yes, the Unitarian faith is the only faith I have known. I have had trouble understanding the finer points of the doctrinal debates within my church; perhaps I'm just too simple. Regarding miracles, I have witnessed extraordinary, seemingly inexplicable events in my service to the sick and wounded that I regard as miraculous. I must confess that I never could fully understand the doctrine of the Trinity. But I know this much, Isaac—what has motivated me to persist in my nursing duties through all the difficulties and hardship of this war has been seeing the face of Jesus in those who are suffering. Whether they have white or black faces does not matter. Yes, His face can *even* be found among Rebel soldiers."

CHAPTER THIRTY-NINE

"If you want to find Jesus, go in de wilderness,
Go in de wilderness, go in de wilderness . . ."

From a Slave Spiritual

"Major Burgess, I am deeply gratified to see that you are thriving here at the Corps d'Afrique hospital."

"Fr. Corby, it is my great privilege to help care for these brave sons of Africa. When I witness their smiles and laughter even amidst their suffering, I'm reminded of my friend Sam's good-natured optimism. But . . . Father, you've been a bit sly, not giving any forewarning of your visit. I thought you had been called back to Notre Dame by your superior."

"Indeed, Isaac, I was recalled in the fall and like a good soldier, I obeyed. Sometimes, with obedience comes a reward, and my reward was a blessing to return once more, if only for a brief visit, to minister to my men. And how could I pass through City Point without visiting my favorite Quaker doctor? Don't you think my timing is impeccable? Here it is, nearly March in the year of our Lord one thousand eight hundred sixty-five, winter is nearly over (at least the birds singing outside think so), and it doesn't take a military genius to realize that General Grant will soon be administering the *coup de grace* to General Lee's Army—so how could I possibly stay away?" The Irish Brigade's beloved chaplain gave Isaac a big grin and then became pensive.

"I can't conceive of a more welcome surprise than to have you knock at my door, Fr. Corby. Considering all the competing demands upon your time, to be included in your itinerary is a great honor and gives me great joy. Now that you are here, there are two very special people I want you to meet. You don't mind if I kidnap you for the afternoon? Since it is the weekend, my duties are lighter and I have an excellent assistant surgeon—mind you, another Quaker—to whom I can delegate my responsibilities while we visit."

"Isaac, I'll be the willing and happy victim of your kidnapping scheme. Before we go to meet these special people, may I ask how you are doing with that little task I gave you some months ago?"

"What little task? Forgive me, Father, if I have neglected something you requested of me."

"How are you and that rascal General Forrest getting along?"

"Oh, that *little* task! That humble adjective takes on a new meaning in this context. At first, I found it extremely difficult to even think about the man, let alone pray for him. But to include him and myself, together in the same prayer, changed everything. Through that experience I have learned that Nathan Bedford Forrest and I aren't so different."

"Good. Carry on."

Nappy warmly shook Fr. Corby's hand as they were introduced by Isaac. By way of contrast, Louisa offered a rather limp handshake, then stepping back, scrutinized the Irish Brigade's chaplain. "So, you're the Catholic chaplain I've heard so many good things about from Isaac. Why, you've nearly made him a Catholic!"

"Would that be such a terrible thing, Mrs. Heyward?" Fr. Corby smiled diffidently.

"The Protestant in me would respond with a most definite yes, but as Isaac's friend from childhood, I must admit that you have been a wonderful friend and counselor to him. You've brought him back from the brink of despair, and for that allow me to give you a proper thank you!" And Louisa's initial lukewarm greeting was transformed into a warm embrace as religious prejudice gave way to sincere gratitude.

With a growing sense of awe, Fr. Corby listened to Nappy give an account of his life before and after meeting Louisa. Realizing he had been staring at Nappy's eye patch, his face reddening, the chaplain asked with hesitation, "Do you have much residual pain from your wounds?"

"Sir, don't be ashamed of your natural curiosity. I'd stare at me if I were you. The fact is I make quite a sight. I thank God that this empty eye socket and the wounds in my right shoulder and leg give me very little pain." Noticing that Fr. Corby's attention had shifted to his gloved left hand, Nappy added, "Now this hand of mine is another story. I wear a glove much of the time, partly to protect it and partly as a reminder to be

careful using it. All the other wounds have healed up nicely, but this rascal will seal up and then break open and ooze a bit of blood from time to
time. Before it opens and bleeds, the pain returns. Right now, it's closed.
You're welcome to take a peek at it." Before the chaplain could answer,
Nappy had removed the glove, revealing a circular, discolored scar in the
palm of his left hand.

Involuntarily gasping, Fr. Corby exclaimed, "Why, that wound is
just like the stigmata!" Now, it was Nappy and the others who stared in-
credulously at the Catholic chaplain.

"Stig-mat-a?" Nappy slowly pronounced the syllables of the unfamiliar word.

"Forgive me, Napoleon. In my experience as a military chaplain, I
have seen many wounds, some so gruesome I wish I could forget them.
But upon seeing this wound and hearing the history of its behavior, it
reminded me of saintly Christians in the Catholic tradition who sometimes receive the marks, or *stigmata*, of our Lord's suffering and crucifixion in their bodies. For one moment, I saw in your hand the imprint of
a nail in His hand."

"But Fr. Corby, this is the *only* wound like the stig-mat-a that I have."

"Yes, of course, although it is interesting that among all your
wounds, it is the only one which has not healed completely."

"Isaac has been urging me to let him knock me out with chloroform
and explore the wound. He thinks there is some foreign material or dead
bone there that might be preventing its healing." Nappy shifted his gaze
between Isaac and Fr. Corby for their reaction.

"It's just a suggestion, Nappy. You must decide when and if you want
me or another surgeon to explore that wound." Isaac replied, breaking an
awkward silence.

"Yes, Napoleon, our mutual friend and wise surgeon has offered you
sage counsel . . . but what a remarkable wound!" Shifting the conversation
in another direction, Fr. Corby said, "I am not sure, Napoleon, that I have
ever had the opportunity to meet someone so intelligent and literate who
has come from such a background of profound deprivation as you have.
Would you be willing to share some insights about your transformation
from unlettered slave to enthusiastic scholar?"

Nappy paused to squeeze Louisa's hand and, smiling, said, "Fr.
Corby, I owe an enormous debt to this lovely woman here sitting beside
me. It was she who identified a spark of intelligence and curiosity in a
contraband whose vocabulary had been limited to the barest necessities

of existence enriched only by the orders, rebukes, and curses of the over-seer. It was she who fanned the flame of my growing desire to learn . . ."

"Nappy, it was you who responded to my small efforts and worked so hard. Now, stop bragging about your wife; it is quite unseemly," Louisa scolded with a smile.

"You see, Fr. Corby, what happens when you marry an angel; she scolds you! And a scolding justly deserved.

"Now I must return to the experience of an ignorant slave *prior* to encountering literacy, a world hitherto unknown to him. I'm not sure I have ever shared the following impressions with anyone, even Louisa, so please bear with me as I attempt to take you into a world where words are not the primary means of knowing. What's the philosophical term? . . . oh, I do remember—*epis-te-mol-o-gy*, a wonderful word Isaac taught me. The epistemology for a slave whose vocabulary has been intentionally and severely restricted by his master must come through other means, not words. But, you may rightly ask, how can one think without words; after all, concepts, ideas, perhaps even our fantasies require words to find expression. Since my near encounter with death at Fort Pillow, I've re-flected quite a bit about the requirement of words for thought. From my own experience before and after acquiring a rudimentary literacy, I can affirm that as an uneducated slave deprived of the necessary vocabulary I could not *think* in the usual sense of the word.

"But it is important to make a distinction here between epistemolo-gy, how we know something, and thinking about that something. Literacy has opened a whole new world to me, for which I am eternally grateful, but words also impose limits—just look up any word in a dictionary and you will appreciate my meaning. Not too long ago, a revelation came to me from a passage in the psalms: 'Be still and *know* that I am God.' Oh, Fr. Corby, do you Catholic folks read the Bible?"

"Yes, Napoleon and the passage you quote conveys the same mes-sage in our version: 'Be still and *see* that I am God.'"

"*Knowing* and *seeing*, I like both words very much. Neither word necessarily involves *thinking*. Before Moses, the great contraband preacher at Corinth, Mississippi, opened the Scriptures for me as I was learning to read and write, my understanding about God was a vague notion that He was maybe even meaner than my master and didn't seem to care about my suffering. But something happened to me one day that introduced me to a way of knowing without words. I had unfortunately annoyed the overseer, who would periodically take out his frustration on one of the field hands to 'keep us obedient.' His favorite posture for punishing slaves was to tie our hands together and then hang us by our extended arms from an overhanging tree limb, which would compel us to stand on our toes during a whipping. He would then leave his exhausted victim struggling to maintain this same posture for several hours. All the field hands were required to be present and witness the 'chastisement' to inspire their obedience. On pain of receiving the same punishment, no one was allowed to come near the victim after the whipping until the overseer cut him loose.

"After the 'chastisement,' I was in great pain, very thirsty, and desperately trying to keep on my toes to avoid even more pain from the extreme tension on my shoulders and arms, if I relaxed even a little. I remember vividly that anger and hatred were the prominent emotions I felt when he finished the whipping. But these gave way quickly to my thirst and a growing sense of despair. When would he come back, or would he leave me there to eventually die? I didn't need a big vocabulary to contemplate this latter possibility, for he had done this to others on occasion.

"I felt utterly alone, abandoned—even the presence of the detested overseer would bring hope. And then something happened that words fail completely to describe. Louisa, bless her heart, tries to teach me a new word almost every day. In-ef-fa-ble, that's it, *ineffable*, beyond words, but we can't stop from trying to use words to explain everything, and here's my attempt.

"You might think the day on which one is nearly whipped to death would be dark, dreary, horrible in every respect. Well, this wasn't so in my case. It was a gorgeous spring day, the magnolias were blooming, the sky a deep blue, birds were singing in the tree above me, and bees were buzzing around flower beds, completely oblivious to my misery. I don't know how to describe it, but at the very moment I became aware of the joy all around me, I felt a presence. It felt like my mother was there caressing me the way she would do when I was a little boy, before she was sold away from my brother and me. I looked around, listened hard, but there was no one there—and yet someone was there with me. The presence didn't leave me until I was cut down from the tree. From that moment, I *knew* there was Someone who cared about my fate. I didn't have the tools of a literate man to reason out the existence of God, *I just knew*. The second time I had that experience was when I was buried alive at Fort Pillow. I was too injured to use my newfound literacy to find peace, but that same Presence came to comfort and save me. This time I could give Him a name."

CHAPTER FORTY

"WHO are you, dusky woman, so ancient, hardly human,
With your woolly-white and turban'd head, and bare bony feet?
Why, rising by the roadside here, do you the colors greet?"

WALT WHITMAN, "ETHIOPIA SALUTING THE COLORS"

"O Captain! my Captain! our fearful trip is done,
The ship has weather'd every rack, the prize we sought is won,
The port is near, the bells I hear, the people all exulting,
While follow eyes the steady keel, the vessel grim and daring;
But O heart! heart! heart!
O the bleeding drops of red,
Where on the deck my Captain lies,
Fallen cold and dead."

WALT WHITMAN, "O CAPTAIN! MY CAPTAIN!"

AS ISAAC WAS ROUNDING on his patients during the late afternoon of March 24, 1865, he was startled by the sudden appearance of a breathless Helen Gilson at his side. Quite agitated, she blurted out her message. "Major Burgess, I just came from our ward for Rebel soldiers, where I was feeding one of the emaciated deserters. He was quite distressed, insisting that he didn't want me to come to any harm. He then told me that before deserting, he had overheard some of their officers planning an imminent attack on our defenses. I thought I should report this news to you immediately."

Isaac's prompt reporting of Helen's intelligence up the chain of command was essentially ignored. At brigade headquarters, he was told, "We have been receiving similar reports from the flood of deserters coming from the Rebel lines over the past two weeks. By the looks of the scarecrows who are deserting, I say let 'em attack. They can't possibly have enough men of fighting strength to do much damage."

In the early morning hours of the next day, Confederate General John B. Gordon's troops did their best to dispel any doubts regarding the Rebel soldiers' willingness to fight. Attacking Fort Stedman, one of the Federal forts closest to the Rebel lines, Gordon's troops, under cover of darkness, achieved a temporary breakthrough, which expanded briefly to the flanking Union forts. Their objective was to split the Union forces, get in their rear, and attack the supply lines at City Point. Ultimately, seeming Union overconfidence was vindicated as initial Confederate gains could not be sustained when fresh Federal troops were rushed to the scene and Federal artillery directed a brutal crossfire at the Rebels. Now trapped in the overwhelming counterattack, nearly two thousand Rebels were taken prisoner. Isaac and the other operating surgeons at the City Point hospitals were swamped with wounded soldiers, many of whom were Confederate.

Ironically, General Lee's gamble with the attack on Fort Stedman paid handsome rewards for Grant's army. Realizing that Lee had weakened his line to support Gordon's attack, General Grant ordered generalized assaults upon the Petersburg defenses as part of the response. Lee's whole defensive line now stretched beyond repair could not hold, setting up a confrontation on April 1. With the defeat at the crossroads of Five Forks, Lee lost a significant portion of his army as well as control of a critical supply line, the Southside Railroad. He now had no choice but to abandon Richmond and Petersburg.

The speed with which the seemingly interminable siege had been transformed into the hot pursuit of a wounded and bleeding prey was dizzying. Trapped for so long in the boredom of siege warfare and sensing the end was near, Grant's Army of the Potomac was eager to pursue Lee's dwindling forces. The enthusiasm for the chase was shared by the Army of the James, now under the command of General Edward Ord since General Benjamin Butler's departure in January. When Ord left behind half of the XXV Corps, now comprised entirely of colored troops, his low regard for the Negro as a soldier became evident. Even the few colored troops who did participate in the chase were kept in the rear of the pursuit.

Initially, there was considerable resentment among officers and men, but they would discover that staying behind had its own compensations.

"Requesting permission, sir, to rejoin our regiment."

"Sergeant Heyward, would you abandon your duties here at the hospital for a *recreational stroll* to Richmond?" Isaac Burgess asked, unable to repress a grin.

"With your permission, I would, sir."

"And so would I, if I didn't have so many sick and wounded patients who need my attention. You may go but on one condition. Promise me that the 22nd USCT will be among the first to enter the city."

"I'm certain we'll do our best to be first, sir."

"With all those explosions upriver, I hope you're not marching into danger."

"I hope not too, but it can't be helped. I'll take what comes my way. I just can't miss the opportunity of being one of the first of Uncle Sam's colored soldiers to enter the Rebel capital. Otherwise, what will I tell my grandchildren someday? Sir, would you do one additional favor for me? Would you please explain to Louisa why I'm going and that I will see her soon?"

"I don't think she will need any explanation. After all, I expect she may be quite interested in hearing that same account a bit sooner than your grandchildren." Isaac, abandoning his officiousness, rose from behind his hospital desk and, warmly shaking Nappy's hand, said, "Be safe, my friend, and give my regards to Jeff Davis!"

With the defenders' trenches abandoned and no enemy in sight, the soldiers of the 22nd USCT were in high spirits as they approached the outskirts of the dying Confederacy's capital. Large parts of the city were still burning from fires set by departing Rebel soldiers and arsonists. Although some white regiments shared the prime honors with a Negro cavalry regiment from Massachusetts commanded by Colonel Charles Francis Adams, grandson of President John Quincy Adams, the 22nd USCT was still among some of the first regiments to enter the bastion of Southern rebellion. Nappy was deeply moved to see the large numbers of Negroes lining the streets. Some were shouting and others weeping for joy, as they tried to comprehend the incomprehensible—rank upon rank of black soldiers in Union blue marching in perfect formation up Main Street where slave coffles had so recently tread.

The spectacle also drew other eyes. Peeping furtively with fear and suspicion from behind windows or from doorways, for those brave enough to venture slightly from their homes and hiding places, the white population was witness to the social revolution occurring that day. Where the Negro had once been in the background, on this day of Jubilee the white community vied with each other to occupy the shadows.

Wishing to confirm that the vision of black soldiers in blue uniforms was more than an apparition, the colored folk of Richmond began to cautiously approach the soldiers and reverently touch them. One elderly man shouted, "Deys real fo' sure! Massa Linkum musta sent dem hisself to lib'rate us." The apocalyptic events of the prior night when masters in haste abandoned their human property in the scramble to catch the last train for the *temporary* capital of Danville now began to make sense. With this epiphany, someone else in the crowd shouted, "Las' night we slept as slaves, but now cuz o' dese black sojers we wake up free!"

Nappy was marching close to the regimental standard bearer, who proudly carried aloft the regiment's unique flag. Another person in the crowd, seeing the flag, shouted, "See dat flag dere. Now dat's de way it should be; the colored sojer ticklin' de ribs of massa wid his bayonet! But wait, what's dat written on de flag?" Another black voice from the crowd slowly sounded out the Latin phrase: "*Sic semper tyrannis!* Why, that's the motto on the flag of Virginia. Marse loved to repeat it all the time. It means 'thus always to tyrants.'" Pointing proudly toward the 22nd USCT's flag, he shouted, "This here's the new flag of Virginia, but we'll keep the motto!" Loud laughter followed while some of the braver white faces disappeared once again behind locked doors.

Despite the chaos of the burning city surrounding them, the soldiers kept strictly to their mission of maintaining order and preserving property. The soldiers set to work at once to put out fires or complete the destruction of buildings too unsafe for occupancy. Later that day they split their rations with the starving populace. Nappy marveled at how the haughty suspicion of the white citizens seemed to melt away as soon as the black soldiers offered to share their rations. He smiled at the ecstatic expressions on the faces of local citizens when they were able to once again taste real coffee sweetened with sugar. While not effusive in their gratitude, once they realized that the black soldiers were respectfully maintaining order and saving what they could of the city's businesses and infrastructure destroyed by *their own soldiers*, many of the white citizens quietly thanked them for the food and their assistance.

By sunset, Nappy had been able to assess the most devastated parts of the city. He wondered why defeated soldiers fleeing their own capital city would choose to destroy it rather than preserve it for the peace that would inevitably come. *Is there so much malice in their hearts that they would even deprive their children of the future benefits from these industries they have destroyed? How much resentment will they harbor toward my people, if they are willing in their insane rage to destroy their own children's inheritance?*

A very tired Nappy, who had worked late into the night with the military fire brigades, was surprised and delighted the next morning by the news that President Lincoln had arrived in Richmond and was walking to the White House of the Confederacy. *If I'd known you were coming, Mr. President, I'd have warned you that Jeff Davis has skedaddled. The old rascal won't be there to greet you,* Nappy chuckled.

Energized by the possibility of seeing the president, Nappy hurried off to intercept the entourage as it slowly made its way through a massive crowd of dancing, rejoicing Negroes that was growing by the minute. Turning a corner, Nappy encountered a wall of humanity, above which he could make out the stovepipe hat of the nation's chief magistrate. Drawing closer, he caught glimpses of Lincoln as the president graciously attempted to acknowledge all the people greeting him. The emotional intensity of the crowd reminded Nappy of a religious revival. One woman who managed to get close enough to touch him cried out, "Now I know I'm free, for I have seen Father Abraham and felt him." Losing sight of him at this point, Nappy was thankful that such a man was president.

It didn't take long for the leadership at the City Point hospitals to appreciate the extent of civilian need in Richmond. Sergeant Heyward was detailed with other black non-commissioned officers to help organize a much-needed food distribution system for the starving population. Louisa was released from her teaching duties to join Nappy in the work. By April 8, the program was distributing more than ten thousand rations daily to the hungry citizens. One day later they were delighted to hear of Lee's surrender at Appomattox Courthouse. "It's finally over!" Louisa exclaimed when they received the news. Nappy smiled grimly and replied, "I hope so, my dear, but I'm afraid that even though the military campaigns may have come to an end, there is another war for the hearts and minds of the people that has just begun. And the Negro will remain at the center of the action."

Nappy and Louisa were amazed at how quickly the mood of a city devastated by war could change after the restoration of order. While the black population was still rejoicing over their liberation, even the general disposition of the white citizens of Richmond had improved considerably with the regular distribution of rations—with food came hope. All this changed almost instantly when news of President Lincoln's assassination reached the city. Surviving only for a few hours after being shot by John Wilkes Booth at Ford's Theatre on Friday night, April 14, the president died early the next morning.

For many, the news was met with stunned silence, followed rapidly by intense grief. Both white and black soldiers found it very difficult to maintain decorum and contain their sorrow. Perhaps the most visible and audible signs of the profound sadness were manifest among the newly liberated colored inhabitants of Richmond. For several days, adults down to small children could be seen wandering the streets, disconsolately weeping and mourning their loss. Black bunting was present everywhere, and even the poorest hovel was decorated in some manner to demonstrate a community's solidarity in grief. Realizing that they might become the targets of Yankee wrath over the assassination, white citizens, now gripped with fear, stayed off the streets. To ensure their safety, if not to demonstrate real sorrow, they decorated their homes with black as well.

For Nappy, who had been in such close proximity to a living, breathing President Lincoln only a few days before, the news of his death was at first incomprehensible. While Louisa wept freely in his arms upon hearing the sad news, he could barely move, frozen in a grief that seemed to forbid tears.

"Nappy, you're so quiet and pensive. What are you thinking, my darling husband?"

Groaning deeply, Nappy held his wife tight. "Louisa, I told you most everything that I experienced those first two days after Richmond fell, except about one incident that had a profound effect on me, which I've been pondering ever since. When President Lincoln was heading to Jeff Davis's house, he paused to rest briefly during the long walk. I was close enough to see an elderly Negro approach him. Politely doffing his hat, he bowed to the President, and said, 'May de good Lord bless you, President Linkum.' The president promptly returned the courtesy, removing his tall hat and bowing to the old man. This gesture greatly delighted the crowd but hit me like a revelation. When the president leaned forward during his bow, I caught a glimpse of that extraordinary face. I'd read descriptions in newspapers about how ugly he was, but my main impression was how much deep sadness was buried there—the fate of so many borne by one man. And if it was ugly, it was also strangely beautiful—ugliness, sadness, and beauty all jumbled together. In that single gesture, a simple bow, President Lincoln ennobled our entire race. Clearly, there was no artifice of the politician seeking votes in what he had just done. That bow came directly from his soul. At that moment I realized that Father Abraham had adopted all of us colored folk, including me, who had never known a father. But now Father Abraham is no more, we have lost our adoptive father, and I am once again an orphan."

Amid their sorrow, extraordinary news came to the 22nd USCT. General Weitzel, the commander of the XXV Corps, had been given the honor and privilege of selecting a colored regiment to escort President Lincoln's hearse from the White House to the Capitol to lie in state before starting the long journey home on April 21 to be buried in Springfield, Illinois. The general had selected the 22nd USCT for this great honor because of its "excellent discipline and good soldierly qualities."

Even the regimental medical officers managed to slip away for the event, which began at 2 p.m. on Wednesday afternoon, April 19, when President Lincoln's embalmed body was transferred to a hearse. Church bells tolled and military bands played a somber funeral dirge as the 22nd USCT solemnly accompanied their fallen president to the Capitol, with heads bent and guns reversed. An occasional tear escaped involuntarily from the eyes of soldiers concentrating intensely on their duty while they flowed freely among the onlooking crowd during the two-hour ceremony.

The next day, Isaac joined Louisa and Nappy as they waited in line to say farewell to President Lincoln as he lay in state in the Capitol rotunda. "Did you hear that some members of our regiment have been sent to Maryland in search of the president's assassin?" Isaac asked Nappy in a whisper.

"No. I had not heard yet. I'm deeply grateful for the honor of accompanying our fallen president to the Capitol and *very* grateful that others will pursue his assassin."

"My colleagues tell me that Secretary of State Seward will likely survive the wounds he received from one of the other assassins."

"Oh, what will happen to this poor wounded nation without our president?" Louisa whispered mournfully. As they came close to the catafalque upon which the president lay, Nappy's face brightened as he whispered excitedly, "Look, all the sadness is gone from his face! He is at peace. Goodbye, Father Abraham, thank you and God bless."

EPILOGUE

"I here declare my unmitigated hatred to Yankee rule—to all political, social, and business connection with the Yankees and to the Yankee race. Would that I could impress these sentiments, in their full force, on every living Southerner and bequeath them to everyone yet to be born! May such sentiments be held universally in the outraged and down-trodden South, though in silence and stillness, until the now far-distant day shall arrive for just retribution for Yankee usurpation, oppression, and atrocious outrages, and for deliverance and vengeance for the now ruined, subjugated, and enslaved Southern States!"

PENULTIMATE ENTRY IN THE DIARY OF EDMUND RUFFIN,
JUNE 17, 1865, PRIOR TO HIS SUICIDE

A WARM RAIN BEGAN to pelt a solitary mounted figure whose horse sauntered along heading southwest in the hot, humid Virginia weather—summer had arrived early and appeared to have no intention of departing any time soon. Indeed, it was still technically spring on that sultry day in the middle of May 1865. Hearing the distant rumble of thunder, the rider thought it might be time to seek shelter and, seeing a farm up ahead, urged his horse on in that direction.

As he drew near to the farm, the rider could see that the place had fallen on hard times. Before he could call out to announce his presence, a young woman stepped out from under the shade of the farmhouse porch and leveled a shotgun at him. "Your kind are not welcome around here! Give me a good reason not to kill you right this instant."

"Ma'am, for one thing, I am unarmed, and for another, I am a medical officer. Perhaps I might be of some service to you. I was approaching your farm only to seek temporary shelter from the storm that is about to break upon us."

Eyeing Isaac Burgess with continued suspicion, the woman used her shotgun to point in the direction of a ramshackle barn that might offer a modest chance of keeping dry. "You can take your horse in there. But, first let me examine your belongings for weapons. I have no reason to trust the word of a Yankee."

Satisfied that he was indeed unarmed, she directed him again toward the barn with her shotgun. "You clear out as soon as it stops raining. I'll be watching you from the porch."

Assuming that she likely was the widow of a Confederate soldier, Isaac thanked her for her *hospitality* and waited out the storm by dismounting and crouching with his horse in the one dry corner of the barn. As the wind whipped through the many gaps in the decrepit boards holding the barn up, he hoped it wouldn't collapse and crush him. Thankfully, the storm was no more than a vigorous cloud burst and passed quickly. Again, expressing his gratitude to the taciturn widow, he mounted his horse and quickly moved on, hoping to be out of shotgun range before any malicious thoughts might overwhelm his hostess.

By mid-afternoon, Isaac reached the outskirts of his destination, Danville, Virginia, a small city made notable by two events in its recent history. First, old tobacco warehouses had *hosted* Union prisoners of war during the last year and a half of the war, until prisoner exchanges were reinstated in February 1865. Second, for a few days in the prior month it achieved the notoriety of being the last Confederate capital. Isaac's first stop was to report to the captain commanding the small Federal garrison occupying the town.

"Sir, I hope your personal business here is successful," the captain smiled, wondering what the nature of that business might be but afraid to pry into the affairs of an officer senior to himself. Not inclined to gratify his curiosity, Isaac thanked the captain for arranging his billeting with a local family for the short visit.

Realizing that he still had time to search for the Thornton farm on the Greensboro Road, he mounted his horse and headed south out of town, following the simple directions that Jimmy Thornton had given him. Finding the farm, or what conformed perfectly to the young Rebel's description of it, he was frustrated to discover that the windows to the house had been boarded up and that no one was living there. As he wandered over the property noting multiple signs of neglect, he became concerned that it had been abandoned for some time, possibly many months. He wondered whether Mrs. Thornton had gone on to join her male family members in the next life.

Discouraged but not ready to give up his search, he returned to his billet for the night. His host was one of the local Danville physicians, who was pleased to chat about medical matters with another colleague, apparently despite his being a Yankee. Isaac was plied with questions about the radical changes that had occurred in hospital care and military medicine because of the war. When his host discovered that Isaac had been most recently serving in a colored regiment, he referred to his own interest in *Negro medicine*. As quickly as he could, Isaac tried to change the topic, sensing the inevitable conflict that would come. However, to his surprise, the older physician stated bluntly, "I came to Virginia a decade before the war after finishing medical training in the North. In fact, as a Northern man, to gain credibility with the local community, it was necessary for me to give lip service to many of the Southern medical precepts regarding the health of Negroes. Between you and me, I have not seen the physiologic differences between the races touted by so many of the Southern physicians. Certainly, I have not seen any real differences in the internal anatomy, healthy or morbid, when I have performed autopsies on both races. It would be heresy for me to say such things here in public, and likely my practice would suffer greatly as well. I just hoped you would be able to enlighten me from your extensive experience with Negro soldiers."

Finding a kindred spirit, Isaac warmed to his task briefly summarizing for the doctor the many innovations he had seen during his time in the army. He then went on to review his experience with colored soldiers, even mentioning his misgivings about the anthropometric studies sponsored by the US Sanitary Commission.

"Dr. Burgess, this conversation has been extremely illuminating for me. Being isolated in this slave culture for so many years, I am thrilled to hear a different, more rational perspective. It sounds like we agree that to assess any real differences in the physiology and pathology that are unique to a given race, the nutrition, hygiene, education, or in other words, the overall well-being of the races to be compared, should be brought up to the same level before making comparisons."

"Yes, that nicely summarizes my thinking on the subject. For fair comparisons between races, these social determinants of health must be equalized first. The great German physician and scientist Rudolph Virchow has done excellent work in this area."

"You have given me many wonderful ideas to contemplate, Major. Is there anything that I can do for you?"

"Doctor, I am looking for a person whose farm is outside town on the Greensboro Road. I went out to the farm this afternoon, but I found it abandoned. Do you know a Mrs. Thornton?"

"The name sounds familiar. I may have treated her in the past. There are so many abandoned farms these days. Too many of the menfolk went off to war and never returned. The best person to help you find Mrs. Thornton is Rev. Dame, the Episcopal rector here in Danville. He is a very kindly man who has organized programs to help the local poor regardless of their religious affiliation. He is an early riser; you should be able to find him in the rectory or the adjacent church office, a short walk from here tomorrow morning. He will likely know Mrs. Thornton. You should also know that his compassion extends even to Yankees. He personally ministered to the suffering Union prisoners until the exchanges resumed last February."

Isaac would always remember the Rev. Dr. George Dame as being blessed with a graying, very full beard, and a twinkle in his eye. The rector of the Church of the Epiphany was already in his office the next morning, sorting through requests for philanthropic aid. Smiling at the major in Union blue, he asked Isaac how he could help him.

"Sir, I was referred to you in the hope that you might be able to help me locate a widow named Thornton. I went to her farm on the Greensboro Road late yesterday and found it abandoned. Do you know her? Is she still alive?"

"Major . . ."

"Sorry, please allow me to introduce myself: Major Isaac Burgess, Surgeon, 22nd USCT, at your service."

"Major Burgess, I do know Mrs. Thornton. Not only is she a widow, but in addition to losing her husband, she has lost both sons in this terrible war. She is not one of my parishioners, being of the Baptist persuasion. But no matter, I have organized a committee of philanthropically minded individuals in our town to help address the great human need in this time of woe. Our mission is to care for one another and the stranger knocking at our door, regardless of their religious affiliation or lack thereof."

Looking Isaac over with curiosity and perhaps with a bit of suspicion related to his blue uniform, he asked, "How might you be acquainted with Mrs. Thornton?" Isaac paused, looking directly into the eyes of the Episcopal rector, and decided he must trust the Southern clergyman.

"Sir, can you spare a little time to hear my story?"

"Major Burgess, I can even spare more than a little time, for I suspect you have quite a tale to tell."

So, Isaac told him the whole story of his connection to Jimmy Thornton. After listening quietly, the Episcopal minister's eyes met and held Isaac's gaze for a short, intense moment of silence. In that moment, Isaac encountered the memorable twinkle, accompanied by a slight smile.

"Major, that is quite a story you just shared. I want to commend your intention to return Jimmy Thornton's New Testament to his mother, and especially your desire to ask her forgiveness. I can direct you to the home she has been staying in as a guest since the time she could no longer manage her farm. I would only caution you regarding her response."

"Does Mrs. Hazel Thornton live here?"

"Do you have business with her?" came the suspicious response.

"Yes, I have something from her son James to give her."

Coming from another room inside a voice called out, "Did someone say something about my boy Jimmy?" A frail middle-aged woman appearing older than her years, whose hair had prematurely turned white, ambled slowly and painfully to the door where Isaac was standing with the lady of the house. Scowling at the sight of a soldier in Union blue, she waited to hear if this Yankee really had any information about her Jimmy.

"Mrs. Thornton, I am the surgeon who operated on your son James and cared for him after the operation. I wanted to visit and tell you in person what a beautiful Christian your son was. He died full of faith in the Lord and confident in God's love for him."

"My boy always wanted to be a preacher; he was a strange one. He'd never want to hurt any of God's creatures, and still they dragged him off to the army. He weren't more than sixteen years old."

"He carried this New Testament with him, which I brought you for a keepsake." Hazel Thornton reverently took the New Testament in her hands, running her fingers gently over the front and back covers. "Mrs. Thornton, he wrote some beautiful words commenting on the Scriptures in the back. Would you like to see?"

"I can't read any of it. I don' know my letters. Have you bin lookin' in my son's Bible?"

"Yes, I apologize if that offends you."

"Well, it jes' ain't right fer *you* to touch it. It's sacred."

"Mrs. Thornton, there is more that I need to tell you." Hazel Thornton gave Isaac a sharp look and said, "Well, spit it out then. You seem to know a whole lot more 'bout my son than I'd expect most Yankee surgeons to ever know. What more kin you do to hurt a grievin' mother?" Isaac then quickly confessed his role in Jimmy's death. Mrs. Thornton stared at Isaac, speechless with rage. Finally, calming a little, she asked, "Did my boy forgive you?"

"Yes, ma'am. He did with all his heart."

"That's jes' like my dear boy, God bless his soul. But, if you are seeking my forgiveness, you shall not have it! I cannot, I will not reconcile with the Devil. For you, sir, are the Devil, as are all your Northern brethren. May God damn you in this life and for all eternity!"

With that *benediction*, Hazel Thornton seized her son's New Testament and threw it with all her strength at Isaac's face, raising a large welt on his cheek.

"Pick it up! Take it, you Yankee scum! You contaminated that Holy Bible jes' like you killed my boy!" The disconsolate Union surgeon and repentant sinner hastily picked up the New Testament and quickly retreated as the door was slammed shut in his face.

Later that afternoon, the Rev. Dr. Dame found a small envelope with a note and some Yankee greenbacks in it on his desk. The note read:

> Dear Reverend Dame,
>
> The caution you offered me this morning is now well appreciated. I confessed to Jimmy Thornton's mother, but unlike her son, no forgiveness from her was forthcoming. I am forgiven by the son and cursed by the mother. I can only hope that God's mercy reflected in her son's forgiving spirit will outweigh her curses, for I stand on the razor's edge between heaven and hell.
>
> Your obedient servant,
> Isaac Burgess, M.D., Major, 22nd USCT
>
> P.S. I have enclosed some money to help address Mrs. Thornton's needs. I will send more each month. Please keep this arrangement anonymous.

CHAPTER NOTES

GENERAL HISTORIES OF CIVIL WAR MEDICINE

Adams, *Doctors in Blue.*

Cunningham, *Doctors in Gray.*

Bollet, *Civil War Medicine.*

 For a recent, detailed assessment of the impact of the Civil War on the development of scientific medicine in America, see Devine, *Learning from the Wounded.*

 For a fascinating collection of essays highlighting various medical innovations and innovators during the Civil War, see Schmidt and Hasegawa, *Years of Change and Suffering.*

 The Medical and Surgical History of the War of the Rebellion represents an extraordinary primary source through its compilation of cases treated and reported by military surgeons during the Civil War and prepared in several volumes in the years following the war.

 For a deeply moving and insightful history of the Civil War from the perspective of the extraordinary human suffering and death that in many ways defined it, see Faust, *This Republic of Suffering.*

 For histories of the Civil War based on the actual words of the participants, see Simpson et al., *Civil War Told by Those Who Lived It*; McPherson, *Negro's Civil War*; Ward, *Slave's War.*

CHAPTER ONE

For General Grant's disconsolate rest on the battlefield, see Foote, *Civil War, Vol. 1: Fort Sumter to Perryville*, 344.

Incompetent surgeons plagued both the Federal and Confederate armies. In addition to its inherent deficiencies, antebellum medical education was far from standardized, such that quacks, charlatans with minimal to no training, could essentially call themselves physicians. For some physicians, the ready availability of *medicinal* whiskey in the pharmacopeia of both armies posed an overwhelming temptation. Whiskey was erroneously thought to be helpful as a *stimulant* in the treatment of shock, the cause of which (i.e., blood loss) was not fully understood at that time. For a fascinating account of military justice proceedings addressing alleged physician incompetence or malfeasance during the Civil War, see Lowry and Reimer, *Bad Doctors.*

The Union Party was a combination of Republicans and Democrats supporting the war effort to restore the Union. To gain a deeper knowledge of the convoluted politics of Indiana during the Civil War and for an absorbing account of the skill and cleverness of its wartime governor, see the online account by A. James Fuller of the University of Indianapolis, entitled "Oliver P. Morton and Civil War Politics in Indiana."

CHAPTER TWO

The military action described in chapters one and two follows closely the account given by Colonel Grose in his military memoir *The Story of the Marches, Battles and Incidents of the 36th Regiment Indiana Volunteer Infantry.*

Wild pigs added to the horror and suffering of wounded and dying soldiers on the battlefield (Niderost, "Grant's Ordeal").

For engaging but often morbid descriptions of the horrific assault to the senses imposed by combat during the Civil War (frequently presented in the soldiers' own words), see Adams, *Living Hell.*

For a description of how topical morphine powder was used and administered for pain relief on the battlefield during the Civil War, see Bollet, *Civil War Medicine,* 239–40, and Adams, *Doctors in Blue,* 51. These modern authors reference a contemporary source in describing topical administration of morphine: Gross, *System of Surgery,* 621.

The use of topical morphine to relieve pain in wounds is undergoing a small renaissance today. For example, see Ciałkowska-Rysz and Dzierżanowski, "Topical Morphine," and Kowalski et al., "Morphine."

Although the term "friendly fire" is a more recent invention, attacking one's friends in battle occurred during the Civil War, usually by accident (i.e., *amicicide*, as used by a War Department scholar; see second reference below). Perhaps the most spectacular instance of amicicide was the wounding by skittish Confederate troops of General Thomas "Stonewall" Jackson during a nighttime reconnaissance during the battle of Chancellorsville. Confusion caused by non-standardized uniforms early in the war also resulted in incidents of friends firing on friends, e.g., at the first battle of Bull Run (Manassas). For examples of specific instances during the Civil War, see Garrison, *Friendly Fire in the Civil War*, and for an historical overview, see Shrader, "Friendly Fire."

CHAPTER THREE

Year of Jubilee refers to God's instruction to Moses in the Torah (cf. Leviticus 25:10) proclaiming liberty every fifty years. "And ye shall hallow the fiftieth year and proclaim *liberty* throughout all the land unto all the inhabitants thereof: *it shall be a jubilee* unto you; and ye shall return every man unto his possession, and ye shall return every man unto his family."

CHAPTER FOUR

For a fascinating account of Assistant Surgeon Bernard Irwin's creation of the first functioning field hospital after the battle of Shiloh, see Fahey, "Bernard John Dowling Irwin."

Often soldiers would employ humor to cope with their misery, thus the name they gave a new "dance routine" involving loose bowels, known as the "Tennessee quickstep." See Foote, *Civil War, Vol. 1: Fort Sumter to Perryville*, 330.

Sanitation was poor in the large military camps, especially early in the Civil War, prior to the efforts of the US Sanitary Commission. Crowding and the limited sanitation contributed to the spread of diarrheal illnesses, among other communicable diseases, at a time when the association between bacteria and infectious disease had not yet been established.

See, for example, Schroeder-Lein, "Latrines," for a description of the challenges posed by latrines.

While hypodermic syringes had been invented prior to the Civil War, they were not commonly available to surgeons early in the war.

Isaac could have given Captain Wormeley more rapid relief of his pain with an injection of morphine but had to struggle to get him to swallow tincture of opium (laudanum) instead. See Dalton, "Hypodermic Syringe," for additional discussion of syringes and morphine administration, and Mahr, "Opium Eaters," for a broader discussion of the wide and sometimes indiscriminate use of opiates like laudanum in the nineteenth century to treat not only pain but other disorders like diarrhea and insomnia. Opioid dependence and addiction were increasingly common in America during the second half of the nineteenth century, including among Civil War veterans.

Regarding the availability of hypodermic syringes and their use in the Civil War, see Lewy, "The Army Disease." By the end of the war, approximately two thousand syringes had been distributed to approximately eleven thousand physicians in the Union Army. Most of the opium and morphine administered by Civil War surgeons was either topically administered directly as a powder into wounds or orally. Hypodermic injections were increasingly administered near the end of the conflict. Thus many, if not most, surgeons had little to no experience with the use of hypodermic syringes during the war.

Penelope Wormeley's chiding remark to Isaac about the Religious Society of Friends' *Testimony Against War* is a reference to Friends' early and uncompromising witness against violence and participation in war. For example: "And this is both our principle and practice, and hath been from the beginning, so that if we suffer, as suspected to take up arms or make war against any, it is without any ground from us; for it neither is, nor ever was in our hearts, since we owned the Truth of God; neither shall we ever do it, because it is contrary to the spirit of Christ, his doctrine, and the practice of his apostles, even contrary to him for whom we suffer all things, and endure all things." From a declaration by George Fox given to King Charles II, January 1661. Quote taken from Steere, *Quaker Spirituality*, 107.

CHAPTER FIVE

Soldier-nurse Tom's quote from the Bible in response to Penelope Wormeley's angry rant is from the Old Testament book of Proverbs 16:18: "Pride goeth before destruction, and an haughty spirit before a fall."

Fire-Eaters—a term used before and at the time of secession to describe the most aggressive advocates for secession of the Southern states from the Union. For more about the Fire-Eaters, see Heidler and Heidler, "Fire-Eaters."

CHAPTER SIX

The epigram quoting George Fox at the beginning of this chapter is an early reference to the Quaker doctrine of the *Inner Light* to which Rebecca refers in her letter to Isaac.

For a fascinating memoir of Laura Haviland's antebellum abolitionist activities, her interracial school (the Raisin Institute), and her later relief work among the contraband camps during the Civil War, see Haviland, *Woman's Life-Work.*

The verbatim quote, from actual correspondence written by Dr. Moses Gunn about his wartime experience as a Union Army surgeon, is presented in a book of his correspondence and eulogies upon his death by his wife, Jane Augusta Terry Gunn. See Gunn, *Memorial Sketches,* 157–58.

CHAPTER EIGHT

For more details of the firsthand experience of the Union surgeon, William Child, quoted in the epigram, during and after the battle of Antietam, see Marzoli, "When Will It End."

Also, Dyer, *Journal of a Civil War Surgeon,* 38–41, offers additional details regarding the horrific sights and smells following the battle from another medical eyewitness, J. Franklin Dyer, Surgeon of the 19th Massachusetts Volunteer Infantry.

Isaac Penington (1616–79) was a Cambridge-educated intellectual and an early member and leader in the Religious Society of Friends. He wrote much concerning the Friends' doctrine of the Inner Light; for example, in a letter from 1673: "O my Friend, mind this precious Truth inwardly, this precious grace inwardly, the precious life inwardly, the precious light inwardly . . . the inward voice of the Shepherd in the heart, the inward seed, the inward salt, the inward leaven . . . whereby Christ effects this. Distinguish between words *without* concerning the thing, and the thing itself *within*; and wait and labour then to know, understand, and be guided by, the motives, leadings, drawings, teachings, quickenings, &c. of the thing itself within" (emphasis in the original). Steere, *Quaker Spirituality*, 145. Isaac Burgess's quote from Isaac Penington may be found on p. 148 of the same volume.

For a recent biography of Jonathan Letterman that describes his remarkable career and contributions to battlefield medicine, see McGaugh, *Surgeon in Blue*.

Fr. Corby's actions during the battle of Antietam, including his offering absolution to the Irish Brigade soldiers before the assault on the *Sunken Road*, hearing confessions during combat with the whiz of bullets passing all around him, his description of the field hospital near the straw stack, and the soldier with the open wound of his brain are taken directly from Corby, *Memoirs of Chaplain Life*, 112–13.

CHAPTER NINE

The first epigram for this chapter, *"Man must be free; if not through the law, then above the law,"* was the motto of the *Anglo-African* newspaper published in New York between 1859–65. See Penn, *Afro-American Press and Its Editors*, 86.

Samuel Johnson has found lodging with a deacon from the African Methodist Episcopal Church (now Quinn AME or Quinn Chapel AME) on East Third Street (a black congregation) in Frederick, Maryland. The church, like so many other houses of worship, also served as a hospital after the battle of Antietam. While Samuel Johnson was a Baptist, there were no Black Baptist churches in Frederick at that time.

More details about the history of this church can be found in the recently revised edition of Reimer, *One Vast Hospital*.

Sam's quote from a debate published in the *Anglo-African* can be read in its greater context in MacPherson, *Negro's Civil War*, 32–33.

The following is a paraphrase from Luke 10:42: "Clearly, our sisters, as the good Lord said, *have chosen the better part*, which will not be taken from them . . . ." In the Authorized (King James) Version, the original reads, "But one thing is needful: and Mary hath chosen that good part, which shall not be taken away from her."

CHAPTER TEN

The epigram refers to "Balaam-like proclivities." Balaam was a diviner hired by the Moabite king, Balak, son of Beor, to curse Israel. However, instead of cursing Israel, through divine intervention, including a talking ass, Balaam ends up blessing Israel, much to the dismay of Balak and the Moabites. His story is related in chapters 22–24 of the book of Numbers, the fourth book of the Torah in the Old Testament.

The eloquent, at times flowery, rhetorical style used in the epigram is a common feature of nineteenth-century polemical writing and speech. References to biblical and Classical themes were commonly employed. Later, in his speech to the Irish officers, Sam uses a similar style to present his arguments.

Free persons of color were frequently in danger of being caught without written proof of their free status (i.e., free papers), making them vulnerable to kidnapping and the possibility of being sold into slavery. These dangers increased after the Compromise of 1850 with the enactment of a more strenuous Fugitive Slave Act, which further emboldened unscrupulous individuals to kidnap free persons of color and destroy their free papers. Options to protect the written evidence of their free status were limited, one option being recording and preserving additional copies of the documents in local county courthouses. Maryland, a border state loyal to the Union, was nevertheless still a slave state during the Civil War. President Lincoln's *Emancipation Proclamation*, which took effect on January 1, 1863, did not apply to those slave states not in rebellion against federal authority (i.e., the border states of Missouri, Kentucky, Maryland, and Delaware). The slaves in those states depended on the action of their state legislature (e.g., Maryland, November 1, 1864) or ultimately the ratification of the 13th Amendment to the US Constitution (e.g., Kentucky) for their formal emancipation.

For more on the profound cultural changes affecting the Society of Friends during the nineteenth century, including changes affecting social mores, dress, and the use of plain speech, see Frost, "From Plainness to Simplicity."

Sam's discussion of the theological defense used by Southern slave owners for slavery, highlights the fact that the Civil War began nearly twenty years earlier, before the formal clash of armies as a theological conflict when several major Protestant denominations (e.g., Methodists, Baptists, Presbyterians) split along sectional lines over the issue of slavery. The theological issues underlying the Civil War have been the subject of a careful historical analysis by Noll, *Civil War*.

Pope Gregory XVI (1765–1846)—his papal encyclical "In Supremo Apostolatus" condemning slavery, translated into English (Gregory XVI, "In Supremo Apostolatus").

For a fuller discussion of the history of the papal condemnation of slavery prior to the beginning of the Atlantic Slave Trade, see Panzer, *Popes and Slavery*.

For another perspective in which papal tolerance or tacit support of at least some aspects of the slave trade has been reviewed, see Mensah, "Popes' Complicities."

For a fuller discussion in its historical context of the commentary on Ecclesiastes 2:7, in which Gregory, the fourth-century bishop of Nyssa, vigorously condemns slavery, see Garnsey, *Ideas of Slavery*, 80–85.

CHAPTER ELEVEN

The Temperance Pledge by the 63rd NY Volunteer Infantry Regiment of the Irish Brigade: "I promise, with the Divine Assistance, to abstain from all intoxicating liquors, and to prevent as much as possible, by word and example, intemperance in others." For a detailed, sympathetic account of the 63rd's difficulties in keeping their pledge, see Vaticano, "63rd New York State Volunteer Regiment."

For a history of the *Anglo-African* Newspaper, see Jackson, "A Cultural Stronghold.'"

Thomas Morris Chester is the best-known and best-documented black newspaper reporter who gave firsthand reports from the battlefield about the military action in the Civil War. For an account of his life and work during the Civil War, see Henig, "The First Black Battlefield Reporter."

CHAPTER TWELVE

Fr. Corby's attempt to reassure the frightened private before the battle of Fredericksburg: "Do not trouble yourself, your generals know better than that," is found in Corby, *Memoirs of Chaplain Life*, 131.

". . . the gross insensitivity of the sale's pitch of the embalmers made my blood boil. One entrepreneur after handing out his business card offered his services in case any of them might be making 'an early trip home.' In such an event, he assured his prospective customers that they would be 'nicely boxed up and delivered to loving friends by express, sweet as a nut and in perfect preservation.' See Ural, *Harp and the Eagle*, 123–24.

"But it was as if Shakespeare's Mark Antony himself were here to 'cry "havoc!" and let slip the dogs of war.'" A quote from William Shakespeare's play *Julius Caesar*, Act 3, Scene 1.

See Ural, *Harp and the Eagle*, 127, for the account of the African American woman and her children being hit by Rebel solid shot on Sophia Street in Fredericksburg on December 13, 1862.

The fragment of General Meagher's oratory before the battle of Fredericksburg is also found in Ural, *Harp and the Eagle*, 125.

Liberty Town is mentioned in Ural, *Harp and the Eagle*, 128.

In their plain speech, Quakers referred to days of the week by number, avoiding the common names, which had pagan origins; thus, First Day was equivalent to Sunday.

Fr. Corby's reference to the "slaughter pen" is from Corby, *Memoirs of Chaplain Life*, 132.

CHAPTER THIRTEEN

Fr. Corby's amusing story of the man and his horse lost during the "Mud March" is taken from Corby, *Memoirs of Chaplain Life*, 135.

The description of Lieutenant O'Brien's traumatic esophageal cutaneous fistula and its successful closure with conservative management is found in Corby, *Memoirs of Chaplain Life*, 132–33.

A description of the Saint Patrick's Day festivities on March 17, 1863, is found at 138–45, and a description of a military mass in Corby, *Memoirs of Chaplain Life*, 99–102.

CHAPTER FOURTEEN

The account of Forrest's attack in late December 1862 on the Federal forces at Trenton, Tennessee, follows that of Hurst, *Nathan Bedford Forrest*, 108–10.

CHAPTER FIFTEEN

For a broad analysis of the suffering of contrabands and the challenge they posed for the Union Army and US government during the Civil War, see Manning, *Troubled Refuge*. For a brief description of General Benjamin Butler's clever use of *contraband of war*, with reference to refugees from slavery seeking asylum in the Union lines, see Manning, *Troubled Refuge*, 32.

Two other historical accounts of the contraband camps and the plight of refugees from slavery during the Civil War provide additional details to this neglected story: Taylor, *Embattled Freedom*, and Downs, *Sick from Freedom*. The latter book highlights the horrific effects of crowding, poor sanitation, and often inadequate health care on the well-being and survival of the contrabands.

For Levi Coffin's firsthand description of his relief work during the Civil War, see Coffin, *Reminiscences of Levi Coffin*, 619–50.

"Perhaps, most unfortunate, when the able-bodied male slaves attempt to flee for the Union lines, they become the primary subjects of pursuit. Rebel soldiers will sooner shoot them down than let them escape to provide similar service to the Federal forces." Compare with Coffin, *Reminiscences of Levi Coffin*, 630: "As the slaveholders fled . . . they took with them their able-bodied slaves, and when these tried to escape and reach the Union lines, they were pursued and fired upon by their masters, who had rather shoot them down than let them go free."

CHAPTER SIXTEEN

Descriptions of the work of Colonel Eaton and the many other dedicated individuals and organizations who helped the refugees from slavery in the Mississippi Valley, especially at the Corinth Contraband Camp, in this and subsequent chapters, have drawn heavily on two sources: Eaton's own memoir of his Civil War experiences—Eaton, *Grant, Lincoln, and the Freedmen*—and the classic study by Walker, "Corinth."

The National Park Service, as part of the Shiloh Battlefield, hosts an excellent separate museum in Corinth, Mississippi, dedicated to the Corinth Contraband Camp and Corinth Battlefield. Although original buildings are not preserved, visitors can walk the perimeter of the camp, where markers explain different aspects of life in the Corinth Contraband Camp (National Park Service, "Corinth Contraband Camp").

"The Spirit of the Lord God is upon me; because the Lord hath anointed me to preach good tidings unto the meek; he hath sent me to bind up the brokenhearted, to proclaim liberty to the captives . . ." Isaiah 61:1.

"The Lord bless thee and keep thee. The Lord make his face shine upon thee, and be gracious unto thee. The Lord lift up his countenance upon thee, and give thee peace." Numbers 6:24–6.

Louisa's use of the Latin expression *tabula rasa* is a reference to *An Essay Concerning Human Understanding* by John Locke (Locke, "Essay Concerning Human Understanding").

For a discussion of the *noble savage*, see Editors of Encyclopaedia Britannica, "Noble Savage."

CHAPTER SEVENTEEN

For more on greenbacks, see Museum of American Finance. "Greenback."

Colonel Alexander's prior Southern connection, living in Mississippi during the 1850s, is noted in Walker, "Corinth." See footnote 16 on p. 8.

"The extent to which something once was, but no longer is, is the measure of its death; and the extent to which something once was not, but now is, is the measure of its beginning." Augustine, *Confessions*, 259.

CHAPTER EIGHTEEN

Rev. Carruthers and the missionaries sent from Oberlin to the Corinth contraband camp are mentioned in Walker, "The Story of a Contraband Camp," 12–14. Also, for a very brief bio, see Find a Grave. "George North Caruthers."

CHAPTER NINETEEN

In Memphis, Levi Coffin reported seeing escaped slaves who had sustained gunshot wounds and other trauma at the hands of their pursuers being cared for in contraband hospitals. "While I was visiting one of the colored hospitals . . . in the suburbs of the city, which had been appropriated to the use of the sick and wounded freedmen, a company of slaves was brought in, some of them suffering from gunshot wounds." Coffin, *Reminiscences of Levi Coffin*, 630.

For a fascinating account of the groundbreaking work of Dr. Middleton Goldsmith on the use of bromine for the treatment of hospital gangrene during the Civil War, anticipating some aspects of the future work of Lister in antisepsis, see Trombold, "Gangrene Therapy."

In Goldsmith's actual report to the surgeon general, *A Report on Hospital Gangrene, Erysipelas, and Pyaemia*, he hypothesized a connection between the three conditions, but his approach to the problem was limited by the lack of understanding concerning the role of bacteria in wound infections at the time.

For a discussion of antebellum plantation slave hospitals, see Kenny, "'A Dictate of Both Interest and Mercy?'"

For a description of Adjutant General Lorenzo Thomas's visit to the Corinth contraband camp in mid-May 1863 and contemporary comments on his actual recruitment speech: Walker, "Corinth," 14–15.

On the loyalty oath, see Hyman, "Deceit in Dixie." The widespread deceit involving oath-taking by Southerners during the conflict was sufficiently common that it was a campaign issue after the Civil War, which helped keep Republicans in power for many years.

For a fascinating discussion of artistic (and propagandistic) portrayals of oath taking from the time, see Clapper, "Reconstructing a Family."

For an extensive discussion of the many often-conflicting loyalties that influenced Mississippians' decisions regarding taking the loyalty oath during the war, see Ruminski, "Southern Pride and Yankee Presence," 59–113.

His doctoral thesis has subsequently been published as Ruminski, *Limits of Loyalty*.

CHAPTER TWENTY

Antebellum Tennessee was divided by geographic features and various industries into three regions: East, Middle, and West Tennessee. Where cotton production was the dominant activity, in the western portion of the state, the number of slaves was the highest and literacy among blacks was the least prevalent. Going further east, there was considerably greater diversity in both agriculture and the trades, which created opportunities for some slaves to learn trades, be hired out, and eventually generate enough personal income so that some even purchased their freedom. Literacy among the slave population in this diverse labor market was valued, or at least tolerated to some degree, among the whites, and there were instances of a few schools where enslaved children could attend. In contrast to the rest of the slaveholding South, no formal laws existed in Tennessee, Arkansas, or Texas explicitly outlawing slave education, although it was usually strongly discouraged in the cotton-growing areas. For a detailed discussion of slave education in antebellum Tennessee, see Kato, "Slaves and Education," and DeGregory, "We Built Black Athens." Many of the rapid changes and events that happened during the late spring and summer of 1863 at the Corinth Contraband Camp (including Levi Coffin's visit in late May) are described in Walker, "Corinth," 5–22.

Levi Coffin visited Corinth, in addition to other contraband camps, in late May 1863. He "had previously forwarded boxes of school-books, clothing, blankets, and farming utensils" to a contraband camp at La Grange, Mississippi south of Memphis as well as to Corinth (p. 631). At La Grange, before moving on to Corinth, he was able to interact with some of the newly arrived contrabands and make the following observations. "Although their destitution was extreme, I heard no murmurs or complaints. Their hearts seemed full of praise to God for their deliverance from slavery; they regarded it as an answer to the prayers they had sent up so often in their days of cruel bondage. I was touched by their simple expressions of thanksgiving, and felt my eyes fill with tears" (pp. 632–33). In describing his visit to Corinth, he states, "Colonel Alexander, superintendent of contrabands at this place, received me cordially. . . . Several teachers and missionaries were stationed here, and about three hundred children attended school. The cabins and tents of the contrabands were kept clean and were visited often by the distributing agents and teachers. It was truly an arduous field of labor; numbers of newly emancipated slaves arrived every day, and there was much destitution and suffering. Colonel Alexander and I rode out to view the farm and gardens cultivated by the freedmen—about one thousand acres were under cultivation, one hundred and twenty-five in garden. . . . A regiment of colored soldiers was organized and equipped at this place. . . . Their colonel told me that they were the most orderly and best-behaved regiment in camp; it was the first time that their manhood had been recognized, and they were anxious to prove that they were worthy of the confidence reposed in them. . . . There were many stanch abolitionists among the Northern soldiers stationed here, and when off duty they spent much time teaching the colored soldiers to read. . . . I spent about three days at Corinth, visiting the schools and teachers, attending the religious meetings of the freedmen, and visiting many of them in their tents and hospitals . . . . The evening before I left Corinth I witnessed the arrival of a large company of contrabands, many of them clothed only in rags, and suffering for want of food . . ." Coffin, *Reminiscences of Levi Coffin*, 636–37.

Description of the field hospitals at Gettysburg, including the tragic consequences of their close proximity to the frontline, are drawn from Kirkwood, *"Too Much for Human Endurance."*

CHAPTER TWENTY-ONE

A vivid account of the immediate aftermath of the battle of Gettysburg, the difficulty of retrieving the wounded and dead following the battle— including the activity of rebel sharpshooters on the fourth of July and the violent storm that day—can be found in Kirkwood, *"Too Much for Human Endurance,"* 183–200.

In his own surgical practice, the author has witnessed the rare occurrence of a gunshot wound to the abdomen traversing the fascial planes between muscles and exiting the abdominal wall without entering the abdominal cavity.

CHAPTER TWENTY-TWO

Seven thousand wounded Confederates were left behind when Lee began his retreat to Virginia after the battle of Gettysburg. McPherson, *Battle Cry of Freedom*, 665.

A total of twenty-two thousand wounded were being cared for in the field hospitals of the Union Army at Gettysburg in the days immediately following the battle. See Coco, *Strange and Blighted Land*, 6.

Tetanus was a rare complication encountered in the care of Civil War wounded who had been exposed to the barnyard environment where the causative bacterium, *clostridium tetani*, was present in the soil. In contaminated wounds the bacterium released the tetanus toxin, which produced the symptoms. A short vignette describing one of the victims of tetanus after the battle is presented in Kirkwood, *"Too Much for Human Endurance,"* 74.

In a speech given years after the war, W. W. Keen, a surgeon who had served in the Civil War, described the advances in bacteriology which were yet unknown at the time of the war and which would later revolutionize the care of battlefield wounds. For the text of his speech, see National Museum of Civil War Medicine, "Post-War Speech."

Sadly, tetanus remains a cause of suffering and death in developing countries where immunization is not consistently practiced. For example, see Woldeamanuel, "Tetanus in Ethiopia."

The humorous story of the soldier-patient having the *effrontery* to survive a "fatal" wound, told by Dr. Reynolds, is related in Corby, *Memoirs of Chaplain Life*, 156.

The Hinshaw and Barker Brothers were real individuals who, as Southern Quakers, refused to support war in any form. Being conscripted under Southern draft laws into the Confederate Army, they were forced to march under guard with Lee's Army of Northern Virginia in its second invasion of the North, all the time steadfastly refusing to render any service that might be of military use. The full account of their experience and that of many other Quaker pacifists who suffered for the Friends' *Testimony Against War* during the Confederacy can be found in Cartland, *Southern Heroes*. Their specific story begins in chapter ten at p. 195. They were assigned to the 52nd North Carolina Infantry Regiment, Pettigrew's Brigade. Rather than join the retreat of Lee's defeated army toward Virginia, which began on the 4th, they found refuge with a Quaker family for nearly a week after the battle. They were captured by Union Cavalry the 9th or 10th of July 1863 and taken to Harrisburg, Pennsylvania, on the 11th of July. Before being taken to Harrisburg, *they have their brief fictional meeting with Isaac Burgess*. Northern Quakers interceded on behalf of the Quaker POWs, and they were eventually released and pardoned by President Lincoln. See p. 248 of *Southern Heroes* regarding their release from Fort Delaware POW camp. The author's direct Hinshaw ancestors had migrated to Indiana from North Carolina well before the Civil War. However, the Hinshaw and Barker brothers may be his distant cousins.

CHAPTER TWENTY-THREE

For a description of the hordes of battlefield *tourists* who descended upon Gettysburg in the days after the battle, see Coco, *Strange and Blighted Land*, 7–8.

One of the worst instances of racially motivated violence against persons of African descent in American history, the New York Draft Riots, occurred between July 11 and 16, 1863. Troops were rushed from Gettysburg to quell the violence. The assault on Fort Wagner (one of the Confederate fortresses guarding Charleston Harbor) by the 54th Massachusetts Infantry (Colored Regiment) occurred on July 18, 1863.

Sam's reference to "Father Abraham" in his letter to Isaac had its origin in a recruitment song. "*We Are Coming, Father Abraham*," a poem by the Quaker poet James Sloan Gibbons, was set to music in 1862. For a discussion of this song and its many uses during the war, see Cohn, "Abraham Lincoln and the Music of the Civil War."

For detailed accounts of the Battle of Helena, Arkansas, see the following sources: Foote, *Civil War, Vol. 2: Fredericksburg to Meridian*, 600–6; Lovett, "African Americans"; Bears, "The Battle of Helena"; Christ, "'They Will Be Armed.'"

The McGuffey readers can be accessed online. For example, the *First Reader* that was commonly used in teaching basic literacy to contrabands can be downloaded at https://www.gutenberg.org/files/14640/14640-pdf.pdf.

For a full description of the distorted form of Christianity offered by masters and Southern Protestant churches to slaves prior to the Civil War, and the slaves' realization of an authentic inner spiritual experience independent of formal slave catechisms, see chapters five and six in Raboteau, *Slave Religion*.

"Physician, heal thyself." Francis Reynolds has quoted Luke 4:23.

By citing the example of the Protestant Henri IV's conversion to Catholicism in the late sixteenth century as a necessary step for being accepted as king of France, Francis Reynolds has offered an explanation to Isaac that his religious status as a Protestant has also been an impediment to his promotion within the Catholic Irish Brigade. Henri IV's conversion is reviewed from a psychological perspective in Dickerman, "The Conversion of Henry IV."

Fr. Corby's description of his experiences during the campaigns of the fall of 1863 can be reviewed in Corby, *Memoirs of Chaplain Life*, 201–7. Loss of the altar stone was a significant problem for a Catholic priest. It contained a relic (usually that of a martyr) embedded in the stone and created sacred space for consecration of the bread and wine of the Eucharistic Mass. For a fuller discussion of altar stones in the pre-Vatican II Catholic Church, see Klemon, "Altar Stones."

CHAPTER TWENTY-FOUR

The description of the execution of the bounty jumper is adapted from Fr. Corby's accounts in his memoirs of other military executions he was obliged to attend and the stories of condemned prisoners he served (see for example, Corby, *Memoirs of Chaplain Life*, 126–27).

CHAPTER TWENTY-SIX

For a discussion of the medical debacle created by the massive casualties from the Wilderness and the conflicting orders prolonging the transport of critically injured soldiers, see Gwynne, *Hymns of the Republic*, 65–73.

For a firsthand account by a Civil War nurse of the chaos attending the wounded after the battles of the Wilderness and Spotsylvania Courthouse, see Woolsey, *Hospital Days*, 149–54.

Sources for descriptions of the Overland Campaign, May–June 1864, include Walker, *History of the Second Army Corps*, 407–523, and Foote, *Civil War, Vol. 3: Red River to Appomattox*, 146–317.

CHAPTER TWENTY-SEVEN

The biblical reference is to the story of Joshua making the sun stand still—see Joshua 10:13: "And the sun stood still, and the moon stayed, until the people had avenged themselves upon their enemies . . . So the sun stood still in the midst of heaven, and hasted not to go down about a whole day."

". . . he, which is filthy, let him be filthy still . . ." Louisa has made a reference to the New Testament book of Revelation 22:11.

For a fascinating account of the USS Red Rover Hospital ship on the Mississippi River during the Civil War, see Wynn, "Mercy on the Mississippi."

For the story of Mary Ann "Mother" Bickerdyke and her cleanliness reforms in Union hospitals, see McIntire, "She Ranks Me."

The title of the article is a quote from General Sherman, who had great respect for Mother Bickerdyke.

The account of the wounded survivors of the Fort Pillow massacre cared for at Mound City General Hospital is drawn from the depositions given by the physicians and wounded soldiers taken by members of the Congressional Committee on the Conduct of the War on April

22–23, 1864. Wade and Gooch, *Reports of the Committee on the Conduct of the War.*

Disposition of the Report on the Fort Pillow Massacre and Returned Prisoners:

"May 9, 1864.—*Ordered*, That the report, with the accompanying evidence, be printed in connexion with the report of the committee in relation to the Fort Pillow massacre, and that twenty thousand additional copies be printed for the use of the Senate."

For an excellent discussion of the actions of the Congressional Committee on the Conduct of the War specifically pertaining to the Fort Pillow massacre and treatment of federal prisoners of war by the Confederates, see Tap, "These devils are not fit to live."

CHAPTER TWENTY-EIGHT

The epigram is a quote from correspondence between Nathan Bedford Forrest and the Union Army general Cadwallader Washburn, who was in command of Memphis after replacing the incompetent General Stephen Hurlbut. The exchange occurred following the battle of Brice's Crossroads (June 10, 1864) in which rebel soldiers giving no quarter to US Colored Troops was again at issue.

As a palliative care physician, it has not been uncommon for the author to hear accounts from surviving loved ones of comforting encounters with the recently deceased, often occurring during dreams.

Common feeding regimens for wounded soldiers, especially in liquid form, included eggnog, milk punch, beef broth, etc. Milk punch recipes of the time typically included sweet milk, various dilutions of brandy or rum, and spices (e.g., nutmeg) without the addition of the egg which would make it eggnog (Civil War Talk, "Milk Punch").

When discovered wriggling within wounds, maggots elicit universal revulsion among physicians, nurses, and their patients. However, surgeons since the Renaissance, if not earlier, have often noted that after their departure, maggots frequently left wounds in a better state than before they were present. For comments appreciative of maggots' beneficial effects in wounds during the Civil War from two noted Confederate surgeons, Doctors Joseph Jones and J. F. Zacharias, see Chernin, "Surgical Maggots." Dr. Zacharias has even been credited with the first medicinal use of maggots in wound care: "During my service . . . at Danville,

Virginia, I first used maggots to remove the decayed tissue in hospital gangrene and eminent satisfaction. In a single day they would clean a wound much better than any agents we had at our command. I used them afterwards at various places. I am sure I saved many lives by their use, escaped septicemia, and had recoveries." The quotation is located in Chernin, "Surgical Maggots," 1143.

Medicinal use of maggots became popular after World War I, before the advent of antibiotics, and even now is making a comeback (see the following references for overviews). A crucial discovery has been the need to use sterile maggots, since maggots planted in wounds by flies *in the wild* may carry dangerous bacteria, including *clostridium tetani* (the causative agent in tetanus). Bonn, "Maggot Therapy"; Nigam, "The Principles of Maggot Therapy."

The description of the battle, Forrest's treachery during the truce negotiations, and the subsequent surrender and massacre of the garrison of Fort Pillow follows the detailed account given in Ward, *River Run Red.*

Nappy's sworn testimony is based primarily on the actual testimony of Private Daniel Tyler, Company B, 6th US Colored Heavy Artillery, and is supplemented from the testimony of Sergeant Benjamin Robinson, Company D, 6th US Colored Heavy Artillery at Mound City Hospital on April 22, 1864. Sgt. Robinson was the witness of Forrest's and other rebel officers' presence at the massacre and the one who heard his boasting. Daniel Tyler reported *not* seeing rebel officers during his wounding.

Tragically, the fate of Daniel Tyler was to be "buried" again in a military prison in Memphis for being absent without leave after briefly returning to his regiment. This time he did not survive the *burial alive* in prison. Unfortunately, he did not have a *Louisa Johnson* to advocate for him. See Ward, *River Run Red,* 340–41 for the ironic details of his tragic fate.

In his account of Sam's bravery and death, Nappy quotes John 15:13 (KJV).

For a statistical review of the losses that confirms the Fort Pillow tragedy as a massacre, see Cimprich and Mainfort, "The Fort Pillow Massacre."

CHAPTER TWENTY-NINE

The anonymous epigram at the beginning of the chapter is taken from Foote, *Civil War, Vol. 3: Red River to Appomattox,* 238.

In addition to intense grief related to his best friend's death, Isaac Burgess may also be suffering from what is now called post-traumatic stress disorder (PTSD). The symptoms of insomnia, rage, and emotional numbing that have become increasingly disruptive to his wellbeing and function as a medical officer—especially after his close call with the rebel sharpshooter at Gettysburg—at least reflect depression and anxiety. Mental illness was poorly understood during the Civil War. It is possible that some cases of *nostalgia*, an incapacitating yearning for home (especially thought to afflict younger soldiers), would now be considered PTSD. "Insanity" was an imprecise term used by regimental surgeons to describe individuals exhibiting highly erratic or abnormal behavior that could result in transfer to the Military Hospital for the Insane in Washington DC, where they might then be discharged from the service. For further reading, see Dean, "'We Will All Be Lost and Destroyed'"; Carroll, "Civil War Soldiers"; Clarke, "So Lonesome I Could Die."

For an excellent account of a Civil War veteran who likely suffered from PTSD, and the drastic effect of his mental illness on his post-war life and marriage, see Andersen, "'Haunted Minds.'"

Moral distress, a form of psychological distress distinct from but closely related to PTSD, has been recognized in military veterans who have witnessed or been engaged in horrific aspects of war (e.g., atrocities, mass casualties) wherein the veteran's own moral code has been compromised. Isaac Burgess's experience likely included aspects of both PTSD and moral distress. For recent studies of moral injury/distress and how it may complicate PTSD as well as contribute to spiritual distress at the end of life, see Koenig et al., "Assessment of Moral Injury" and Chang et al., "Spiritual Distress of Military Veterans."

Sources for the description of the fighting on the 19th of May include Walker, *History of the Second Army Corps*, 486–88; Foote, *Civil War, Vol. 3: Red River to Appomattox*, 238–42.

For another contemporaneous account, written by a witness from the II Corps, see Military Historical Society of Massachusetts, *Wilderness Campaign*, 296–300.

CHAPTER THIRTY

Mother in Israel—honorific title for a woman minister within the Society of Friends who was recognized and revered for her spiritual gifts and leadership.

New Testament quote: "I am the resurrection, and the life: he that believeth in me, though he were dead, yet shall he live" (John 11:25 KJV).

In addition to the poignant firsthand account by the Civil War nurse Jane S. Woolsey of the chaos attending the wounded after the battles of the Wilderness and Spotsylvania Courthouse referenced in the chapter notes for chapter twenty-six above (Woolsey, *Hospital Days*, 149–54), also see the memoir of William Howell Reed, a civilian working with the US Sanitary Commission, chapters one and two of Reed, *Hospital Life*, 9–44. He gives a vivid eyewitness description of the chaos exacerbated by limited medical logistics and resources at Belle Plain, on the Fredericksburg Road, and later the town of Fredericksburg, due to the massive and continuous flood of wounded soldiers that began with the Battle of the Wilderness and extended well into May 1864.

CHAPTER THIRTY-ONE

For more about the epigram, see Shaker Museum, "'Tis a Gift."

Formation of granulation tissue is a crucial element in the healing of open wounds by secondary intention, i.e., where the wound edges cannot be approximated surgically, either due to a large gap from missing soft tissue like Ezekiel Burgess's wound and/or because of a grossly contaminated wound. In healing by primary intention, the edges of a clean wound have been approximated with sutures. Granulation tissue is a complex mixture of capillaries with proliferating endothelial cells, keratinocytes (skin cells), fibroblasts (cells critical to scar formation that exert a contractile effect, contracting the diameter of an open wound to facilitate its closure), and immune cells. Its characteristic pink color and smooth surface herald a stage of wound healing that is resistant to infection (putrefaction for Isaac Burgess) and at much lower risk for bleeding. See the following for a modern reference explaining the nature of granulation tissue: Alhajj and Goyal, "Physiology."

For a description of the temporary use of Fredericksburg for supplies, medical care and transport in May 1864, see U.S. Army Surgeon

General's Office, "Appendix CLI," of *Medical and Surgical History*, starting at p. 1042 in the PDF.

For a more detailed discussion of the action at the North Anna River, see Walker, *History of the Second Army Corps*, 491–97.

CHAPTER THIRTY-THREE

"Marriage is a great mystery . . ." Pastor Jones is referring to Ephesians 5:32 (KJV).

"In another place, the good Apostle urges us to *bear one another's burdens and so fulfill the law of Christ.*" This is a reference to Galatians 6:2 (KJV).

CHAPTER THIRTY-FOUR

The epigram for this chapter is a quote from Dr. Burt Wilder, who served as a medical officer in the 55th Massachusetts Infantry, a black regiment stationed primarily in South Carolina during the Civil War. He had many scientific interests, which are described in his military diary and letters home. He was a strong advocate of the equality of Negroes throughout his career, not only as citizens but also in defense of their full humanity as a biologist and professor of neurology at Cornell University. His was an advocacy (and minority voice) in distinct opposition to the prevailing scientific consensus after the Civil War, both in the North and South, of Negro inferiority, which was drawn from contemporary interpretations of Charles Darwin's *Origin of Species* (1859) and Herbert Spencer's highly influential *Principles of Biology* (first volume published in 1864).

For more information about Dr. Wilder's military service, see Reid, *Practicing Medicine in a Black Regiment.*

For an early twentieth-century scientific presentation by Dr. Wilder refuting the dominant eugenic theories claiming black racial inferiority based on brain characteristics, see Wilder, "The Negro Brain."

By the end of the Civil War, a quarter of sailors in the US Navy were black. The prejudice and resistance to black men serving in the US Army were much less evident in the US Navy. Free blacks had always been able to serve and from the beginning were accorded a much higher degree of equality (e.g., sharing common quarters and mess with the white sailors) than their compatriots in the army. For a brief review of black sailors' service in the US Navy during the Civil War, see Quarles, *Negro in the Civil War*, 229–32.

CHAPTER THIRTY-FIVE

For further reading about the controversial politician-turned-Union general, Benjamin Butler, see the following: Holzman, "Ben Butler in the Civil War"; Longacre, "Black Troops"; and Horowitz, "Ben Butler and the Negro." This last article documents the dramatic about-face that occurred in the Massachusetts politician's attitudes toward blacks and slavery in a very short time because of the war.

For Benjamin Butler's own perspective and defense of his fascinating, controversial, and tumultuous military and political careers, see Butler, *Butler's Book*.

Regarding General Benjamin Butler's toad-like appearance, see Longacre, "Black Troops in the Army of the James, 1863–65," 1.

The ways of God are not as our ways: Louisa has paraphrased a quote from the seventeenth-century English clergyman and member of the Royal Society Joseph Glanvill (1636–80), who in turn was likely referencing Isaiah 55:8 ("For my thoughts are not your thoughts, neither are your ways my ways, saith the Lord"). Edgar Allan Poe used the quote in the beginning of his story "A Descent into the Maelstrom." Here is the quote as used by Poe: "The ways of God in Nature, as in Providence, are not as our ways; nor are the models that we frame any way commensurate to the vastness, profundity, and unsearchableness of His works, which have a depth in them greater than the well of Democritus.—Joseph Glanvill." See Poe, "Descent."

For the description of the Union Army's action against the Petersburg defenses on June 15, 1864, I have largely followed Rhea, "Cold Harbor."

For another source that presents an eyewitness account of the black troops' prowess as soldiers during the fighting at Petersburg on June 15, 1864, and examines the issue of not taking prisoners in revenge for Fort Pillow, see McPherson, *Negro's Civil War*, 225–29.

For more information about General Edward Hinks (Hincks), see *Yankee Volunteer: A Virtual Archive of Civil War Likenesses*, collected by Dave Morin (Yankee Volunteer, "Edward Winslow Hinks").

To learn more about medical cadets in the Civil War, see Hasegawa, "The Civil War's Medical Cadets."

From review of the official record of the field and staff officers serving in the 22nd USCT, the following medical officers served in the regiment at some point:

- Charles G. G. Merrill, Surgeon

- Martin Phillips, Assistant Surgeon

- James C. Moore, Assistant Surgeon

- Stewart Cowper, Assistant Surgeon

From this list, it appears that the regiment may have been more fully staffed than many colored regiments during the Civil War. In general, it was difficult to recruit competent medical officers for US colored regiments in the Civil War. See Quarles, *Negro in the Civil War*, 203–4.

For Isaac's musings about the Ninevites and their dramatic repentance, see chapter three of the book of Jonah in the Old Testament.

CHAPTER THIRTY-SIX

Jimmy Thornton's note on Matthew 11:12 includes a reference to Christ's statement that "the kingdom of God is within you." This is a quote from Luke 17:21.

Rebecca's observation that "it seems not unreasonable to speculate that rebel saboteurs might have been seeking a form of retribution with the explosion of the ordnance vessel at the City Point wharf" was later confirmed. A horological torpedo (i.e., time bomb) had been planted by Confederate agents on an ordnance vessel at the City Point wharf on August 9, 1864, as an act of retribution for the mine explosion that initiated the Battle of the Crater on July 30. Beside the tragic loss of life, it caused significant, prolonged logistical chaos in the handling of Union ordnance as concerns for unforeseen safety issues forced storage of ordnance further away from the means of transport to the battlefield.

For a detailed account of the Battle of the Crater, see Robertson, chapter six: "From the Crater to New Market Heights."

For an account of the Battle of the Crater from the Colored Troops' perspective, see Quarles, *Negro in the Civil War*, 301–4.

Here is the text of General Grant's letter two days after the explosion at the City Point wharf, detailing the casualties:

> City Point, VA, August 11, 1864
> The following is a list of casualties from the explosion of the ammunition barge on the 9th instant: Killed, 12 enlisted men, 2 citizen employees, 1 citizen not employed by Government, 28 colored laborers; wounded, 3 commissioned officers, 4 enlisted men, 15 citizen employees, 86 colored laborers. Besides these there were 18 others wounded, soldiers and citizens not belonging about the wharf. The damage to property was large, but I have not the means of reporting it."
> U. S. GRANT, Lieutenant-General.
> To Major-General HALLECK,
> Washington, D. C.

For a glowing account of Forrest's Memphis Raid in August 1864 by an admiring historian, see Holmes, "Forrest's 1864 Raid on Memphis."

As much as a quarter of Forrest's force participating in the Memphis raid were wounded and left behind by their commander, many of whom received medical care at Fort Pickering, where Penelope Wormeley and Rebecca Burgess were providing nursing care, primarily to sick and wounded colored soldiers. For an eyewitness account of a Union Army chaplain confirming the losses and presence of Confederate wounded at Fort Pickering following Forrest's raid, see Richardson, *Abolitionist's Journal*, 91–93.

In Rebecca's confession she refers to the rebel soldiers as *goats*. This is a reference to the account of the last judgment in Matthew 25:31–46.

> When the Son of man shall come in his glory, and all the holy angels with him, then shall he sit upon the throne of his glory: And before him shall be gathered all nations: and he shall separate them one from another, as a shepherd divideth his sheep from the *goats*: And he shall set the sheep on his right hand, but the *goats on the left.*
> Then shall the King say unto them on his right hand, Come, ye blessed of my Father, inherit the kingdom prepared for you from the foundation of the world: For I was an hungered, and ye gave me meat: I was thirsty, and ye gave me drink: I was a stranger, and ye took me in: Naked, and ye clothed me: I was sick, and ye visited me: I was in prison, and ye came unto me. Then shall the righteous answer him, saying, Lord, when saw we thee an hungered, and fed thee? or thirsty, and gave thee drink?

When saw we thee a stranger, and took thee in? or naked, and clothed thee? Or when saw we thee sick, or in prison, and came unto thee?' And the King shall answer and say unto them, 'Verily I say unto you, inasmuch as ye have done it unto one of the least of these my brethren, ye have done it unto me.'

Then shall he say also unto them on the left hand, 'Depart from me, ye cursed, into everlasting fire, prepared for the devil and his angels: For I was an hungered, and ye gave me no meat: I was thirsty, and ye gave me no drink: I was a stranger, and ye took me not in: naked, and ye clothed me not: sick, and in prison, and ye visited me not. Then shall they also answer him, saying, Lord, when saw we thee an hungered, or athirst, or a stranger, or naked, or sick, or in prison, and did not minister unto thee? Then shall he answer them, saying, Verily I say unto you, Inasmuch as ye did it not to one of the least of these, ye did it not to me. And these shall go away into everlasting punishment: but the righteous into life eternal." (Authorized [King James] Version)

Later, Isaac, in his musing about Helen Gilson, refers to verses 35 and 36 from the same passage in describing her acts of mercy.

The following are Helen Gilson's actual words written in a letter but quoted here for Isaac Burgess's benefit. "The dust is intolerable . . . No roses here, nothing of beauty, only a parched and arid plain, a mile square of hospital tents, filled with sick and wounded men."

For more information about the remarkable, and sadly, short life of Helen Gilson: Coddington, "Helen Louise Gilson"; History of American Women, "Helen Gilson"; Smith, "Depot Field Hospital"; and Civil War Talk, "If Walls Could Talk."

For more details concerning Miss Gilson's work in creating the Corps d'Afrique Hospital, see the contemporary description by Reed, "Chapter Five: 'A Woman's Ministry,'" in *Hospital Life in the Army of the Potomac*, 80–89.

CHAPTER THIRTY-SEVEN

For more details regarding the educational programs for refugees from slavery that were instituted by Union military commanders during the Civil War see Blassingame, "The Union Army."

Nappy's homily: The image of shaking Jeff Davis over the mouth of hell but asking the Lord to not drop him in is taken from an actual homily by a black preacher. See Ward, *Slaves' War*, 295.

"By the skin of their teeth": an idiom taken from the book of Job 19:20.

For a concise description with an excellent map of the battle of New Market Heights, September 28–9, 1864, see American Battlefield Trust, "New Market Heights."

And for a further discussion of the brief breakthrough and valor of the colored troops, see American Battlefield Trust, "New Market Heights."

For Benjamin Butler's medal honoring the Army of the James' Colored Troops for their courage in the Petersburg campaign and his strong advocacy for black soldiers in general, see Longacre, "Black Troops in the Army of the James, 1863–65," 1–8.

Regarding the formal encouragement of cleanliness amongst the colored troops, here is a quote from an official report by Chaplain Burrows and others: "The officers made a concerted effort to improve sloven habits formed by the troops in slavery. Hence, there was a great emphasis placed on personal pride, appearance, and cleanliness. To provide motivation, the cleanest man of each guard detail was excused from the detail and given a three-hour pass. A full day's pass was given to the cleanest man at each company's morning inspection. In addition, the cleanest man in Corps reviews received a twenty-day furlough and the two cleanest men in each division received fifteen-day furlough." Blassingame, "The Union Army as an Educational Institution for Negroes," 157.

In John Wesley's sermon "On Dress," he states that "cleanliness is indeed next to godliness," in quotation marks. Although he helped popularize the phrase, its original provenance is unclear. Mosaic law addresses ritual uncleanness in chapter 15 of Leviticus, so the association between cleanliness and godliness in some sense (ritual or otherwise) has ancient origins. See Wesley, *Sermon on Dress*, 5–6.

The XXV Corps was established on December 3, 1864, when the black troops in the Army of the Potomac were transferred at General Benjamin Butler's request to form a unified black Corps within the Army of the James. For more details, see Longacre, "Black Troops in the Army of the James," 2.

CHAPTER THIRTY-EIGHT

When originally mustered for service, the "Harvard Regiment" (20th Massachusetts Volunteer Infantry) included such illustrious individuals as Oliver Wendell Holmes Jr., later associate justice of the US Supreme Court and "Pen" Hallowell, the "fighting Quaker," who would later serve briefly as the colonel in command of the 55th Massachusetts Infantry, the second all-black regiment raised by the staunch abolitionist Governor Andrews of Massachusetts. For an engaging account of Oliver Wendell Holmes Jr.'s life, see Budiansky, *Oliver Wendell Holmes.* The biography gives a vivid description of Holmes's military service as a young man during the Civil War and paints a rich portrait of the cultural and intellectual milieu of the Harvard Regiment, which underwent considerable change over the course of the war.

For an excellent history of intellectual currents within the North during the Civil War era, see Fredrickson, *Inner Civil War.*

For discussions of the anthropometric measurements and the range and volume of data collected in the US Sanitary Commission study, see Schwalm, "Body of 'Truly Scientific Work,'" and Haller, *Outcasts from Evolution.*

For a contemporary analysis of anthropometric studies by a Civil War surgeon who performed them, see Hunt, "The Negro as a Soldier." Also, see the discussion of Dr. Hunt's work in Haller, *Outcasts from Evolution*, 32. I have utilized this quote from Dr. Sanford Hunt in Isaac's debate with his medical colleague: "Does the large brain, by its own impulses, create education, civilization, and refinement, or do education, civilization, and refinement create the large brain?"

For Herbert Spencer's equivalent use and substitution of "survival of the fittest" for "natural selection," see Spencer, *Principles of Biology*, 444–46, 474. Charles Darwin recognized the equivalence of the expression "survival of the fittest" with "natural selection" in his later writing. For Spencer's speculations and discussion of Alfred Russell Wallace's evolutionary thought, especially linking brain development with racial superiority, see Spencer, *Principles of Biology*, 468–69. The epigram for the chapter is taken from Spencer's footnote on p. 469.

For an overview describing the evolution of Unitarian doctrine in the nineteenth century, see Ahlstrom, "Chapter 24: The Emergence of American Unitarianism."

CHAPTER THIRTY-NINE

After returning to Notre Dame University in obedience to his religious superiors, Fr. Corby made a brief visit to the Army of the Potomac, arriving February 25, 1865, at City Point as documented in Corby, *Memoirs of Chaplain Life*, 270.

The word "epistemology" was only in recent use during the Civil War period, being first used in 1856. See https://www.merriam-webster.com/dictionary/epistemology.

CHAPTER FORTY

For a description of the entrance of Union forces into Richmond on April 3, 1865, and the Negro population's response to their liberation as well as Lincoln's visit the next day, see Quarles, *Negro in the Civil War*, 330–35. For the quote from the Negro woman who saw and touched President Lincoln during his April 4 visit to Richmond, see p. 335. The remarkable encounter in which Lincoln reciprocated the bow and greeting of the elderly Negro is also documented on p. 335.

Regarding the food distribution program to the starving citizens of Richmond, see McClure, "'So Unsettled by the War,'" 138.

For more details regarding Abraham Lincoln's assassination and funeral, see Hodes, "Lincoln's Assassination," and for the diary of Mary Henry, daughter of the Secretary of the Smithsonian, see Remembering Lincoln, "Mary Henry Diary."

Benjamin Quarles quotes the president's secretaries' observation regarding Lincoln's appearance in death "of profound happiness and repose, like that so often seen on the features of soldiers shot dead in battle." Quarles, *Negro in the Civil War*, 343.

EPILOGUE

Note on the epigram: Edmund Ruffin was a prominent secessionist, advocate of slavery, and Southern agricultural reformer. Despondent after the collapse of the Confederacy and suffering from chronic illness, he prayed for death and ultimately planned on suicide.

His "last" diary entry quoted in the epigram was actually the penultimate. He finished the one quoted in the epigram at 10:00 a.m. on June

17, 1865, but his planned suicide was interrupted by an unexpected visit from neighbors. Returning to his desk, at 12:15 p.m. on the same day, he wrote a short addendum to his diary summarizing and repeating what he had said before. He then put a rifle in his mouth, and after an initial percussion cap failure, he successfully took his life on the second try. For more information, see Lively, "Edmund Ruffin."

The Rev. Dr. Dame's ministry of mercy to Union prisoners of war (POWs) was remembered with deep gratitude in a memoir by a former Union Army POW (Sprague, *Lights and Shadows*). On p. 121, Sprague notes the Episcopal minister's impressive beard. "Rev. Dame of Danville . . . a gentleman of very striking appearance, with a beautiful flowing beard, that would have done honor to Moses or Aaron."

Another admirer of the Episcopal minister, Alfred S. Roe, a private in Co. A, Ninth New York Heavy Artillery Volunteers, wrote in a memoir published in 1891, with great respect for Rev. Dame's ministry of compassion to the prisoners,

> Dr. Dame, the Episcopal rector, New Hampshire born . . . calls almost daily on us, and, on his asking me what he can do for me, I suggest a book. The next coming brings *Paradise Lost*—there being a degree of fitness in his selection that I don't believe occurred to him. In December last I called on the aged clergyman and said to him, grasping his hand, "You don't know me; but I was sick and in prison and ye visited me." With what cordiality came the response, "Is that so? I am glad to see you. Come, let us sit and talk." For nearly an hour, we discourse of these remote times, and he tells that wherever it was possible he sent a letter to the friends of the dead prisoners. Whatever of improvement there was in our treatment above that given to men further South, I think was largely owing to him. To my mind he filled, in the broadest sense, the definition of the Christian. Though Northern-born, his early going to the South, his education at Hampden-Sidney College, his marriage and long residence in Virginia, all combined to make his prejudices in favor of secession; but he was more than rebel or federal, he was a Christian man . . . . His talks to the men were always most respectfully received, and when in the following April, the Sixth corps entered Danville, no one received more considerate attention than the Rev George W. Dame. (Roe, "In a Rebel Prison," 34–35)

Rudolf Virchow (1821–1902), German physician, statesman, revered father of modern pathology and public health, summed up his revelation about the broad connection between social factors (e.g., poverty, lack of education, poor hygiene, inadequate nutrition) and the origin of disease in a pithy phrase: "Medicine is a social science and politics is nothing else but medicine on a large scale." See Taylor and Rieger, "Medicine as Social Science," 548. For more background regarding Rudolph Virchow's innovative ideas that lead to the development of social medicine, now known as public health, see Virchow, *Collected Essays on Public Health*. For an excellent biography of Virchow, see Ackerknecht, *Rudolf Virchow*.

BOOKS BY THE AUTHOR

NONFICTION

Suffering and the Nature of Healing
Touch and the Healing of the World
Thriving in the Face of Mortality: Kenosis and the Mystery of Life
Journey to Simplicity: The Life and Wisdom of Archimandrite Roman Braga

FICTION

Neither Bond Nor Free: A Novel

BIBLIOGRAPHY

Ackerknecht, Erwin H. *Rudolf Virchow: Doctor, Statesman, Anthropologist*. Madison, WI: University of Wisconsin Press, 1953.

Adams, George. *Doctors in Blue: The Medical History of the Union Army in the Civil War*. Dayton, OH: Morningside, 1985.

Adams, Michael. *Living Hell: The Dark Side of the Civil War*. Baltimore, MD: Johns Hopkins University Press, 2016.

Ahlstrom, Sydney E. "Chapter 24: The Emergence of American Unitarianism." In *A Religious History of the American People, Volume 1*, 471–88. Garden City, NY: Image, 1975.

Alhajj, Mandy, and Amandeep Goyal. "Physiology, Granulation Tissue." National Library of Medicine. https://www.ncbi.nlm.nih.gov/books/NBK554402/.

American Battlefield Trust. "New Market Heights: Union Breakthrough; Sept 29, 1864." https://www.battlefields.org/learn/maps/new-market-heights-union-break through-sep-29-1864.

———. "New Market Heights: Sept 29, 1864." https://www.battlefields.org/learn/maps/new-market-heights-sep-29-1864.

Andersen, Judith. "'Haunted Minds': The Impact of Combat Exposure on the Mental and Physical Health of Civil War Veterans." In *Years of Change and Suffering: Modern Perspectives on Civil War Medicine*, edited by James Schmidt and Guy Hasegawa, 143–58. Roseville, MN: Edinborough, 2009.

Augustine. *Confessions*. Translated by R. S. Pine-Coffin. New York: Penguin, 1979.

Bearss, Edwin, C. "The Battle of Helena, July 4, 1863." *The Arkansas Historical Quarterly* 20/3 (1961) 256–97.

Blassingame, John W. "The Union Army as an Educational Institution for Negroes, 1862–1865." *Journal of Negro Education* 34/2 (1965) 152–59.

Bollet, Alfred. *Civil War Medicine: Challenges and Triumphs*. Tucson, AZ: Galen, 2002.

Bonn, Dorothy. "Maggot Therapy: An Alternative for Wound Infection." *The Lancet* 356 (2000) 1174.

Budiansky, Stephen. *Oliver Wendell Holmes: A Life in War, Law, and Ideas*. New York: W. W. Norton, 2019.

Butler, Benjamin. *Butler's Book: Autobiography and Personal Reminiscences of Major General Benjamin Franklin Butler*. Boston: A. M. Thayer and Co., 1892.

Carroll, Dillon J. "Civil War Soldiers and Dreams of War." *Civil War History* 66/2 (2020) 103–24.

Cartland, Fernando G. *Southern Heroes: The Friends in Wartime*. Cambridge, MA: Riverside, 1895. https://archive.org/details/southernheroesoroocartuoft.

Chang, Bei-Hung, et al. "Spiritual Distress of Military Veterans at the End of Life." *Palliative and Supportive Care* (April (2014). DOI: 10.1017/S1478951514000273.

Chernin, Eli. "Surgical Maggots." *Southern Medical Journal* 79/9 (1986) 1143–45.

Christ, Mark K. "'They Will Be Armed': Lorenzo Thomas Recruits Black Troops in Helena, April 6, 1863." *Arkansas Historical Quarterly* 72/4 (2013) 366–83.

Ciałkowska-Rysz, Aleksandra, and Thomasz Dzierżanowski. "Topical Morphine for Treatment of Cancer-related Painful Mucosal and Cutaneous lesions: A Double-blind, Placebo-controlled Cross-over Clinical Trial." *Arch Med Sci* 1 (2019) 146–51.

Cimprich, John, and Mainfort, Robert C., Jr. "The Fort Pillow Massacre: A Statistical Note." *Journal of American History* 76/3 (1989) 830–37.

Civil War Talk. "If Walls Could Talk: Helen Gilson and Marie's House." Oct. 7, 2016. https://civilwartalk.com/threads/if-walls-could-talk-helen-gilson-and-maries-house.127889/.

———. "Milk Punch." https://civilwartalk.com/threads/milk-punch.80169/.

Clapper, Michael. "Reconstructing a Family: John Rogers's Taking the Oath and Drawing Rations." *Winterthur Portfolio* 39 (2004) 259–78.

Clarke, Frances. "So Lonesome I Could Die: Nostalgia and Debates over Emotional Control in the Civil War North." *Journal of Social History* (Winter 2007) 253–282.

Coco, Gregory A. *A Strange and Blighted Land. Gettysburg: The Aftermath of a Battle.* El Dorado Hills, CA: Savas Beatie, 2017.

Coddington, Ronald S. "Helen Louise Gilson: Where Others Dared Not Go." Library of Congress. https://guides.loc.gov/civil-war-soldiers/gilson-osgood.

Coffin, Levi. *Reminiscences of Levi Coffin: The Reputed President of the Underground Railroad.* 2nd ed. Cincinnati: Robert Clarke & Co., 1880.

Cohn, Jordan. "Abraham Lincoln and the Music of the Civil War." *New Errands: The Undergraduate Journal of American Studies* 6/2 (May 2019). DOI: https://doi.org/10.18113/P8ne6261227.

Corby, William. *Memoirs of Chaplain Life.* Chicago: La Monte, O'Donnell & Co., 1893.

Cunningham, Horace. *Doctors in Gray: The Confederate Medical Service.* Gloucester, MA: Louisiana State University Press (1958). Reprinted with permission by Peter Smith, 1970.

U.S. Army Surgeon General's Office. "Appendix CLI: Extracts from the Report of the Depot Field Hospital of the Army of the Potomac, from May to October 1864." *The Medical and Surgical History.* https://archive.org/details/MSHWRMedical1/page/350/mode/2up.

Dalton, Kyle. "The Use of the Hypodermic Syringe in the Civil War." National Museum of Civil War Medicine, June 7, 2023. https://www.civilwarmed.org/hypodermic-syringe/.

Dean, Eric T., Jr. "'We Will All Be Lost and Destroyed': Post-Traumatic Stress Disorder and the Civil War." *Civil War History* 37/2 (1991) 138–53.

DeGregory, Crystal A. "We Built Black Athens: How Black Determination Secured Black Education in Antebellum Nashville." *Tennessee Historical Quarterly* 69 (2010) 124–45.

Devine, Shauna. *Learning from the Wounded: The Civil War and the Rise of American Medical Science.* Chapel Hill: University of North Carolina Press, 2014.

Dickerman, Edmund H. "The Conversion of Henry IV: 'Paris Is Well Worth a Mass' in Psychological Perspective." *Catholic Historical Review* 63/1 (1977) 1–13.

Downs, Jim. *Sick from Freedom: African-American Illness and Suffering During the Civil War and Reconstruction*, New York: Oxford University Press, 2012.

Dyer, J. Franklin. *The Journal of a Civil War Surgeon.* Lincoln, NE: University of Nebraska Press, 2003.

Eaton, John. *Grant, Lincoln, and the Freedmen*, New York: Longmans, Green, and Co., 1907.

The Editors of Encyclopaedia Britannica. "Noble Savage." *Encyclopaedia Britannica*, Apr. 24, 2019. https://www.britannica.com/art/Romanticism.

Fahey, John. "Bernard John Dowling Irwin and the Development of the Field Hospital at Shiloh." *Military Medicine* 171/5 (2006) 345–51.

Faust, Drew. *This Republic of Suffering: Death and the American Civil War.* New York: Alfred A. Knopf, 2008.

Find a Grave. "George North Caruthers." https://www.findagrave.com/memorial/496 33351/george-north-carruthers.

Foote, Shelby. *The Civil War: A Narrative.* 3 vols. New York: Vintage, 1986.

Fredrickson, George M. *The Inner Civil War: Northern Intellectuals and the Crisis of the Union.* New York: Harper & Row, 1965.

Frost, J. William. "From Plainness to Simplicity: Changing Quaker Ideals for Material Culture." In *Quaker Aesthetics: Reflections on a Quaker Ethic in American Design and Consumption,* edited by Emma Lapsansky and Anne Verplanck, 16–40. Philadelphia: University of Pennsylvania Press, 2003. https://works.swarthmore. edu/fac-religion/376/.

Fuller, A. James. "Oliver P. Morton and Civil War Politics in Indiana." Indiana Historical Bureau. http://www.in.gov/history/3996.htm.

Garnsey, Peter. *Ideas of Slavery from Aristotle to Augustine.* New York: Cambridge University Press, 1996.

Garrison, Webb. *Friendly Fire in the Civil War: More Than One Hundred True Stories of Comrade Killing Comrade.* Nashville: Rutledge Hill, 1999.

Gregory XVI. "In Supremo Apostolatus: Condemning the Slave Trade." 1839. Papal Encyclicals Online. https://www.papalencyclicals.net/greg16/g16sup.htm.

Grose, William. *The Story of the Marches, Battles and Incidents of the 36th Regiment Indiana Volunteer Infantry.* New Castle, IN: Courier Company Press, 1891. https:// archive.org/details/storyofmarchesba00gros/page/n11/mode/2up.

Gross, Samuel. *A System of Surgery: Pathological, Diagnostic, Therapeutic, and Operative, Vol. 1.* 4th ed. Philadephia: Henry C. Lea, 1866.

Gunn, Jane Augusta Terry. *Memorial Sketches of Doctor Moses Gunn by His Wife.* W. T. Keener: Chicago, 1889. https://dn790003.ca.archive.org/0/items/memorial sketchesoogunnja/memorialsketchesoogunnja.pdf.

Gwynne, Samuel C. *Hymns of the Republic: The Story of the Final Year of the American Civil War.* New York: Scribner: 2019.

Haller, John S, Jr. *Outcasts from Evolution: Scientific Attitudes of Racial Inferiority, 1859–1900.* Carbondale, IL: Southern Illinois University Press, 1995.

Hasegawa, Guy R. "The Civil War's Medical Cadets: Medical Students Serving the Union." *Journal of the American College of Surgeons* 193/1 (2001) 81–89.

Haviland, Laura S. *A Woman's Life-Work: Labors and Experiences.* Cincinnati: Walden & Stowe, 1881. https://tile.loc.gov/storage-services/service/gdc/lhbum /24792/24792.pdf.

Heidler, David S., and Jeanne T. Heidler. "The Fire-Eaters." Essential Civil War Curriculum. https://www.essentialcivilwarcurriculum.com/the-fire-eaters.html.

Henig, Gerald S. "The First Black War Reporter on the Front Lines" *Civil War Times* (Jan. 2008) 40–45. https://www.historynet.com/thomas-morris-chester-first-black-battlefield-reporter/ .

History of American Women. "Helen Gilson." Catholic News Agency. https://www.womenhistoryblog.com/2008/03/helen-gilson.html.

Hodes, Martha. "Lincoln's Assassination Stuns the Nation." *Humanities* 36 (2015). https://www.neh.gov/humanities/2015/marchapril/feature/lincolns-assassination-stuns-the-nation.

Holmes, Jack D. L. "Forrest's 1864 Raid on Memphis." *Tennessee Historical Quarterly* 18/4 (1959) 295–321.

Holzman, Robert S. "Ben Butler in the Civil War." *New England Quarterly* 30/3 (1957) 330–45.

Horowitz, Murray M. "Ben Butler and the Negro: 'Miracles Are Occurring.'" *Louisiana History* 17/2 (1976) 159–86.

Hunt, Sanford B. "The Negro as a Soldier." *Anthropological Review* 7/24 (1869) 40–54.

Hurst, Jack. *Nathan Bedford Forrest: A Biography*. New York: Vintage, 1993.

Hyman, Harold M. "Deceit in Dixie." *Civil War History* 3 (1957) 65–82.

Jackson, Debra. "'A Cultural Stronghold': The 'Anglo-African' Newspaper and the Black Community of New York." *New York History* 85/4 (2004) 331–57.

Kato, Junko I. "Slaves and Education: Tennessee as a Slave State Where the Instruction of Slaves Was Not Prohibited." *Tennessee Historical Quarterly* 77 (2018) 110–31.

Kenny, Stephen C. "'A Dictate of Both Interest and Mercy?' Slave Hospitals in the Antebellum South." *Journal of the History of Medicine and Allied Sciences* 65 (2009) 1–45.

Kirkwood, Ronald D. *"Too Much for Human Endurance": The George Spangler Farm Hospitals and the Battle of Gettysburg*. El Dorado Hills, CA: Savas Beatie, 2019.

Klemond, Susan. "Altar Stones Reminiscent of Mass in the Early Church." Catholic Spirit, July 5, 2018. https://www.thecatholicspirit.com/news/local-news/altar-stones-reminiscent-of-mass-in-the-early-church/.

Koenig, Harold G., Nagy A. Youssef, and Michelle Pearce. "Assessment of Moral Injury in Veterans and Active-Duty Military Personnel with PTSD: A Review." *Frontiers in Psychiatry* 10 (2019). DOI: 10.3389/fpsyt.2019.00443.

Kowalski, Grzegorz, Malgorzata Domagalska, Krzysztof Słowinski, Monika Grochowicka, Marcin Zawadzki, Sylwia Kropińska, Wojciech Leppert, and Katarzyna Wieczorowska-Tobis. "Morphine (10, 20 mg) in a Postoperative Dressing Used with Patients After Surgical Debridement of Burn Wounds: A Prospective, Double-Blinded, Randomized Controlled Trial." *Advances in Wound Care*. DOI: 10.1089/wound.2023.0037.

Lewy, Jonathan. "The Army Disease: Drug Addiction and the Civil War." *War in History* 21/1 (2013) 102–19.

Lively, Matthew W. "Edmund Ruffin Fires His Final Shot of the War." Civil War Profiles, June 17, 2015. https://www.civilwarprofiles.com/edmund-ruffin-fires-his-final-shot-of-the-war/.

Locke, John. "An Essay Concerning Human Understanding." National Constitution Center. https://constitutioncenter.org/the-constitution/historic-document-library/detail/john-lockean-essay-concerning-human-understanding-1690.

Longacre, Edward G. "Black Troops in the Army of the James, 1863–65." *Military Affairs* 45/1 (1981) 1–8.

Lovett, Bobby L. "African Americans, Civil War, and Aftermath in Arkansas." *Arkansas Historical Quarterly* 54/3 (1995) 304–58.

Lowry, Thomas, and Terry Reimer. *Bad Doctors: Military Justice Proceedings Against 622 Civil War Surgeons.* Frederick, MD: National Museum of Civil War Medicine, 2010.

Mahr, Michael. "Opium Eaters and the Civil War." National Museum of Civil War Medicine, Aug. 16, 2022. https://www.civilwarmed.org/opium-eaters-and-the-civil-war/.

Manning, Chandra. *Troubled Refuge: Struggling for Freedom in the Civil War.* New York: Vintage, 2017.

Marzoli, Nathan A. "'When Will It End': A Civil War Surgeon and His First Experiences with War at Antietam." National Museum of Civil War Medicine, Sept. 14, 2021. https://www.civilwarmed.org/child/.

McClure, John M. "'So Unsettled by the War': The Aftermath in Virginia, 1865." In *Virginia at War, 1865*, edited by William C. Davis and James I. Robertson, Jr., 138. Lexington, KY: University of Kentucky Press, 2012.

McGaugh, Scott. *Surgeon in Blue: Jonathan Letterman, The Civil War Doctor Who Pioneered Battlefield Care.* New York: Arcade, 2013.

McIntire, Tracey. "'She Ranks Me'—The Story of Mother Bickerdyke." National Museum of Civil War Medicine, Apr. 8, 2024. https://www.civilwarmed.org/mother-bickerdyke/.

McPherson, James. *The Negro's Civil War: How American Blacks Felt and Acted During the War for the Union.* New York: Ballantine, 1991.

McPherson, James M. *Battle Cry of Freedom.* New York: Oxford University Press, 1988.

The Medical and Surgical History of the War of the Rebellion. Washington, DC: Government Printing Office, 1870.

Mensah, Isaac S. N. "Popes' Complicities in the 'Negro' Slave Trade, 15th to 19th Century." Master's thesis, University of Ghana, 2019. https://ugspace.ug.edu.gh/server/api/core/bitstreams/317881c5-0906-4578-8995-81fe3d09dc8e/content.

Museum of American Finance. "Greenback." https://www.moaf.org/exhibits/checks_balances/abraham-lincoln/greenback.

National Museum of Civil War Medicine. "Post-War Speech by Civil War Surgeon W. W. Keen on Military Surgery." https://www.civilwarmed.org/keen-surgery/.

National Park Service. "Corinth Contraband Camp." https://www.nps.gov/shil/planyourvisit/contrabandcamp.htm.

Niderost, Eric. "Grant's Ordeal at the Battle of Shiloh." Warfare History Network, Mar. 2019. https://warfarehistorynetwork.com/article/grants-ordeal/.

Nigam, Yamni. "The Principles of Maggot Therapy and Its Role in Contemporary Wound Care." *Nursing Times* 117/9 (2021) 39–44.

Noll, Mark. *The Civil War as a Theological Crisis.* Chapel Hill: University of North Carolina Press, 2006.

Panzer, Joel. *The Popes and Slavery, The Church in History Information Centre.* https://catholicbooks.wordpress.com/2013/09/09/online-ebook-the-popes-and-slavery-by-joel-s-panzer/.

Penn, I. Garland. *The Afro-American Press and Its Editors.* Springfield, MS: Willey and Co., 1891.

Poe, Edgar Allen. "A Descent into the Maelstrom." https://poestories.com/read/descent.

Quarles, Benjamin. *The Negro in the Civil War*. Boston: Little, Brown, 1953.

Raboteau, Albert J. *Slave Religion: The "Invisible Institution" in the Antebellum South.* New York: Oxford University Press, 1978.

Reed, William Howell. *Hospital Life in the Army of the Potomac*. Boston: William V. Spencer, 1866.

Reid, Richard M., ed. *Practicing Medicine in a Black Regiment: The Civil War Diary of Burt Wilder, 55th Massachusetts.* Amherst and Boston, MA: University of Massachusetts Press, 2010.

Reimer, Terry. *One Vast Hospital: The Civil War Hospital Sites in Frederick, Maryland After Antietam*, Frederick, MD: National Museum of Civil War Medicine, 2024.

Remembering Lincoln. "Mary Henry Diary." Apr. 15, 1865. https://rememberinglincoln. fords.org/node/551.

Rhea, Gordon C. "Cold Harbor and the Advance to Petersburg." *Essential Civil War Curriculum*. https://www.essentialcivilwarcurriculum.com/cold-harbor-and-the-advance-to-petersburg.html.

Richardson, James D. *The Abolitionist's Journal: Memoirs of an American Antislavery Family*. Albuquerque: High Road, 2022.

Robertson, William G. "From the Crater to New Market Heights: A Tale of Two Divisions." In *Black Soldiers in Blue: African American Troops in the Civil War Era*, edited by John David Smith, 169–99. Chapel Hill: University of North Carolina Press, 2001.

Roe, Alfred S. "In a Rebel Prison: Experiences in Danville, VA." In *Personal Narratives of Events in the War of the Rebellion, Being Papers Read Before The Rhode Island Soldiers and Sailors Historical Society*, 34–35. Fourth Series, No. 16. Providence, RI: Rhode Island Soldiers and Sailors Historical Society, 1891.

Ruminski, Jarret. *The Limits of Loyalty: Ordinary People in Civil War Mississippi.* Jackson, MS: University Press of Mississippi, 2017.

———. "Southern Pride and Yankee Presence: The Limits of Confederate Loyalty in Civil War Mississippi, 1860–1865." Doctoral thesis, University of Calgary, 2013.

Schmidt, James, and Guy Hasegawa, eds. *Years of Change and Suffering: Modern Perspectives on Civil War Medicine*. Roseville, MN: Edinborough, 2009.

Schroeder-Lein, Glenna R. "Latrines." Civil War Rx. https://civilwarrx.blogspot. com/2014/03/latrines.html.

Schwalm, Leslie A. "A Body of 'Truly Scientific Work': The U.S. Sanitary Commission and the Elaboration of Race in the Civil War Era." *Journal of the Civil War Era* 8/4 (2018) 647–76.

Shaker Museum. "'Tis a Gift to Be Simple, but Things Aren't as Simple as They Seem." Feb. 10, 2021. https://www.shakermuseum.us/tis-gift-simple-things-arent-simple -seem.

Shrader, Charles. "Friendly Fire: The Inevitable Price." *US Army War College Quarterly: Parameters* 22/1 (1992) 29–44.

Simpson, Brooks, et al. *The Civil War Told by Those Who Lived It*. New York: Library of America, 2011.

Smith, Adelaide W. "Chapter XI: Depot Field Hospital," 107–9. In *Reminiscences of an Army Nurse During the Civil War*. New York: Greaves, 1911.

Spencer, Herbert. *The Principles of Biology, Vol. I*. London: Williams and Norgate, 1864.

Sprague, Homer B. *Lights and Shadows in Confederate Prisons: A Personal Experience, 1864-5*. New York: G. P. Putnam's Sons, 1915.

Steere, Douglas V., ed. *Quaker Spirituality: Selected Writings*. Ramsey, NJ: Paulist, 1984.

Tap, Bruce. "'These Devils Are Not Fit to Live on God's Earth': War Crimes and the Committee on the Conduct of the War, 1864–1865." *Civil War History*, 42/2 (1996) 116–32.

Taylor, Amy M. *Embattled Freedom: Journeys Through the Civil War's Slave Refugee Camps*. Chapel Hill: University of North Carolina Press, 2018.

Taylor, Rex, and Annelie Rieger. "Medicine as Social Science: Rudolf Virchow on the Typhus Epidemic in Upper Silesia." *International Journal of Health Services* 15 (1985) 547–59.

Trombold, John M. "Gangrene Therapy and Antisepsis Before Lister: The Civil War Contributions of Middleton Goldsmith of Louisville." *American Surgeon* 77 (2011) 1138–43.

Ural, Susannah J. *The Harp and the Eagle: Irish-American Volunteers and the Union Army, 1861–1865*. New York: New York University Press, 2006.

Vaticano, Patricia. "A Defense of the 63rd New York State Volunteer Regiment of the Irish Brigade." Master's thesis, University of Richmond, 2008. https://scholarship. richmond.edu/cgi/viewcontent.cgi?article=1702&context=masters-theses.

Virchow, Rudolf. *Collected Essays on Public Health and Epidemiology*. Vol. 1. Edited by Leiland J. Rather. Canton, MA: Science History, 1985.

Wade, Benjamin F., and Daniel W. Gooch. *Reports of the Committee on the Conduct of the War: Fort Pillow Massacre. Returned Prisoners*. US Senate. https://www. gutenberg.org/files/41787/41787-h/41787-h.htm.

Walker, Cam. "Corinth: The Story of a Contraband Camp." *Civil War History* 20 (1974) 5–22.

Walker, Francis A. *History of the Second Army Corps*. New York: Charles Scribner's Sons, 1887.

Ward, Andrew. *River Run Red: The Fort Pillow Massacre in the American Civil War*. New York: Penguin, 2005.

———. *The Slave's War: The Civil War in the Words of Former Slaves*. New York: Mariner, Houghton Mifflin, 2008.

Wesley, John. *Sermon on Dress*. Boston: McDonald, Gill, and Co., 1800. https://archive. org/details/sermonsondressoooowesl/page/6/mode/2up

Wilder, Burt. "The Negro Brain." In *The Proceedings of the National Negro Conference from 1909: May 31 and June 1*, 22–66. https://librarycollections.law.umn.edu/ documents/darrow/Proceedings%20of%20the%20National%20Negro%20 Conference%201909_%20New%20York_%20May%2031%20and%20June_1.pdf.

Military Historical Society of Massachusetts. *The Wilderness Campaign*. Boston: Military Historical Society of Massachusetts, 1905.

Woldeamanuel, Yohannes Woubishet. "Tetanus in Ethiopia: Unveiling the Blight of an Entirely Vaccine-Preventable Disease." *Current Neurology and Neuroscience Reports* 12 (2012) 655–65.

Woolsey, Jane S. *Hospital Days*. New York: D. Van Nostrand, 1868.

Wynn, Jake. "Mercy on the Mississippi: The USS Red Rover Hospital Ship." National Museum of Civil War Medicine, May 21, 2020. https://www.civilwarmed.org/ redrover/.

The Yankee Volunteer. "Edward Winslow Hinks." https://dmorinsite.wordpress.com/ edward-winslow-hinks/.